I0766356

WEEP FOR
Love
BY
DAVID KENNETH WALDMAN

Copyright Page

Name: Waldman, David Kenneth, 1952- author.

Title: Weep for Love / David Kenneth Waldman.

Description: First edition. | San Francisco, California: Rebecca House International Publishing.

[2024] Summary: Weep for Love is a fictional romance novel that creates an alternative version of the author's encounters with women. A realistic romance novel captures an in-depth portrait of a life that swirls around a couple in love. Not filled with tiresome tropes: real-life love involves family, friends, work, and of course, the heart of a romance, set in an alternative reality. Instead of avoiding any resemblance to a specific woman, the character traits, feelings, and personal descriptions are an amalgam of dozens of women. There is no relationship to one particular woman, event, or association. The author constructed the male protagonist's character, and it bore no resemblance to any person except the author. My main protagonists wrote and directed this story, and I put down the words of their actions and thoughts.

ISBN Paperback 978-0-945522-09-6

ISBN Hardback 978-0-945522-11-9

ISBN E-Book   978-0-945522-10-2

Library of Congress Control Number: 2021943285

Weep for Love is a work of fiction except when it narrates the attributes of the male protagonist, whose personality is based on the author's lived experiences. Names, characters, businesses, places, events, book cover model, and incidents are either the products of the author's imagination or used in a fictitious manner. If there is any similarity to any living or dead person, then that is pure coincidence, i.e., by chance, it was not intended.

Table of Contents

Rebecca House

'Where imagination comes alive'

A social enterprise of To Love Children

Publishers since 1984, San Francisco, California

davidkennethwaldman@gmail.com

A portion of the sales of all books' profits goes to To Love Children, a 501 (c) (3) nonprofit, which in 2006 obtained Special Consultative Status from the Economic and Social Council of the United Nations.

Founded by the author in 2002, its mission is to advance educational opportunities for vulnerable girls living in poverty.

Dedicated to Brooke

Your Love lay in an open heart, foreseeing endless romantic possibilities.

Wishes can come true, especially incredibly impossible ones.

"You were made perfectly to be loved."

Elizabeth Barrett Browning

Prologue

"The truth of the human heart." Nathaniel Hawthorne

"Imagine that you will awaken someday to learn that your life has rushed by at a pace disturbing to realize and cruel. The most intense moments will seem to have occurred only yesterday, and nothing will have erased the pain and pleasure, the impossible intensity of love and its child-like joy, and the loneliness of passions unrequited and unspoken. Thus unanswered." Meg Rosoff

Poets inspire us to pause and ponder the shifting multicolored sky at sunrise, awakening our romantic tendencies. Or, by chance, you become aware of a rare lunar rainbow. Don't lament the end of a day, from the changing colors at sunset to evening twilight. Consider a starry night sky through the eyes of *Vincent van Gogh*. Love surrounds me when my eyes open to recognize its multiple colors.

Weeping tears are a deep-seated expression of feelings when there are no words to express them. Thus far, I had not known how to bear a loss of love. Instead, look to my muse for her artistic understanding of adoration. The emotions of passion inspire songwriters, poets, and novelists, immersing us through words, poetry, or music, which is always about love. But unluckily, no romantic songs or poetry adequately voice a lover's feelings about the intimacy of love.

David Benjamin Bradley postponed a quest for romance after his last relationship ended. Amicably, but it was nonetheless another chance at romance denied. *Weep for Love* is a story of two people pursuing a passionate romance, which is emotionally exhausting.

Delayed starting any new relationship, so my career became an enduring obsession.

Women friends often repeat their favorite trope, and your time will come. Never realizing it is ever-present, waiting for time is an oxymoron. Time is already here.

Disregarding a simple truth, romance was elusive due to a lack of experience with what true love is and is not. The reality is even more complicated.

A love affair is open to imagination, creating endless romantic possibilities.

David Benjamin Bradley believed meeting good-looking women was not his problem. Ascertaining a woman's desire remained harder to discover. Romantic love remains well hidden. It was safer to stay unemotional and steer clear of commitment, as it may risk disappointment.

Weep For Love captures an in-depth portrayal of a couple's love affair. Not mollified with tiresome emotional tropes. Love is woven throughout tragedies, miscarriages, trauma, jealousy, character flaws, the blues, joy, and hope. An authentic love story encompasses family, friends, coworkers, and the heart of a romance.

The main protagonists narrated their love stories and wrote about their actions and thoughts.

"It begins with a character; all I can do is trot along behind him, trying to put down what he says and does." William Faulkner

Suzanne Siobhan Brooke is not a natural person, but is a fictional character. Based on an amalgamation of women's individualities, who are cherished and loved. David Benjamin Bradley is a complex fusion of imaginary and author-lived experiences.

Literary license freed me to fictionalize events, personalities, love affairs, and dreams realized, thus making possible a happy-ever-after or a prelude to the beginning of one.

Males who do not want to draw attention to their gender write romance novels under a female nom de plume. How is it plausible to write a romance novel and not be faithful to yourself? When did it become a thing that males could not capture the essence of romance?

"All thoughts, all passions, all delights, whatever stirs this mortal frame. All are but ministers of Love and feed his sacred flame." Samuel Taylor Coleridge

A person's life may experience unexpected detours that may not lead to the romance your heart craves. It is of no matter to the cosmos your pleas for a love affair. Notwithstanding dreams and longings for love, life is full of capricious consequences.

Romance does not always guarantee lasting happiness in the end. The future is filled with unknowns, which are unlikely to be determined in advance. Regardless of how your life unfolds, a human need for love and affection is ubiquitous.

"We must be willing to let go of the life we have planned, so as to have the life that is waiting for us." E. M. Forster

Sexual scenes result from the fervor of the protagonists' love for each other. Satiated with pleasure, you have no voice for words. You reach a state of joy, blending into each other's arms. Sex morphs into lovemaking.

Romance novels' descriptions of acts of love exaggerate sexual love. Words alone cannot capture the ecstasy of lovemaking, and using euphemisms instead of innocuous phrases of actual descriptions of sex is a theater of the absurd.

"A romantic novelist uses words to alter reality into consequential facts, as long as it does not infringe on the truth of the human heart." Nathaniel Hawthorne

The enjoyment of sexual pleasure woven into the story matches the protagonists' love for each other. The author did not write sexual love scenes to offend. Not calling something by its proper name does not eliminate the sensual sex portrayed.

A love affair is not effortlessly attained, so foolish not to trust your dreams. However, a comfort zone of dreams avoids the risk of unrequited love and deprives you of emotional sensations of affection.

By chance, you meet a captivating woman with intelligence and inner beauty. In a word, intuition can be relied upon to provide courage, thus depart imaginings of love into the arms of a lover.

Dating may become the beginning of a romance. The onset of love first unfolds with a passion leading into a fanciful version of romantic love.

However, I do not claim to be an expert on love. *Weep for Love* is my interpretation of a love story that connects the realism of love and family with a poignant romance.

Dispel all preconceived notions about romance novels. Leave ample time to visualize and appreciate pleasure in one of the many truths of romantic life.

Remember, "We were children once, playing with toys." The Low Spark Of High-Heeled Boys - Traffic

Enjoy reading,

David Kenneth Waldman

One
Never-Ending Romance

"No, this is not the beginning of a new chapter in my life; this is the beginning of a new book! That first book is already closed, ended, and tossed into the seas; this new book is newly opened, has just begun! Look, it is the first page! *And it is a beautiful one!"* C. Joy Bell C.

On a warm spring morning, an unexpected phone call changed my life.

"Dr. David, sorry this is the last minute to impose on you, but would you write and deliver a speech on my behalf? The United Nations Summit on Sustainable Education for Refugee Children is next week. You would be perfect as it is your expertise."

"Absolutely love to as long as there is advanced notice. What is the due date for a prepared speech?"

"You are scheduled to speak on Monday morning on Shaping the Future of Girl Education through Empowerment."

"You are aware today is Thursday."

"Yes, David, my staff prearranged everything to ensure it will be easy to attend. Therefore, there should be no concerns. Personally prepared your itinerary and arranged your temporary pass for the United Nations. My staff has your plane tickets and hotel reservation awaiting your approval. All travel expenses are covered, including a stipend.

Miss Jacqueline Caroline Brooke, our nonprofit organization's Director of Refugee Education, will meet you at JFK airport as soon as you exit baggage claim."

Unbelievably, delivering my first speech at the United Nations. However, a long-term romance recently ended, leaving me indifferent.

"Miss González, thank you for this opportunity. Unfortunately, it's not a good time."

"David, you are impressive, along with Jacqueline, who manages details and answers questions. She conducts all meetings except the one speech you deliver. You will enjoy collaborating with her."

Reluctantly, despite feeling down, my instinct was to accept this opportunity. Intuition led me where I needed to be. Hardly ever was a mistake. So bid adieu to my blues.

"Miss González, honored to give this speech."

My hometown is a perfect place to reawaken my frayed San Francisco energy. A city that never sleeps revitalizes my Bronx resilience with the cacophonous sounds of people hailing taxis.

A sense of urgency prevails amid a sea of yellow cabs, cars, and limo drivers in bumper-to-bumper traffic, and with city buses fanned out in all directions.

New York City's fast-paced life blended melodies of ethnicities into a symphony. Multiple accents were heard on Manhattan streets, filling the air with musical opuses. George Gershwin's *Rhapsody in Blue* comes to mind.

New Yorkers expected straightforward talk without anyone taking personal offense. As a native son, I learned to express my feelings in words framed as cold, hard truth. It did not always win friends or influence everyone.

Characteristics of a New York City lexicon were not indicative of the state, just as San Francisco does not represent California. New Yorkers are not easily offended by expletives or rudeness. It was not unusual for a New Yorker to share and express emotions with people they had recently met.

However, adopting Mom's British slang quieted some of the harshnesses of how this New Yorker speaks. My favorites are 'bloody hell' and 'bloody awful,' words rarely spoken in California.

A New Yorker is prone to behave similarly with strangers as with friends or acquaintances. Even so, people interpreted New Yorkers' talk as rude and did not accept it as a colorful description of a person's opinions.

On the other hand, exasperating a New Yorker is relatively easy. New York street etiquette is well-defined.

Contrary to New Yorkers' sensibilities, strolling on a congested street and suddenly stopping to look at the skyscrapers is frowned upon. A trivial transgression is stepping down on the wrong side of the subway stairs. It causes disdain.

Nevertheless, going to New York was a decision never regretted. An uneventful flight on a Golden Gate Airline 787 from San Francisco to New York allowed me sufficient time to edit and practice my speech.

JFK is my favorite airport to fly into, with an iconic view of the New York City skyline. Utterly weary, up all night writing, the battle to keep my eyes open, I finally lost. Unfortunately, I slept through the landing, only waking up startled at the thumping of the plane's tires hitting the tarmac.

My hometown is famous for being one of the world's favorite cities, and it would be remiss to leave out that New York has the absolute best pizza and MLB baseball team in the country. This is our arrogance to Chicagoans and Bostonians, a New Yorker's truth and pride. Even so, my New York state of mind and direct way of communicating have been restored. The city became a perfect setting for a serendipitous romance.

Welcome to New York City, Dr. David Benjamin Bradley. "Pleased to meet you. I'm Jacqueline Caroline Brooke. Is this all your luggage?"

"Yes, I travel light."

"Sweet, my car is in the green parking garage, close to this terminal, an easy walk."

Charmed by Jacqueline, my attention focused on her, not what she was saying. My long-term unsuccessful relationship faded into memory.

Jacqueline's electric blue eyes were enticing. Her smile warmly captures a love of life.

Her attractiveness is enhanced by her long, wavy, beige-blond hair flowing down her back, tight blue jeans, a pink silk blouse, and sexy brown suede ankle boots. Her charismatic personality added to her desirability.

Shortly, she would reveal more complexity.

Mesmerized by Jacqueline. "Sorry, you said 7:00 a.m. for breakfast?"

Not paying attention to Jacqueline speaking was not my best first impression. She was captivating, with a friendly demeanor and lovely Irish brogue.

Yet a sadness prevailed, unnoticeable, except for someone who suffered anguish.

With ample time to become acquainted, as rush hour meant that time spent in traffic to mid-Manhattan could extend to 90 minutes.

Little control over words that escape my mouth, probably not my most subtle pick-up line.

"My preference is David."

"Wonderful, my Sisters and friends call me Jacquie.

David, Oh My God, devastation from those horrific wildfires, with the sky turning orange as if it were outraged at the destruction of the forest and people's lives. How can anyone cope with the calamity of losing their home? Your loved ones are safe, but your family's home loss and sentimental objects like photos are irreplaceable."

"Frankly, Jacquie, I cannot imagine how people have any strength to rebuild their lives. How do you offer reassurance to a family? How does one make it uncomplicated for families to recover their lives?"

A lonely tear formed at the corner of her eye and slowly flowed down Jacquie's cheek.

Jacquie's empathic gift was revealed: "David, there is kindness in your dark blue eyes. I feel safe with you."

It looked as if her tears wanted to follow the first one. She needed to share a well-hidden hurt.

"If you want to talk, I'm a good listener."

Endeavoring not to cry did not prevent sobs and tears from ultimately escaping.

"My blind date ended as soon as I could get away. He took advantage of me."

Years of pent-up emotion needed to be released. Jacquie wanted someone to be a silent listener.

"Tried to speak, but an invisible emotional shield blocked my words. Powerless and silent for over five years, no one, except my Sisters, realized what I lived through. But not details because it would upset them, and they could not amend reality."

Cheerful less than an hour ago, tears flowed onto her cheeks, and she patted them away with a tissue. Tears transformed her happiness into memories that caused sorrow. While wanting to appreciate her loves and fears, what made her laugh instead was,

"Tell me about your family."

Jacquie went from tears to smiles. Her family life was indispensable, and she had an especially close relationship with her Sisters.

"Dad was surrounded by women, four daughters, my mother, and grandmother. My family is a cherished part of our lives. As a young girl, Nana immigrated to America from Rosscarbery, a small town in West Cork, Ireland.

Mom was raised in a traditional Irish home, so my Sisters and I grew up absorbed in the literary works of W.B. Yeats, Thomas Moore, James Joyce, C.S. Lewis, and George Bernard Shaw. My favorite 19th-century women romantic poets are Jane Austen, Charlotte Brontë, Elisabeth Gaskell, George Eliot, and Mary Shelley. Mom immersed us in Irish art, music, literature, and language.

Jacquie's favorite C.S. Lewis quote, "It may be hard for an egg to turn into a bird: it would be a jolly sight harder for it to learn to fly while remaining an egg. We are like eggs at present. And you cannot go on indefinitely being just an ordinary, decent egg. We must be hatched or go bad."

"Wow, thought he just wrote books."

"My Sisters and I listened to classic '60s and '70s rock and roll music. The youngest, Suzanne, adored The Beatles and was fond of their songs. She played them on the piano, enjoyed their lyrics, and sang them frequently. Her talent to bring out the sentiment of *Beatles* songs was impressive."

I wish my time with her wouldn't end so abruptly.

"Over a long dinner, maybe we can talk about what you were like as a girl, *and if wishes were horses, beggars would ride.*"

"David, this is my favorite old Scottish proverb."

Never underestimate an Irish woman's wit, intelligence, sense of humor, grace, beauty, and gentleness that flows from her heart.

"Tell me about your Sisters. Who was born first?"

"Born first, Mom gave birth every two years. Noreen Jennifer Brooke was the second-born. She has an adorable five-year-old daughter, Jessica. The three of us girls went to her with our troubles. She is completing her nursing courses and hopes to work at San Francisco General Maternity Hospital.

Victoria Deirdre Brooke, the third-born, is a fiery redhead who proudly flaunts her freckles and blue eyes and is fearless. Unconventional, open-minded, and loving, she has kept every Sister's secret.

We relied on Vickie to protect us from Dad's bitterness just in time to hide in the barn. Vickie was always a comfort to us girls with her depth of compassion and empathy. As a teenager, a judicious insight to understand our disappointments.

You will adore my Sisters, as each of us has a distinct personality. Yet we have a lot in common.

My baby Sister, Suzanne Siobhan Brooke, was born last. As the oldest, I had the joy of caring for my Baby Sister. Which enabled me to spend a lot of time with her. From the first day she came home from the hospital, she was never a fussy baby; she always smiled.

Suzanne is the wittiest, most emotional of our Sisters, self-confident, and an audacious risk-taker. A pretty girl who enjoyed pretending to be married. She wanted me to marry her to a favorite doll in make-believe weddings. This little girl of five told me this was practice for when she would marry her beloved one day.

Compassionate with a gift of being hyper-empathic and gracefully managing it with prudence, she volunteered at ten to help elect a Congresswoman.

She is silly and makes us laugh when any of the Sisters is sad. Her cheerfulness was easily recognizable, marked by a part giggle and laugh, a joy to hear.

Mom helped as I fed, diapered, put her in bed at nap and sleep times, and held her when she cried. As a result, closeness is sustained by a mutual devotion to Sisterhood and friendship.

Suzanne is the prettiest and exudes a sense of femininity and sensuality. Boys and men would want to date her. However, my baby Sister held on to her faith. She knew her dream man, with whom she would fall in love and marry. Oh, and Suzie had a natural propensity to get into trouble."

"Trouble is a recurring theme since childhood, something we decidedly have in common."

"Let me get you checked in and settled in your hotel room. Since this is your hometown, would you do us the honor of selecting a restaurant for dinner? But first, must call the boss to tell her you arrived safely."

Neglected to eat dinner and instead talked throughout the night. Was Jacquie the woman of my dreams? She enchanted me despite my self-imposed fear of rejection.

Look forward to working together.

Sadness returned to Jacquie after her phone call. She wanted to finish talking about her horrendous date. She shed tears for a few minutes before she could compose herself.

"Reluctantly agreed to go on a blind date with a policeman named Paul."

'Please, Jacquie, a double date just this one time. Just dinner, promise, and we leave together. This guy I'm dating has a friend, and asked if I knew someone to set him up.'

Jacqueline sobbed, barely able to relive the story of her nightmare. Tears continued to flow down her cheeks.

Using all her emotional strength, with a slight quiver in her voice, "he raped and disparaged me. Threatened my life if I went to the police."

'Besides, no one will believe you.'

"Imprudent and afraid to report the rape, so all evidence was lost. As soon as my pregnancy was confirmed, my first thought was to obtain an abortion.

Alone and pregnant in a San Francisco health clinic, I faced a consequential decision that would affect my unborn child and me for the rest of our lives. Vulnerable, scared, and conflicted, wanting the baby, yet my memory of the look on his contorted, angry face still haunts me."

Jacquie folded her legs under her, next to a box of tissues.

"You don't have to tell me details. It upset you."

Relationships are built on trust and mutual care for one another. David, I want to tell you. Grabbed my bag, ran out of the clinic, and drove across the city.

Anxiously walked into my therapist's office during her group therapy session without knocking. Cannot remember anything except that she led me to her private office."

'Jacquie, finishing this session in a few minutes. Then have two hours before my next appointment.'

"Dr. Rose listened with unspoken compassion. David, her wisdom enlightened by her empathy, a remarkable ability to bring light and healing to deep-rooted pain hidden in the darkest recesses of my heart. Her advice is why I have my baby girl."

'You have a look of being violated.'

"Rose had recently begun a group for women who were abused or raped, and what she said took me by surprise."

'You will not be on your own. Plus a secured, good-paying job and the love of your mom, Nana, and Sisters. You have their support and affection to raise your baby girl.'

'What should I do? Started loving my baby. She is a month and a half, and I hear her saying, "I'll be there to comfort you." Rose, is this crazy?'

Jacqueline sobbed, and between breaths, 'My baby said I chose you to be my mom.'

'Jacquie, your baby, wants to grow up with your love. Pregnancy is a blessing, not rape. God provides what we pray for, but not always in the way we expect. Go home and talk to your sisters, and take in their love. You already know your answer. Your Sister's love and inner strength will give you courage.

"Rose told you your unborn baby is a girl?"

Joyously with no trace of recent tears, "My beautiful daughter Annabelle Ashley Brooke is the love and joy of my life. She is a four-year-old with an old soul.

David, I'll understand if you don't want to start building a relationship."

"Jacquie, tell me all about Annabelle. I hope to meet her soon. The weather is usually dependable and sunny in the Springtime in San Francisco. We might go to the zoo if it's warm. Anywhere you and Annabelle choose."

"Oh, David, are you sure?"

"It doesn't have to be the zoo. Bet your daughter would love going to an amusement park. Why don't you decide with Annabelle when you get back home?"

"She is with Noreen, who is babysitting.

Men do not want a woman who keeps her baby from rape. Or bless me for being one with God."

"Jacquie, I'm not like most men. Tell me about your love."

"Annabelle, frankly, is beyond belief. She is playful as a kitten, and loves the way she thinks. With an artist's heart, my baby girl now visualizes what she is capable of.

Annabelle loves drawing and singing, and recently started ballet dance and piano lessons. It is hard to keep up with her.

She is a caring and kindhearted child who sits on my lap when I'm sick. At bedtime, she climbs into my bed and says, "Mommy, you should not be alone." Mommy, you should not be alone. My teddy and I will keep you company and look after you."

Jacqueline told me my unconditional acceptance of Annabelle was when she started to fall in love.

Our mutual sexual attraction transformed into an intimate relationship as lovers. Her soft hand took hold of mine. As we walked toward the bed, a spark of excitement went through us. Anticipating our first kiss, unbuttoned her silk blouse, revealing her soft, round breasts, which enhanced her sensual appeal. Took off her bra and sensually touched her breasts to tease her nipples.

Jacquie's kisses were soft and danced delicately on my face, alternating with long, passionate kisses.

"David never felt this much sexual desire with a man."

Gently pulled off her boots and unbuttoned her jeans, and unhurriedly pulled them off. Took hold of the bottom of her tight-fitting jeans, gently pulled off her pants, and slid off her panties.

As we drew our bodies closer, we joined in a gentle, embracing gesture.

Jacquie enhanced our mutual desire as her luscious lips captured mine. She used her tongue to invite me to a French kiss.

Her nakedness aroused my longing. After unbuttoning my shirt, Jacquie kissed my neck and, with her soft tongue, played with my nipples. Lingering kisses on my lips heightened my excitement as her long fingers stroked my crotch. A deep sigh of pleasure escaped. She loosened my belt and sultrily unzipped my pants. Taking a long time to kiss me, she tossed my briefs to the floor.

Jacquie's moist mouth captured my penis. Skilled at delaying my orgasm and heightening my sexual desire. If she felt me getting too aroused, she parted her legs, allowing me to use my tongue. Jacquie enticed me by playing with my anus with her long fingers.

Switched to rubbing her breasts against my inguinal area. The word stuck with me. An old girlfriend preferred the word "instead of the groin. Rather, Jacquie enjoyed the word crotch as it held a sexual connotation for her.

The warmth of her stomach, soft, wet mouth, and hands squeezing my buttocks were intoxicating. She wet one of her fingers and slowly slid it into my anus. Making love in multiple positions intensified our lovemaking. Our passion was like a ballet, each movement complementing the other.

"David, I'm cumming." Joining her intensified our orgasm.

Jacquie and I had an exquisite sexual and loving romantic—best friend relationship. Our lovemaking lasted until the first rays of sunlight of a new morning. Tonight marks the beginning of our romance. And they were the happiest six months of my life.

Always asked for Annabelle when Jacquie stayed over on weekends. Everything we did included her and enhanced our joy."

"You don't mind?"

"Jacquie, your little girl captured my heart. You and I are comforted when she is with us."

Annabelle loved being with me and her mom. At my home in San Francisco, her bedroom was filled with her favorite books, dolls, and toys, and we spent endless hours delighting in our play.

Annabelle asked about The Bronx because she enjoyed the sound of my accent. This exceptional little girl has a knack for speaking like a native New Yorker.

We spent a reasonable amount of time together. I loved Annabelle as my own.

Jacquie's humor and *joie de vivre* make me laugh. Enjoy her playfulness and her ability to ease my sadness with laughter. Our love for each other grew more profound, more joyful, and unconditional.

"David, my love deepens when you give of yourself so lovingly to Annabelle. You are more attractive and desirable when you do. Yet, worried, your blue eyes only come to life when we make love, or you are with Annabelle. Honey, my desire is for you to be happy."

Our life together was blissful, marked by endless conversations and an incessant care and love for each other.

We often went on treasure hunts for antiques as an excuse to drive all over northern California. Jacqueline and I enjoyed visiting the Redwood Forest and Annabelle's favorite, Santa Cruz's Beach Boardwalk. The three of us frequently walked on China Beach, with its picturesque view of the Golden Gate Bridge.

Since we both worked long hours, going to the movies or a Broadway play in San Francisco at the O'Donnell Theater on Fillmore Street was a cherished luxury. For Annabelle, this was a new experience.

At our favorite restaurant in Chinatown, Annabelle always ordered an egg roll and vegetable chow mein. We always share a cookie and cream gelato in Little Italy for dessert.

"David, the cream makes the cookies taste good."

Playdates with Annabelle included amusement parks, picnics, and playgrounds. Usually, our day ended by watching one of her favorite movies.

Noreen frequently visited with her daughter Jessica, who was a year older. Annabelle always enjoyed her sleepover at Aunt Noreen's home. The girls love each other as Sisters.

Upon being introduced to Noreen, she started talking as if we had known each other for years. Right away, I was fond of Noreen and loved spending time with her.

"David, while my Sister prepares dinner and the girls play in Jessica's bedroom, come and sit next to me. I'd like to tell you no secrets are kept; my Sisters share everything. Even Vickie will call a Sister meeting if knowing a secret is in our best interest."

"There should be an awesome Best Sisters' award for not engaging in sibling rivalry."

"Silly goose, when Jacquie first met you in New York, she told me how excited she was to meet someone who respected her and how much you love Annabelle."

"Do you mean everything? Does it include our first night together?"

"Jacquie said you were fantastic in bed, and it was early morning when you ordered room service."

"You did mean everything."

"David, I have grown fond of you and appreciate your love and care for my niece and Sister."

"Are all Sisters as charming? With the pièce de résistance, you are gorgeous. Your attractiveness lies in your capacity to love and laugh. Did this come off as a pathetic pick-up line?"

In a playful tone, "Yes, but I wanted you to. You and Jacquie are happy. That's what matters."

"Dinner is ready. I'll go get the girls to wash their hands." Then, surprised to hear, "David, you have my permission to hug and kiss my Sister."

A hug from Noreen is hard to put into words. Her kiss was delicate, and the warmth of her lips touching mine was sweet, like listening to her affection through her body.

"Noreen, your hug and tender kiss confirmed our friendship."

"Your gift of words, one could easily believe you were born Irish."

Noreen, cherish your compliment. Or was that a polite way of saying full of Blarney?"

With a delightful giggle, "a little of both."

Jacquie said, "Annabelle asked if you would read her favorite bedtime story, Cinderella."

A fairy tale she never grew tired of hearing. Tucked Annabelle in bed and sneaked in two instead of one chocolate chip cookie her mom allowed. She always goes halves with me, so we both get a cookie.

Next, we checked the closet and under her bed for monsters so she could fall asleep. Each time we checked, she would tell me about the funny names of each of the monsters we searched for each night.

"Can we check for Cookie Snatcher Monster now?" Watches a popular children's TV show, which has creative names for its characters. That told me about Jacquie's love, artfully prolonged, as she turned off her night lamp and went to sleep.

Honestly, it is impossible to keep anything secret from Jacquie. She was always aware that the second cookie was for me. When it came to Annabelle, she let me spoil her.

Jacquie and Noreen enjoyed Sister's talks. My mom called it having a good old chinwag.

The best aspects of Noreen's kitchen include a comfortable breakfast nook, ideal for relaxing after a meal at the end of their tête-à-tête. Jacquie and Noreen loved having hot cocoa waiting for them.

At bedtime, lovemaking always ended in spooning. Our favorite way to fall asleep.

Our relationship didn't neatly fit into a single category: romance, lovemaking, or friendship. Thankfully, an unrestricted merging of all three made what was to come barely endurable.

Annabelle was happy. Jacquie and I grew closer and more intimate, deepening our affection and creating an intermingling of three hearts.

The thing about romance, particularly when it catches you off guard, is simultaneously both animating and disquieting. Jacquie promised we would spend a weekend at her home in South Lake Tahoe, and that day never arrived. We both accepted that our fate was not marriage, and our relationship sealed in love would last forever. Though it was inevitable to hear the words,

"Love, it's unclear what destiny has in store for us, but trust our paths are one."

These heartfelt words did not alleviate the disappointment of the emotional loss of our romance.

Jacquie often spoke of her fondness for Jaz, who spent last year in Paris studying world-famous fashion designers.

She was deeply in love with Jaz. They separated because an insurmountable distance became too much of an obstacle.

"David, after reuniting with Jaz, it became clear we made a dreadful mistake. Jaz wants me to take some time out of respect for you and our love. Having faith, we realize that our destinies are intertwined. Do you trust me?"

"Yes, of course, completely."

"You will meet someone. Keep hope alive. David, you will soon appreciate why this was meant to happen. Tears will dry, and your lovely blue eyes will sparkle again. I love you, and am afraid to lose you."

"No, you will not. Whatever life has in store for us in our future, we have something no one can take away. Our love lies embedded in each other. Both hearts are intertwined, and my intuition tells me there is nothing to be apprehensive about."

Well, those were just poetic-sounding words and my sincere desire.

"Yes, we are passionately connected in our love. David, are you good?"

"No. Though knowing you are back with your loved one bestows some comfort. Confidence in our love will keep us close."

Jacquie started to tear up and tenderly asked,

"David, would you become Annabelle Ashley, my wee beautiful girl's uncle? She loves you and thinks of you as her dad. And when she was promised to ask you to be her uncle, she jumped up and down on her bed. My baby is devoted to you, and Annabelle's and my love will keep us bonded."

"Love, nothing could make me happier!"

"Annabelle attends a new preschool close to our home in South Lake Tahoe. There, one day, your destiny becomes apparent., Honey, our love endures. You fear not seeing me, the same fears I have."

"We are family, and you and Annabelle are my blessings."

Why our relationship transformed was not yet known. Jaz, Jacquie, and Annabelle loved each other and helped mitigate my loss.

Acknowledging their love did not diminish my heartache. Nevertheless, love needs to multiply for it to become everlasting.

Held hands and had intimate conversations. Jacquie and I laughed and hugged, which sealed our new relationship.

Jacquie loves that I'm sensitive to Jaz's emotions. Jacquie is reassured that we're adjusting to a new us. A new beginning for Jacquie and me. She kept her promise that we would never lose our intimacy. Even with her reassurance, my heart shattered, and I found myself torn between happiness for their relationship and sadness at the same time.

'Love each of my Sisters to bits and look out for each other.'

Jacquie has her Sisters who have her heart intermigled. Tears were barely quelled, but I was reassured she was safe and loved.

"David, promise me you don't get disheartened."

"Sorry, love, I cannot give you that assurance."

"Reassure me, you'll come to me if you are saddened or need me. Give me your word. You don't stay isolated if you cannot jump off your carousel of blues. Promise, when you call, I will always come to you."

"My word, always be there for you, Annabelle, and Jaz. However, the suffocation of blues buries me in a cloak of silence. Your love is my lifeline, and you have my word to go to you when I'm blue. But, Jacquie, cannot always keep my promise. I already miss you."

"Me too. I'll call you often. David, I love you. Take care of yourself, Annabelle, and I need you.

Are you all right?"

"No, my world just stopped spinning."

"Mine too, but must remain strong for you and Annabelle."

With tears in her eyes, Jacquie hugged me and kissed me tenderly.

"Talk soon around bedtime to ease you and me into our new relationship."

Driving home, the evening seemed darker, the streets emptier. Ate a slice of Sicilian pizza with mushrooms, onions, and green peppers, accompanied by a chocolate cherry soda. Watched a favorite, William Powell and Myrna Loy movie, *The Thin Man*. Which broke an aloneness of one in a city of hundreds of thousands of diverse voices. Starting a new work week with a broken heart.

Always looked forward to having dinner with Annabelle and Jacquie one or more nights a week.

At one of our dinners, Jacquie seemed restless and disquieted.

"Do you want to tell me what is troubling you?"

"Paul texted and wants to have weekends with Annabelle. And found out about my love affair with Jaz and threatened to smear my reputation as an abusive mother. Has confidence in a sympathetic judge granting shared custody rights."

"That never happens. Do not worry."

Jacquie wanted me to vow, not to antagonize Paul. "David, please, let the courts handle this. Our family lawyer, Mrs. Nixon, is the best child protection lawyer in the country. She filed a restraining order and built a case against him for raping me. The Judge imposed a 150-foot restraining order around Annabelle and me to prevent physical retaliation. Based on his verbal threats and not the fact that he raped me.

Solely because Paul was in the police force, there was politics. Decided my daughter's life would not be tied up in court to win a brutal battle as a woman.

Sweet David, you will despise Paul. The mere thought of him is repulsive. Usually stays away but occasionally shows up. It is unnerving and upsetting.

Pregnant with Annabelle, a blessing out of a horrific rape. After her birth, I started therapy to be taught how not to be abused by his madness. Paul is a mean, despicable, sorry excuse for a human, a nasty, jealous man.

David, you are my first true romance with a man. Your loving support for Jaz and me as we build our lives means a great deal to us. However, your caring impulse is to protect me from harm, and fear for your safety. Make a solemn promise to not fight Paul if provoked. He worries me with his uncontrolled contemptible hate. Somehow manages to barge into my life when everything is calm."

"No guarantee, but sincerely try not to engage in a dispute with Paul. Unless he becomes an imminent threat to you, Jaz, or Annabelle, is all I can say, and remain honest."

The day a restraining order arrived, Jacquie and I were slightly reassured.

As days and weeks passed, Jacquie and I spoke and texted with each other at least once a day. Each night, our phone call gave us both a sense of comfort. A truism is that time heals all emotional wounds. Yet, the bloody axiom never said how much time. A month slipped into a month with a new name. It no longer mattered what Jacqueline texted. It always lifted my spirits.

"Love, exciting news, an invitation for you and me to a dinner party at Senator Julia Harrison's home. Call me tonight, xoxo JCB."

"Love to go with you, but…"

Jacquie ignored everything after she heard me insert a but.

"You remember my youngest Sister, Suzanne."

"Sorry, no love, cannot say I do."

"David, speak about her all the time. Stop kidding. Remember the day we met and told you my Sister worked at ten years old as a volunteer in the election of the Senator in her first political race to become the Congressional Representative of the 81st District, Sacramento."

"Yes, of course, as a proud older Sister, feeling elated about her triumphs."

"Suzanne was recently promoted as an assistant speechwriter and reports to Senator Julia Harrison and her Director of Speechwriting. Now Senator Harrison is a front-runner in the Presidential primary season.

Well, my Sister was the one who got us invited.

Shared with Suzanne, you are six feet tall, slender, and muscular with long chestnut-brown hair and dark blue eyes. She has seen pictures of you and remarked how handsome you are."

When Jacquie's voice seemed to smile, I knew she had a secret.

"Whenever my sister and I spoke, Suzie always looked forward to hearing about you. Casually mentioned that your unflagging honesty and sincere kindness, intelligence, and perceptiveness have made you successful as a social entrepreneur, author, and educator. David, perhaps I should have added that I love your witty sense of humor and limitless capacity for empathy.

You two have much in common. Creative, risk-taker, spontaneous, compassionate, with a sense of humor, stubborn, romantic, sexy, and loving. Oh, and how we had fantastic sex when we first met."

"Was that all? Jacquie, you forgot trustworthy, cheerful, loyal, brave, reverent, and thrifty.

"David, please be serious. How you were described to Suzie makes you uncomfortable. I'm genuinely sorry. Was anything said inaccurately? You cannot catch a wife with modesty as bait."

"Wife? Jacquie, love, what are you talking about? How did an introduction to your baby Sister become matchmaking?"

"Sorry, wrong turn of phrase. Perhaps adding our lovemaking was a wee over the line."

"You think?

Which man would not want a beautiful woman to tell her lovely Sister, he is every woman's vision of a lover and wants to be in bed with me."

"Was this Bronx sarcasm, or are you angry with me? David, I apologize, but this is how I see you. Are you embarrassed?"

"No."

"Does no mean not feel embarrassed or not angry with me?"

"Jacqueline Caroline Brooke."

"Love how you say my name with your Bronx accent."

"You made me sound better than other men. What you shared with your Sister does not leave me much room to impress. Your Sister has a mental image I cannot live up to. As this was only supposed to be an introduction, what are you implying? This is not a blind date, so please don't emphasize my virtues."

"Too late, love. Readers of your best-selling books, rave book reviews, numerous speeches at conferences, news coverage on your international work for children, and you are just beginning your career."

"News coverage does not brag about my sexual prowess. Mind you, it may lead to commercializing me as a sexual commodity. But if this is what women must endure, it is impossible to understand how women cope with unscrupulous sexual harassment.

Jacquie, this is the best you have been at avoiding my question. Why does meeting your Sister mean she has my biography?"

"There is sadness in your voice. What is troubling you? Suzanne is excited to meet you, not a caricature of you. David, please tell me."

"Rejection, my worst nightmare, is starting a relationship with a woman I have fallen deeply in love with, who would leave me. Not ready to meet anyone new. Do not want a girlfriend. My life is working, and everything is good. Finally, my life is uncomplicated."

"No, you are not content. You make others happy, Annabelle, Noreen, Jessica, and me, but refuse to think of yourself. David, it is only my baby Sister. You met Noreen, and she adores you. I adore you. There are just two more Sisters I want you to meet."

"Love, what part of not wanting to meet anyone prevents you from believing me? Not ready, plus your Sisters do not do anything by halves. Okay, naively thought that when we met, we would stay together forever. You captured my heart, and I love you and always will. Promise you will be the first to know when ready to be in romantic love again."

Jacquie whispered softly, "I could never leave you. Our relationship grew more intimate, so please don't withdraw from me.

You cannot kiss an Irish girl unexpectedly. You can only kiss her sooner than she thought you would. An Irish proverb translates to I love you. Annabelle loves you, and you do not have a monopoly on the mindset that you lost something precious.

Our loving and incomparable relationship gets me up in the morning. I love that we are still close. You accepted my love for Jaz, which means everything to me. It is how I was able to go back to her."

"You two are meant for each other. Only want you to be happy.

Starting to date again is like juggling fire batons. Inevitably, getting burnt is a likely outcome; it' getting burnt is a likely outcome, it is not a safe place to hang out. How much manipulation of a fire baton before the right woman appears?"

"David, have faith you will find someone."

"A burden of blues tugs at me and hinders a second chance to redefine romance, sensuality, and love. Jacquie, the simple truth is it's incredulous for me to imagine the likelihood of finding a love mate after you."

"Before long, a woman will appreciate the depth of your capacity to love. Your confidence emerges when you are ready to accept this. Spiraling more profoundly into the blues hides this from you. This is not a setback. It is a new opportunity for love. That day will arrive soon. Your intuition and heart let you in on the secret."

"Jacquie, compared to a Senator, who is way above my pay grade, though your invitation is appreciated. Thank you, but not interested in attending. This is your auspicious occasion. You can tell me all about it."

"Only one other person I know is as obstinate as you. Once you have decided, you tell yourself you can never see yourself as I do. A woman at this fundraising dinner appreciates how lucky she found you and fell in love with you."

"Cherish you, Jacquie. Fairy tales with happy, ever-after endings were great as a kid. You get to go to sleep believing all is right with the world. Alas, no longer a kid."

"You can't have confidence in a river remaining the same when you see it again."

"Sweetheart, yet it is, in essence, the same river. Change flows like a river. You taught me this, hold on to faith until you....."

"Jacquie, this is the fifth time in person or talking on the phone. You have stopped in mid-sentence. You don't want to share something with me, and wouldn't like to find out in public.

What do you mean some woman at this event will fall in love with me? It's foolish to argue against myself for not finding another Jacquie. Yet, you need to accept that it's not probable. Plus, you're up to some matchmaking. I love you, thank you, but no thanks."

Her giggle was comforting, but also meant my argument was lost.

"Trust your heart as much as I do. Endangering your life because it's where girls who are vulnerable need opportunities. Your mission is to advocate for the right to education of vulnerable girls in remote rural areas of East Africa. We are both twenty-five, yet I have neither completed nor started a doctoral program.

Work in war zones regardless of danger. Your courage and compassion put your life at risk, even with security precautions. As you say, it is just what I do. That is the David I love. How many times have you said it is not about me?

David, I trust that you are making a difference in transforming the lives of vulnerable girls and motivating children to never give up on their dreams.

Focus on the phenomenally varied and impactful life you've had. You'll be able to see the difference you made. Reviewing your life through the eyes of someone you did not know. You would be floored and super impressed, and it is your life!

Why hasn't the right woman yet appeared in your life? I don't have an answer for you; perhaps you're meeting at a crossroads. My vision includes the entirety of you, which you keep well hidden. Soon, you will accept what you consider improbable.

Loving taking risks is not antithetical to you, even if your sadness emerges. Do not define yourself as despondent. Because in your heart, you understand who you are."

"I love you every moment we spend together, and cannot keep up with your wit and intellect, but I did not have to. You trusted my life experiences would intrigue your Sister. She wanted you to be happy and invited me. That is right, isn't it?"

With her giggle, she unpretentiously said, "You are an Irish person's match in wit and intellect."

"Jacquie, why is Senator Harrison so familiar to me?"

"Perhaps because her name has been mentioned while talking about my Sister dozens of times."

"There is no way I'm ready for this affair. Besides, how could your Sister trust that the Senator would be interested in meeting me? What could persuade her to talk about me to the Senator? Her credibility to put in a good word could get sullied."

"Beloved, didn't tell my Sister to invite you."

Unfortunately, I won't get a response from Jacquie. Knowing not to underestimate her and trusting that details will become known.

"David, cannot wait for you to meet my baby Sister. One day, you shall understand why Suzanne has faith in you. She recently turned 20 years old and is sophisticated, multi-talented, loving, and easy to get along with. Frequently spends time singing lovingly as a duet with Annabelle."

"You are holding something back, and why do you want to surprise me? Or do you want to wait for the right time? Sorrowfully, my intuition is uncertain while immersed in dark blue hues."

"Have faith in me."

"Truly, with no hesitation. So, you are not going to tell me."

"No, I'm not. Love, we can talk all night, but first let me give you the party details. The Senator's address … she lives in Northeast Sacramento County. The fastest way is over the San Francisco-Oakland Bay Bridge. You stay on I-80 East to US 50 East. It is an hour and 55 minutes drive, longer with traffic."

"Jacquie, what is wrong? You sound uneasy."

"Nothing, just eager to see you and my Sister."

"Jacqueline Caroline Brooke!"

"You never say my full name, which I love, unless you are earnest."

"You are superb at changing the subject to avoid giving bad news."

"Didn't want you upset, and would tell you later."

"How much later? Tomorrow is Thursday, and this fundraising affair is Saturday."

"Okay, only if you agree, you won't react with a 'Bronx attitude' and do something impulsive to protect me."

"Sweetheart, I promise. What could be so bad?"

"Paul was able to get an invitation, and most assuredly, will intimidate and bully. Lost control when receiving a restraining order, and rape charges were filed. Raged at the Judge, which did not impress her. Hoped he was still in jail. David, I'm scared. What if he succeeds and takes my baby from me?"

"Stand corrected, Jacquie. It could be this bad.

Guarantee it will never happen. I will not allow it, so there is no assurance. Might wallop your nemesis' face a few times."

"Honey, you will not have to, like you were going to anyway. I'm not worried about the security as they will check each guest as they enter. Plus, you will be there, so everything will be all right."

Jacquie spoke reassuringly; nevertheless, her worry was noticeable.

"Tell me more about Suzanne."

Whenever she spoke about her sister, her demeanor was calm.

"Tomorrow after work, leaving a few days early to spend time with Suzie.

Anxious to talk in person. With Suzie's schedule, it was a challenge to coordinate Sister talks."

"Senator Harrison has been her mentor and boss since my Sister was ten years old. That takes up a lot of her time."

"Speaking of young ones, can Annabelle come?"

"Sweetheart, this is a Black-Tie affair and way past her bedtime. Instead, she was assured a night to watch her favorite movie with Uncle David and me."

"I miss her."

"She is annoyed because you and Aunt Suzie will be together, and cannot take her. My love said, 'Mommy, this may affect my social-emotional development.'

There's no need to speculate who couldn't refuse her and just say no. David, don't want my baby to repeat words she does not understand."

"Whoops, Annabelle overheard me talking to a colleague and said she wanted to understand. So, I explained, and she kind of understood."

"Sweetie, tell her that is grown-up talk. Then you do not have to say no."

"Jacquie, so what is your concern?"

"The love of my life is brilliant. David, should she be assessed to measure how gifted she is?"

"Annabelle has not yet begun to explore her talents and intellect."

"I do not understand. If she is gifted, why not?"

"Okay, let me give you an example. You could say I had potential if you first met me when I was twenty."

"You're sure."

"Undoubtedly, not a good influence on you. Have to watch my sarcasm. You would not have been aware of my accomplishments over the next five years. How talented have I become compared to five years ago? Am I more gifted now?

It is only a snapshot of her talents at the moment. Love, she will do so much more."

"Can I share my pride in her talents?"

"You already do. You frequently answer questions arising from your love's curiosity.

Did you hear her singing a song taught to her about how she can do anything if she never gives up?"

"David, recently, 'Mommy, there goes my rubber tree.'

Thought she meant she tipped over a plant. "*High Hopes,*" 'Whoops there goes another rubber tree plant,' is her new favorite song.

David, you are cherished. A similarity of gifts admired in Annabelle is the same as the one you possess. You once told me that you can see the same qualities in someone you have. However, you could not recognize values you don't have. You would not recognize them. Yet if you did, you couldn't relate.

Oh, David, you are so clever. I love how you explain complicated things so they become easy to understand. Annabelle and I are lucky to have you as our uncle. Please let me know what to do. Counting on your instinctive male trait of wanting to fix things for women."

"So, you could not resist sarcasm. I should have realized sooner that this has nothing to do with Annabelle. You diverted my attention to her, rather than respecting my wish not to attend. You have gotten me talking about Annabelle instead of protecting you from Paul. Plus, it was a perfect time to give me a pep talk. Jacquie, hence, my love for you, please release me from attending this dinner party."

"Suzie is aware you write children's books. She read them and was impressed. She gave copies of them, plus a draft copy of your memoir, to Senator Harrison. She told my sister she was looking forward to meeting you."

"Jacquie, this isn't reassuring me. If the Senator had read a draft of my memoir, she would have learned of my blues history, making me feel vulnerable.

Love to attend this donor affair at the Senator's home. However, there is a conference starting early Saturday morning."

Jacquie was skeptical of my flimsy excuse for not attending, citing a scheduling conflict.

"How exciting! What is the name of this conference? Perfect, I'll meet you there on Sunday morning to have brunch. It's okay, Sweetie, you don't have to make up an excuse for me. You can tell me if you do not want to attend this dinner party."

She was not amenable to any excuse; finally, she relented and remained silent.

"You have nothing to worry about. The Senator is too busy to have time to read your memoir.

Love, my sister shared with the Senator, you make a difference when you empower teenage girls who suffer from bullying, low self-esteem, or have a false image of their body.

You are never going to meet all the teens you helped, who are exposed to intolerable gender bullying, suffer dark episodes, and contemplate suicide. Even at times of mental anguish, you accomplished much for others. I love you, Cher Ami."

Jacquie's thinking is not predictable. Her wit, stubbornness, intoxicating personal charm, and warmth become a beacon of reassurance in the face of adversity. In other words, Jacquie would not take no for an answer. Reluctantly, I acquiesced.

"Oh, by the way, remember this is a black-tie dinner. Text you soon with details. Annabelle and I love you. Bye for now."

It was Wednesday evening, and my tuxedo needed to be dry cleaned. As fate would have it, this was to be a night that forever transformed my life.

"It isn't possible to love and part. You will wish it were. You can transmute love, ignore it, or muddle it, but you can never pull it out of you. I know by experience that the poets are right: love is eternal." E.M. Forster

Two
The Day My Life Changed

"Goodbye? Oh no, please. Can't we go back to page one and do it all over again?" A.A. Milne

Leaving home, driving across the San Francisco-Oakland Bay Bridge, as a reddened sun slid silently under the Pacific Ocean at the point it touched the western sky.

The scenery blended seamlessly into a dark, star-filled sky on a ride from San Francisco to Sacramento. Anticipated driving on the US-50 corridor, so-called the *loneliest road in America*.

Average traffic for a Saturday evening to the Senator's home took two and a half hours, enough time to listen to my favorite Jazz station on Blue Star FM.

Unsurprisingly, regardless of dreams, difficulties arrive. C'est la vie life happens. Yet obstacles are surmountable, and there is always hope.

"Listen to the mustn'ts, child. Listen to the don'ts. Listen to the shouldn'ts, the impossibles, the won'ts. Listen to the never haves, then listen close to me... Anything can happen child. Anything can be." Shel Silverstein

No foreseeable signs to indicate what was to unfold tonight. A simple fact is that unanticipated consequences are needed for your life to change.

A cloudless night under a January Wolf Moon, at Sierra Woods Estate, the home of Senator Julia Harrison, seemed fantastic, not ominous. Wished Jacquie were driving up with me. Lingering doubts of not belonging were irrational, so I ignored them.

Relaxing with Jacquie, who was reading the Sunday San Francisco Journal.

'David, you know Suzanne works for Senator Harrison. Her husband, Dr. Robert Kelly, is one of the country's leading surgeons for trauma-related injuries. Let me read this to you. Oh my, it's not speculation. The Senator is considered a presumptive winner of the upcoming Presidential primary season.'

Not every day do I get an invitation to a credible presidential candidate's home for a formal fundraising dinner. Jacquie sent me a description of their home.

'David, check this out. Twenty acres of land, enriched by Alder, Aspen, Cedar, and Pine trees, offer a spectacular view of the Sierra Nevada mountains. The property features a 10,000-square-foot home, as well as several guest cottages, one of which was converted into her main campaign headquarters.

Incredible fireplaces in the living room, primary bedroom, and family room, movie theater, sunken spa, steam room & sauna, and an outdoor kitchen. Awesome, right?'

Born in Modesto to a middle-class family, the Senator moved to Sacramento when she was two. Dr. Kelley has a substantial inheritance, donating hundreds of thousands of dollars yearly to impoverished children, as well as to urgent causes such as climate change, wildlife extinction, and environmental issues.

Voted for the Senator, and incredible to receive an invitation. Jacquie assured me she would introduce VIPs to become acquainted with.

Fantasy time is over. My home was once filled with joy. Living in a small three-bedroom house in the outer Richmond district, I am surrounded by the never-ending soothing, low-pitched sounds of fog horns piercing the night fog of the Pacific Ocean.

Annabelle loved helping prepare meals and cook. We let her open the box and put the pasta into a pot of cold water. She had trouble keeping spaghetti on her plate, never mind on her fork.

'Uncle David, why is the spaghetti so sloppy?'

Her solution was simply to use her left hand, laughing each time she grabbed some to eat.

Our relationship became more intimate. Babysitting for Annabelle became a highlight of my week. When Jacquie worked late frequently, I got to spend time with my niece, a precocious and adorable four-and-a-half-year-old.

'Uncle David, are you happy?'

'Why would you ask? Content to be with you and your mom.'

'No, are you sad you don't have a little girl?'

'You never have to worry about that.'

'Don't like it, you live alone, I'll become your little girl forever.'

'Hey, you two, if we are going to get to the movie theater on time.'

Annabelle was strapped into her child seat, happily chatting with Madeline, her favorite doll.

'What did the love of my life say?'

'Nothing.'

'Okay then, why tears?'

'Just have something in my eye. She said I love you. The love of your life has a loving way, and Sweetheart, she has captured my heart, sensing my moods, especially when I'm sad.'

Sensing strong feelings, Jacquie remained silent.

'Annabelle asked if I was happy. Taken aback by her saying I don't like you living alone, and I will be your little girl forever.'

'Annabelle's four-and-a-half-year-old soul taught me what matters in life.'

A police car's flashing red light through my rearview mirror broke my daydream. Clearing a path for an Ambulance whose siren told vehicles to pull over. Moved out of the way into the right lane.

A new year has been added to the twenty-first century, and I have already been invited to a Senator's home who is running to become the next President of the United States. How much better could this year be? I wondered what fate had in store for my future.

"What we do not confront in ourselves, we will meet as fate." Carl Jung

"David, you told me your path takes unexpected twists and turns. Passion, joy, and love turn up in the unexpected, and become a night of…"

"Of what?"

"Trust me."

"You are keeping something from me, and trust me, it's a ruse to change the subject."

"Did you get your tuxedo dry cleaned? Any problems?"

"No problems, Jacquie. You don't belong attending this dinner party. Recovering from the blues, barely having the energy to drive there, and dreading the long drive back."

"Don't worry, everything is planned."

"What is? Once again, you are being mysterious."

"Got to check on Annabelle. We both love you. See you soon. You have the directions?"

"Yes."

"Promise to meet you at the door and introduce you to the Senator and people you need to be on familiar terms with."

Our relationship transcended friendship and romance, coalescing into a uniquely intimate bond. My love for Jacquie and concern about her worries left me with a dilemma. Not sure how to avoid contempt when meeting Paul. It was not possible to guarantee Jacquie that I wouldn't confront him.

On a blind date, this despicable man forced violent sex on Jacquie. The F**king Bastard raped her. But confident and thankful, Paul would never be part of Annabelle's or Jacquie's life.

Against better judgment, I surrender to Jacquie's expectation to be on my best behavior.

Parked my car with a quick getaway in mind. Strategically positioned it so no one could block me when ready to leave. Purposely, walked toward the Senator's home.

Jacqueline said my choice to take a sauna or hot tub at the end of the night and would join me.

'David, don't drive home. The party may go on late into the evening. You can sleep with me in my room. The Senator gave me the use of one of the bedrooms.'

'Isn't this chancy? Should we? There are reporters and TV cameras.'

'Don't worry, security showed me how the Senator gets upstairs privately. Or we use one of the cottages.'

Far from being insecure, the mansion was impressive up close. An accurate descriptive word is breathtaking.

No one has yet seen me in front of the Senator's imposing, arched, double mahogany wooden doors. About to turn and leave just as the door opened.

Two Secret Service agents stood before me, a female and a male. She asked for my photo ID and Secret Service clearance badge, checked her clipboard, scrolled a finger down the page, then turned the page and said, "Welcome, Doctor. The Senator is looking forward to meeting you."

"Please call me David. Doctor is for professional reasons."

"Yes, sir."

"Close enough. Just David."

"Are you a relative of Jacquie, Dr. David?"

"No, sir, just David, a friend of Jacqueline."

The agent had not said anything more and used a wand for security.

"Do you chat with each guest, asking if they are related to Jacqueline? Did I say something silly aloud?"

The female agent's eyes smiled. Sorry to say, this man has no sense of humor.

"This way, sir."

"Oh, left a few gifts in my car. How can I be so absent-minded?"

"Give me your car keys, and I'll retrieve them for you."

"It's a bouquet for the Senator and two boxes of chocolates, Jacquie, my niece, and Jaz's favorite."

"Not a problem, sir, I've also been absent-minded about remembering presents left at work for my wife."

From that moment on, he and I became good friends.

The female agent led me inside, where two more Secret Service agents stood, talking into the lapels of their suit jackets.

In a cocoon of safety, a sense of sanctuary of faith. Tight security was expected. After all, the Senator was a Presidential primary winner.

However, security was not for my protection.

Intuition warned me to stay alert. Turning to leave, Jacqueline rushed to block the door. She instantly blankets me in the warmth of her nurturing spirit, which somewhat calms my fears.

She was surprised at my arrival. "David, thank you for trusting me." All doubts receded with her kiss and comforting hug, assuming my concern was a side effect of feeling blue.

This would be a good evening, secure in Jacquie's joie de vivre.

Someone was tapping my shoulder. The male agent leaned over and whispered, 'Behind you' were car keys, two boxes of chocolate, and flowers.

"Love, this is for you and Annabelle, and a box of Belgian dark chocolate for Jaz. The flowers are for Senator Harrison."

"Oh, sweetheart, your niece loves chocolates, and thanks for remembering Jaz."

"Let me kiss you to say thank you for her and me. Eager to personally introduce Suzanne, my Baby Sister."

"Who?"

"David, please stop that and wait for me. You know her importance to me, so don't wander over to chat."

"Jacquie, acquiesce and shall wait since you won't reveal your reasons."

"Love, the Secret Service has talked with Paul and told him to behave, or they will arrest him."

A genuinely unbiased impression of Paul reminds me of *Bluto, Popeye's* nemesis, for the love of *Olive Oyl*. He was brutish-looking, lacking any redeeming social qualities.

I placed my prejudice on hold, though he had attacked Jacquie, and stayed professional. Committed to being open and fair-minded. I lie as if this native New Yorker would repress his emotions in this situation.

My protective instinct intensified for my niece and her mom. Annabelle's biological father is contemptible. Having witnessed his demeanor, determined to provoke him into a fight and get him arrested.

Jacquie is uncomfortable with me meeting Paul. Afraid of his uncontrollable temper, which instantly flares in an outpouring of unjustified anger. Before saying something, he turned and walked away.

My acrimony for Paul would not safeguard Jacquie, so I hesitated and glanced to satisfy myself that she was okay. Jacquie looked relieved, knowing I was here for her.

"David, you were miles away. Where were you?"

"With *Popeye* and *Bluto*. Sweetie, you look exquisite tonight."

"Sweetheart, thank you for the compliment. But, please, David, let security handle Paul as he is unpredictable."

"How are you always aware of what is on my mind?"

"Your face has a look of antipathy."

"Is this the word of the day? Sorry, don't know what it means, so how can I get my face to look like that?"

"Cheeky David, in other words, your resentment."

"Sincerely apologize. This is your auspicious evening. Promise to control hostility, be discreet, and behave."

I meant to say that I would try.

"David, why *Popeye*? Never mind, Jaz sends her love."

"Jacquie, please give my love back to Jaz. Not promising to leave you unprotected."

You are impossible. Make yourself at home. Sorry, just a few more guests to greet. David, please socialize."

Guests? Jacquie was at ease talking to the Junior Senator and Governor from California, the Mayors of Los Angeles, San Diego, San Francisco, Sacramento, Modesto, and California Congressional Representatives, with wives or husbands, and people whom I didn't recognize.

We are content with our intimate relationship and cherish the time we spend together. Our intimacy was limited to occasional kissing, and romance evolved into a unique closeness and special friendship.

Yet, worried about being pulled into a blue hole of despair. Even wearing a tuxedo was not a suitable time to meet dignitaries.

Jacquie recognized my discomfort, interrupted a conversation with a Congressperson, and walked over to me. And held my hands.

Her voice softened, lovingly, "You are extraordinary, the equal of everyone here tonight."

She kissed me on the cheek and returned to her conversation with the Congressperson. Proud of Jacqueline. She is a compère host for Senator Harrison.

Walked through a large central hallway to the living room with no distractions to prevent me from socializing. Not a fan of alcoholic drinks, God and I had a bargain and traded to stop drinking if she let me live through a nightmarish hangover. An occasional beer was enjoyed on Thanksgiving and New Year's Eve.

Loved a chateau mantle fireplace with a fire crackling, freeing sparks to escape up the flue on a chilly winter evening. Circulating among guests, I noticed a walnut-brown leather sofa and coffee table that would be perfect somewhere you can put your feet up and watch football. A violin quartet played music and performed a captivating repertoire of a cappella pieces. Their melodic voices echoed in the room with songs of love.

Chatter from guests was imperceptible. The acoustic quality of their mellow voices created a warm ambiance.

Cable news and print reporters mingled and made a pleasant minor din in the hope of an interview with Senator

Harrison, confident of getting a byline for a story sent to their editors by a pending deadline.

Couples danced, and it was enjoyable, like watching ballet movements in sync with the music. Jacqueline socialized, welcoming prominent people. There's no need to hurry to introduce anyone to me.

Having assured Jacquie, I'd try to behave, remain calm, and not provoke Paul, an intuitive warning to not cause trouble. Sound advice if followed. But, shit, Paul decided to talk to me.

Paul's face was flushed red with an imprint of a hand. Flashing Red Warning Lights should have had me walk away, precisely the one person who shouldn't be near me.

"The bitch, all I did was try to hug her and get a friendly kiss, and she slapped me."

Trying not to laugh, definitely didn't care. Nonetheless, curiosity canceled warnings, ignored at my peril.

"Which woman?"

Directed a disdainful stare at a woman standing not more than twenty-five feet away, talking to five people. An elegant-looking woman, standing five feet eleven inches tall, wore sexy high heels that added a few additional inches. She was slender, with wavy reddish auburn brown hair that fell softly down her bare back, standing five feet eleven inches tall, and wearing sexy high heels that added a few additional inchestanding five feet eleven inches plus tall sexy high heels that added a few extra inches, slender, with wavey reddish auburn brown hair, fell softly down her bareback below her shoulders. The loveliness of a melodic brogue highlighted her attractiveness.

She was an unbelievably gorgeous woman, a woman confident in her own beauty. Sexy with sensuality, her endless laughter was highlighted. Her happy giggle sounded somewhat familiar.

An invisible cord drew me closer. Afraid to take a breath or move, this angel fades from my sight. Witnessing a long-held dream from my heart come true, she stood before me.

Her elegance, beauty, Irish intonation, and delightful smile captured me. Photos, however, did not capture her sophisticated demeanor or her refined deportment of sophistication. Everyone vanished from my sight except this angel.

Paul brusquely broke my trance. Wary of getting into an argument with Paul, I face a binary choice: behave or break my pledge to Jacquie.

"What a cold-hearted bitch. Bet she is a lesbian. That's why she wouldn't kiss me."

Well, there goes my last opportunity to behave, barely able to rein in my Bronx rage. At least the record will show I didn't provoke. Paul's disparagement of lesbians, plus a woman whose Sister he raped, was unbelievable and intolerable. Tried to kiss Jacquie's sister in public, and it's infuriating that Paul walked away from justice.

"Bet you fifty dollars you could not kiss her. No man can."

"Take your bet and another fifty dollars. After kissing her, she and I will dance."

How thoughtless to bet on a woman you've not even met.

Sensual and beautiful, a model for any fashion page, yet with a soothing demeanor, the girl next door radiated kindheartedness and passion. With her adorable giggle, she stood transfixed. There was no hint she even recognized her allure. Was it because she was Jacquie's sister, which made it easier to approach her?

Gorgeous women admit imperfections that others overlook. At this moment, none mattered. I hoped Suzanne would use her Irish wit and smile to make it easier for me to approach her.

Wearing a black satin formal evening dress added to her sensual appeal. A long, sexy naked leg showed from a slit on the left side of her dress. Seduced by her bare sexy shoulders, her beauty was stunning. Rendering me unable to speak.

Frozen, my eyes focused on her delightful smile, framed by the red of her lips, oh, those bluest blue eyes. Incapable of uttering a sound. Stepping closer, I realized that Jacquie would realize Paul tried to hit on her Sister once we kissed. Suzanne would not appreciate having a bet on her because I wanted to provoke the bastard. There was no time to explain how a bet turned into the hope of her touch as we danced.

She turned to face me and gazed into my eyes. "Oh, Dr. David! I've been looking forward to meeting you. Jacquie has told me how you first met and always speaks about you."

"You don't mean all the details of our meeting."

There were no secrets the Brooke Sisters kept from each other. Suzanne's giggle was appealing, and secrets no longer mattered.

"Just David."

She smiled. In a playful tone. "Hello, just David."

Suzanne wanted me to be relaxed. She put me at ease. Even though nervous, like a cat placing a paw in a fast-running stream.

"Knowing how this may sound presumptuous, hell, it's straightforward of me, but may I kiss you and ask you to dance?"

Mesmerized by her, Suzanne was no longer a bet. Hard to suppress deep-seated emotions as she drew closer to me, and we kissed. A kiss lingered long on my lips. She took my hand, and we walked onto the dance floor to dance to Roberta Flack's "*The First Time Ever I Saw Your Face. My love.*"

There couldn't be a more perfect song for a movie, if ever directed a romantic film.

Suzie would later share a long-held dream. Expected the man she had waited for her true love to kiss her and ask her to dance. The lover of her dreams was finally dancing with her. You can't make this stuff up, as it was too unbelievable even for a romance novel.

Paul walked deliberately with contempt and defeat as we danced and approached Suzanne and me.

"You Son of a Bitch! You won," and slapped two fifty-dollar bills in my left hand.

"Won. What did you win?"

Her smile vanished, and the recklessness of trying to defend my friend and her Sister's honor would cost me my chance to dance with Suzanne.

"What did he place in your hands?"

"Not anything."

Opened my right hand, hoping this would satisfy her.

"Now, your left hand."

Lovely as long as it lasted, dancing with a captivating woman.

"A hundred dollars! That's all you bet on me. Thought we both had felt something extraordinary to start to get to know each other, and you assumed only a hundred dollars was a good bet?"

Hold on a minute, was this her Irish wit?

Suzanne was upset and didn't want to tell her Sister. Paul had already tried to have sex with her that evening. Trying to de-escalate a situation? Or sensing she understood my anger at her Sister's nemesis.

Suzanne sensed an emotional connection, anticipated and held me lovingly, and we started to dance again. Gently placing her head on my shoulder. She wanted to get closer. Was Jacquie's sister the woman of my dreams? Hopefully, this was a second chance at romance. Suzanne softened into my arms, and my life changed forever.

Dancing with a gorgeous woman in a black gown, she softly sang "The First Time Ever I Saw Your Face."

Jacqueline's futile effort tried to stop him. Paul dashed across the room, and he tapped me on the shoulder. Turning my head, I then found myself on the floor with blood on my lip.

Secret Service agents quickly removed Senator Harrison from the living room.

"David, please, stay down and let the Secret Service handle this."

Okay, now it's personal, and I lifted myself off the floor. As agents sprinted across the large room, they punched me in the stomach and my face. The floor became familiar, everyone stopped moving, and time slowed down. Standing for the second time, determined to fight back.

Paul aimed a handgun at Suzanne, and it happened so quickly. Scared that I couldn't get there in time, leaped before her. Can't remember the sound of the shots. A burning sensation in my chest and another shot to my stomach, and collapsed onto the floor.

Suzanne knelt to shield me and pleaded, "Agent, please call for an ambulance and get Dr. Robert."

Drifted in and out of consciousness, words heard before lost awareness, with tears rolling down her face,

"Dear God, David, please stay alive. Don't want to lose you. We just met."

The Senator's husband, Dr. Robert, arrived at that moment.

"Suzie, need to stop the bleeding. Have the Secret Service inform the ambulance that they may have a Code Blue."

People close to death have reported seeing their life flash before their eyes. Instead, Roberta Flack's song played out in my head.

Jacquie later shared that the Senator's husband refused the Secret Service to leave to attend to my life-threatening injuries. Dr. Robert was the only Doctor close enough to respond immediately; without him, may not have survived. The doctor, in a low voice, had a peaceful look before fading into a deep corner of my mind.

The two Sisters stood with trepidation as the ambulance doors shut. The siren blared a long, drawn-out warning that someone was in critical condition. Suzanne wanted to ride in the ambulance with me, but was not allowed.

Dr. Robert calmly said, "You and Jacqueline come ride with me. We will follow the ambulance in my car."

Rushed into the emergency room at Bayswater Medical Center, the attending emergency room doctor was concerned about the patient's blood loss.

Jacqueline stood steadfast by her Sister. Senator Harrison arrived and comforted the sisters. The Senator wondered if she could get an update from her husband.

"Senator, it's been over an hour. Doctor Robert said it should only take an hour."

Reassuring Suzie, "Robert is in surgery with surgeons who are experts dealing with gunshot wounds."

Suzanne sank deeper into her chair, trying hard to cry quietly, not for herself but for me.

Time crawled, as minutes slowly ticked by, unbearable for Suzanne and Jacquie. The ambiguity of life offered us a glorious love affair, impatient to be held and cherished at this moment.

Finally, three hours later, the Chief of Surgery and Dr. Robert emerged from the emergency room, removing their masks. Suzanne and Jacqueline were holding hands, dreading the news that was about to come.

The Chief of Surgery is aware of the fear in the Sisters' eyes. "Please sit."

Suzanne remained resolute, tears welling up, ready to stream down her cheeks. Jacquie wrapped her arm around her baby Sister.

Doctor Robert, in a reassuring voice, said, "Suzie, the bullets caused more damage than I first thought, and I almost lost him twice. Took the two bullets out and stopped the internal bleeding. David's vital signs are stable. However, he remains in Intensive Care, and will not know more until he wakes up."

Frightened and alarmed, holding back tears, "Doctor Robert, you mean if he wakes up?"

Doctor Robert replied gently, "Suzie, I meant when he is awake. Promise to keep you updated as soon as I know."

Suzanne ran to the elevator just in time to get inside as the doors closed. David was still unconscious on a gurney. She was obstinate and would not delay being by my side.

The emergency room Head Nurse asked, "Who is his next of kin?"

Afraid to answer, fearful that a quiver in her voice would expose raw emotions and unleash a flood of tears.

"Guess it would be me. David has no living relatives except his mom. All close friends are scattered over the country and worldwide."

Is Suzanne his fiancée? If not, she cannot visit the ICU."

Senator Harrison was already on the phone with the Hospital Director to get permission for Suzanne. She arranged for me to be moved into an intensive care private room.

Suzanne stayed with me all night and into the late afternoon of the following day. Sitting by my side, holding my hand. And between sobs, "Please don't die, I just met you. I can't lose you now."

When I woke, not sure of the time, the blinds were partially closed, and a faint, diffused winter light streamed in between the half-closed Venetian blinds. Suzanne had closed her red, swollen eyes from crying and slept with her head resting on the bed.

Gently stroking her hair, "My gorgeous Blue-Eyed Lady, you did not lose me."

"David, thank God, was so frightened. My blue-eyed lady? Oh, my eyes."

"Jacquie, oh dear God, please tell me she is safe."

Tears welled up, blurring my vision. Praying she was out of harm's way.

"David, she will be in soon. She is waiting for Jaz."

"Thank God!"

"This wasn't the way I wanted to seduce you.

Suzanne, it hurts. My chest and stomach hurt."

"I'll call for the doctor to give you something to alleviate your pain."

"Hi, can we have a do-over and finish our dance?"

"Can you wait until you can stand first?"

"Yes, now with you by my side. When did you get here?"

"Last night, the same time you did, Dr. Robert, the Senator's husband, drove Jacquie and me here."

Half-heartedly tried to admonish him in a soft tone, but with wet eyes. "What were you doing, jumping in front of a loaded gun? Don't tell me you are a superhero. Oh, David, seeing you get shot twice, don't have words... yes, I do, terrified for you. Grateful you protected me, oh God, David, at the risk of your own life."

Holding my hand tighter, Suzanne started crying and wiping her tears with her other hand.

"It's all right, Suzanne. You are safe."

"David, crying for you. Helpless, just watching you fall to the ground."

"You kneeled over me to protect me, not knowing if that endangered your life. Shouted for Doctor Robert. Someone, please call for an ambulance.

"You heard me?"

"Suzanne, clinging on to consciousness, ensuring you were out of harm's way, so we could finish our dance."

"Is this the best you can do? Heard so much about your renowned New York wit."

"Are you okay, Suzanne? You had a dreadful fright. Scared, couldn't reach you fast enough to get in front of you. In that moment, I only cared about saving your life. I'm serious, I want a romantic end to our dance."

"I know, so do I. And you are first on my dance card when no guns point at me."

"What happened? Why didn't he open fire on you and Jacquie? She was right behind him."

"Don't know. It all happened so fast. David, I was in shock."

"Suzanne, hold my hand. I'm glad you are here. Can we talk?"

"Oh, New York man, we have plenty of time to chat.

Are those tears in your eyes?"

"No, I have something in my eye."

"Yeah, they are called tears."

Dr. Robert entered smiling, which diminished Suzanne's concern.

"Dr. Robert, David is in severe pain."

"David, let me examine you for a pain management plan. First, wanted to see how you are doing before prescribing painkillers. The anesthesia is slowly wearing off, which is why you have pain. Prescribing a low-dose opioid, the nurse will dispense it. Then let's see how you manage your pain tomorrow.

A low-dose opioid will make you sleepy. The Doctor on the night shift can determine if you also require a sleeping pill. Allowing you to sleep through the night. You may remain drowsy from the after-effects of the anesthesia and pain medication for the rest of the day. Probably fall asleep this afternoon. This is normal and nothing to worry about.

David, the surgery lasted three hours, and you were resuscitated twice. You were kept in surgery to ensure no bleeding or damage from bullet fragments that may have been hidden. Your vital signs are all normal. However, keeping you in intensive care for the rest of today enables me to closely monitor your recovery.

David, the bullet in your chest lodged close to your heart, and you sustained life-threatening injuries, but the good news is you are over the worst.

Your recovery will take time. Before you ask, a hospital dietitian goes over your diet with you. You need lots of protein, which opens up a wide range of food choices. However, all indications are that you are on the mend. Your only job is to follow the Doctor's orders and rest. You are a lucky man."

"Doctor, why did you tell Suzanne surgery would take only an hour? Was it to keep her calm?"

"Said nothing to David."

"You were unconscious and in the emergency room. Should this get written up in a medical journal?"

"No, thank you, Doctor. Sorry, but liked your answer. Sarcasm reminds me of home. Rest assured, I didn't hear a voice telling me to go into a light. Though did hear you saying, 'Nurse, hand me a hemostat to control his bleeding, Stat.' And called for a Code Blue each time I went into cardiac arrest."

"David, since she was young, Suzanne had faith in how her love mate under specific circumstances would appear. From what Suzanne told me privately, along with this recent experience, let's leave it for metaphysicians to clarify."

"Doctor, don't need an explanation. I'm just sharing with you and Suzanne. Thank you, Doctor, for saving my life. Grateful you brought Suzanne and Jacquie when the emergency responder told Suzanne, 'Sorry, miss,' and closed the ambulance door. Jacquie took her hand as they both felt discarded. You said you would drive them to the hospital."

"Doctor Robert, did that happen in surgery or when he was in the ambulance? How could David have any knowledge of events?"

"Suzanne, you, David, and I can talk about this when he is more robust.

David, let's just keep this between you and Suzanne. The Senator may face uninvited questions from the media if this overshadows her campaign for even a few days. Ostensibly, this is not a miracle."

"Of course. Where is the Senator? I need to apologize."

"David, the Senator left when she received news that you are recovering in the intensive care unit. Her agenda is demanding with senatorial duties and the need to win the primary. The Senator's senior assistant will call daily for an update and report back."

"Doctor, why is your wife, sorry, I mean Senator, paying so much attention to me? Didn't even have a chance to meet her. Not to mention leaving blood on your living room's hardwood floor."

"Suzanne walked into my wife's campaign office when she first ran for the 81st Congressional District in Sacramento. This young, confident-sounding girl said,

'Miss Harrison, I want to volunteer to get you elected, and come some days after school and weekends.'

'Why are you interested in my campaign?'

'Because I believe in your platform to educate vulnerable children. And you will be a great President one day. So, want to be there when you do.'

That was ten years ago, and she had been working for the Senator in a paid position when she turned fourteen. That is the reason. I'll check back on you before leaving the hospital later this afternoon."

"You heard me during the night?"

"It was hard not to, and you repeated, please don't die. Can't lose you, not now, all night."

"Suzanne, tell me about the ten-year-old girl who sounded confident with a gift of prescience."

"David, there is plenty of time now. Rest, not going to leave your side."

When the nurse arrived with the prescribed meds, she explained that David was in a light coma and could not have heard Suzanne.

Suzie and I understand differently.

"Take the painkillers and rest. Staying right here, so you are comforted."

"Suzanne should argue with you to go home, but in too much pain. Do not want to win the argument."

David's eyelids started to droop, wanting to reclaim his reputation for his New York wit.

"Suzi, have something that concerns me."

"Whatever worries you, Jacquie will take care of it."

"Do you suppose they will give me back my deposit on the tuxedo with two bullet holes and some blood?" Reluctantly, closed my eyes and fell asleep.

Jacquie came into the room and whispered,

"Sis, will he be okay?"

"Oh, Jacquie, I was afraid David was killed and lost him, and it was all my fault."

"Suzanne, you would not be responsible; I wouldn't allow for him not to attend this dinner. If he hadn't been there, you might have lost your life, Sis. David will tell you that he wanted to come, but he needed a bit of coaxing.

David said that about his tuxedo. Sweetheart, David owns the Tux. Oh, Suzanne, his crazy New York humor has resurfaced. Our David will be okay."

Three
A Kiss, A Dance, A Blue-Eyed Eye Lady

"He was afraid to love because, every time he does, someone breaks him a little more." Shivani Saharia

Convalescing was gradual but with significant milestones, such as standing and walking. Still ambivalent about sharing inner thoughts, it was too soon. On the flip side, being determined yet afraid, I was unable to protect my beautiful, blue-eyed lady. Suzanne never left my side, eating meals and sleeping beside me each night.

Jacquie visited after work and stayed overnight on weekends.

Out of the blue, "Please tell your Sister to go home. Suzie is exhausted and should not delay her work with Senator Harrison."

"David, why? She brings you comfort and nurses you to heal faster than alone."

"If not for me, she would not have experienced this trauma. Her life was put at risk, so I'm going away to recuperate. Before you walked in, spoke to Senator Harrison, apologized for any blood stains, and took responsibility by placing her and her husband and VIP guests in harm's way."

'Senator, please call Suzanne and ask her to go home and back to work. She loves working for you.'

"Her reply was unforeseen."

'David, Suzie has never been as happy since you came into her life, bloodstains and all. When the party date was announced, she became excited, continued speaking of destiny, and could not wait to meet you. Trust there is a reason you met under dreadful circumstances.

Jacqueline, Suzanne, and you are invited for a private dinner at my home. Guaranteed, the security will tighten. An unexpected breach and precautions for the parameter failed, and a gun entered our home. David, as soon as you recover, I want to meet you in person.'

'Senator, thank you. Suzanne holds you in high esteem.'

'You are fortunate to start a relationship with Suzanne. She walked into my office at the age of ten and never left. My husband and I are fond of her. Our family adopted Suzanne, and she is part of our hearts. Her fiery passions brought optimism to my campaigns. A staff member will call you to check on the progress of your recovery and will inform me.

David, rest. People are waiting for me.'

'Senator, let me apologize for delaying your busy agenda.'

'Glad we could speak and hear you are stronger. Please relay my regards to Suzanne and Jacqueline. Goodbye for now.'

It's easy to recognize Suzie's unconditional loyalty to the Senator. The Senator's affection and respect for Suzie are heartfelt. Suzanne worked long hours for weeks at a time without a weekend off. She was devoted to the Senator, and she was with her.

Is Suzanne the woman of my dreams, now, when Jacquie was the woman just a short time ago?

Unfortunately, I was too emotionally weary to begin a relationship with Suzanne. Another rejection would be insufferable.

"Honey, where will you go, and who will care for you?"

"New York to work at RH International, my publisher. They offered me an office to work on revisions for my older books. A childhood friend is a nurse and is married to a doctor. They invited me and promised to oversee my recovery."

"Did you call your mom to inform her?"

"Not yet. Decided to wait so as not to worry my Mom.

Jacquie, please, no argument. My mind is made up.

New York City is my childhood home. It's comfortable and familiar, which will speed up my recovery. Please tell my Sweetpea I'll call her often."

"Of course, she won't understand why she can't be with you. When are you going to tell my Sister?"

"Jacquie, do not have any courage left. Please speak to her for me?"

"Then why leave, David? This is not the reason. You have to do that yourself, if you must, stipulate to the following..."

All the preconditions Jacquie set were agreed to. She will have my phone number and address.

"David, we know each other too well to believe this is what you want."

"This was not an easy decision. Your sixth sense discerns outcomes before me. Nevertheless, my affection and love for you cannot cover my guilt.

A broken agreement put you and your Sister in jeopardy. You and Suzanne are the ones who understand that taking the bet was a way to protect honor, instead of waiting for you.

Oh, Jacquie, my heart was drawn to her."

"That was my hope."

"It's hard to balance a fear for her safety and my growing affection for Suzanne. There is no way I'll allow her to remain at risk."

"Suzanne, let you kiss her on the lips seconds after meeting you. She has stayed with you every day these past three weeks. She is now sleeping in the nurses' quarters and would not want me to tell you."

"Tell me what?"

"The first time we met at JFK airport, I shared with you that my Suzanne, at five years of age, loved to pretend to get married and have me perform the ceremony.

As she grew older, the virtues of the man she was destined to fall in love with became increasingly evident. When asked, how can you be so sure? She boldly declared I'll gaze into his dark blue eyes, we kiss, and ask me to dance."

As implausible as it seemed, Jacquie was unrelenting in protecting her Sisters' veracity.

"Suzanne is resilient, so people naturally suppose little, if anything, can upset her. The opposite is true. She is fragile and vulnerable, yet she holds onto her faith. Sound like anyone you know? One day soon, you will have appreciation for my Sister, who occasionally suffers from different dark shades of blues but has it under control."

"You wanted us to meet, possibly as a potential lover?"

"Yes, because knowing you and my Sister's heart, you were intended to meet."

"Getting shot was not part of your arranged blind date."

"David, you almost died. Please don't joke. Frightened to lose you. Paul is ruthless, and you didn't hesitate to save her from a dire and imminent threat to her life.

You are meant to be together. Suzie is an Irish-Catholic woman from Northern California, and you are a British-Jewish man from New York. You are perfect for each other. She felt the same as you while dancing. Both of you are obstinate, with the caveat that you always find a way to make each other happy."

"Jacquie doesn't make any sense. You just said we come from different worlds, yet we would find ways to make each other happy. What about today?"

"David, trust you to come to the right decision."

Suzanne nervously queried as she walked into the room.

"Honey, can I help with your decision? It sounded important."

"Suzie, did you have a good sleep?"

"Yes, thank you., You sounded anxious, so what is this decision?"

"Well, I just shared with your Sister that there is an opportunity to work in New York. With your range of responsibility to support the Senator's presidential campaign, I was disinclined to ask you to come with me."

Jacquie's eyes smiled as if this was close enough without David telling a harmless lie. Somehow, he finds it impossible to fib. A self-imposed atonement, it seems, for lying to his mom a few times as a boy.

A difficult dilemma. Do not want to disappoint Suzie by leaving without her. Unyielding in ensuring she remains safe.

"Suzie, can you get an extended leave of absence and come to New York with me?"

"New York! Often dreamt of seeing Broadway plays. Would you take me to see this Bronx of yours where you grew up?"

Sat on my bed, restraining tears welling up in her blue eyes, and caught me off guard about how deeply seeded her emotions ran. Tears were not ones of joy. Her look told me she knew my real reason.

It would take me a while to appreciate her hyper-empathic gift.

Spoken in a soft brogue. "That was not what you and my Sister were discussing."

"David, you are nervous we are getting too close, too quick. Paul tried to kill me because I rejected him and was with you.

Jacquie, are you and David aware of the news?"

"Suzanne, please accept that there is no way I'll place your life in jeopardy! Despite my affection."

"Paul was as mad as a box of frogs and resisted arrest. Cable news reported he was cornered, started shooting, wounded an officer, and was shot dead late last night."

Suzanne glanced over at her Sister for concord.

Jacquie was not gentle in her reproach, "David, he was fanatical, of all people, you knew this."

Suzanne walked over to the open window, giving her time to collect her thoughts. Her go-to is not to blurt out her thoughts without being concerned with the consequences of her words. A well-developed personality trait, she would attempt to teach me. To keep control, don't speak the first words that come to mind.

In an affectionate tone, "You no longer have to protect my Jacquie or me. If you'd like, I'm more than delighted to visit New York and take time to develop our relationship. David, my confidence in us is unshakable. In the not-too-distant future, it will become clear why you need not have qualms about starting a romantic relationship. This is our beginning, not an ending."

"My dearest unknowns are part of life. You are not alone anymore. You and Suzanne have something most couples never have or frankly will never have, and you will discover this in your own time. There is no promise of a fairytale ending. You and my Sister have to create one once you recognize your blessing comes from the warmth of your love."

"Suzanne, say romance if it is what you want to say, knowing how independent-minded you and your Sisters are.

Angel, a hesitancy to get closer is palpable. Afraid rejection triggers a trap door hidden under my feet, which opens to a swirling blue sinkhole, with no way to climb out. Please be patient with me. A loss of romance with Jacquie is still fresh.

My life transformed on the evening of our meeting. Nothing mattered except to kiss you and have our first dance. There was less time than a hummingbird's heartbeat to save you, even though I ended up close to death. There wouldn't be any unwillingness if this were to occur again."

"Why then, David, please help me understand how to be with you." With a tear-stained face, "Why are you distressed? A romance would nurture our love. David, you want the same."

"If you left me, unable to protect my heart, leaving me vulnerable. It's not a fear of relationships; it's just a dread of a Romeo and Juliet-style relationship. Passionately unpredictable and enamored with each other, you know how this play ended.

Trying to explain is like describing color. Still need time to heal. After Jacquie and I transitioned from a romantic to a unique best-friend relationship, we still experienced a different type of intimacy, but it meant a different kind of intimacy, no longer a romance. We are not in a romance movie. This is real life. Please, go slow as not being part of your decisions causes unfounded fear, but nonetheless, it is tangible."

"David, what decisions? Sweetheart, are you ready to say the true reason?"

"Our relationship started with me almost getting you killed. All because."

"Because of what?"

"First, to defend your and Jacquie's honor. Took a bet hoping you'd kiss and dance with me. When our eyes met, it was no longer a bet. Well, you already know the rest. You were almost killed. Couldn't live without you."

"David, it was exactly your bet that enabled me to trust your kiss and dance."

"Okay, didn't make any sense."

"One day soon, it will. Jacquie said your much-loved movie has one of my favorite quotes."

"Rather spend one lifetime with you than face all the ages of this world alone."

Jacquie hugged and kissed us.

"This is a movie *trilogy,* knowing how it ends. David, you know my Jaz would love to meet you. David and Suzanne, you are invited to dinner a week from Saturday.

I have to leave now and go to work. Please call me tomorrow when you return home and you've settled in. Love you both, talk to you soon, ciao."

"More than happy to slow down as long as we are together. It means everything to me.

May I share my good news with you? Senator Harrison authorized an annex office in our home for me to remain close while you recover. My boss, who one day will become President, always astonishes me. Having faith in her since I was a girl."

"Our home? Not my home, Suzanne. It is yours."

"What would you like to eat for lunch? Read the hospital menu and had an idea. Let's have our favorite pizza toppings."

"Are all your Sisters brilliant at changing a subject from a topic they do not want to answer?"

Spending time with Suzanne is like trying to catch your shadow. She does not allow time to chat about things she doesn't want to hear. Intelligent, creative, and decisive, she commits wholeheartedly once she makes up her mind. Her intuition and heart confirmed her decisions, and she never revealed more than necessary until the right time.

Suzanne wants our relationship to develop, as it mostly happened in intensive care and a hospital room. Her wit and intellect, with an unending capacity for love, should comfort me. Is she my love mate, and why does that scare me? Never wanted to be with a woman more than Suzanne.

"Love, let us order a thick-crust Sicilian vegetarian pizza. Is it okay to have mushrooms, onions, green peppers, and pineapple on my half?"

We frequently have our pizza made this way. She even gave it a nickname, the DS pizza.

"What did you say?"

"Shall I order a vegetarian pizza for us, and sneak it up into the room?"

"No, before that."

"Didn't say anything before that. Oh, I said love."

"That is the first time you called me love."

Suzanne leaned in closer, kissed me, and whispered.

"The first time was our first kiss and dance to our song, *First Time Ever I Saw Your Face, My Love.*"

She sang our song on our drive to her home in South Lake Tahoe. Her tranquil singing is refreshing, like walking on cool grass on a hot summer's day.

A pure sound, the innocence of an angel.

Discussed sweltering summer days, how the moon turns blue, starry nights, boats without oars, fairy tales, and whether Tinkerbell is real. And why is the ocean blue? Have we ever seen pigs with wings? She and I laughed at my attempt to paraphrase Lewis Carroll.

Our mutual love of Jazz led her to sing Ella Fitzgerald's "Blue Moon" and "Cheek to Cheek."

Over the past three weeks, she had shared many of her wishes.

"David, my dream is to debut as a professional singer. And Love, wouldn't it be wonderful for us to live in New York City in a building with a door attendant one day."

As we pulled in front of one of the four garage doors at Woodland Cottage, she turned and said, "My father will love you after he gets over you slept with his elder daughter, and now, soon, his youngest."

Four
The Pleasure Of Love

"So she thoroughly taught him that one cannot take pleasure without giving pleasure and that every gesture, every caress, every touch, every glance, every last bit of the body has its secret, which brings happiness to the person who knows how to wake it." Hermann Hesse

Suzanne's bedroom is an exorbitantly luxurious 750-square-foot living space, with a fireplace and a king-sized bed. Her favorite space was where she read and watched her favorite movies. A four-seat sofa matched an oversized ultramarine blue comfy chair, perfect for a couple.

A balcony with a spectacular panoramic view of the lake, and across a grass field, a two-story, beautiful custom-built red Barn home with a cupola and a separate attached Horse Barn.

A sizeable walk-in closet could have been a small second room. Surprisingly, a diverse wardrobe of dresses, gowns, pantsuits, robes, lingerie, exercise, casual, and dress shoes. Inside the closet, a dresser with a matching vanity table and mirror holds all her personal lotions, makeup, and essentials. The bedroom is incredible, particularly personalized with a feminine touch and hard to describe without visuals.

"David, there is ample space in the closet for you. Take my hand."

The door in her bedroom led to a magnificent bathroom. A drop-in whirlpool bathtub, decorated with Azulejos Portuguese blue and white tile, large enough for four people, with a separate glass-enclosed shower.

"We'll have a hot bubble bath tonight. It will help you relax and sleep better. You are still in pain, and Dr. Robert said moist heat would help."

"But a sexy naked woman in the tub is a better curative."

"Silly, don't assume you will get lucky tonight."

Her adorable giggle gave me my answer.

Suzie's home and land were free and clear, with a mortgage paid in full.

"Mom added each Sister's name after each birth to ensure each had equal ownership. So our home belongs to the four of us.

Being the youngest, my sisters gave me the primary bedroom."

"It's all breathtaking, would love to stay here when I drive up to be with you."

Oh shit, I said that aloud. Since it was only my first day out of the hospital. Suzanne quickly changed the subject, taking the edge off my reluctance.

"Good, hoping you would feel at home."

Fortunately, my blue-eyed lady delighted in making me happy. But, still, for God's sake, "Suzie, please go slow. Not ready to commit to living here full time."

Suzanne already read my body language and facial expressions and was ahead of me.

"Of course, when you come up from San Francisco. David, there is a splendid view of the Sierra Nevada mountains. Our land has a lush green meadow for my two beloved horses and a lakefront pier where we jumped off and swam as children."

Keen to meet Victoria, closest in age to Suzanne. Each lovely sister had a distinct personality and became one Sisterhood. As the last-born, Suzanne reaped the benefits from their counsel and love. Was it possible to truly feel a part of her family?

"Family was even a bigger word than I imagined, wide and without limitations if you allowed it, defying easy definition. You had family that was supposed to be family and wasn't, family that wasn't family but was. Honest love from family, yet to be filled to abundance by unexpected supporting players." Deb Caletti

She took my hand and talked without catching her breath to avoid my dwelling on imagined worries.

"A bedroom, once our playroom, could become a lovely nursery."

Overwhelmed, immersed in a relationship, especially since she promised to allow time for me to adjust.

Caught between a growing affection for Suzanne and a deep-rooted fear, she disappears as floating, short-lived soap bubbles inevitably do.

Bubbles can't outlast fear. They only focus your awareness briefly.

"Please show me. I would love to see the bedroom."

Her eyes smiled as she put her arm in mine and said, "It's down the hall."

Suzanne was a whirlwind of liveliness. Embraced her dreams of a political career and, at the same time, pursued her multiple passions.

She raises money for vulnerable children. And sells her paintings at art shows and nurtures her love of singing and performing at small local venues and festivals.

Keeping our relationship open to flourish is a challenge, not letting myself succumb to fear and thus barricading my door to a romance. Discovered myself joyfully slipping into her embrace of love. Exquisite to be seduced by Suzie, my love partner.

Suzanne kept speaking to prevent me from focusing on my fear of losing her. Romance does not account for an indifferent universe that does not care or even recognize me. The universe doesn't owe me a happy life. Second chances at true love are rare.

"The most disconcerting thing about the universe is not that it is hostile but that it is indifferent, but if we can come to terms with this indifference, then our existence… can have genuine meaning. However vast the darkness, we must supply our own light." —Stanley Kubrick.

She gently interrupted my thought. "New York man, my first cousin, Megan, and her husband live in a spacious three-bedroom farmhouse. David, she looks forward to meeting you."

My mind was whirling, wondering how I found my way into this fairytale. It was just too picture-perfect. Everything seemed ideal, sorry to say, but fear of rejection doesn't typically check in with reality.

"Suzie, you are an Irish cupid."

She softly recited an old Irish proverb.

"David, may you have a world of wishes at your command. God and his angels are close at hand. Friends and family, their love impart. And Irish blessings in your heart!"

Holding hands with Suzie restored my joy. Strolled slowly down the staircase, one hand on a magnificent mahogany banister, and out the front door, where a young couple waited.

"David, this is our Megan."

Megan has long, dark, sumptuous auburn hair, enticing blue-green eyes, and a seductive, warm smile. Her eyes were amiable, and her affection genuine. Though surprised by a mutual sexual attraction.

A more prolonged-than-expected kiss from Megan was sensual and sexually appealing. Ryan's ostensible interest rang hollow.

Suzie was happy that Megan and I liked each other, although not to this extent. She showed discomfort as she watched Megan kiss me, even with her approval. Megan wanted me to accept her. It was easy to do.

"Suzie told me all about you, Dr. David."

"Just David."

"Promise you will come for dinner the first chance you and Suzie get. Trust we will become close friends. Suzanne never stops talking about you. All you have accomplished is impressive."

Suzie proudly boasted, "Megan is in the second year of her Internship in a Psychiatry Residency program."

"Exciting, looking forward to chatting with you. You can tell me all about your internship."

Her kiss, aware of Suzie's feelings, careful not to send unrealistic expectations to Megan, was concerning. My experience told me it was not a one-off. There was more to unfold.

Her eyes spoke the truth of her kiss; she wanted more. I hoped Suzie would defuse an emotional situation in which I had gotten caught up.

"We are about to take a walk to show David our property, not all 525 acres, just a few places, particularly growing up."

Suzanne kissed Megan goodbye and started whispering. Stepped away to afford privacy.

"David and I would love to come for dinner. Yes, we will arrange a date. Bye, love."

Walked hand in hand into the barn to meet her Quarter horses, a mare, and her filly foal, Suzie's two loves. Suzanne helped raise the mare and her filly foal from birth.

Whisper recently turned ten and is my passion and love, her reddish-brown coat. Her name was given because all I needed to whisper, she understood. Shadow is her five-year-old daughter. She is a beautiful, chocolate brown. I'm fond of them both.

Suzanne, a natural horse whisperer, petted both horses and fed each an apple.

Suzie spoke gently, "Whisper, this is David, my boyfriend. Born in New York City, who doesn't have experience with horses. Be friendly. Shadow, come, don't be shy."

She was serene when with them. They are an integral part of her life.

"Thank you for the introduction. Suzie, they are beautiful."

"You can ride Whisper in the morning. Megan will let them romp in the meadow the rest of today."

"Suzie, is it true they understand and are aware of feelings?"

"Yes, how did you get familiar with horses?"

"For a future visit with Jacquie and Annabelle. Jacquie told me my baby Sister treats them as family, so read up on equine facts."

"Whisper is friendly and wants to let you ride her. You will grow to love both. Go ahead and ask Whisper. It helps when she recognizes your voice."

Softly, "Whisper, looking forward to our ride tomorrow."

She nodded her head up and down, bringing her face close to mine so she could smell me.

"David, aren't they wonderful?"

Being part of Whisper's family meant a lot to Suzie. She kissed Whisper goodbye just as Ryan threw high-quality hay into the meadow.

Megan did not have to place a bridle on them. She spoke softly, and they nodded in agreement, following her into the meadow.

With her arm through mine, her long, wavy, reddish, auburn brown hair shone in the sunlight.

"Suzanne, your tight-fitting blue jeans are eye-catching.

Once your blue eyes looked into mine, I wanted nothing more than to kiss your delicious red lips. Wishing our first dance would not become our last."

Chattering monkeys, in my head, clamoring for my attention, were distracting, to say the least. 'Why would this adorable woman want you?'

Two diametrically different upbringings: hers, growing up in the country, and mine, city life. Suzanne lives a multi-colorful life I couldn't offer. The only horses I knew were the New York City Police horses; her experience was quite dissimilar.

Her talent of hyper-empathy meant she sensed feelings even if I tried to hide them. Suzanne's dark blue eyes softened. "The exquisiteness you appreciate in me is the same imposing qualities you possess."

Suzanne stopped and turned to kiss me. We continued walking, my arm wrapped around her.

"Suzie, your talk with Megan sounded poignant. Could you share what you and Megan whispered about?"

"She told me she is falling in love with you. Asked permission to spend time with you."

'Never felt like this before, Suzie. Could I have an Irish kiss and hugs with David? It would create an intimate bond of friendship.'

"How did you answer her?"

"If you didn't, David would be disappointed. Of course, every man does, but you are a married woman and would claim you as a trophy. If you were successfully seduced for a night of pleasure."

"What is an Irish Kiss?"

Suzie whispered.

"One finger or two, and this didn't upset you."

'David looks at me like he is sexually attracted.'

'Sweetheart, the same when you look at him, but David would never come between a happily married couple. You love Ryan and would never leave him.

David's fantasy is to have sex with every attractive woman. Yet, never would David have fallen deeper in love with me than he could admit. You and David both want a friendship. Precious, he would protect you from any man because you are my cousin. That is important to him. With your personality and being gorgeous, it helps.'

'Why aren't you jealous?'

'Because David would never hurt me.

Scared, a woman I didn't know could seduce him away. Then I'd be jealous.'

"Suzie, any man who leaped in front of a woman to protect her from getting shot is astonishing. I was enraptured. The black dress with bare shoulders and no straps accentuated your boobs, and a long slit down one side revealed a long sexy leg. My reaction was to ensure you would again be able to wear the dress."

"Now, a true reason."

"That was it."

Suzanne, always patient, stopped and waited for my words to link up with my heart.

"Hoped to romance you, anticipating a likelihood of a relationship."

"David, so afraid to be left alone. Don't ever do that again!"

"Excuse me? Like that will ever happen when your life is in danger."

"I'm serious."

"I know you are. I'm too. It wasn't about the dress or how beautiful you are.

It was our first kiss. You also wanted not to be our last. Kissed you with an open heart, hoping to send a message to reach your heart through my lips."

"Love, frightened, silly me, please find a way to keep me safe without harming yourself. Or is this Bronx tough guy thing to protect his blue-eyed lady?"

"Suzie, no guarantee. If possible, we will protect you from harm. Do you suppose your temper resembles my disposition, and never bore us to tears?"

Suzie realized we had the exact same nature and started laughing.

"Suzanne, why did you tell Megan I want sex with any good-looking woman? And consider her sexually desirable. This will boomerang as trouble if she has these thoughts and feelings."

"New York man, because she is in love with you, her kiss aroused you."

"How could you be aware of my thinking?"

"Because I watched how you kissed her and became jealous of her, not you."

"Suzie, forgive me. I kissed her back, enjoying it, and I'm sincerely sorry."

I love you, still searching for the suitable words to describe what you mean to me. Don't want one kiss to escalate now you approve of an Irish kiss. Suzie, I apologize for letting her go further with her kiss."

"David, I trust you, and it's in your eyes that there is something else you want to tell me."

"No, well, there is, and no, it's best not to say anything."

"David, was that a double negative because there is something you want to say?"

"You first need to appreciate the unspoken rules of the street. Survival meant don't kiss a wife or girlfriend."

"Guessed, this was what you wanted to say as I noticed it too."

"Expecting at least a tap on my shoulder to interrupt her kiss. Instead, Ryan acted like he didn't care."

"David, why did he respond that way?"

"I don't know, but my intuition tells me this isn't the end. When in a relationship with Jacquie, Noreen kissed me. She and I felt the warmth of a special friendship, and I adore her. Megann kissed as a woman who wants to sleep with me."

"Who is the woman who wants to sleep with you?"

"Suzanne, please stay focused on Megan and not my love life. You have no worries. Love would never do anything to upset you."

"David, this is my private sanctuary when I need to be alone. No one has ever been allowed to come here, not even my Sisters. A quiet space to meditate, paint, sing, have time to myself, or when I need to cry.

You could walk right past and never be conscious. My Sanctuary was here, with ten-foot-high vines covering an old stone wall. The trees behind the wall give the impression that you are as safe as houses. Love, hold my hand, careful of the vines, as the entrance looks like part of the wall.

This is the code to open it. Even if someone gets this far, without the correct code, no one can enter unexpectedly."

Suzie's Sanctuary is more extensive than first imagined. A bay window faces the lake, and the house is 1250 square feet with a twelve-foot ceiling. A twenty-first-century energy-efficient home with solar panels on the roof. Instantly feel at home with its resplendent furnishing, starting with a three-seat outdoor oak bench.

A broad iron and oak wood spiral staircase led to a bedroom in the loft, and a queen-size canopy bed with quilt blankets provided a sense of warmth and comfort. Wooden shutters closed from the inside, ostensibly, for extra protection from fierce winds and the chill of winter's frequent snowstorms. Lace floor-length curtains added a touch of femininity to dress up the living room. Two backup generators and a cord of wood for the fireplace are used for heat and ambiance.

Over the last few years, Suzanne has added amenities to make her home cozy.

A pantry stocked with food and household goods, filled with everything any home needed, enough for two people to live for two months. A refrigerator and a separate freezer packed with her favorite foods. Three half-filled oak wood wine racks with her and her sisters' preferred wines.

When a cold front or snowstorm threatens, an extra-wide, grey flannel-lined, navy blue sleeping bag, large enough for two, with dark red woolen blankets inside, keeps her warm down grey flannel-lined navy blue sleeping bag large enough for two with dark red woolen blankets inside keeps her warm down to minus 30 degrees Fahrenheit.

Suzie often slept here, regardless of the weather, instead of in her bedroom.

She designed a warm and welcoming home, showcasing her unique style. Furnishings include a soft, brown mahogany leather sofa, a wood-burning fireplace, and an old-fashioned wooden antique table that serves as both a work and dining room table. A concert piano with music sheets of her favorite songs, as well. A concert piano with music sheets of her favorite songs. Plus sheets of early attempts at writing original songs.

In one corner of the room was a vintage, dark blue and gold Mother Goose wooden toy chest, similar to the one that had been in my childhood bedroom.

A wooden pine-stained bookshelf with various novels, music CDs, and art magazines scattered on a coffee table made this her consummate getaway to relax and create.

A small art studio accessible from both the inside and outside housed dozens of finished and unfinished artworks. Suzanne hung her paintings of the Sierra Nevada mountains, as well as her pride and joy: oil paintings of her beloved Sisters, Mom and Nana, Annabelle, Jessica, Whisper, and Shadow.

"New York man, remember the sketches done in your hospital room?"

"Suzie, of all your talents, you are an artist extraordinaire. This is the first time I've seen completed work, all of which is spectacular and of art gallery quality. Perhaps, love, one day, would you paint us?"

"Promise to have something finished soon to hang in our bedroom."

Proud of Suzie's artistic talents, I suddenly released powerful, profound, unexpected, deep-seated emotions. Started to shake, got teary, and began to cry.

Underestimated how much healing was needed to recover from the shock of two bullets. Simultaneously adjusting to a relationship with a woman who never left my side. Suzanne finally shared her private life with me, which overpowered my deep feelings. Silly, this got me to cry, and not being shot twice.

Loved every moment with Suzie, never felt as content. Nevertheless, still fretful that one day she would leave me. Fear of rejection was ominous.

A college friend once told me God never gives us more than we can handle. So, who decides how much is enough, God or me? I never received a response, but that doesn't matter. Didn't think there was an answer.

"Are those tears?"

"No, got something in my eye."

"Yeah, they are called tears."

She sat quietly, allowing me time to gather myself. She handed me tissues to wipe my tears.

"Started to write a new novel."

"I love that you are writing again. What type of novel?"

"A romance novel. Just started composing the plot during my hospital stay."

"Oh, New York man, a romance novel. What inspired you?"

"Truly, it was you at the beginning of our romance. The novel starts with our first kiss and dance.

One day, I may find the right words to harmonize my feelings with your saying, "Please don't die, I just met you." You will be the first person to read it when it is done. Would you read draft chapters as they are finished?"

"Do you have a title?"

"*Weep For Love.*"

"David sounds like a beautiful romance title. Want me to read your manuscript?"

"Yes, tell me if your inner voice and feelings were captured. Taking tears welling up in your eyes as a yes?"

"No one except my Sisters, mom, Nana, and a few close girlfriends or the Senator ever cared about my feedback."

"Angel, you are being too humble; many people value your advice, wit, and sense of humor."

Leaned over and gently stroked her cheek, and we kissed. She placed her head gently on my shoulder.

After a few minutes, she took my face in her soft hands and kissed me.

"What was that for?"

"From your girlfriend."

"Suzanne, your beauty beguiled me, but your heart made enduring connections to mine."

"Honey, would you marry a gorgeous woman just to sleep with her? The man of my dreams is creative, intelligent, empathic, makes me laugh, and accepts and loves my silliness, not only my looks. A man who lets me give him a baby to start our family."

Embraced her love and held her closer to me.

"David, you are my beloved. My weeping is not for myself but for the hope of a future together. Please, this is the beginning of our relationship. You have found the woman of your dreams, and this scares you. This is real. It is also what you believe and deserve.

Sweetheart, a romance novel. Oh, David, don't fear, this is a floating soap bubble that bursts. We are genuine, and our love is enduring."

"Suzie, my heart has shattered into countless pieces too many times. It's different being with you. To give you flowers, romance, and poetry is an endeavor to encapsulate my love. Fearful but resolute not to lose you.

However, love is not a momentary occurrence. Lovers try to grasp fleeting romantic moments in songs, books, and films.

True love cannot break. Love belongs in your heart. Love is made up of hundreds of acts of affection. A romance becomes a love story when it synchronizes with each lover's heart."

"Would I marry a woman as gorgeous as you? For sex and candy for the eye."

"New York man, eye candy."

"Oh, silly me, dear Suzie, it's you I love. Your beauty shines from your heart out into the world."

"David, let us extend our love to include a family."

"Not yet as assured of what happens in the future as you are. The past is our memories.

Suzie, our love exists in the present. In this moment and the next...."

"What is clear is that David is to expand our love to our future children."

"Honey, at this moment, your love is sharing your secret Sanctuary.

Suzie, you are my love mate and have my heart."

"Sweetheart, would you read something in my diary written ten years ago?"

Stopping and kissing a few times before reaching the leather sofa. Floral garden-designed quilt blankets neatly folded with goose-down pillows laid on top of a childhood toy chest, where her secrets were kept safe. An antique tin box faded yet retained the colors of a lithographed scene from a 19th-century romantic artist. She sat close to me with the box resting on her lap.

"Suzanne."

"Hush, Love."

Suzanne's diary was wrapped in a waterproof bag to prevent moisture from damaging her private thoughts. She flipped through the first few pages until she reached her first entry.

"David, read; please don't say anything."

Dear Querencia, (name of diary)

Writing my deepest-held secret. One day, I will meet a man to become my beloved husband. He will be intelligent, kind, loving, and whisper tenderly romantic words to me. He will have dark blue eyes.

His name is David. I love the name David because he wrote poetry and psalms. He will kiss me and ask me to dance. That is how I will know my beloved. When I meet him, I'll share my most secret place. I'll share my most secret place with him, and we'll kiss and kiss and maybe show him this so he knows he was always in my heart. Truly and sealed with a kiss. Suzanne at ten years old.

No words were necessary; there were no words to voice a desire in Suzie's eyes. She had a long-held yearning to become sexually intimate with her beloved.

"Love, you cannot translate the joy of sex into words or songs of love. Words alone cannot testify to an exhilaration of mind and body during sexual intimacies.

Sex is most exhilarating during an act of lovemaking."

"David, can we please pause for a moment? Honey, this is my first time. I'm still a virgin.

Teach me the art of lovemaking."

"Yes, sweetheart, we'll delight in our lovemaking. Suzie, I cherish and love you.

"Men have tried to seduce me or tried sweet-talking all the time. As a girl of sixteen, men, mainly those 50 years and older, tried to verbally force themselves on me. Men wanted to control and own me, and have sex, which was disturbing and frightening. My Sisters, especially Jacquie, came to protect me.

Only wanted one man fated to be my love mate to become intimate with me. David waited to make love and for you to take my virginity. Because we're meant for each other."

"Suzie, glad you did not lose your virginity by coercion or force."

"Never sexually frustrated, sometimes slept with Jacquie. She told me that she had shared our intimate relationship with Jazquie.

Jacquie anticipated, 'The man you love is a gentle lover and finds it satisfying and irresistible that you are innocent in lovemaking. Your lover meets all your desires, includes everything in your lovemaking, and thus enhances intimacy with him, beyond your dreams.'

David, would you share in my fantasies? My nipples and breasts, lips, and vagina are extremely sensitive. Please show me and let me lead in our foreplay.

Oh, David, so inexperienced. Teach me how to have oral sex. Is that ok?

Lots of French and Irish kisses, too, and can we try out unusual positions to have you inside me? Make me cum masturbating, and want to do the same for you. David, gently, please let me experience if I like anal sex.

New York man, I'm afraid you would see me as sexually awkward and not please you. Jacquie waited until she turned eighteen before introducing erotic lovemaking. We even watched erotic movies, and read the *Kama Sutra,* and What must you think of me? Knowing all of this about Jacquie and me, are we still good? David, do you still want me?"

"Oh, my sweet blue-eyed lady."

"Love, why are you smiling? Nervous about pleasing you."

"Sweetheart, you are an exceptionally incomparable woman. I appreciated that you took a risk and were transparent and vulnerable. You are unsure of my reaction, yet you implicitly trust me.

Regret that you were sexually harassed. How terrible it must have been. Genuinely can't appreciate how this affects a woman's psyche.

And do I still want you? Oh God, yes. You have already pleased me, and Suzie, we have not yet started our lovemaking."

"David, I'm silly. Please tell me you love me and want to take my virginity and make love to me."

"No, you are not silly, which I adore, by the way. You are sexually innocent, yet you are far from naive, not if Jacquie taught you lovemaking. You are a woman in love who wants her lover to desire her.

Precious, want to pleasure you in our lovemaking. Your trust is a gift of love, smiled as you sounded both profound and anxious.

I love you, Suzie, and want to make love. Despite fears of rejection, I am not afraid of commitment.

It's okay, we are good. Had my share of sexual experiences, most fantasies satisfied, except being with you."

"Honey, how many women did you satisfy? Oh, God, which fantasies?"

"My blue-eyed lady, I'm with you and wanted to make love since first seeing you. Our first kiss was passionate and sexual, and because of my love for you, I now want to share my love through my passion.

A start of a new relationship causes uncertainty, yet an incomparable romance is here to luxuriate in its warm embrace."

"David, sexually and emotionally turned on by your kisses. Patiently waited to lose my virginity with my lover. Happiest with you and looking forward to being with you when we're apart. You're with the blue-eyed lady you dreamed of all these years."

Unhurried, sensual, and erotic, she removed her blouse but left her bra on. Unbuttoned skin-tight jeans, with my hand in her panties, caressing her vagina, she moaned with pleasure. Slipped a finger inside her, which was wet with anticipation. Sex was spontaneous and enhanced our enjoyment.

Suzanne's luscious lips kissed my waiting lips, a soft, distinct moaning sent waves of bliss flowing through her. Guided my hands to touch and fondle her during a sensual kiss. Massaged her firm buttocks and lightly caressed her breasts. Our foreplay was erotic, and as her breasts pressed closer to mine, her chest rose and fell slowly. Caresses awakened a long-awaited desire that was finally attained.

She nervously opened my belt, unbuttoned the top of my pants, and teasingly pulled my zipper down.

Suzie, lying on the floor, revealed her yearning. Ivory lace push-up bra perfectly accentuates her beautiful breasts. Women's cleavage is sexy and enticing, and women have mastered the art of taking off a bra. Hers had me stymied.

"Love, it unhooks from the front."

The clasp released, and her bra slipped off.

Fondled and kissed her boobs. Sucked seductively on each nipple, taking cues if not gentle enough.

"Love, oh, keep massaging my boobs and suck and lightly pinch my nipples."

Our fondling was sexually stimulating with surges of anticipation.

"All I care about is making love and being your first lover."

She was in a sensual and playful mood and wanted to make the most of our first time together to make the most of our first lovemaking.

"Even knowing would be with an experienced lover, I'm nervous, don't know how to do anything with a man. Being a virgin, what if I could not please you, David?

Lovemaking was learned from Jacquie, movies, and the Kama Sutra."

"Sweetheart, just be yourself, passion and instincts guide you."

"David, please tell me you want me. But first, do you still want a relationship with me?"

"Suzie, emotionally aroused with you in my arms. There is no one I wanted as much. Nervous too, have known beautiful women, but I have never been as enraptured. Want you not just for sex, sharing your first memorable lovemaking, or growing our relationship. I want you because it's you. Our lovemaking will express what words couldn't justify: the phrase I love you."

"You are not going to tell me how many women."

"No. I'm not. Look into my eyes. You are remarkable, disarmingly charming, and have an irresistible brogue. You ask questions you don't want to hear answers to. Nothing will be kept from you about my life. Later, we can discuss any concerns and promise not to keep secrets. It may take time for me to talk about certain things."

"New York man, I, too, promise to share and not keep anything private about my life. I trust and love you. When you don't want to answer, you remain silent. This gives me my answer, and oh, David, I'm still nervous, not having any sexual experience with a man. Growing up with six females provided lessons in self-reliance and independence.

I want you to make love to me.

Will it hurt? Promise to go slow and let me catch my breath."

"Suzanne, it's okay to tell me what you want. I'll be gentle, and not all virgins bleed or hurt. Our lovemaking will keep you in the moment of pleasuring you. You will delight in receiving and giving pleasure."

"Silly me. I love you. Please be patient with me. Show me how to give you oral sex.

This moment, in my lover's arms, has only been a dream. My dream has manifested, and to tell the truth, I couldn't have imagined you being a New York man."

Her giggling helped Suzie relax.

"Every woman and man seeks to be with their first lover.

Remember Kahlil Gibran's quote, "Let love be like a moving sea between the shores of your souls."

Trust your natural sensual and erotic instincts."

I placed my hands gently on her face, caressing her soft skin, and ran my finger over her lips before starting to kiss. It was like my first kiss; all the others now seem just practice.

"If you make love the way you kiss, you have nothing to worry about."

"Did we start?"

She looked at me and laughed.

Love this playful woman lying beside me, and she loves me. Her soft brogue helped make her feel cozy around her. My dream of finding romantic love was no longer elusive.

"David, please tell me you want me. Am I someone you want to love? Would I be able to have multiple orgasms?"

"Suzie, sweetheart, slow down. It's all right. If presented with choices, I'd choose to be with you. Don't worry, just enjoy our lovemaking.

I love you. Let me hold you sensually and softly, fulfilling your desires.

My dear sweet Suzie, you have revitalized my capacity to love. Most of all, I want to be with you even if we don't make love now.

Suzie, you have set your expectations high. First-time lovemaking is always memorable. Even after numerous times of lovemaking. Angel, let's see about your multiple orgasms."

Her vagina was wet and ready, and her nipples were hard in anticipation. Lifted her arms and gently placed them over her head to prevent her from touching me. Using just my hands and mouth, she had her first orgasm. It drove her crazy with a longing to intensely kiss, which created a mutual desire; simultaneously sexually and emotionally arousing.

She leaned back and wrapped her long, sexy legs around mine. Arms and legs became entwined, and she rubbed her pelvis against my crotch. Our kisses became passionate, and she slowly unbuttoned her tight-fitting jeans. "Angel, raise your butt," and her blue jeans were off.

Spoken tenderly, "Angel, I love you."

Kissed her neck and twirled my tongue around her nipples, increasing her sexual arousal.

"A little more, please don't stop, faster. David, I'm cumming, moaning in bliss, and she had her second climax. Unhurriedly and seductively took off her suggestive lace panties and tossed them to land near her bra.

"Love didn't realize my orgasm could come in waves and get so wet. David, your penis is so hard; I want you throbbing inside me. Don't worry, love, you are wearing a condom, and you started taking the pill when you were in the hospital."

Moaned and spread her legs wide. She was wet with desire. Gently, slowly, and erotically touched her clitoris with the tip of my penis.

"David, oh, so good. Please put it inside me."

Sexual excitement increased as my penis rubbed softly against her vagina and elevated her rapture. Suzie wanted to take my penis and insert it inside her.

Two lovers sharing in her first lovemaking, she took control of losing her virginity. Taking hold of my penis unhurriedly, guided it inside her.

Hard to portray our lovemaking without resorting to hyperbole. Tiresome tropes and cliches cannot adequately explain sexual ecstasy or convey the essence of a shared frame of mind.

"David, slowly, all the way, deeper, want to feel you pulsating."

Started to move quicker. My penis inside her tight vagina was unbelievable ecstasy.

"Harder, oh, Love, cumming, David, try and climax with me."

Our first orgasms were in sync; no words give justice to the erotic feelings experienced.

"Sweetheart, not in my wildest dreams could I imagine losing my virginity as a feeling of such joyfulness. Elated, my love, having waited for you, to take my virginity."

Held each other closer until my penis slipped out.

"Angel, your hymen did break."

"It didn't hurt. Is this blood from breaking my hymen?"

"Not every woman experiences pain the first time. Glad you didn't."

"David, how do you know every woman is different?"

Kissing her with fervor, distracting her.

"Suzie, let's not talk about other women. It is you whom I wish to be with."

"Sorry, David, I don't want any other man. My loving, gentle, and sexy New York man. Our lovemaking was exquisite. Love how you pleasured me when you took my virginity."

"Angel, what did you feel?"

"Couldn't imagine sexual desires were satisfied in unexpected ways. Excited knowing I could climax this much being hypersensitive. David, you fulfilled yearnings beyond my imagination. I'm silly; sex gets better each time, doesn't it? As an inexperienced lover, I shared my deflowering. Is that the right word?"

"Deflowering you intensified our first lovemaking."

"But love, you can't help being envious. You are an experienced man skilled at the art of lovemaking. Beautiful women try to seduce you, and I'm afraid some woman will take you from me. Men sometimes don't come back after their sexual conquest. Were you unhappy that I was a virgin and inexperienced in lovemaking? Are you happy with me?"

"Yes, Suzie, euphoric, my angel.

Oh dear sweet Suzie, you are not a conquest. Skilled in sex is not the art of lovemaking. You are the only one I wanted to make love to.

Lovemaking is when you give something precious to each other, your love.

Sweetheart, you are switching roles. Where is the confident, seductive woman who captured my heart?

We were pleased that our first lovemaking was impromptu, natural, tender, and loving. Would not have wanted our first time to be any different.

Susie, you are sexy, sensual, feminine, loving, and simply gorgeous, and your loveliness, elegance, tenderness, love of life, brogue, sense of humor, Irish wit, and desire to learn the art of love. Curiosity sparks your intellect and unabashed passion from your silliness. Suzie, heard a depth of feelings when you say you are silly."

Men fear rejection and lack confidence because you are breathtakingly stunning. Suzie, your beauty is intimidating, yet there are taller, more handsome men who would want to romance you and bring you sexual pleasure. So why would someone as attractive as you want to date just any man? Suzanne, you were waiting for the man of your dreams. Alone, approachable, and can choose anyone. Honey, how can you be assured it's me fated to be with you?"

"David, did you see me as Jacquie's Sister, or was it me?"

"All thoughts were about making love to you. Caught by your allure before Jacquie introduced us, because you captivated me."

"David, do you believe in love at first sight?"

"Suzie, why all the questions?

Which comes first, love or romance? Out of a romance comes a more profound love. First, there is a chemical rush of the first meeting, dating, and plenty of sex. Endorphins pave the way to love. Believe in the embers of love ignited at first sight.

Love how beautiful and sexy you are. The first time I saw your face and eyes, our first kiss revealed your sweetness. Drawn to you and wanted us to start our romance."

"Thank you for saying that."

"How could you have confidence it was me you were expecting? Yes, I believe in love at first sight. However, love is not something that can be demanded at will. It grows out of giving and spending time together. The quiet midnight talks, holding hands, and spontaneously kissing, a man who holds your hair back as you react to excess drinking, someone who is kindhearted. Each day, you want to make her happier. Love is lots of things.

Love is more than endorphins. You recognize love when frenetic lovemaking bonds with permanency and fate.

Suzie, why are you insecure?"

"Oh, David, I've never been insecure. Since we met, I'm afraid to lose you. Reassured because the tears you shed betrayed you connected with me so profoundly, it scared you."

"Love, yes, it scared me. Am I in a dream?

My fear evaporated as I looked into your eyes. Honey, my fear is that the blues will return with a vengeance if I lose your love.

Jacquie perceived a necessity for me to be introduced to romantic love, which I thought was improbable. The moment my eyes met yours, an invisible cord tugged me forward. It was your laughter and beauty that choked my voice, preventing me from speaking. Suzie, you radiate a glow from a love of life that takes my breath away. Obviously started to breathe; otherwise, couldn't say all of this to you now."

"David, thank you for making me smile."

"You captured my heart. However, it has not yet become real. Our love will grow and blossom into different expressions of affection. Our most mind-blowing sex is just wordless expressions of love.

Promise to always do what I can to make you happy. Not jealous or overshadowed by my beautiful blue-eyed Angel, loved by everyone who meets you. She is friends with a Senator she believes will someday be president. Just the opposite, admire and take pride in your capacity to love. And revel in the diversity of your talents and intellect.

Sharing now makes me feel vulnerable. Do you believe strongly in our destiny, or is this just a fantasy, and I'm talking rubbish? Want to believe strongly in our destiny. As a survivor of broken dreams and relationships, I need time to accept my new reality. When jumping in front of you, the only thought is to protect you. Your life is precious to me. Fated to make a transformative difference with your art, singing, and public service.

It was not a sacrifice of my life for yours. It was a gift of love. Your life wrapped up in mine, yet separate and cherished."

"David, afraid a man who is so unique, loving, handsome, and foolish is pursued by women prettier than I. Who has a more diverse repertoire in their lovemaking, giving you the pleasure you can't resist? You will leave me.

New York man, this won't be the last time we face these same emotions of fear.

Yet your words come from your heart. Only want to be cherished and loved by you. You want to grow our intimacy and relationship as I do. What is holding you back? Why won't you let me come any closer? Revealing this, you allowed yourself to become vulnerable. David, you say this because you don't want me to let go of you."

"Foolish?"

"You did jump in front of a deranged man with a gun. Who raped my Sister and wanted to kill me? When there were Secret Service agents twenty-five feet away."

"Point taken, but not close enough to save your life. Jumping in front of a gun is not a thing when I kiss and dance with a woman."

"Why are you fearful when I'm just as afraid of losing you? But it brings me closer. Want to understand why it pushes you away?"

"Because I'm protecting my heart, rejection prompts deep, dark blues, not of your making. Reaching out in despair of blue darkness, looking for a way back to my life. Regrettably, finding a light to guide me is not so easy."

"David, can't quell your inner fears. Instead, as a beacon to guide you back to me, you have my heart and the light of my love. As a young girl, confident in my romantic dreams, I looked and waited for you."

"How did you recognize it was I you were expecting? How could you possibly know?"

"My New York man, Jacquie, talked about her joy and love of having you in her life. She is more in love and intimate with you now than when you first met, and she has never rejected you. My Sister and I have an out-of-the-ordinary relationship. As the lastborn, she looked after me. Jacquie always knew who I was waiting for.

Her love for you and me recognized that we needed to meet. With everything she told me, I grew more confident. But when you kissed me and asked me to dance, there was no longer any doubt. The woman you've been waiting for. Trust you appreciate who I am."

"Want to, and part of me already believes. My heart is part of your heart. Still, there is a thin line between dreams and reality. Just have to open your eyes. Yet, I live with you now, already closer to you, but not totally for what you hope. You are currently in my arms, and Suzie, my life changed, and will never be the same. My fate was to be with you, Jacquie knew before me. She told me to hold on to my faith and that I would meet the woman of my dreams.

Sweetheart, when you were asleep in the hospital, holding you, wondering how this could be possible. Even sleeping, you sense my doubt and roll over to kiss and hold me closer.

A part of me is afraid to believe. Don't have the full strength back to fight my demons. Promise to always love, stand by, and support you in accomplishing your dreams and those to whom you have yet to give a voice.

Suzie, your fear of a woman seducing and taking me from you is impossible. Why risk losing everything with you? Whatever any man could want in a relationship with a woman is with you. Never, of my own accord, distress you. No woman can take your place. Blessed you are in my life. Your fear is the same as mine. You'll look to others to fulfill your needs."

"Love, a woman who waited for the man of her dreams, had no need to date. No one appealed to me. As an attractive woman, shying away from unwanted advances is emotionally wearing.

A complete woman without a man because of confidence in myself, my loving Sisters, nieces, friends, my career, artistic talents, my beautiful Whisper, and Shadow. Waited as long as needed until my love arrived. My dream man would come into my life, I didn't know how or when.

David, it was your approach I was waiting for. You are my gift of immeasurable love and affection, and you are sexy in your passionate lovemaking.

You have captured my heart. Happiest being with you.

Your feelings originate from your dark blue eyes, as well as your words and actions. How do I get you to trust we belong together?

The woman you write about in your poems. You recognize me, the relationship you hoped for. Yet, you won't let yourself trust me. Never would leave you because of your fear of losing me or unintentionally pushing me away.

Exchange a kiss for a kiss and give you the space and time you want. The woman you've ever wanted for a love mate; intelligent, empathic, loving, funny, playful, witty, sexual, and sensual, and she will help you reach your potential greater than you thought possible because of our love. Happy we have each other."

"Since meeting you, who is this new David? Give me time to adapt; my world turned inside out. A few weeks ago, my life was another David. You have returned to your home, and everything is different for me. Afraid to find myself adrift between worlds. Don't know who this David is. Oh, shit, what if I'm not the man of your dreams? How can you be sure?"

"Love, it is not now or never. It is forever. We have a stronger soul, heart, and mind connection than your fear of losing me."

"David, you are my New York man. I love you. Stop talking and kiss me."

Breathing in her love, hoping it would be enough.

"Love when you are ready, but sweetie, will not stop seducing you to say what your heart wants, and my heart longs to hear."

On our walk back to Woodland Cottage, we stopped to watch her beloved horses revel in the quiet of a setting sun. Neither of us said a word. Our lovemaking and intimate conversation have already taken place.

"I love you not only for what you are but for what I am when I am with you. I love you not only for what you have made of yourself but for what you are making of me. I love you for the part of me that you bring out." – Elizabeth Barrett Browning.

Five
Jazmine

"Love her and let her love you. Do you think anything else under heaven matters?" James Baldwin

Jazmine Felicity Dubois prefers to be called Jaz.

"Suzie, she is anxious and looks forward to you and David coming to dinner. She is the love of my life. Jaz is French with royal blue eyes. As a brunette, she sometimes wears her hair in a side braid. Jaz is sensitive, creative, open-minded, playful, serious, entrepreneurial, intelligent, and reflective. My Jaz has a beautiful French sense of humor and giggles at her jokes.

Jaz founded a romantic theme clothing boutique with stores in London, Paris, New York, Rome, and San Francisco. She is opening a store in Quebec this year. She says women want to wear romantic clothes and feminine dresses for dinners, dancing, or the theater, even in Canadian weather.

As a five-year-old, do you remember whom you wanted to dress up as on Halloween?"

"I wished to dress like *Cinderella,* and you lent me your costume. What does that have to do with Jaz's clothing boutique?"

"She named it Boutique le Cendrillon, French for The *Cinderella* Boutique."

"Jacquie, on Union Street, passed a boutique selling romantic clothing, rushing to a meeting for the Senator. Bet this must have been her San Francisco store."

"Love the name. Sis, she sounds wonderful. So pleased you two are together."

"Suzie, she and I are deeply in love. We want to live together at Woodland Cottage and have our wedding ceremony there.

At three years old, her mother died, and her father shamelessly left her at an orphanage. Jaz was a motherless child and a father who rejected her. A loving childless couple soon adopted her. Suzie, guess her religion?"

"No way, Jewish. Sis, so why are you worried?"

"Will David be jealous of Jaz?"

"He is protective of your feelings and mine and doesn't take an interest in Jaz's sexual orientation. If she were not a lesbian, he would jump into bed with her. You appreciate that he will fall in love with her.

Sis, our David is nonjudgmental. David frequently speaks about being overjoyed that you are reunited as a couple with a woman you love, as exceptionally wonderful as Jaz. You know this. So what is upsetting you?"

"Dad, have yet to tell him I'm bisexual, and Jaz is a lesbian. David doesn't care about my personal sexual preferences. As long as I'm happy and loved."

David would have said, "No, still not getting it."

"Both Mom and Dad and Nana agreed to come. Noreen, Victoria, and Megan told me they would support us. Can you arrange to be home with David? I'll be reassured, ostensibly he has a way of calming down a situation, what to do if it all goes ass-backward."

"Of course, love, we plan to be home when you arrive. Are you ready now to tell me the truth?"

"David defended my honor and yours by humiliating Paul when he tried to have sex with you. Well, Sis, he jumped in front of you after being knocked to the ground twice, got shot, and almost died."

"Are you afraid his Bronx temper will emerge against Dad if he demeans Jaz? David trusts you know how to tune him out."

"He will not sit still and not say anything if this happened, and with Dad's homophobic hatred and antisemitism, I'm worried it will create a terrible outcome."

"Oh, dear Sis, thank God Dad doesn't even own a gun. Even if he did, he wouldn't understand how to put bullets in it."

After a second of silence, the Sisters burst out laughing.

"Sis, Jazmine will tell Dad she is a lesbian. Regrettably, she refuses to tell Dad she is my lover without her standing by my side."

"You worry about Dad's rage, oh, never mind, you don't care but are concerned Jaz does."

"Yes."

"Suzanne, you were far away and started to look worried."

"The phone conversation with my sister last night. I said you would love Jaz because Jacquie loves her. I didn't want her to worry that you would do some Bronx protection thing."

"You didn't say I want to go to bed with her? Suzie? You did. You are not allowed to play with my libido."

"New York man, be serious. David, she dreads that Dad will have one of his hateful bursts of anger and say things to Jaz. You won't be able to stay in your seat."

"Please, Love, let Jacquie manage your dad. She understands how to cope with his rage. Promise won't say anything to create chaos for Jacquie and Jaz when they are home in Woodland Cottage."

"Love, not worried about you. It's Dad."

"You are the only one besides Jacquie who appreciates my sensitivity to Jaz's feelings. Suzanne, let me explain why your Sister changed her relationship with me and told me to trust her. Although it may hurt my heart in the short term, I will one day understand.

Jacquie believed I'd be okay because she trusted we would be together. This gave her the courage to reunite with Jaz. Otherwise, she would not have left our relationship, and I would not be with you now. That is, if she did not go back to her love. This may sound confusing."

Suzanne gently stroked my hair.

"Why we met is Jaz and Jacquie's deep love for each other. Jacquie was elated to reunite with Jaz. 'She is the most wonderful woman.' She would have stayed with me if I hadn't let her go.

It helped me stop worrying because she had met her soulmate. Their love for each other and Jacquie's love for you and me are sacred. Jaz means a lot to me as she, without knowing, brought you and me together. Does this make sense?

Love, you and I were inevitable as a couple because of Jazmine. I'll never allow your dad to demean her. If Jaz's feelings are offended, or she is made unwelcome, it would be the same if you or Jacquie were treated that way by your father."

"No, you don't sound silly. Your faith, we were meant for each other because our minds rationalize in multiple dimensions."

"Yes, if that is code for making things sometimes more complex than is necessary, like an Irish and Jewish Yin Yang, bonded because we trust and respect each other's thinking."

"My New York man, I love you in ways still trying to describe."

"I asked Jacquie if you talked to Suzanne about being engaged."

"How do you know they are planning to get married?"

"Well, you and Jacquie always talk about her love for Jaz. But, love, you have passion in your voice when you speak to me. The rhythm and accent when Jacquie talks about her become more lyrical than when talking about work. Feelings replicate from the tone of your voice when speaking."

"David, you never fail to surprise me with the extent of your experience and knowledge. You will love her. Love, when were you certain?"

"Just now, you confirmed my guess. The two of you don't give anything away, you don't want me to find out."

"It's impossible to keep a secret from you if we leave clues, no matter how opaque. Jacquie and I have no doubts you will love her and accept her for who she is."

"Then why is Jacquie upset?"

"Jaz is concerned you won't accept her because of your past love affair with Jacquie. An intimacy that never ended. Your love for each other, even though as friends, occasionally becomes cozy. Jaz is not troubled about your intimacy with Jacquie. Love, she imagines you will be jealous of her."

"You want me to have a love affair with Jaz to make her feel more secure?"

"David, please, Jaz is certain you will pretend to tolerate her but never accept her with your heart."

"Jacquie already is aware of my empathy concerning Jaz's feelings. Sorry, still don't see a problem."

"Love, it means a lot to Jaz if you become friends. You and Jacquie are still in love. Jaz is nervous about coping with your affection for her lover. Jacquie is still close to you, and Jaz fears Jacquie could restart her romance with you."

"So it seems, not the only one who gets irrational about love. Jacquie's affection deepened because it gave her peace of mind, and I was okay, which freed her to return to Jaz. Enjoying her love for Jaz because they are both meant for each other."

"Sweetie, which is how you make her feel welcome. Your sincere joy for their relationship. It will mean more to Jaz coming from you. Nothing Jacquie or I say calms or reassures her."

"Let Jacquie take care of this. I'm not a love therapist or marriage counselor and don't want to get in the middle of this reassuring thing you have in mind."

"Jaz grew up in a culture where it's not unusual for men and women to have affairs while married. Liaisons are sexual and romantic and sometimes lead to marriage."

"Not following you."

"Love, she has never received respect from males except for gay men who love and treat her with dignity. A person in her own right. Homophobia runs deep in the French culture."

"Nope, still not following the problem Jacquie and Jaz cannot resolve."

"Jacquie told her she should not tell Dad she is a lesbian and keep it secret. Dad will never accept Jaz. Jacquie wants to let the family know that Jaz and Annabelle have moved into Woodland Cottage.

Jaz believes all American men are biased, just like French men. David, you understand fear alters imaginings to seem real."

"Is it all right to let Jaz decide if she wants to talk to me about her fears?

"You're impressive, Jaz will love you, and she already does. My Sister speaks about you all the time."

"Please, no pressure on her."

On the evening of the dinner party, Suzie changed her outfit and shoes a half dozen times.

"Does this look like a Sister going to dinner with her Sister and lover?"

She laid out what to wear, promptly placed it into the closet, and took out blue jeans, a dark grey vest, and a white shirt.

"David, would you wear your red tie as it makes you look handsome?"

"Is this a look that puts Jacquie and Jaz at ease? A tie would make my outfit look too formal."

"Is this red one OK?"

"Perfect. Why don't you open the two top buttons to look casual?

Your grey shirt would be perfect. What do you think?"

"What about the tie?"

"On second thought, you are right. The tie looks too formal. Thanks, love, for making me happy and getting your red tie. Anyhow, it will clash with my outfit."

Suzie doesn't need to be correct. Instead, she tries to make me happy. Her outfit changed a seventh time."

Once dressed, we had over an hour before having to leave. So we sat on our favorite comfy sofa chair, where we watched movies, read, or cuddled with Suzie on my lap.

"Never told you what to wear, apprehensive about tonight's dinner, and want everything to be wonderful."

"An hour before we have to leave?"

"Uh oh," glancing at her watch," my bad, two and a half hours."

"There is a simple fix for an anxious girlfriend who had us get dressed early. Love, come closer to me."

"Promise you won't wrinkle your shirt or my dress."

We didn't undress. Romance for Suzie meant passionate kissing. Her kissing is sensual, and our affectionate conversation and much-loved cuddling are our favorite lovemaking. There are no words to do justice to how she kisses erotically.

"Could we just stay here like this all evening?"

"Sweetheart, this is just a prologue to our lovemaking date."

Suzie remained nervous for Jaz and Jacquie.

"How do you stay calm? What is your secret?"

"No secret, just you are with me. Jacquie and Jaz are preparing an enjoyable evening. Love, how about a preview of our date when we get home?"

"Here is a small down payment." She ran her fingers through my hair, kissed me, and unbuckled her seat belt."

"David, did you remember to bring the flowers?"

"In the trunk to keep them cool. This red rose is for you, your favorite, a box of dark Swiss chocolate for Jaz, Jacquie, and Annabelle."

Holding a bouquet of roses in her left hand, we embraced, tongues exploring sensual sensations of what was to come.

"Love birds, delicacies are in the kitchen. The meal can last just so long in the oven.

David and Suzanne, appetizers will be ready shortly."

"Sis, we will be right in."

Jacquie kissed my lips and gave a light kiss on my cheek.

"Lover, you are getting a lot of kisses today."

"It is your luscious lips I desire and the pleasure of running my hand along your sexy body."

"Where are we going?"

"The bedroom is this way."

"Our bedroom is five miles away. Guaranteed an unforgettable night of lovemaking. I love you. Here is another down payment of what's to come."

"Suzanne, why is David standing there?"

Her kiss played over in my mind's eye.

"David's look is familiar. Little Sister, should you get him or me? Jaz is in the kitchen and nervous about everything being impeccable."

"Jacquie, did you tell her I drink soda from a bottle?"

"She believes I said this to make her worry less."

Having retrieved flowers from the trunk, "Oh no, forgot the card."

"Love, it is in your left shirt pocket."

Having just arrived shortly after sunset, a twilight sky grew quiet, and birds suddenly stopped singing. As we entered Jacquie and Jaz's home, the sky grew darker and more ominous. Abruptly, lightning and thunder heralded a downpour of rain.

Suzie and I get cozy whenever there are storms and sing to the rhythm of the rain's sound.

"Suzie, is it all right for another kiss, and linger longer in my kiss with your lover? Jaz also wants to have a long kiss."

"Jacquie, Suzie, hello! Standing right here."

"Hush."

Jacquie's loving kisses and hugs are hard to put into words. Our affection deepens our heart-to-heart connection.

Met the love of my life, Suzie, even though I couldn't imagine it was believable after a relationship with Jacquie. Nevertheless, Jacquie knew it was inevitable, as did Suzie.

In a soft voice, face tenderly touching mine, her soft lips close to my ear, "Love, what is the problem? When will you let your heart and not your fear of rejection ask my Sister to marry?"

"Jacquie, please let's focus on your Jaz."

Would not have quickly gotten away if not for her worry about Jaz's anxiety.

"Ok, later then."

"What will you two do later?"

"Sis, take David's hand, and he will take the other."

The three of us walked into the dining room. An exquisite setting with rose petals spread down the middle of the table, Suzie kissed her Sister.

"Oh, Jacquie, exactly how you described it. Elegant, warm, and inviting, it's beautiful."

A little girl was on my mind instead of a table setting.

"Where is my Sweetpea? Aunt Suzie and I looked forward to hugging her and encircling her in love and kisses."

"Annabelle is with Noreen, having a sleepover with Jessica."

"David, your niece had me promise to place her latest drawing in your hands."

"Sis, she inherited your and my hyper-empathic ability."

'Mommy, give this picture to Uncle David first. He will share it with Aunt Soosi.'

She still has some trouble saying 'Suzanne'. "When asked why Uncle David first, she said, 'Mommy, Uncle David knows.'

Suzie sensed an emotional message in Annabelle's picture and came over to hold my hand.

"David, she wanted to go to play with Jessica. 'Mommy, tell Uncle David I love him.'

Jacquie handed David the pastel drawing that Annabelle had wanted.

"God only knows what is in my baby's mind."

David was careful with her drawing. Tears welled up. She handed over her picture to Suzie as he started to walk toward the kitchen.

"Sis, I did not tell her what to draw. I couldn't keep this from him. Even knowing how this would affect him. A four-and-a-half-year-old, admittedly an exceptional four-and-a-half-year-old little girl, wants you and David to have a family."

By the time David walked into the kitchen, his demeanor had changed into his usual self.

"Wow! Suzie, you told me it was the best kitchen ever."

Jacquie and Jaz fashioned a warm, welcoming kitchen, the heart of their home. The refrigerator door was covered with Annabelle's drawings and paintings. A Ben Franklin pot-bellied stove fire was lit, filling the air with sweet scents in a kitchen where brioche, croissants, and pies were baked.

"Jacquie, can we move the dinner to the kitchen?"

Suzie whispered, Honey, you're speaking out of emotion without considering the time and effort it takes to set an elegant dinner table.

"Wouldn't it be wonderful the next time we come to dinner? We should have it in the kitchen."

The Sisters let the comment about eating in the kitchen pass because it was a promising idea.

Jaz hadn't noticed me as she deftly placed the main dish into the oven. Her voice lit up the kitchen, soft singing contrasted with the darkness of a thunderstorm.

Silently stood at her side, not to startle her.

"Oh, David, you caught me with my hands covered with flour dough."

She was finishing the last touches of her mother's recipe for home-baked brioche bread, ready for the oven.

"David, our main course is my signature dish, a roasted pork with a raspberry gastrique (sweet and sour sauce) with roast vegetables of eggplant, bell pepper, garlic, onions, and plum tomatoes."

"Jaz, honestly, French cooking was never my preferred cuisine. You need to appreciate the totality of the ingredients, love each vegetable, understand the chemistry of cooking, and know the right temperature and cooking time. Additionally, you must recognize that the dish's presentation is as important as its taste.

Know the chemistry of cooking, including the optimal temperature and cooking time, and understand that the dish's presentation is as important as the taste. It seemed to me there was never enough food on the plate."

With a surprise-sounding but loving tone, "David, in addition to the main dish, you have fresh home-baked brioche bread, your favorite Stilton cheese, and for me a piece of cheese from Normandy, a Camembert, and for Suzanne and Jacquie a Walnut Cheddar from Effin, Ireland, a Merlot wine, and Peruvian Dark Roast whole bean coffee. Tiramisu was invented in the 19th Century in an Italian brothel and is known as an aphrodisiac for our dessert.

Dinner was carefully planned and prepared to entice an appetite. As a French woman, I have mastered French cuisine and wine, and I don't go hungry."

We lost control and started to laugh.

"Understanding French cooking through a chef's eyes is like lovemaking; did I get that right?"

"I'm happy. Jacquie frequently spoke of your romantic side."

Jaz's smile radiated a sweet kindness.

David had seen photos of her and later told Suzie they did not do justice to her beauty or capture her essence.

Jaz's smile exuded sweetness, and she was overjoyed to see Suzie.

"Suzanne, may I have permission to kiss your David the French way? And add a little more of the American way?"

"You don't need my permission, ma chère Amie. David would be disappointed if you did not."

"Everyone does realize standing right here."

Jaz responded, "Oui mon amour."

"David fretted about meeting you."

"Why?"

Jacqueline and Suzanne flashed their hushed look.

"Jaz, to tell you the truth, I was concerned I would not make a good first impression, and it is important for me that you feel comfortable when we meet."

Kissing her left cheek and right cheek ended in a heart-to-heart hug.

Suzanne held the kitchen door open as Jacquie kissed Jaz and left her with a box of tissues. Tension in Jaz's shoulders demonstratively relaxed. Tears welled up in her royal blue eyes, emphasizing her cheekbones.

"Suzanne and I will work on finishing touches for our dinner table. The roses would look best on our pantry cabinet during dinner."

"Merci mon amour, dinner will be ready shortly, and we shall eat at 8 o'clock."

"Suzanne and I want to catch up with a Sister talk. David, you and Jaz take time to get acquainted."

"Can we walk out to the porch? A rainbow graces the sky after rainstorms deplete their thunderclaps and flashes of lightning. A sign that signals the end of the fury of the storm."

I took a quote out from my wallet, written on the back of a worn-out business card, and handed it to Jaz.

"Look for me in the whirlwind or the storm. The more violent the storm, the quicker it passes." Paul Coelho.

She was charming, with her blue eyes and smile.

"David, may I kiss you hello?"

She kissed me sensually on my lips, searching for approval. Outside, we sat on a swing in silence.

"Wanted us to meet, but was nervous, and you made it easy for me. Did you mind if I kissed you on the lips?"

"From a beautiful woman, no, I kissed a new friend."

A single tear flowed onto her cheek.

"David hoped so much to be friends and develop a loving friendship. Concerned you would not accept me into your and Suzanne's home."

She still held my hand, but her grip loosened, not afraid of me pulling away.

"This is my favorite place to sit alone and dream or write poetry. I'll show you if you want."

"Yes, would like that."

"Suzanne says you write the most romantic poems and love letters."

"That is nice of you to say. Suzie told me she let you read them. It's okay, as nothing stays secret with her or her Sisters. You have charmed Suzanne; she can't wait to spend more time with you."

Jaz radiated a glow of love and trust, and we quickly became close friends, as if we had known each other for years.

"Jaz, you are my new best friend."

"David, insecure and afraid you would say all nice things only to make Jacquie happy."

"If circumstances were different, and I had not met Jacquie or Suzanne, I would hope to seduce you and not stop making love to you."

She began to laugh and could not stop.

"David, I'm sorry I laughed. Suzanne told me this meant you wanted us to become close friends."

'He has an unexplained emotional sense and can feel people's hearts. My love wants you to stop worrying about being accepted because you already are. A close friend is waiting for you to share joys and comfort sorrows.

David loves to make children laugh because he wants to bring them joy and happiness. He has an incomparable way of putting people at ease and getting them to smile. He believes that humor is the golden thread that keeps a relationship blossoming through wonderful and sad times.

"David, do you like to sit on a swing on warm summer nights, whispering to your love?"

Still not ready to share her worry, she waited, knowing Suzanne and Jacquie would make certain dinner would not be overcooked.

"David, I understand why Suzanne and Jacquie fell in love with you. I already have, and I'm glad you are my friend.

I'm a lesbian."

Suzie reassured Jaz, 'David doesn't pass judgment about sexual orientations. It would never occur to him because he has zero interest and doesn't care, except for your happiness. He never understood why people care.'

"David, why did you get upset with Annabelle's drawing? I regarded her drawing as beautiful."

"She drew Suzanne and me in front of Woodland Cottage, with a shining sun and a rainbow."

"I don't follow."

"She drew a baby in Suzanne's arms and us as a family."

She handed over the box of tissues.

"If this upsets you, we can change to another topic."

"Something tells me we're going to become close friends because of this talk. Suzie and I hope to have a baby, a daughter. My life would be empty without Suzanne.

Jacquie told me that while recovering from my wounds, people assumed Suzanne was resilient. And nothing could affect her.

She said they were mistaken. Suzi is vulnerable and suffers from mild depression. We make quite a couple, both vulnerable, yet together, nothing could separate us. Always would search for a way back to each other."

"David, I've never met anyone like Jacquie, which is true for you and Suzanne."

Pleased to gain her trust, she accepted I was indeed her friend.

"I love her so much, and we plan to be married at Woodland Cottage. Jacquie wanted me to wait until I was comfortable telling you."

"Jaz, you and Jacquie are fortunate to have each other. Always respect your feelings. There is no one more perfect for Jacquie."

Finally, we are getting closer to what is troubling her.

"David, hand me the box of tissues s'il Vous plaît."

"Can you hold me and let me place my head on your shoulder?"

"Of course."

"Jacquie told me her father did not take well that you had an intimate relationship with his eldest and youngest daughter. He bellowed at you because you are Jewish.

Placed in an orphanage, my adopted parents raised me in Jewish and French culture."

"His anti-Semitic hate is meaningless to me, so I ignore him."

Jaz will decide in her own time to share what is troubling her.

"I love you and Suzanne; Jacquie had already spoken with Suzie. I wanted to wait until you arrived with Suzie to make my request. Noreen, Victoria, Megan, her mom, and Nana will also be there. We want this home as our second home, an investment for Annabelle one day."

"Not family, Jaz. He hates me and calls me the Jew. As a Jewish lesbian, bet his head ought to explode."

"David, at an early age, told my parents I'm a lesbian. Dad asked Mom, 'She still can be Jewish if she wants, right?' My parents plan to attend our wedding, and Mom will love your Bronx accent and New York sense of humor. Mom's best girlfriend and family live on Manhattan's West Side."

"Having loving parents and family is a blessing. Annabelle told me she has two mommies. She said that was a good thing. 'Uncle David, Mommy Jaz wants to adopt me like you.'

Jaz, does it even matter what her dad says? Property has never been his. The Sisters legally own it."

"Without his blessing, I cannot move in."

"Approval is unlikely, let alone his blessing. Where will you both live?"

"Jacquie thought we could live here. It is not as large, but we have four bedrooms, so Annabelle can have her bedroom."

Jaz started crying. "Could you hold me? Jacquie said she always felt safer in your arms."

Jacqueline and Suzanne opened the back door at that moment.

"Dinner will be, Love. Why is it that whenever you are alone with Jacquie and now her intended, you are kissing or hugging? Both beautiful women."

"Suzie, s'excuse, sensed a warm friendship in his arms."

Jacquie kissed me and took Jaz's hand.

Suzanne smiled, "Love being in his arms, too. Jaz, welcome to your family."

As we entered the dining room, Suzie said softly, "Honey, look at Jaz's place setting."

Jaz placed a bottle of Chocolate Cherry soda, my favorite, in front of me and one for herself.

"David, it's exhilarating for my first time to drink out of a bottle. Like an honorary Bronx woman."

"Jaz, how do you have soda in your fridge? Isn't this a transgression in France?"

"Friends make their friends comfortable. Suzanne told me you're not a wine enthusiast and love to drink soda from a bottle. I thought you wouldn't do so unless I joined you. Was this okay?"

"Jaz, yes, more than okay, merci beaucoup."

Jacquie got up and hugged her.

She mimed. How did you get her to drink from a bottle?

In a whisper, "Didn't I say this is why she is extraordinary. This is the woman you love being herself."

"David, please, no more bad habits," she couldn't help laughing.

"Jaz, speaking for Suzie and me, we couldn't be happier you have come into our lives. Drinking out of a soda bottle is an act of love and a symbol of friendship. Don't tell anyone who is French because they already reckon Americans are crude and uncivilized."

Jaz smiled as David wanted her to feel comfortable and loved.

Suzie spoke softly, "David, how do you do that? Using humor to relate to people's emotions."

A delicious home-cooked French meal beckoned, although I dreaded a cheerless after-dinner talk.

Jacquie, in her rare Irish motherly tone, said, "Let's leave the dishes and take our coffee and dessert to the living room."

Just as Suzie and I got comfortable on the sofa, Jaz started the conversation calmly.

"David, please speak to Jacquie's dad before she says anything."

"Dad is going to accuse me of being a lesbian. He doesn't care about what a bisexual person is. Jaz should remain quiet."

"Jaz, rest assured, I'll be there; however, I cannot stop her dad from being impudent. It's good sense not to have to speak to him first. You have my promise to stand by you and speak up in defense of defending your honor. It would not end well if I were to be a go-between."

"Love, why not? You are the only one who understands what to say."

"Suzie, you and your Sisters are better at what to say."

"Responding with a not-so-gentle Bronx tone set against an Irish man's strong will, hostility is expected, to say the least.

Frankly, doesn't matter what is said. Your dad does not care, let alone change his mindset. Just because, I didn't lose my temper when he bellowed, 'You Jew.' First, you had an affair with my firstborn, and now my lastborn."

"Yes, because you did not lose your temper and just walked away."

"Love, tuned him out, having heard worse growing up, and it was me he attacked, and from a father's point of view, he has an argument. Unfortunately, he lost credibility because he used his insincere love for you and your Sisters as an excuse to launch an anti-Semitic diatribe."

"Jaz, on behalf of Suzanne and me, we are elated and can't wait for you to move in. Annabelle had already adopted you as her second mommy. And she is over the moon with her *Cinderella*-themed theme for her bedroom.

Suzanne shared that the family wants to welcome you home. You already have my love and friendship, as well as Suzie's; we will always be there if you need us. My guarantee won't let him demean or bully you."

"Yes, happy to be family. However, cannot move in with his disapproval."

Suzanne knew there must be some deeper reason, and David waited for Jaz to decide when to tell him. Otherwise, she never would escape his vitriol.

This may take time. Please go along and glance of trust.

"Your dad hasn't yet gotten over my sleeping with two of his daughters. His firstborn and now his lastborn. It would be emotionally challenging for any father. Don't care if he attacks or focuses hate or vile words on me.

Sorry, can't assure you my reaction if your dad verbally spews hate at any of his daughters or Annabelle. You and your Sisters, to some degree, learned how to tune him out. Consequently, his bullying got bolder. You were little girls, so he took advantage of his daughters. Your mom and Nana are figuring out what to do."

"David, how did you find out?"

Suzanne was becoming upset. No matter how demeaning her father got, she never gave up hope that he would change.

"Your strength of will, love, compassion, honesty, empathy, and more came from your mom and Nana. A good practice is never to stand in front of a mother protecting her children. Two moms will come up with a solution."

"To solve what? Love, please, why are you so confident?"

"Suzanne, close your eyes, place one hand on your heart and one on mine, and let the truth surface. Jacquie, as firstborn, you already understand."

Suzanne opened her eyes and glanced at Jacquie.

"David is right, isn't he?"

"Suzanne, when Jaz and I talked about our wedding plans, Mom and Nana were concerned Dad would sabotage the wedding.

'Jacquie, your mom and I want an end to your dad's outbursts of rage. Megan referred us to the Director of our local mental health clinic, whom she interviewed for a class assignment.

The Director wouldn't make a diagnosis over the phone. However, she said it sounded like a textbook definition of Intermittent Explosive Disorder—an impulse-control disorder with episodes of unwarranted anger. She explained that people explode in a rage despite a lack of apparent provocation or reason.

Since this disorder is typified by hostility and recurrent aggressive outbursts, your mom and I agreed to find a permanent solution to stop his duplicities. It worsened over the years, and we no longer will accept or cope.'

Nana queried, 'Can you remember when your father read you a bedtime story? Comforted when you had nightmares, went to school on parent-teacher nights, celebrated any of your birthdays?'

Mom sounded resolute, 'The four of you girls made excuses for your dad, and he used them to bully his way when he wanted something from you, except for our fearless Vickie, who protected you all by hiding you during his displeasure and rage. Soon, I'll share other mitigating factors Nana and I have already taken. We already have a final resolution.

Your dad started when you were young, so you naturally believed his deceptions. He was always a good father. Because he told you, girls, you didn't notice him, or he arrived late.'

Nana lovingly added, 'Your mom was always there for each of you.'

Mom was incensed, 'Your dad manipulated his daughters to believe his excuses. To get you not to accept what you experienced with your eyes as true.'

Jacquie, reassuringly, "Mom told me the house was always hers. It was her signature on the mortgage documents."

"Jaz, sweetheart, Woodland Cottage will always be our home wherever we choose to live. The mortgage has been paid in full. One hundred percent ownership was transferred to the four girls, which was worth a lot of money. Mom first transferred the title solely to me. Then each time a Sister was born, she added her name."

"Suzie, you already knew this is your property too. Always has since mom was the one making mortgage payments."

Jaz, discomfited, "Father left me in an orphanage, and was fortunate when new parents adopted me. My parents taught me not to lose myself in hate. I would be the one who suffers, and the person despised wouldn't care.

His animosity, intolerance, and being forced to watch as your dad intimidates Suzanne, bullies David, and makes life unbearable for Jacquie and me, would be intolerable."

Suzanne wanted me to be calm; however, there was no way to respond coolly.

"Jacquie, Suzie, my response will be automatic if your dad attacks Jaz. So, there is no guarantee that I will remain quiet if he should demean Jaz.

Consequently, a woman who gave a friend a bottled soda antithetical to her sensibilities is capable of saying what should be said.

Jaz, you and I developed trust and friendship within a brief time. You and Jacquie decide what's best for your life together. Suzie and I support whatever decision you make. It will be our joy for Suzanne and me when you finalize your move to Woodland Cottage because you and Jacquie wish to do. Do not let his animosity drive you out of your new home. Your decision, but I assure you if that S.O.B. says one word out of place."

"David."

"I'm sorry, love."

"Jaz, if their dad is verbally abusive, or bullies, disrespects, or shames you, I was schooled in The Tenets of the Bronx Street and learned how to respond."

"David, what do you mean, tenets of the streets of The Bronx?"

"Jaz, if he should say one wrong word, he will understand the meaning of being raised in the streets of The Bronx. He does not intimidate me, nor am I afraid to say 'back off.'

My vow is that you will not be alone if he implies, threatens, or intimidates you. You can't show weakness to a bully. However, you must recognize when and how to reduce your retaliation risk. No one will chase you from your home."

"Jaz, love, my David will defend your dignity and take on incoming verbal abuse."

I was too bone-weary to get undressed and only managed to take off my vest. Suzanne went into the bathroom and returned wearing sexy red satin lingerie, which intensified my yearning. She lowered the lights, lit sensuous incense, kneeled to untie my shoes, and removed my socks. Mesmerized by her charisma, Susie completely controlled my heart, mind, and body. Gently moved me to the sofa, where we remained standing.

"Come closer, love."

Leaned nearer and, loosening my belt, drew down my zipper and removed my jeans. She placed her hands on either side and slowly tugged at my sexy man briefs. Really, this is what Suzie calls them.

Sultrily unbuttoned my shirt and removed it promptly. Embraced me tenderly and started kissing my face until her lips softly met mine. She kissed my neck and teased my nipples with her tongue. Then kissed me delicately on my mouth.

One of her thin straps from her lingerie slipped half off her shoulder, and she stepped back to slip off the other strap.

"Lover, you lift it over me."

Suzanne got a pillow, placed it before her, and I kneeled. Kisses had her chest quivering in anticipation, positioned where her pleasure was. Using my tongue, she moaned as she got her first orgasm. She sighed, fully gratified.

Suzie slipped into my arms, allowing my hands to gently caress her, taking time so she could relish sensual feelings. Twenty minutes after her second climax, weak from all the caressing and two explosive orgasms, she set free my lust with her sexy red lips, with breasts gently heaving.

"Love, get me soapy and fondle me."

After watching Japanese erotic videos, 'so sexy and a turn-on. I want us to do this.'

Now, a sensual divergence of our lovemaking, Suzie took a small bath bucket and filled it with soapy water. A small brown wooden stool was placed behind me to sit on.

First, she got soapy, followed by putting soap foam all over my body.

"David, rub your penis between my boobs."

Slowly slid over me with her breasts. It was hard not to enter her then and there.

Motioned me to sit, took my soap-covered arm, and placed it between her legs. Sliding back and forth, used my arm to masturbate.

"Suzie, come straddle my leg."

As she came closer to cumming, she went faster after some minutes, with multiple orgasms, and collapsed into my arms. For what seemed a long time, she finally stopped trembling. Waited for her to slow her breathing.

"David, make love to me."

"Angel Love, let me kiss you. Suzie, our lovemaking for your pleasure."

With her soft hand in mine, I helped her into the bathtub. Added more hot water mixed in with her favorite aromatherapy rose crystals.

"Love ran out of bubble baths, so I borrowed Annabelle's."

"David, the water temperature is just right."

"*Goldilocks*," may I make love like the Papa bear?"

"Silly, stop delaying and come to me."

Knowing this would drive her crazy with lust.

"Love, place yourself against the bath pillow on the backside of the tub."

"David, my love, please come into the tub."

Her body lifted slightly off the bottom of the tub. Massaged her boobs, placed my hand between her legs, and gently fondled her vulva.

Suzie had shown me her most sensitive erogenous zones, which triggered orgasms. She closed her eyes and moaned with desire.

Sitting in front, turned to face me, and climbed on top of me. She took hold of my penis and inserted it into her vagina. At first sensual and slow, she bounced faster and faster until she couldn't contain her climax any longer and moaned, Oh, David, I'm cumming.

Suzie brought me close to cumming and slowed down and started over. She wanted to get me aroused but not to ejaculate, and by the fourth time, freed my desire to orgasm. It didn't take long to get me aroused as my hips pushed into her with my penis in sync with her movements. When she rose off of me, I quickly put my penis in her mouth and rotated her tongue around the head of my penis.

"Suzie, I'm cumming." She opened her mouth to catch every drop of my semen. Some landed on her face and on her boobs. Gently wiping her face with a washcloth rinsed under the bath tap with warm water. We were in bliss.

"Love, leave some on my boobs."

Our lovemaking was a sexual dance without prior choreographing, responding without words. Drained of sexual energy, lowering further into the bath water. Suzie reached over me and lay across my lap to turn the bath faucets to add hot water.

"David, can we stay here forever with me lying on top of you?"

Time passed unhurriedly, and unexpectedly, we heard our breakfast tray cartwheel roll into our bedroom. We stood, and she took my hand as the water drained.

Suzie assessed the right temperature to rinse us off in the shower. The water temperature was perfect. She placed her arms around me, erect nipples against my bare skin, and her hands on my buttocks.

"Oh, wait a sec."

She wrapped her wavy, reddish auburn brown hair onto her head. Suzanne resumed holding me close, turned on the shower, and brought us into ecstasy.

First, she grabbed her long lavender towel and stepped out of the shower. She gently held my hand, unsure about how steady she was after our lovemaking. Took hold of my blue towel, and we dried each other.

"David, have a surprise for you."

"Suzie, is it more sex?"

"Silly goose, later."

"Take my hand and no peeking, okay? Oh, David, you didn't keep them closed for two seconds."

Walking naked a few steps into our bedroom, stopped, turned, to face what she wanted to be the first thing I saw.

"Keep behaving and no peeking."

It sounded like our double closet doors opened.

"Honey, keep your eyes closed."

Used a type of blindfold she wore on a plane. Slipped it over my eyes, so no opportunity to peek.

"Let me put on your silk robe, and please leave it partially open."

"Suzanne, can I take off the blindfold?"

"Patience, New York man. In a few seconds.

Now, love, take off your blindfold and show me your dark blues."

Wearing her favorite pink silk kimono, showed her long sexy legs.

"It is more sex."

Suzanne stepped aside, revealing her favorite vino chilling in a silver bucket. Drinking together is more romantic than letting her drink a glass of wine alone. Of course, my favorite South African beer was also chilled, knowing I rarely drank, but when I do, it's beer.

Our favorite sharp cheddar cheese, delicious ripe red strawberries, dark, white, and milk chocolate, and sesame water crackers complement wine and beer. A small envelope for a business-sized card lay on the tray.

"You never cease to amaze me. How were you able to? The wine is even chilled."

"A secret."

After lovemaking, we occasionally treated ourselves to a sumptuous snack. We have no maids, no one except us, and the house is locked up. Suzie was playful and waited for me to work this out.

"No one except your Sisters, Mom, and Nana has a key, which is why you closed the bathroom door, not our bedroom door. Oh, your Megan."

Leaning against the headboard, putting strawberries in each other's mouths, and sharing a small glass of *cabernet Sauvignon.*

"Love, open the envelope."

One of my favorite childhood vintage board game cards lay in my hand.

"You took all my energy with our lovemaking. What is this supposed to mean?"

"To tell you the truth, I had a cute idea, but when the card arrived, I forgot."

How I love her giggle and laugh.

"Sometimes I'm silly."

"Glad you are."

Took our bed tray and placed it on the breakfast cart.

"Honey, where are you going?"

"To pee, come and keep me company."

She removed the bed cover, pulled up our Mulberry Silk Comforter, and snuggled together to keep warm. Candles flickering, one by one, went out.

"Love, would you light a fire?"

"Do we have any more of the three-hour-long logs? After lighting the log, David, could you turn off our bed lamp?"

Cuddling less than five minutes, "Love, are you sleepy, or can we talk?"

"Okay, what would you like to talk about?"

"David, will Jaz be all right?"

" Jacquie loves her, whatever she decides to do."

"Love, please don't get upset at my jealousy. Do you believe Jaz is pretty?"

"Not as close as pretty as you."

"This is important for me. Jaz is a beautiful, sensual French woman and was flirting with you."

"Woke in her a heterosexual passion?"

"David, please be serious. Jaz held your hand and wouldn't let go. Her kiss lasted a long time."

"Yes, honestly, she is gorgeous, so are Jacqueline, Victoria, Megan, and Noreen, and your mom is stunning. Why are you worried? If anyone should be jealous, it's me., Every man you talk to is trying to seduce you."

"David, do not flirt or pay attention, and my heart is set on you."

"Angel, feel the same way, and don't send sexual signals. In playfulness, you let women know that I want to have sex with beautiful women. Recognize that you want to break a never-ending cycle of feeling jealous.

Now, Jaz, a woman you adore and the love of Jacquie, so this is not about Jaz. You are fearful that a woman can seduce me away. Dearest love, I sincerely empathize with you. Jealousy can ruin a relationship. Trust alone cannot quell jealousy. Jealousy controls all emotions and becomes the dominant emotion. Rationality is nowhere to be found.

Suzie, you never have to worry or get jealous. It is unimaginable for me to ever upset a woman whom I waited for a lifetime.

Love, both men and women love you, and worry, some attractive dude, wealthier, better-looking will."

"My mom?"

"Don't you agree she is gorgeous? Where do you suppose you got your looks, values, and empathy? Your mom taught you about love? Also, you inherited her bluest eyes."

"Would you want to sleep with my mom?"

"Why? Did she say something? Suzie, what is disturbing you?"

"Do you want to sleep with my Sisters, Megan or Jaz?"

A sob overwhelmed her and started to choke up, and her eyes could no longer keep her tears from escaping.

"Angel, come into my arms, let me hold you. I love you. We have romantic and spiritual love and are each other's best friends. Our passion is forever. Never thought it possible, a second chance to redefine romance to transcend sex.

Enjoying what has always been part of your life, close sibling relationships. Love from your Sisters is something I have never experienced. Adore and love them as my sisters, confidants, and friends. You appreciate how much this means to me, unconditionally adopting me into each of your hearts. Absolute trust in your Sisters and value their counsel.

Suzie hoped one day to have her own family. Your Sisters are already part of our romance and thus have deepened our love.

Do not want to sleep with any of them. Nor any woman. It is you who takes my breath away. Suzie, I love you. And 'trust us' is not an empty platitude. It is a sacred pledge my heart made. You flood my capacity for love, sex, and our intellectual and spiritual life."

"David, feel the same and more, yet you are a man with strong sexual desires, and another woman could easily seduce you."

"Yes, honestly, a sexy, gorgeous woman may seduce me. Indeed, not my heart, love, affection, and the life we are building. No woman can tempt or take me away from you. Or would ever betray our promise of fidelity. We have chosen each other in our dreams, and fate found a way to bring us together.

Suzie, you are a beautiful, sensual, and sexy woman, yet you remain vulnerable. Your spontaneity outpaced my ability to keep up with you. Your deep-seated emotions drew me into your heart. Your cute giggle inside your laugh reveals a layer of unspoken excitement. Still short of breath at the elegance of your femininity.

The moment I laid eyes on your bluest blue eyes, I knew you were my heart's desire. My dearest love, I want to fall into your arms and be caught by your passion. When we kissed and danced, asking me to stay alive and staying with me in the hospital was our prelude to romance.

Adore and cherish every moment we are together. You started to mend my broken heart and didn't let my fears prevent me from knowing you are my love mate. It is you I want.

Being sexy and beautiful comes naturally to you. Oh, Suzie, what can be said, for you not to doubt my love? Understand a fear of losing my love to another woman.

Your unlimited capacity for unconditional love and your silly romantic nature entice me. You make me laugh and set free my imagination with your intellectual curiosity.

Could never leave you or want to. No one could replace the vast emptiness in my life if we were not together. Mind you, being gorgeous and having mind-blowing sex is lovely; however, it's not why I love who you are. Trust me, as I trust our love."

"David, this was not easy for you to become vulnerable. You have opened your heart, soothed me, and I feel safe to share my fears. Oh, my lovely New York man, you are the love I've waited for since I was ten years old. Now you told me I'm the woman you dreamed of who came into your life."

"Suzanne, as we danced, love songs became one with you in my arms. This must be a dream of dancing with my blue-eyed lady. You have delighted my heart. Holding you in my arms was a dream come true.

Wearing your black satin gown, you exuded elegance, and every man and woman was in awe of your beauty and poise. Yet, you regarded me as if you had known me your entire life. The world disappeared except you and me on the dance floor."

"David, love you so much, afraid a beautiful woman one day will take you from me. Not any of my Sisters. Yet you like to talk to women. And you were in bed with Jacquie just a few hours after meeting her."

"Suzie, your Sister brought us together and understands your fear. Something we have in common, and one day will dissipate, a promise.

Honey, have more women friends because some men are, well, to be truthful about my sex, males, don't know how to cherish a loving woman. In short, quite a few are insensitive and misogynistic clods.

These men view sensitivity and equality as masculine weaknesses and silence any connection to true feelings. The American male ego is relatively simple to understand."

"We are perfect for each other. It's just, and please, please don't get upset. Not trying to make you feel rushed about how fast we nurture our relationship. But you do want the same.

What prevents you, David, is your fear; you don't want me to reject you for another. Didn't fall for a man with two life-threatening bullets in him. Fell in love with you at ten years old."

"Suzie, have faith in our love. Yes, you're right, I want the same for our relationship. We have a passion that remains largely unexplored. There is no reason to become upset.

Suzie, can we now get some sleep?"

"Love, promise me you will speak with Dad before he gets into one of his rages."

"The only time he acted to protect you, he got shot twice. Proud of your slap, left five fingers to mark his face."

"David, please, it still upsets me, and thank you, there is a compliment in there somewhere."

"Won't upset a delicate situation, and I'll only say something if your dad gets riled up and bullies you, Jaz, or Jacquie.

If your Sister and Jaz decide to say they are a couple, there is no other outcome. No one can talk rational sense to your dad."

"You, if anyone can. David, please, will you at least try?"

"Promise, with the stipulation, Jaz decides what she wants to say. She has me and your family to protect her."

"David, when did we make love last?"

"About an hour ago."

"Let's kiss and see how it goes."

Six
Enduring Emotional, Romantic Love

"Where to look if you've lost your mind?" Bernard Malamud

A sense of foreboding hung in the air as Suzanne and I arrived. The family room atmosphere was tense, like that of a courtroom, rather than a regular family gathering. Noreen and Victoria sat together, conversing with no joy. Jacqueline, Jaz, Megan, and Ryan sat on the fireplace ledge. Her mom, dad, and Nana are due to arrive any minute. It was not the family's usual get-together, as everyone was on edge.

The front door slammed, and in walked Mom, Nana, and Dad, who begrudgingly dragged himself inside. He looked like a disgruntled schoolboy being taken to church when he wanted to play soccer with friends.

Jaz, at her bravest, hoped to find the best words to present herself to her lover's dad.

'Jacquie wants to say to her father, we are in love and live together at Woodland Cottage. The idea will infuriate him; homophobia is a disease of hate. Oh, David, she doesn't want me to tell her dad about my being a lesbian.

I'm a lot more than my choice of a bed partner. Emphatically, David, won't deny I'm a lesbian. Though my

Jacquie wants to protect me from his rage, if someone judges my sexuality, I can adequately defend myself.'

As soon as everyone was seated, Victoria, with lovely wavy red hair and warm blue eyes, was fearless regarding her dad. Vickie has never been intimidated by her father and protected her Sisters from dad's frequent anger outbursts when they were young girls and led them into the barn's safety.

"Papa, Jacqueline, and Jaz called a family meeting."

"Who is Jaz?"

"As I was saying, please listen to what Jacqueline says."

"What gobshite are you talking about? You want me to listen! I always listen."

"Nana was unafraid. "Timothy Patrick, you listen, but you never hear."

Whispering, "Your dad will never contradict her. Or dare to say a word to her that is out of place."

"Hush, David, your friends Jacqueline and Jaz need you. Please do not joke tonight."

"Love, just making a family observation."

Suzanne stood next to Victoria; a show of unity proved to be a miscalculation. You don't trample on Superman's cape.

Promised not to say anything, thus unable to stop an approaching train wreck.

"Why is the Jew here? He's not family."

All the family's eyes swiftly turned to me, nervously waiting for my reaction, hoping I wouldn't make a difficult situation worse. Suzanne shifted closer to me.

"So, love, how well do you believe this is going? Don't want to remain silent when I want to tell your dad Feck off."

"Guess now is not a good time to announce my conversion to Judaism when we start our family."

Suzanne wanted to express her love and for me to remain calm.

"What do you want to say? I'm listening."

Victoria turned to Jacqueline. "Do you want me to stand with you?"

"Vickie, cheers, I'm okay."

"Dad, this will not be easy to hear, let alone accept. Pray you don't get cross."

"Daughter, you are talking gobshite."

"Jaz is moving into our home."

"The pretty one sitting next to you. Where does this woman sleep?"

"Dad, in our room."

Started a countdown from five. Suzanne squeezed my hand tighter.

"Is this woman a lesbian?"

Honestly, I was not surprised to think he could make it to four. So, I started to prepare for the worst outcome.

"Dad, bi-sexual means..."

With utter disdain, "It means your Jew boyfriend turned you into a lesbian."

Fearful of his anger outbursts, no one dared except me to correct his anti-Semitism or rants about gay love, which obviously he doesn't understand, nor is he willing to accept.

In my best calm voice, not to imply judgment.

"No, Timothy, you don't know what it means. Your daughter and Jaz have enduring emotional and romantic love. A bisexual woman likes both men and women, which means loving or sleeping with either sex. What father wouldn't be overjoyed that his firstborn found someone to spend the rest of her life with?"

Unfortunately, my natural tendency to speak my mind surfaced. Truthfully, always kept my cheekiness--chutzpah close at hand,

"Or have you lost your mind? Wonder how you can sleep at night."

Outraged, "Don't you dare reprimand me!"

Keeping cool, it takes a lot for me to get angry after years of living in New York City. Knowing how to cope in a city with explosive emotional situations before it goes south.

Remained as serene as possible, in an easy-going voice,

"Someone has to. You are a verbal oppressor, and you can no longer scare the shit out of your family."

"It was all your fault, and now my daughter is a lesbian."

Suzanne whispered, "David, please don't escalate. Dad gets infuriated when challenged."

After our fantastic love-making last night, Suzanne hoped to have convinced me to speak in a less confrontational tone.

Nana caught on first and winked at Suzanne, whispering, "It's ok, Luv. Let him redirect your dad's anger.

"Sit the feck down. Don't want this Jaz woman living in my home."

Megan leaped up, took my hand, escorted me back to my seat, and sat close.

Jaz calmly stood next to Jacqueline and took her hand.

"Mr. Cantwell (*Brooke was the girls' mom's maiden name*), I'm a lesbian. It is who I am. Your daughter and I love each other."

On the edge of my seat, prepared to jump up.

"Look, whatever your name is, shut your mouth and sit the feck down. This is a family matter."

Megan and Suzanne held my hands in a valiant attempt to keep me seated.

"Ryan, you're letting a Jew hold on to your wife? Already made Jacqueline a lesbian."

Nana gave a Don't you even utter a word look. Ryan promptly shut his mouth.

With all due respect, I could summon "Timothy."

"It's Mr. Cantwell! I will not have a gay person in my home."

Suzanne was proud of my self-control. However, it was just a matter of minutes giving a full-throated defense of Jaz.

"Timothy, Jaz wants your blessing to move in because she respects elders."

"A Jew will not tell me how to run my family."

"David, this is getting out of control. Please don't say anymore."

"Jaz or whatever your name is, get out of my home. Give you my blessing. Don't want a lesbian corrupting my firstborn. How about this, get the feck out of my fecking house!"

Jaz quickly turned on her heel and went outside.

Not only did he cross a red line, but Timothy blew right past it. This meant he said something so despicable that he could not help but avoid being antagonistic.

"What the F*CK are you doing? You have asked the love of your firstborn to leave, and she has the self-respect and grace to do so."

"Don't you dare criticize me!"

"Shut the F*CK up!"

"No Jew will tell me how to speak in my home."

"Jacqueline handles the crap you spew; you are a self-righteous, pompous piece of shit. You can call me Jew all night, don't give a damn.

When you don't even own this house and land or ever did, how dare you have the chutzpah to verbally assault a beloved member of our family and ask her to leave her home? Like it or not, she is teaghlach-family, my mishpocha, my extended family, and is loved."

Infuriated, "I paid the mortgage."

"Like hell you did, your wife and mother-in-law paid the mortgage, and you moved in like a king."

"I own this house and land, and can throw anyone out on their arse, starting with you."

"You have the audacity to claim ownership, no, shameless, unadulterated gall. The legal documents state that the Sisters own this home and land.

"Not sorry for you and won't mention your love affair with the same woman shortly after Jacquie, your first newborn daughter, came home from the hospital."

Timothy turned bright red and fell silent. Grabbed his coat and left through the kitchen, slamming the door. Driving as fast as possible out of the property.

"Love, how did you guess about his affair?"

Your mom was resigned to this reality. Sorry, Elizabeth. You have already agreed to leave him, so his storming out is not unwelcome news. The girls didn't want to accept that side of him, so they didn't speak about self-evident behavior as they grew up.

Your dad used the Sanctuary for years before Suzanne was born. Notably, Suzie's Sanctuary has a woman's touch. Feminine decorating, including oak wood wine racks, when your dad drinks beer. Partially concealed behind a pantry shelf are cookbooks, crochet doilies on the sofa's arms, a stylish bed with pillows and other accessories, and a female lace bed canopy.

A woman adding feminine items to her home is a different aesthetic choice than a man's. A female's home reflects her personality and stylish sense of filling it with love. A man would not keep a feminine-looking home unless a woman friend frequently stayed overnight. Suzie has grown up seeing these things, so a feminine touch would feel comfortable and normal.

Suzie, Victoria, Noreen, Jacquie, and Megan remained quiet as this was not what they had expected to hear.

"Suzanne, girls, your mother and I said nothing to David. Jacquie has bits and pieces, which we will soon remedy. Your mom and I have already taken steps; we shall shortly speak about."

Noreen suspected David's modus operandi of rationalizing and acting on a hunch. "David, when did you find out?"

"Didn't, well, not 100% sure until he didn't say anything and stormed out of the room. That's when I had confirmation of my suspicions."

"Oh my God, David, you confronted a bully with fits of rage on a hunch?"

"Yeah, raised in The Bronx, you become street smart. Capable of reading people and identifying and evaluating potential dangers to stay safe. Sweet Noreen, bullies, lose their power when confronted.

Your dad is impotent now because his family knows his secrets.

When a gang member picked on me for being Jewish, I grew up where there would be an inevitable fight or flight, running for my life. Wasn't it peculiar for a man who vilifies Jews, as your dad did not once dare to insist on my removal? Nana would have had him packing. A man who is so antisemitic would be more vehement against someone he loathes, not afraid of him."

"Okay, let me say this quick. My friend Jaz, Jacqueline's love, is standing outside in the cold and needs an outsider who doesn't have a history with the family. And needs reassurance.

A man who thinks he is a gift to women is a classic example of a typical male ego. An archetypal pattern of male behavior. A case of your father justifying cheating on Elizabeth. Your dad didn't want to give up a free ride, living rent-free with your mom.

Ladies, what does your father do for a living? Reminisce about my dad and express affection and sadness that he has passed. Sentimental memories of visiting my dad at work as a boy. Many children go to their dads' or moms' place of work."

"How did you know about the house and land ownership?"

"Vickie, the same critical thinking skill you have is inductive reasoning. Moved in, still recovering from my trauma, and you and your loving Sisters instantly adopted me and ensured this was my home. Your mom and Nana welcomed me with open hearts.

Nana, you and Elizabeth knew each other because you were paying the bills and the mortgage. Each time tried to contribute and return the love by paying rent, Nana told me, "Don't worry, everything is in hand."

The phrasing didn't make sense. Expected to hear her say, 'You are already doing so much,' or 'Okay, how about in place of paying rent, doing the repairs, cleaning, shopping, or whatever? 'You are already doing so much, or okay, how about in place of paying rent, doing the repairs, cleaning, shopping, or whatever?

Don't worry is something you say to a child, not to upset them. It should be welcome to want to pay rent. However, refusing my payment indicated something was amiss.

Men sometimes offer remedies to impediments or mansplain to women unnecessarily. Indeed, neither wanted nor needed. However, it seemed suspicious; Nana and Elizabeth also refused a request to access mortgage documents.

When inquiring about the documents, we should also consider their location. In the case that we need to locate them, God forbid, we could find them. Copies are for caution.

Instead, I got pure blarney, and as a New Yorker, I called it by a different name (BS). No persuasive reason not to answer, except if his name wasn't on the mortgage loan documents. You ladies appreciate how sensible your Nana is.

Elizabeth and Nana wanted to protect their girls from how little your father seemed to care for his family. They didn't want their secret plans revealed until everything was in order. The family would get news within minutes."

Megan entered the room wearing Jaz's wrap coat, a wool beret hat, and leather gloves.

Suzanne caringly said, "Love, use your leather jacket in the front door closet. Go, she must be freezing."

"Jacquie, it will be all right. Jaz is not fragile."

"David, I trust no one else to talk to her now. Thank you, sweetheart."

Gently placed her wrapped coat on her shoulders and handed her hat and gloves. Remained silent, standing by her side.

A moonless night sky with twinkling stars like jewels against a canvas of black. We watched in awe at a shooting star racing across a quiet and peaceful night, triggering a cherished memory.

"The first night of my arrival, Suzie and I imagined hidden wonders inside a band of stars spilled across the sky. With reverence, we marveled at our Milky Way. Around each twinkling of a star's light could be ringed planets, ocean moons, comets, and asteroids, turning the night sky into a more dynamic display of amazement.

Mused about a never-ending universe filled with unknown mysteries waiting to be explored. Powerful supernova star explosions are impossible to imagine. These first and second-generation stars seeded our universe with gas containing the elements essential for life. Thus paving the way for the creation of planets and sentient beings. Evolved from stardust, situated on a rocky, ocean-blue planet. We are children of the stars.

Enjoy gazing at a night sky filled with starlight. Amazed how Cosmologists could understand anything, given the complexity of quantum physics to explain our Universe. Only at the beginning of our understanding of the cosmos.

Lovers seek the night sky for its allure of romantic possibilities.

Children wish on a star, S*tarlight, star bright, first star I see tonight, I wish I may....*"

"As a girl growing up in Marseille, France, my parents, after a summer sunset, drove to where it was darkest. Each July to August, view shooting stars and marvel at the beauty of a night sky with streaks of light flashing across the sky. At University, I read about the Perseid Meteor Shower. It would not have been as wonderful if my parents had given it a name, no?"

"Late morning of the first day of my arrival, Suzanne was excited to introduce her two passions. Walk with me to acquaint you with Suzie's friends."

"Whisper and Shadow, Suzie brought me here my first morning at Woodland Cottage."

"Is it okay?"

"We can ask Whisper."

"David, are you teasing me?"

On a dimly lit path, I strolled toward the barn. As the barn door opened, a mare and her filly foal came out from behind a log fence."

"Suzanne had built large, comfortable horse stalls in the back. She likes them having freedom of movement."

In a soft voice, "Whisper, come here. Want to introduce Jaz, Suzanne's friend, whom she told you about?"

Whisper walked over and put her head over the fence to smell me and say hello.

"Shadow, you too," and she walked over and stood beside her mom.

"David, do they understand you?"

"They are Suzie's extended family, raised Whisper and then her filly foal."

Placed my head next to Whisper. "Would you say hello to Jaz? She joined our family. Come closer, she will say hello."

Whisper put her head next to Jaz, so they were face-to-face.

"She wants to remember you. So say anything in a soft voice."

"Whisper, is it OK if I move in? Was that a yes? Sorry if you heard loud voices and a car speeding off."

Whisper bowed her head as if to say, No problem.

"Would you like to give her and Shadow an apple?"

Reached into a hanging bucket, where there are always fresh apples.

"Here is an apple to give her."

"Whisper, can I ride you sometimes? David, she said yes."

"Just open your hand with the apple. She is gentle."

"It was like feeding an old friend."

"Shadow, a nice red apple for you, too."

Shadow was frisky. Whisper looked at her foal, shaking her head. Shortly after, Shadow stopped prancing and walked up to Jaz to get her apple.

"David, did her mom ask her to be polite?"

"Yes. Here is a torch, Jaz, (a small battery-powered electric light). "The path is dark where we are going. I'll take the other torch. Suzanne said it draws attention to the beauty of the stone path. She meant it is safer to walk where the light is on the path."

As we stood outside the gate to enter the Sanctuary,

Jaz wondered, "How is it possible for Suzie's Sanctuary to be here?"

"Carefully follow the stone path."

"David, may I hold your hand?"

"Suzanne wanted assurance of privacy and safety," entered through a hidden entrance opened by code."

"Jaz, wait a second while the lights are turned on."

"Will she be upset with me because I came here?"

"She especially wanted to invite you to share her private Sanctuary."

The coziness of Susie's home, beautifully decorated with books, an antique dinner table, a shag rug in front of the sofa, and the patchwork quilt blankets, was welcoming.

This door leads to a pantry full of food and three oak wood wine racks with bottles of Suzie and Vickie's favorite wines. A kitchen area with a fridge and a stove opposite the sink. A Ben Franklin stove, a pile of wood providing heat and ambiance. As well as a stone fireplace inside the living room, which is used chiefly for warmth and to set a soothing mood.

A sizeable flat-screen TV connected to the internet with speaker bars for our favorite movies and music videos. Oh, the spiral staircase leading to our loft bedroom and Suzie's office. The door downstairs leads to her art studio. Suzie and I love our home away from home.

"David, this is a unique gift. Thank you for showing this to me. It's Magnifique."

We frequently use this as our second home and refuge. Annabelle was the only family member permitted to stay overnight with us. This is her home too, and we have special family nights here.

Suzie shares her heart and only cares about making her Sisters, Megan, Annabelle, Jessica, and me, happy.

Suzie guessed her dad would probably be upset with you if our family gathering tonight became emotional. Suzie wanted you to realize how special you are to her and the family.

Brought you here to share Suzie's and her Sisters' love, so you feel welcome. You are not a guest but a Sister and essential to the family. Suzie doesn't just express her innermost emotions with words. She wanted you to feel exceptional. Her desire was for you to be the first Sister to share her private place."

'Silly me, love, worried about which Sister to ask first to share our Sanctuary. It is important to me because of my affection for my Sisters.'

She wanted to ensure each Sister knew how much each one was loved. She was upset she didn't have a resolution; nevertheless, Suzie was confident she would solve it after a few days of pondering.

'David finally found a solution to my problem.'

'Okay, but it wasn't a problem.'

'Hush, love all my Sisters and Megan and Jaz; however, the looming conflict with Dad wants Jaz to appreciate how indispensable she is to the family and me. We all agreed in a ceremonial sense that Jaz should be invited first. David, isn't this a perfect solution? In some way, could you be the first to take Jaz to the Sanctuary? You will know the moment. It will mean more to Jaz to be with you.'

'So, you went for an over-the-top solution when having everyone come simultaneously would make life easier.'

'David Benjamin.'

'Oh, yes, a perfect solution.'

'David, and why is it perfect?'

'I give up. Why is it perfect? You love all your Sisters and now want Jaz to know she is also loved. Oh, you are brilliant because this is no longer about your Sisters. It's about Jaz.'

'New York man, you New Yorkers are really slow on the uptake.'

"David, S'il vous plaît, hold me like the first time we met."

After a few minutes of sitting quietly, she revealed her secret hurt.

"I'm obstinate about getting her dad's approval because I was emotionally devastated when my real father abandoned me. Unceremoniously placed in an orphanage.

It was fortuitous to find where he lived shortly after my fifteenth birthday.”

‘Daughter, I have no daughter; leave and never return.’

“Slammed the door in my face, and my world collapsed. A woman asked who was at the door. My birth dad said, Just some tramp asking for a handout.”

“Blessed with extraordinary, loving parents. Dad told me not to hold on to any expectations if I were to locate him.

David was only a fifteen-year-old girl; how could he speak to his daughter in this manner? Without his permission, I will never live in a home with such a father.”

“Truly sorry about your father. But Timothy is now gone for good.”

“Because of me?”

“No, Jaz, not because of you. Confronted him with the truth. A bully doesn’t like being challenged and suffering defeat.”

“What you have done for Jacquie and me was loving. Merci. You got him to direct all his hate toward you to protect me.”

“Disrespected and mistreated in your home was not permitted.”

"Merci beaucoup, Is this true? The family still wants me. May I kiss you?"

Suzanne quietly stood by the door inside the room and heard everything. She stepped closer as Jaz's lips touched mine. Suzie waited for her to end her kiss. Her love for Jacquie made Jaz genuinely exceptional.

"Oh, Suzie, really, your family wants me?"

"Yes, Love, you are part of the family."

"Suzanne, can I kiss you, too? You will not mind me."

"May I also have a hug?"

Suzanne later told me Jaz's kiss and hug were sensual, tender, and loving.

"Came looking because Nana and Mom called an emergency family meeting.

Jaz, welcome to your family and home."

"Suzanne, how did you know where to look for us?"

"Love the most predictable man. This is where I wanted David to take hold of my love. Asked David to take you here at the first opportune moment."

Holding hands, the three of us sang, "*Show Me the Way to Go Home*" as we returned to Woodland Cottage.

Seven
Family is what Love is All About

"In family life, love is the oil that eases friction, the cement that binds closer together, and the music that brings harmony." Friedrich Nietzsche.

Suzie's mom asked the family to gather in our bedroom in the unlikely event her husband returned. Couldn't barge in unnoticed. Suzie, Jaz, and I entered our bedroom, and everyone whispered instead of typical joking and laughter.

Transformed our bedroom into a one-of-a-kind off-Broadway theater. Everyone except Mom and Nana was waiting for the curtain to go up. They looked concerned and relieved at the same time, a look the Sisters had never seen.

Jaz sat next to Jacquie. Victoria and Noreen sat together on our comfortable chair.

Megan sat alone. Ryan was conspicuous by his absence.

"Megan, love, come sit beside David and me on the sofa."

Megan's smile returned to her joyful self.

Suzie leaned closer and spoke softly, "Something is not right. Why isn't Ryan here?"

"This is an auspicious family meeting. Nana and I would like to add our abiding love and a warm welcome to Jaz to our family. Annoyingly and rudely interrupted a while ago, didn't have a chance."

"Suzie didn't realize your mom used sarcastic wit when something was serious."

"Of course, she is Irish."

"Jaz, Nana taught me this as a wee child and instilled in my daughters the same Irish blessing. Happy you, and Jacquie, and my grandchild Annabelle are getting settled."

"May the road rise to meet you. May the wind always be at your back. May the sun shine warm upon your face. The rains fall soft upon your fields, and until we meet again, may God hold you in the palm of His hand."

"Jaz, welcome to your new home." She kissed Jaz on both cheeks and hugged her.

"There should be a few tissue boxes in Suzanne's bedroom somewhere."

"Mom, have a box for Noreen and me."

Vickie dried her tears, gave Jaz a few tissues, took her by the hand, and stood with her in front of Nana.

"Jaz, as the family's matriarch, there are few privileges I allow myself. But this is a joyful day for me and now your teaghlach. According to Irish, French, and Jewish family traditions, my granddaughters helped arrange a family celebration to welcome you to your new home."

"Did your Nana say Jewish tradition?"

"Nana knows I studied Judaic culture, and of course, you and Jaz are Jewish."

"You think I should ask Nana if she liked the Yiddish word for an extended non-related family?"

"Are you feeling brave?" As Suzie giggled.

"Sweetheart, there is much of her love and empathy in you."

"What are you two whispering about?"

"I was saying…,"

"Nana doesn't care. She is speaking about you, and you were not paying attention."

"Ok, got it.

Thank you, lovely Sister Noreen."

Noreen flashed a smile, and her lips mimed a sweet kiss.

"David, are Suzie and Noreen finished now?"

In unison, "Sorry, Nana."

"David, you protected my Suzie and got shot, and now you deliberately provoked that foul-tempered fool of a man so his ire would go to you. You are the most loving man or a Meshugana."

"Nana, he was cruel to Jaz, which infuriated me."

"Remember, this is Nana you are talking to."

All the Sisters' eyes turned and glanced at Nana. She doesn't say things like that unless it is consequential."

"Suzie, your David, mom, and I recently met for lunch. He wanted advice on what to do if Timothy started his homophobia and hateful Jewish diatribe. It seems he anticipated what unfolded tonight and wanted to prepare."

"Nana, what did you advise? You already knew his nature wouldn't stay quiet."

"Suzie, Nana can best explain.

"David was resolute to defend you, Jaz, Jacquie, and Annabelle. Nothing said convinced him otherwise.

The last thing we told David definitely not to do was to confront him directly. Of course, he would not sit quietly. David told us he had guaranteed his friend she would not be demeaned. We preferred a peaceful approach to de-escalation and shared our idea with them.

David respected our mother's instincts but didn't accept the prudence of a non-confrontational approach. Some nonsense about The Bronx code of the streets."

"Nana, I assured Suzie would stay inconspicuous and subdued, but if her Dad made one thoughtless, malicious attack that crossed a red line, she would not be held back.

Nana, you stopped arguing with Timothy. Why? Of course, you wanted me to turn his anger away from Jaz and Jacquie."

Megan wondered, "David, how did you find out?"

"Jacquie and Suzie unknowingly taught me their deflection technique and guessed it came from Nana."

Suzie's mom came over to me and kissed me.

"Girls, this may be hard to hear. David convinced me you already knew the truth. Suzie, as the youngest, it was harder for you to believe your father was a bully who mistreated his family."

"Timothy wouldn't dare confront Nana. Whoops, sorry."

"No one knows except your extraordinary David that Timothy and I have been separated for half a year.

As you know, your names were added to the mortgage papers. Our attorney assured us that it was legal proof of ownership and that bank statements showing mortgage loan payments provided additional evidence. This secured your ownership of the land and home. As soon as the mortgage was paid in full, you were clear of his influence.

Your dad was never interested in detail, only in getting his way, so he never bothered to sign the mortgage loan papers. He wasn't aware the house was always in my name. Once Jacquie turned eighteen, ownership was legally transferred to her as firstborn. Your father never had legal rights to the property."

"Mom, we guessed some of this, but this is not why you called a family meeting."

"Suzie, this is hard to admit my worst mistake. When I was younger, your father only wanted me for a few months before he went off, God knows where. After agreeing to part ways twenty years ago, they started a love affair after Suzie was born."

Noreen viscerally tuned into Mom's emotions and wrapped her arms around her. Tears welled up with mom and daughters.

"One day, I will tell you all about him."

"Mom, you mean Uncle Liam?"

"Vickie, he loved you girls and blessed your lives. He wanted to tell you the truth about our relationship. Convinced him you were still too young. Before Liam passed away, he solemnly promised to talk to you girls.

"Mom, why didn't you share this with us?"

"Vickie, I'm fearful your dad would take my girls if your father found out about Liam. Girls, forgive me, I couldn't bear that outcome."

The daughters kissed Mom one at a time, and a silence of hugging said everything.

"Elizabeth, they should hear the rest. You need comfort from your daughters."

"Love, what do you mean?"

"Suzie, why don't you let your mom say it in her way?"

"David is remarkable. Was he born Irish? The final court papers arrived last week. Your father moved in to live with his new girlfriend months before."

"Who would want to have that Son of a..."

"Uncle David, what is all the noise? The loud chatting woke me."

"Oh, Sweetpea, I'm sorry. My sweet love, come here. Let me give you a hug and a kiss good night. Then, kiss your Aunts, Grandmother, and Nana. Mommy Jaz and Mommy will tuck you back into bed."

"Uncle David, will you and Aunt Suzie kiss and tuck me in tonight?"

"My love, promise even if you are sleeping."

"Lover, thank you for seeing her listening at the door before she opened it, and for controlling your language. How did you realize she was at the door?"

"Angel, it's her favorite thing to burst into the room thinking she could surprise me and come run and hug me. She listened first to ensure I would not be distracted. Tonight, she only opened the door a little as I said, Son of."

"How did you see her when you were facing away from the door?"

"Suzie thought it strange she had not already awakened from all the commotion, so I censored my words just in case. Plus, I saw her cute face in the mirror peeking in."

"David, she is the love of your life. When are you and Suzie going to have your baby?"

"Nana, please, not tonight."

"Girls and David, it is after 2:00 am, and Nana and I are going to our bedrooms to go to bed. Don't stay up too late. We will make a late breakfast for you all."

"Megan, please stay over. You shouldn't be alone tonight."

Vickie caught on and diverted Megan, who was about to ask Suzie how she knew Ryan was not home.

"Noreen and I are lighting a fire and sleeping on the sofa. Once we get Jessica from her bed, all four of us will have plenty of room."

Suzie and I kissed Annabelle and tucked her in bed as promised.

We sat on our favorite comfy armchair. Suzie was on my lap, her head resting on my shoulder.

"Love, we should get into bed. It's three o'clock."

"Couldn't we fall asleep here with me on your lap?"

Carried her to bed at 5:00 a.m. She was fast asleep. Managed to take off her jeans and blouse and covered her with our mulberry silk quilt, which she and I love. And lay next to her, holding her from behind, and closed my eyes.

"David?"

"Angel thought you were asleep."

"I was, but I want to tell you I love and cherish you. Thank you for protecting Jaz and confronting Dad."

"Suzie, hush now and get some sleep."

"Love is Ryan having an affair."

"Not certain, but Megan believes it."

"The look she gave me when I said she should not be alone."

"Yes, let's talk about it in the morning."

"Honey, sing me the lullaby you are practicing when you suppose I can't hear you since I'm out of the room."

"Oh, that was the radio."

"Then find another station. They repeatedly play the same song."

"Close your eyes and snuggle closer."

"Is this the first lullaby you will sing when we have our baby?"

Kissed her delicately.

"Sleep and dream of angels."

"Hush, little baby, don't say a word; Papa's gonna buy you a mockingbird.

And if that mockingbird won't sing, Papa's gonna buy you a diamond ring.

And if that diamond ring turns to brass, Papa's gonna buy you a looking glass...."

Eight
I am now an Orphan

"My mother died today. Or maybe yesterday, I don't know. I received a telegram from the old people's home: Mother deceased. Funeral tomorrow. Very sincerely yours. That doesn't mean anything. It might have been yesterday." Albert Camus

I was editing my romance novel in the family room when news came that I had been orphaned.

Jacquie convinces her mom and Nana to eat breakfast at their favorite restaurant, Red Oak Public House, to Jaz and Jacquie's delight.

Suzanne caught up on her sleep and just finished getting dressed.

Jacquie loved cooking with her daughter. "Annabelle, love, would you like to beat the eggs? I'll get Texas bread for you to soak in eggs to make French toast.

Noreen, Jessica, Jaz, Vickie, and Megan helped feed Whisper and Shadow and led them into the meadow. After breakfast, they decided to shop for dinner to prepare the family's favorite seafood pasta with shrimp, scallops, and garlic.

The telephone rang, and Jacquie called Suzanne.

"Sis, can you get the phone? David is writing, and Annabelle and I are making French toast."

After a few minutes, Suzie came downstairs, visibly upset.

"Sis, you look shaken. Who was on the phone?"

"Where is David?"

"In the family room writing, Sis, who called?"

"The head nurse at Shalom Hospital in New York."

Suzie walked into the family room, looking up at Suzie's tear-stained face.

"My mom."

"Oh, my sweet love, David, the Hospital has been trying to reach you all morning."

"I dreaded hearing news of her passing since a year ago when my mother fell seriously ill. My mom finally lost her battle to stay alive."

"The Chief Head Nurse said she left numerous messages on your phone. Your mobile phone battery needs to be recharged or turned off. She found our home phone's direct number among your mom's belongings."

"Suzie, come sit next to me."

"Love, your mother died early this morning, at 3:50 A.M. New York time. Her close friend and neighbor, Mrs. Steinberg, knocked on your mom's door around 11 p.m. She typically checks up on your mom each night before she goes to sleep. When your mom didn't answer, she opened the door with her key.

She found your mom lying on the sofa in the living room. Oh God, David, her telephone book opened with all your phone numbers. All crossed out except for ours."

"Mom would say she couldn't keep up with all of my multiple moves; subsequently, she would put a line through an old address and number."

"Her neighbor called 911, and an ambulance arrived within a few minutes and rushed her into the Emergency Room.

David, they tried hard to revive her several times after her heart failed."

"Love, get the picture, yet not one hoped to have for a long time."

"David, deeply sorry for your loss. Didn't realize you had a Sister. The Chief Head Nurse wanted to reach the next of kin, calling your Sister. However, she found it odd that your Sister did not have your telephone number.

Is there anyone you want me to call?"

"No, my Sister will. Let me save that story for a later date."

"Love, the Chief Head Nurse wanted to speak with you. Remembers you fondly. When you came to the hospital with your mom, the day your dad died. Sweetheart, she said, this little boy didn't shed a tear. It was as if he willed himself not to cry.

The Chief Head Nurse asked if you had anyone in California, and told her you were part of my family. Was that okay?"

"Nurse Dorothea is empathetic and kindhearted. Yes, it was sweet of you."

"She said, 'Please give David my phone number.' Love, she added, 'if the man were the same as a boy, he wouldn't ask for comfort, but wanted a hug when consoled. Started crying and handed him a tissue, and this little boy told me it was okay. Just got something in my eye.'

"Here is her direct phone number."

"Silly thing, she remembered. Will call her now. May I use your private office, using the personal line?"

David came back upstairs after 20 minutes, kissed Suzanne, and, before walking out the door sorrowfully, said, "Suzie, I am now an orphan."

"David, would you like me to come with you?"

"No, thank you, love. Let me be by myself for a while."

Gently closed the front door and walked toward the meadow.

"Jacquie."

"Sis, I heard. Let him be for a while."

"Would you?"

"No."

"Going to be with him."

Annabelle listened by the kitchen door, heard everything, and then hurried past her mom and Aunt Suzie, rushing out the front door.

She found her daddy leaning back on the inside of the wooden fence.

Since the newly arrived adoption papers granted full parental rights, Annabelle is legally and emotionally my daughter. Annabelle and I couldn't have been happier.

Whisper saw him and trotted over, put her head down, and knelt on her knees so David could easily climb up to ride.

David reached for the cord to open the gate, tenderly patted her head, and climbed on her back. Whisper stood and trotted out of the meadow.

In her adorable tone, Annabelle called out, "Daddy."

David turned Whisper to ride back to her. Whisper bent down to make it easier for him when riding her bareback.

"Whisper, just be a few minutes."

Suzie was blessed to have Whisper in her life. She knew when I needed her as she sensed my feelings.

"Girl, glad Suzie introduced us." She nodded and gave her a fresh apple.

"Sweetpea, are you okay?"

"Daddy, sorry about your mommy."

"Thank you, sweetheart."

"She went to see God in heaven."

"Come here, let me hug you. Don't worry, I'm okay. Your mom and Aunt Suzie are outside, waiting to serve your breakfast. Whisper, and I are going for a short ride, back in about an hour."

"Daddy, I want to come with you. Don't like you alone when you are sad."

"Texas French toast, with fresh California strawberries and Vermont maple syrup. Your favorite breakfast."

"Yours too when you were a little boy."

"Tell your Aunt Suzie I'll return soon to start breakfast without me. I'll be okay. I love you."

I wiped away my tears with my hand and again mounted Whisper. Annabelle started walking toward the house, spun around, and called out again. Didn't want her to see my grief, but what she said helped heal my heart.

"Daddy."

Directing Whisper to saunter back to my daughter and slide off her.

As I kneeled, Annabelle ran into my arms and hugged me.

"Daddy, I love you."

"Sweetpea, I love you even more."

Waiting to ensure she was okay as she walked back to her mom and Aunt Suzie.

Whisper nudged me with her nose.

"Ok, girl, where do you want to take me?"

She wanted me to go to Suzie's and my Sanctuary.

"Whisper, can we go someplace else?" She nodded. 'No, this is where you need to be.' Fed her another apple before walking into the Sanctuary. It was a warm Saturday morning under a cloudless blue sky. Enveloped in a sense of calm yet numb with grief, lying down on the wooden bench, lost in remembrance.

Always love to come here. Whisper would bring me here when sad."

Sat up so Suzie could sit next to me.

"This was not where I wanted to be, but Whisper wouldn't move, so I took the hint. Have not yet appreciated how much Whisper was tuned into my moods."

With a gentle, loving touch, Suzanne put her arm through mine. This time it was my head on her shoulder.

"Love, talk to Annabelle when you get back. She is worried about you."

"Of course, wish she didn't hear about my mom. That is a lot for a little girl to process."

"Or a grown man loved you, turned Whisper around after you heard Annabelle call out again, and kneeled to hug her. This made your little girl smile."

"She touches my heart by saying just a few words, and would do anything for her. She is my beautiful daughter. Oh, Suzie, she provides endless love and joy."

"You spoil her by letting her do anything she wants when she is with you. I love you for doing so, and one day we will have our daughter. A sister for Annabelle."

"She now speaks of you as her dad and is overjoyed you adopted her. Annabelle recognizes that, out of habit, she sometimes calls you Uncle David; it's okay because she is accustomed to saying it.

Love, take Whisper. Please go eat breakfast.

I just want to be left alone. I promise to follow you shortly, just a few more hours. Need to immerse myself in my grief and let go of my tears."

"The last thing you need is to be by yourself."

"Suzie, hold my hand. My mom loved you, and that says a lot. You are the only girlfriend Mom loved. Adored Jacquie yet knew she was not the one."

"Last week, called your mom to see how she was doing and if she needed anything. Asked her to tell me about when you were a little boy. Your mom said you were affectionate, always wanting to hug and kiss.

Then, one day, "told David at age four, you are a big boy now, and we don't hug and kiss." And gently pushed you off her lap. A few years ago, she said David was upset and asked why she hadn't told him I loved him.

"She told you that? Wonder why?"

"David, your mom asked if she did the right thing. With serious misgivings because you slid into the blues each time you broke up with a girlfriend. Your mom wanted me to say I love you, and hugging was important to you. So, love, do I give you enough hugs?"

"Suzie, please, not now. May we speak about this later?"

After a few minutes of silence, "First heard you love me when you said $100 is all you bet on me. Suzie, why do you have tissues everywhere and not a box when I need a damn tissue?"

Holding me tenderly, "Take your time."

Wiping tears from my face did not stop those in my eyes.

"An open hand with two fifty-dollar bills was going to decide my chance to finish our dance. The moment you were not offended made our relationship possible. Minus getting shot and almost dying, knew I was falling in love with you."

"You getting shot twice was indeed a buzzkill. David, you smiled. Sorry for your loss, I love you."

Suzie's hugs and gentle kisses were always comforting.

Out of nowhere, she placed her hand on my crotch.

"Looking for something?"

"To see if you are hard."

"Well, your hand answers the question."

"David, are you horny? As long as you can get aroused, I'll worry less."

"Suzie didn't get to say goodbye to my mom."

Sympathetically, "Sweetheart, you spoke to her the other day, most times twice or more a week, or after you arrive home from a business trip. You always stop whatever you are doing to take her call. This alone doesn't help you feel less grief, but one day it will."

"Your mom told me she was happy that of all your girlfriends, you had found me."

'Don't let go of my son. He loves you and will never leave you. David told me you are the one. But, Suzanne dear, he is afraid of rejection, real or imagined, so he holds back.

And, dear, you have mother love.'

"David, what is mother love? What does she mean? Don't understand what she meant. Don't love you as a mother. Your mom knows we don't have a child. You surely don't consider me a mother when making love to me."

"More as a sex Goddess, an angel, and my lover."

"And who are all these girlfriends?"

"Which question would you care for me to answer?"

"The last one first."

"You are emotionally overwhelming me. Want to be alone and not talk, just need comforting, and you ask a question you are afraid of the answer to."

"Yes, but still want you to tell me."

"Honey, you don't want me to tell you my thoughts right at this moment."

She was wearing one of my dress shirts and started seducing me by slowly opening her buttons.

"I love it when you wear my blue shirt. It enhances your blue eyes."

"David, start kissing my neck, won't remember my question."

"New York man, come with me, and I'll lay blankets on the rug."

Suzie stood in front of me and started an enticing striptease. Her soft skin, long legs, and the sexy way she rubbed her breasts against me were tantalizing.

From the first, Suzie's smile revealed warmth and compassion. She captured my heart and soul. The only woman who took my breath away.

"Suzie, want to make love to you."

On my knees, she was lying on her back, legs spread apart, resting on my shoulders. Pleasing her with my tongue, she moaned. Oh, so good, erupted with an orgasm, causing her hips to quiver.

My mouth gently sucked on her breasts and used my tongue on her hardening nipples. Erotically, she inserted three fingers and moved them faster until she climaxed. Suddenly, took off my clothes more quickly than ever. Turned around, bent over the sofa, and raised her perfectly sculpted derriere.

She was no longer a shy woman, a virgin, worried if she could please me.

"I love you, Susie."

"David, introducing new sexual positions and eroticism to our lovemaking, sex becomes more alluring. Make love to me from behind."

She was wet with desire from two climaxes. Slowly rubbed my penis against her vulva and clitoris. Suzie moved her butt to capture my penis.

"David, please put it inside me."

Turned on and after many thrusts,

"I'm cumming!"

Suzie put her mouth on my penis to capture my semen.

Suzie started to masturbate, and she had another orgasm. Tenderly climbed on top of me, taking my penis in hand to guide me to penetrate her. Wiggling her pelvis to keep me hard as long as she could.

"David, I love you so much."

"I love you more, Angel."

We hugged in silence, losing track of time.

"David, breakfast. Would they have left us French toast?"

She worried we were hungry and started to laugh.

Finally, realizing what she had said, she giggled, "I'm silly sometimes," and we kissed.

"David, did you remember to lock the door?"

"Yes, love. Who are you afraid will enter our Sanctuary? Oh Shit, your dad."

"This was a home where a caretaker and his wife lived for 40 years to be closer to their grandchildren. Since we moved in, Dad had used this as his private hideaway and recently asked me if I remembered where it was. He couldn't find the entrance because it was removed and had a new one installed."

"Do you think he ever came here with your mom?"

"Don't believe so. Oh, David, do you suppose he brought his woman friend here?"

"Probably, there is certainly a feminine touch here, not what you added."

"He may want to use it once more."

"No, can't imagine after you and I made love here, the thought of…"

"Love, use the polite words, love stains."

"Yeah, that would freak him out."

"The new security lock for the door and latches for the windows were recently added for additional safety and privacy, and I'm glad I did."

"Suzie, who would want to have sex with your dad?"

"David, even lions, feck."

She surprised herself with how easily she talked this way.

"What time is it? Let's dress, Angel."

"Are you feeling peckish? Can't believe it's noon. Let's have lunch.

What do you want to eat? I'll make something for you."

"Thank you, but not hungry."

"Oh, love, just some juice then."

"Hours of lovemaking and nothing else matters when being with you."

Walking back to the house hand in hand, Whisper has long since been back in her meadow.

"Lover, how many girlfriends?"

"Suzie, love, please not now. You are only on my mind. Let's ask Annabelle to join us for lunch."

"David, she would love to. Sweetheart, I wish I had a chance to meet your mom. We only talked on the phone. She always remarked how happy she was because we were together. She wanted to meet Anabelle very much.

"So, what did you two talk about?"

"What were you like as a boy. Your mom only said a few things. Did she know I'm the lastborn?"

"Yes, why?"

"She once told me you were her last chance to have a baby. Your mom was relaxed with you even as a boy because you were sentimental and let her be herself."

'David was the only one with whom I could share my sentiments and dreams. He always listened and understood. David would always get into trouble. If there were trouble, it would find David unless he found it first.'

"She told me you loved to kiss, hug, and buy her presents. 'Hugging and kisses stopped after pushing David off my lap when he was around five.'

Your mom had deep regrets, as she felt it was her fault that you felt rejected and unhappy. Oh, David, she said she hurt her baby."

"She asked me, wait for it. Do I give you enough sex, kisses, and hugs?"

"Mom felt better after she understood I never blamed her. Just wanted a hug, a kiss along with her hello and goodbye, and most of all, saying, I love you."

"David, why didn't you tell me? Is this why you get the blues? Afraid of me discarding you? Your fear of rejection runs deep, as it triggers sadness. Love, I'll never leave you."

"Suzie, the depth of your love is the same as my love for you. Can't have this intense talk now. Angel 'never' is not reality; there is an ending for everything.

My mom died. Nothing lasts forever. Not even the cosmos."

"Sweetheart, sorry, could not face losing you."

"Suzie, I'm not hungry. Please make Annabelle and you lunch."

"Your little girl knows you did not eat breakfast."

"Suzie, please give me some time to grieve. Don't want to talk. Making love awakens hidden desires and leaves me emotionally drained. Not to mention coming to terms with accepting my mother's death. Not hungry. Perhaps tonight, we can have dinner with Annabelle."

"Can I stay with you and hold you when you cry?"

"Our bedroom or back at the Sanctuary."

Nine
Silence before A Storm

"Storms think that they will scare everyone on their path, but they are very mistaken because they have forgotten the stormy souls who are afraid of nothing!"
Mehmet Murat Idan

Suzanne started working in her home office earlier than usual when her secure telephone rang.

"Suzi, Good morning. How are you?"

"Nervous, Senator."

"What is troubling you?"

"Senator, you only call me on the secure office telephone when what you say needs to remain confidential. And you never call me Suzi in an official capacity.

Yesterday, Camila handed David a large manila envelope marked "For Your Eyes-Only," addressed to Dr. David Benjamin Bradley, before she came downstairs to collaborate with me. Been worried ever since."

"Camila was asked to deliver a security clearance application. David was instructed to get fingerprinted as soon as possible and did so without question."

Suzanne knew a covert action was planned. However, even with top security clearance, she was not permitted to know the details. So she hadn't given it much thought until

Camila arrived and realized a risky operational plan included David.

"Senator, you used Dr. David and included his middle name on the envelope."

"Suzie, it is a standard operating procedure for a name."

"You have worked with me for over ten years and have my implicit trust. This security request comes from the White House."

"With all due respect to the President, you can tell the White House what to do with this request. I'm sorry, Senator, everything has been going so well, we are happy, and I'm scared."

"Suzanne, I have never lied to you, and you are privileged and cleared to have access to everything."

"Senator, why not this?"

"You, of all people, understand it's for your safety out of an abundance of caution."

"David will not be able to fill in details, but he is authorized to provide only enough facts to ensure you understand how long he will be gone."

"Senator, thank you for telling me."

"David is waiting for me to make this call as he is anxious. I need him to feel confident that you are safe, as he already knows you will support him."

"Safe. Will David be safe?"

"Suzanne, meet me in my Sacramento office on Monday for lunch, and I'll keep you updated."

"For heaven's sake, Senator, when does he leave?"

"Sunday, early evening, on a commercial flight, and Suzanne, you are not to go with him to see him off."

"You realize how hard this will be."

"Yes, I do know.

David is a qualified expert and is a perfect person for this mission. It is hard to ask this of you. Can't tell you 100% whether he will be safe. However, promise you he will come home. After explaining the mission's significance, David agreed to go. Suzanne made him sign a confidentiality paper."

"David will keep whatever confidential without the paper."

"This wasn't a directive from the President's office, more of a request. After he signed, I knew better and shredded it."

"Senator, thank you for your trust in him."

"It started the moment he jumped in front of you. As a ten-year-old girl, you understood what you volunteered for. Talk to David. I have a meeting to go to. My husband and I will keep you updated on any developments.

You said once, Mrs. Harrison, if you say, it is good enough for me."

"Never told you when you went home, had tears in my eyes thinking what a remarkable girl. Keep that moment in your heart. I don't make promises I can't keep. And will do everything to ensure David comes home safely. No matter what it may seem at the time.

David was afraid to upset you and refused the mission; he suggested diplomatically where I could put it. You picked up some of his straight-talking vernacular."

"Senator, was that an off-handed compliment?"

"Yes, Suzie, it was. Please call my office at any time, and I will update you as soon as the events are confirmed. I have faith in you and David, and have made this mission a top priority for my staff and myself. Speak with David. I will stay in touch. Goodbye."

Suzanne went straight upstairs and took hold of my hand as we walked silently to our Sanctuary. It was the first time she passed the meadow without greeting Whisper or Shadow.

"Forgot something and will be back in a minute."

Suzie walked toward the fence and noticed Whisper and Shadow on the far side of the meadow. Stood quietly with her hands on the wood rail fence. Whisper saw her and started trotting over, with Shadow following. She once told me that Whisper senses her distress and comforts Suzie.

She tenderly stroked Whisper's head and spoke softly.

"Suzie," and handed her two apples. Fed her beloved horses each an apple, placed her head on Whisper, and cried.

Gripping my hand tighter as we approached the Sanctuary as if she meant never to let go. In the privacy of our Sanctuary, she looked at me, no longer able to hold back her tears. She let them flow. Her nose started to run, so she went inside to get a box of tissues.

"Shit, didn't want to cry."

"A bad influence on your choice of words."

Usually, she would smile, but only more tears would come.

"The phone call must have been from Senator Harrison."

"The Senator shared little about the assignment or its consequences."

"Suzie didn't want to accept it."

"Damn it, David. Then why take it? You had a choice."

"Angel, love, the Senator must have said why."

"Don't sweet-talk me, David. I'm upset. Why didn't you say? You tell me everything. The one time you follow the rules, you put your life into jeopardy!"

Remained quiet.

"Oh, David, sorry to worry you. I'm ok. Just bloody scared to lose you. The Senator said you could not say anything to protect our family, and most of all, me. Nothing to hold on to if you never come back. I want you to give me a baby.

No, you couldn't concentrate knowing if I was pregnant or not. But I want your baby. Don't know what I want. How will we have a baby if you never come back? David, can't figure out if I'm more frightened I may lose you or upset with you for accepting this mission."

Suzanne started back to the house alone.

Megan ran to her. "Heard you saying something loudly to David."

"I'm all right. Want to be alone."

"Suzi, let me walk with you. You're distraught."

"David loves you, Megan."

"Why did you argue? He loves you in ways he doesn't yet understand."

"This wasn't a fight. Trust it wasn't. We never fight. David never says anything when I'm upset."

"Not like this. Love, you look terrified. Let me take you home. After feeding Whisper and Shadow, I'll come back to check on you."

"I couldn't imagine being without you."

"Suzie, you have David., Call if you need me; check in on you later."

Suzanne walked into our bedroom, unsure whether she should cry or shout. She stared through teary, blurry blue eyes and smiled at her sensual portrait of her and David.

Collapsed onto the bed, grabbing hold of David's pillow. Something was inside the pillowcase: an envelope with her name. She opened the envelope after wiping her eyes and blowing her nose.

My blue-eyed Angel,

My love, I will soon depart to go on a government mission. I didn't fall in love with you. Instead, walked into your love with my eyes wide open, wanting to take every step with you as our love unfolded.

Dedicated to you, my love.

Suzanne goes to the stream to see otters play in the flowing water. She waits for her lover with a pure purpose. Her heart reaches out to help her lover find his way. Waiting to feel his body next to her, we are soul-heart bonded. When his lips caress her soft lips, time fades. A kiss, a dance, and then romance.

Love is a quiet thing, embraced by holding hands and endless hugs. Romance deepens intimacy as they watch clouds drift in the sky above. Two lovers become yin and yang.

The stream reminds us that life flows and love is in the water. Love creates visions of babies yet to be born in the rushing whitewater of the stream.

Suzanne goes to the stream to earn its confidence. Her love is the same, yet never the same; the stream flows freely, twisting and turning, bounded by the banks running alongside. Her beloved will free their love as a stream bursts its banks.

Our love will create life.

My love cannot escape from your heart, and as sure as a rainbow after a storm, my love will be kept safe in your heart. Promise to return home to you to look after your heart.

Our love is true, and I love you.

Your Beloved David.

Suzanne heard the front door open and close, but there were no footsteps on the stairs. She placed his letter inside a teak wood box containing love letters. Laughed a little, thinking I would not even want to sit with me after my emotional outburst.

Suzie slowly entered the family room and sat, saying nothing to David. She placed her head on his shoulder. He wrapped his arms around her and kissed the top of her head.

"You missed."

"Don't think so. My kiss landed on the top of your head."

"You missed my lips."

Lovingly kissed as a truce, for it was an unbearable thought for Suzie not to stand by my decision. Promised herself not to upset me before leaving.

"Are you hungry? There are leftovers."

"Thank you, love. Maybe a little later."

"Okay, I can prepare something for us when you are ready."

"Okay, when we are ready."

"Stop it, David, please just stop. How will I live without your affection and kindness? You got a muddled Irish girl who took you down to the river. David, the ode was beautiful. I would be lost without you."

Suzanne needs to be distracted or start to imagine the worst.

"Leaving Sunday, we have the rest of today and all day and night Saturday. My flight is on Shamayim International Airline nonstop from San Francisco airport early Sunday evening."

"Can you disclose where you land?"

In a barely audible whisper. "Frankfurt arriving early Monday morning Central European Time."

"How long will you be away, and when you whisper in my ear again, stop on your way out at my lips?"

"Suzie, five days. I was only allowed to say that somewhere in Western Europe. Adding in the faintest whisper, Geneva."

"Promise me you will come home safe."

"What is safer than Shamayim International Airline? Their security is the best in the world."

"David, you can't promise me because you may not return. Could not live without you. I have a premonition that something is going to happen. Don't even contemplate for a moment to joke one way or another; you will come home, even in a box."

Suzanne's gift of premonition always worried me.

"Why did you break confidentiality and give me these details?"

"Senator Harrison wanted me to disclose enough, so you don't imagine worse. She granted me discretion on what I could divulge. The truth is that it didn't matter if the Senator allowed me. I love you. That is why."

"David doesn't sound like the Senator."

"Asked, won't you get in trouble with the White House? Surprised she would ever use that language."

"What did she say?"

"F*CK the White House."

"In private, she has a mouth on her. She would never use that word with anyone except a small inner circle, her two daughters, her husband, and me. Pleased she included you, which means she implicitly trusts you."

"That is all I should say. Dr. Robert will relay messages as the Senator will communicate directly from the situation... Oh shit."

"White House Situation Room, where the direst events unfold. As if that would keep me calm."

"Since you can't take me to the airport, you can track my landing, and the Senator will keep you updated."

"Sweetie, are you hungry yet? I can make us sandwiches."

There was no time to eat. Hunger did not disrupt our intense desire to make love.

Ten
Premonition

"You open your heart knowing that there's a chance it may be broken one day, and in opening your heart, you experience a love and joy that you never dreamed possible. You find being vulnerable is the only way to allow your heart to feel true pleasure that's so real it scares you. You find strength in knowing you have a true friend and possibly a soul mate who will remain loyal to the end."–Bob Marley.

Separation cannot silence our love, and a heart cannot forget a lover. Suzie's thoughts are filled with unsettling emotions and dread, for there is no hope even in her dreams. So she works late because the Senator needs to get elected President. There is peace of mind that arises from Suzie's faith in the Senator. Most of all, in her beloved David.

The sun's rays faded a while ago, replaced by the warmth of the last rays that warm the early night's chill. Her thoughts slowly drifted back to her work.

Jacquie is concerned about sharing breaking news with her Sister. Mainly after she has finally been able to start work.

Jacquie tried to remain calm when she was not. "Sis, turn on the television to a cable news channel."

Suzanne feared the news and didn't move, so Jacquie turned on the television with the volume lowered.

"Oh God, no, don't want to hear. He promised me he would return."

'Don't pledge when you have no way of knowing.'

'Love, I don't, but trust the Senator. She said experts thought through every precaution.'

'Is the Senator going to wrap you in an impenetrable shield?'

'Suzanne, then trust my intuition.'

'David, I always have from the first day we met.

Is it intuition or your faith and hope? I'm scared. Don't give me platitudes. Give me something I can hold on to.

Hold me and promise you won't get harmed. And let me cry. I cry for you, for us, damn it, David, you can't say for certainty.'

She wanted to be in my arms and I in hers. Suzanne trembled with a fear of the unknown.

'Angel, afraid, too. It would be a lie if I were to say otherwise. However, not ready to lose you, and my fear will keep me alert and safe.'

'Oh, David, this is a platitude and does little to calm me.'

'Nothing I can say now will soothe you or me. No false promises, but there is always hope.'

'What could I hold on to get us through this if it is not my love for you?'

'Suzanne, my heart is tied up with your heart. Our time will come to have our baby. Our baby is our future, our combined love, and she needs us to welcome her into the world. You know this is true; assure you I will return to you. Fate will find a way.'

'That is not enough to protect you. Love, faith, hope in a baby yet to be conceived is not reassuring.'

'You have a concern because your fear is guiding you. Since you don't have much experience living in fear, you have little practice coping.

You are beautiful. Whoever meets you, men or women, falls for your happiness and joy. These are not platitudes; it is who you are. You are a brave woman who uses her sharp wit instead of anger because it doesn't reside inside you. Come with me to the mirror. Whom do you see.'

'Can't see anyone through my tears.'

'Love, those tears are your lens to your true self.'

'I'm sorry.'

'For what?'

'Irish Blarney rubbed off on you.'

'But it is blarney of truth. Let me kiss your wee smile to freeze it, to remember you are okay while on my mission.'

'Oh, David, that is not a thing.

See, you are standing next to me. I see myself. What am I supposed to see?'

'You will know when you see it. Look with your heart now and not your eyes.'

'I don't see, wait, I see, just how deep my heart is filled with your love and my love for you.'

'Keep looking and take your time.'

Anxiously, 'Don't see anything, David. Tell me what you want me to see.'

'It is what you need to see. Why Whisper is tuned into you without words.'

'My trust in our future baby. She is inevitable. Yet still fearful of losing you.'

Being afraid is not an emotion that is your guiding star. It is our love and faith in us.

"CNB Breaking News, an explosion ripped through a Shamayim International gate at Frankfort Airport, where a flight was scheduled to leave at 7:00 a.m. Central European Time. German Police are hunting several suspects, and the President has sent additional FBI agents to the scene. We have no word as to why two FBI agents were already close to the explosion.

The White House requested that the German Prime Minister not release video or photos or hold a press conference. This prevents the terrorists from knowing the information police have."

We now have preliminary numbers of those wounded and killed. However, a release of names is withheld until the next of kin is notified. Passengers, especially those who witnessed the incident, are now being debriefed. American Embassy staff are interviewing each American citizen after being cleared by emergency medical responders."

"Suzie, please turn off the news. David wasn't going to Germany. You said Geneva. Oh my God, Suzie, was this his connecting flight?"

"Sis, I must hear if there is news of David."

"Little is known at this early stage except that the police now call this a terrorist attack. German Police and Special Forces have closed all roads and railway stations to seal off the city.

Just in, a list of people missing and not accounted for includes all Americans, a Rabbi, his wife, two Sisters from Catholic Goodwill, ten girls and their parents, including a young female Israeli citizen, all on their way to Tel Aviv for a youth peace summit.

Tragically, confirmation by German police of a young British couple with their 18-month-old who are deceased. Unverified reports of fifty-one people, of whom are wounded, with relatively few casualties.

We can report some positive news: the airplane had backed away from the gate minutes before a second explosion."

A preliminary report noted a bomb placed in the jet bridge behind the baby strollers. It was timed to go off five minutes after the first explosion. It is believed not to create pandemonium but to kill a maximum number of people."

"CNB can report 105 passengers plus seventy-five onboard with a crew of eight flight attendants, and the Captain and Co-Pilot are safe and are in a secure location, being interviewed and released.

Tears in the Anchor woman's eyes, caught on an open mic, "Thank goodness the plane got far enough away from the gate, as it may have killed everyone."

"Counterterrorist police are searching for five men caught on security cameras. That is all that German and American authorities allowed us to report.

The White House asked the Press not to release names until passengers' next of kin are notified."

"Jacquie, Oh, God, the baby and her young parents.

Sis, David was there."

"Susie, are you sure?"

"He told me he would land in Frankfurt early morning and board a connecting Shamayim flight. This was a quick stopover to deplane passengers, then board new passengers, including David, and continue to Geneva."

"Suzie, turn off the news, and wait until Senator Harrison can update us with accurate details."

Suzie is still in shock after hearing of the baby's and parents' deaths. No words, no tears, just a feeling of dread. Her worst fear came true.

"David promised he would return home to me.

Oh, Sis, so many won't be coming home."

It was the longest week of Suzie's life, and she buried herself in work, spending 15 hours a day on it. Eating little and sleeping only after she cried herself to sleep. She managed to get three to five hours of sleep a night. Having run out of her antidepressants, slipped deeper into hopelessness.

"Dr. Robert, can you prescribe a sedative and renew her meds? Oh, thank you. The two prescriptions are ready."

"Delivering them now and will be there in less than an hour."

"Suzie, Dr. Robert brought refills of your medications and has news to share."

Suzie rested on the sofa with an Irish Duvet blanket that Nana brought from Ireland and gave to her and David. Calms and provides a connection to David.

Dr. Robert came downstairs with Jacquie and asked about her symptoms of depression.

"Jacquie, the good news is Suzie should respond well since she was only off her meds for a few days."

"Doctor, she cries silently for her beloved and alone, not to upset me."

As soon as Suzie saw Dr. Robert, she said in a low voice,

"Oh dear God, Dr. Robert, please tell me he is not dead."

"Suzie, there is no evidence he is dead. The Senator got permission from the White House to release updates on a need-to-know basis. The Senator argued that you need to know. Listen to all of my news. Not having facts only lets your mind imagine the worst.

David was on a diplomatic mission for the U.S. government, representing the President of the United States. His orders were to travel to Geneva to meet with representatives of a terrorist group to negotiate the release of one hundred young girls.

 Girls are kidnapped and used as wives or conditioned to become child soldiers. David had no hesitation in accepting, except for one. He worried about you if he did not come home alive.

GrenzSchutzGruppe 9, a special force arm of the German Counterterrorism Police and the FBI Joint

Terrorism Task Force, has been conducting a house-to-house search.

Due to the Senator's recommendation, the President asked the German Prime Minister, while David was in the country, to monitor the airport, roads, and train stations. Two FBI agents were already with him. The President assured David that the FBI Special Task Forces would also protect him.

Suzie, Jacquie, German police, and the FBI Special Task Force confirmed that five terrorists took David hostage ostensibly to leave the country. The FBI believes the terrorists went to a safe house unknown to German authorities when the police net closed. The FBI employs methods for searching that I'm not privy to.

"Dr. Robert, will they find David so he can come home?"

"Suzie, the Senator and I met a remarkable girl of ten, and we informally adopted you. The terrorists killed innocent passengers and wounded more, who are still recovering. The Senator has made certain of every conceivable possibility, plus some confidential methods to locate David are now in effect. There are no other hostages taken we are presently aware of, and all indications suggest David is alive."

"Dr. Robert, why the *James Bond* tactic? Please, if you have more news, please tell me."

"Suzie told you more than allowed by the President. You have heard what the Senator says to the President when angry.

Will use my secure government phone to update you once the reports have been confirmed. From now on, all calls will be to your government phone. Whenever I can relay any news, I will share it with you in person as much as allowed." With a wink that meant a little more, "Suzie, this is asking a lot of you. Trust the Senator and me."

"Dr. Robert, of course, and please tell the Senator, so does David."

"The Senator already knows."

On the eighth day, Suzie became inconsolable.

"Suzie, the Senator, is on the phone and wants to provide you with new updates and as much news as she now has."

Suzie fearfully looked at her Sister, "Jacquie, please ask the Senator if we can place the call on speakerphone."

"Suzie, there is hope that the latest security updates are promising."

"Senator, please tell me the truth."

"I made you and David a promise that he will come home. Two FBI agents were on the plane with David, leaving San Francisco, and were at the boarding gate when the first bomb exploded.

German police are searching for all routes to potential terrorist safe houses. Twenty FBI counterterrorism agents are now on the ground cooperating with the German Special Counterterrorism Force.

Suzie, I asked the President to place the United States Army Garrison's medical staff in Frankfurt on standby for David to get medical support as soon as possible."

"Senator, appreciate all you are doing to bring David back alive."

"Suzie, glad you are working and focused on my campaign to become the next President of the United States. First and foremost, I want you and David to be safe. One last thing is not a request. You must take your meds regularly and a sedative at night to sleep. Your word."

"Senator, my word."

"Hold on as tight as you can. Stay away from cable news, as it will only upset you. Will call after confirmation of events as they unfold. I have access to the world's best intelligence. Suzie, speak with you soon."

Jacquie took the phone from her Sister. "Suzie, are you ready to take your meds? Let me get them for you."

"Gave my word to the Senator. Please bring me a glass of water, thank you. Then, Jacquie, would you speak with Mom and Nana, Victoria, Noreen, Megan, and Jaz to inform them of what the Senator told us?

Jacquie, will you stay with me tonight?"

"Of course, and call the family."

"Oh, God! Annabelle, what are we going to say to her?"

"Suzie, all she was told was that David went on a business trip and had been delayed. Reassured her by adding 'I will say when he is returning home.'"

"Jacquie, is she asking questions? David tells your baby everything, and she knows he sometimes works for the government. He would not go this long without calling her every day he traveled. She is too bright not to guess something is wrong. For now, David would not want to give her false expectations. Let her hear the truth, though an age-appropriate watered-down version."

"Sweetheart told her she could speak to you to calm her concerns, which cheered her up."

"I love you, Sis. Want to eat my meals in the downstairs family room. This is also where I'm going to continue to sleep. And use the downstairs bathroom to shower.

Jacquie, if I gave you a short list of items needed, would you please get it for me?"

"Only after you agree to a precondition, stay with you and eat all meals with you, and you promise to get out each day and ride Whisper, and I'll ride Shadow."

There was no news for another day, but when the phone rang, it sounded louder than usual.

"Suzie, hold for the Senator."

"Suzie is Jacquie with you? Good, use the speakerphone. These are the most recent details approved by the White House to keep you updated. A terrorist group in Frankfurt, known to the German Special Forces, placed all the bombs. They used encrypted communication methods with the head terrorist cell operating out of Darmstadt. They were sent to disrupt the negotiations.

It seems the Country's negotiators were caught off guard. Our government intelligence service failed to act faster when plans for this meeting were leaked to a terrorist group.

Eyewitness accounts gave similar versions of what occurred. However, each person had a different perspective from their point of view. And now, it is being monitored by video surveillance cameras."

"Dear God, Senator, is David dead?"

"Susie, I would be there and not over the phone."

"Senator, as much as I love you, stay the feck away from me."

"David is an awful influence on your recent proclivity for your choice of words, not normally spoken by you. Don't apologize. Remain strong. Jacquie, how is Suzie sleeping? She doesn't want to worry me."

"Senator, her meds started to work. But she still will not sleep in their bed until David is safe and back home.

My daughter Annabelle comes down each day to spend time with her Aunt. She is the only family member allowed, and their time together is cherished. She reassures Annabelle that her daddy is just unavoidably delayed."

"You and your Sister have a deep affection and love for David. You brought them together. Jacquie, Robert, and I marvel at your strength of will. We appreciate how difficult this is for you and your family.

"Senator and got him almost killed! Sorry, I'm tired and worried about my Sister."

"How do you keep up your hope?"

"Senator, Suzie still clings to her faith in David's vow to find a way back. I hold on to my trust that he will."

"Jacquie, take me off speakerphone and go somewhere private. Tell me when Suzanne cannot hear you."

"Senator, she is taking a shower."

"Jacquie, prefer you not to say anything until I can provide you with 100% confirmation. Can only reassure you, David will come home safe."

"Senator, how? Are you sure?"

"You and your Sister will know soon. Robert should arrive in a day or two. Encourage your Sister to remain confident. You two are remarkable women, hold on a little longer to your faith."

"I have a presidential campaign to win. And need Suzie to get me through election day and beyond. She is my most important priority, which supersedes my political ambition."

"Senator, thank you."

"You will shortly hear from Robert or me., Goodbye."

"Jacquie, was that the Senator?"

"Yes, love, she is worried about you."

"It's all right, Sis. Work with sensitive information, the top secret intelligence I'm not allowed access to. The Senator would only provide hope over the phone."

By the end of the tenth day, Suzie was determined not to lose hope that David would be found alive. Jacquie stayed with her 24/7. She continued to sleep on the sofa, as this was the only way Suzie could fall asleep.

As her eyelids grew heavy with sleep,

"David told me to trust he would come back to me."

"Suzie was past two in the morning. Please take a sedative and get some sleep."

The phone rang suddenly, startling both. Neither Sister moved, preparing for the worst and hoping for the best.

"Jacquie, is Suzie awake?"

"Dr. Robert, she is standing next to me."

"I'm only fifteen minutes from your home. Stay in the office, and Jaz can let me in. Tell her to please meet me at the door."

"Susie, Dr. Robert is coming."

"I'm nervous."

"Dr. Robert would not come this late if bad news. Go ahead and get dressed. Suzie, don't imagine the worst. I'm here for you."

Dr. Robert hurried down the stairs, balancing a tray of three large cups of coffee.

"Jacquie, your Jaz thought it would be a long night."

Suzie and Jacquie stood silently, anticipating the worst, but their hearts told them it would be okay. However, it's hard for a heart to hold back fear.

"There will be updates as a rescue operation has begun. The Senator asked me to do this in person."

Jacquie broke the silence. "Heard the White House would not release news to the media."

"Dr. Robert, is there news about David?"

"You will hear shortly, and Suzie, hold on to your faith just a little longer."

The three sat in silence for an hour. Suzie just held her coffee cup, not drinking from it. Startled when Robert's phone rang, Suzie spilled some of her coffee onto the tray.

"They are close to hearing the code. The Senator suggested this specific code as she wanted it to be clear and unmistakable for Suzie."

A few more agonizing minutes passed.

"The President just authorized placing the call on speaker since we are in a secure location in your office."

Silence for another 25 minutes.

Jacquie and Suzie nervously held hands. After enduring days of no news, anticipation in the room was palpable. Surrounded in unbearable, deafening silence, suddenly, the phone speaker crackled and broke the tranquility of the silence, and seconds later,

"The pizza is out of the oven, over."

Copy, verify, and provide confirmation pizza is out of the oven, over."

"Verified and confirmed, the pizza is out of the oven, over."

"Who is talking?

"That was the Special Forces team leader, and she is reporting to the Situation Room. The President, Vice President, Secretary of State, and Defense, Senator Harrison, Director of the FBI, and key National Security team members are listening."

Twenty more unbearable minutes. It was the last few minutes that were the most difficult.

"DS pizza is now in the delivery van, over."

"Copy, verify, and confirm the DS pizza is now in the delivery van, over."

"David, is he alive? Dr. Robert?" Jacquie and Suzie could hardly breathe.

They waited for the last confirmation after fifteen more excruciating minutes of silence. Finally, the words the Sisters were hoping to hear.

"Confirmed and verified, the DS pizza with mushrooms, onions, and green peppers with pineapple added only on one half, and Chef says it is arriving hot and delicious, over."

"Copy, bring the pizza home. We have a lot of hungry people."

Applause erupted from the Situation Room.

"Broadcasting will cease, but will continue to listen. I'm 10-10 on the side. Signing off until we reach the airport."

Suzanne started crying and hugged Jacqueline, who let all the tears she held back for Suzie's sake flow down her face.

"Sis, he is alive and safe. My David, oh Jacquie, your David is coming home to us."

"Suzanne, taking this off the speaker. The Senator wants to speak with you."

Her face was wet from tears, and she had a runny nose from crying. Suzie took the phone from Dr. Robert.

"Thank you, Senator! Is David okay?"

"The Air Force doctor on the helicopter wanted to examine him to ensure he was in good condition before authorizing it was safe for David to travel. The Special Forces commander is in the Situation Room and monitoring David's transfer until he reaches a U.S. Base. David has been approved to continue to a US Air Force Base in France. Another layer of precaution is to conduct a complete examination. Once the doctor agrees, he will travel to the U.S. Army Medical Center in Germany.

The President has lifted the news blackout, which is now being reported on all TV, cable news stations, international news media, and social media. Suzie, all the terrorists are dead.

Along with David, ten hostages were safely rescued. They were citizens of France, Germany, and the United Kingdom. Regrettably, one woman was deceased.

David will board a U.S. Air Force C-130 Hercules plane to travel to France and then to Germany.

You'll be able to watch it on CBN when the plane lands.

David compromised, after some convincing, to use a wheelchair rather than a stretcher to transport him to the waiting ambulance. Suzie, the doctor, threatened to sedate him if he disagreed."

"Senator, which means he is Okay."

"Suzanne, please wait for all the test results. His vital signs are stable, and there are no internal injuries, but tests are still needed. Though he took many beatings, they will heal. A promising sign is that he is alert.

Suzie, David asked if he could have a specific meal on the way."

"David asked for a DS pizza, Senator, to say I'm on his mind."

"Suzie, you understand your David well. He also requested that a message be sent to you. With your permission, I will read it to you."

"Angel, you were right all along. They are called tears."

"What does that mean? The Doctor was concerned because he was not crying."

"Senator, it means he loves me."

"Is that his New York humor?"

"No, Senator, this was his heart talking."

"Jacquie, he was most anxious for you not to worry. 'Tell Annabelle I am safe, love her, and will call as soon as possible.'

"Thank you, Senator. She will be happy that her dad is coming home."

"This is all the news I have for now.

The President has a C-21 government plane on standby. The same Learjet business people use. The pilot can take off when you and Jacqueline board at McClellan Air Force Base.

The President requested that the White House Press Corps have only one reporter accompany you on the plane.

"Suzie, at my request, the Press Pool selected reporter Roxana Morris, your childhood friend, to put you and David at ease. She agreed only to interview David when asked. Everything will be off the record unless you authorize her to relay any news you give her straight to her editor."

"Senator, may I grant her an exclusive to David and me and provide general comments once in the air to the pool reporters, so she gets to shine both ways? Like, to provide Roxana with a chance at a second Pulitzer for Journalism.

She recently lunched with David and me, and no other reporter would feel comfortable or trusted by David. A Senator would love to chat more, but I've a plane to catch. And Senator, I was right when I predicted at ten that you would make a great president."

"Robert, did she drop the phone?"

"No, she just forgot it was in her hands."

"Julia, Suzie stands beside me and wants to say something."

"How can I ever thank you?"

"You have, by your loyalty, worked with me these last ten years. Suzie, there is more updated information. David will arrive at the hospital in three hours. You will be delayed for 24 hours as you are diverted to Andrews Air Force Base. Robert and I will join you there."

"Senator, this is Jacquie. My Sister started to cry again and couldn't speak. She is afraid you will say he is in a more serious condition, which is why the delay."

"Jacquie put me on speakerphone. Suzie, understand you are upset. I must be brief as I have meetings with the British and German Prime Ministers and the French President. The delay is only one day. You will see him as soon as you arrive at the hospital.

You and your Sister shall stay at your favorite hotel, Lincoln-Adams. Reservations are under your name. At your disposal, you have a government car and driver. You both need to rest and catch up on sleep. Perhaps swim in the hotel pool. Suzie, Washington, DC, is a second home for you. Take advantage of the opportunity and eat at your favorite restaurants for all your meals.

You are authorized to include Jacquie whenever you use your government credit card. I want you refreshed before you meet David. Your arrival in Germany in the morning allows you to go straight to the hospital."

Suzie spoke up, tears still lingering on her cheeks.

"Senator, I'm sorry."

"The doctor on the plane with David confirmed his vital signs are stable and normal, remarkable after what he had to endure."

"Senator, if I don't cry, would you now tell me the truth? You are leaving out some vital information. Hear it in your voice. Please tell me, Senator."

"Suzie, sorry, but nothing is for sure, and I did not want you upset. Not telling you has upset you more. Is Jacquie still next to you?"

"Yes, Senator."

"Suzanne, David has not spoken since a U.S. Air Force psychiatrist examined him on the plane to Germany. After a few innocent questions to gather intelligence, he got verbally loud and angry. David became agitated and started to use his colorful New York street talk.

David saw a syringe prepared to inject him with a sedative, so he stopped, asked a U.S. Air Force nurse to hold him, said he was tired, and closed his eyes. Suzie, what do you make of David asking for forgiveness each time he used an expletive directed at the doctor?

The nurse reported that David winked at her and whispered, 'Thank you for your help.' She took it to mean that she had unwittingly helped him avoid debriefing. The nurse said he copiously apologized and asked if she would please send a message to you."

"Senator, what did David's note say?"

"He wrote, 'Suzanne, I'm sorry, my Irish Angel, where are you, my Suzanne?'

David now just repeats this sentence."

"Suzie, you can translate David's phrase and tell me one day. Glad David is now safe. Robert and I will see you on the plane in Washington, D.C., so farewell for now."

Jacquie turned to Suzie. "Does that sound like our David? It sounds like a boy who didn't want someone to send him to his room, so he changed his attitude. David also tells you he is all right by getting the nurse to look after him. Which enabled him not to be debriefed. Felt terrible not being able to tell her what he was up to, so he expressed regret."

"Suzie, does this sound familiar?"

"David once told me his mother said to stop crying when he was upset as a boy over something or another. David was so upset he couldn't. His mom would say, If you want to cry, I'll give you something to cry about. He said that always scared him into silence and wished someone kind would dry his tears."

"Suzie, not a psychiatrist, but you know his mind, even as a boy, went right up to the line, but at the last moment always steered away, except a few times when not watched."

"Suzie, David does not want to speak to the head doctor. This note and his actions have worked for him."

"This makes me feel so much better. David is already pissing off doctors. Jacquie, help me pack."

Eleven
My Irish Angel

"It had long since come to my attention that people of accomplishment rarely sat back and let things happen to them. They went out and happened to things." Leonardo da Vinci

"Miss, sorry, you are not permitted to see David unless you are his wife. Even then, you need his doctor's permission. The Chief Doctor, who is also the hospital's Director, is currently on his rounds and is not available. Oh, wait, Doctor, this is David's."

"Suzanne."

"Miss Suzanne, David has been moved just across the parking lot to the Behavioral Medical Building. I will call over now and have the attending Doctor speak with you. Miss Suzanne, this soldier will drive you and your sister. It takes less than two minutes. Doctor Robert called and said he and the Senator would meet you there."

"Jacquie, what should I do?"

"Behave yourself until we have gotten his room number. David needs you, and being together will reassure both of you."

The soldier politely said, "I will take you to a private waiting area, and wait in the car should you require me."

"Thank you, Private, for your kindness. Please feel free to return to your regular duties. My Sister and I are good."

Dr. Robinson's first mistake was to pull out a Doctor's Report and start to read to Suzie about torture symptoms, hyper-arousal, irritability, outbursts of anger, mistrust, rage, low mood, and depression. The doctor had read textbook symptoms, not a diagnosis for David. It was time to take matters into her own hands.

"Doctor, need a Chocolate Cherry soda, it helps me relax."

"Turn left out of the room, and halfway down the hall are nurse staff quarters. There is a soda machine you can use."

"Thank you, please continue to update my Sister."

She quickly left the room.

"Miss Brooke, David has a strong survivor instinct."

Stalling for time so my Sister can find David's room. "Doctor, do you mean you have seen signs of defiance? David always said you could take the boy out of the Bronx, but you cannot take the Bronx out of the boy."

"As a man of science, that is a familiar colloquialism. I married a woman from Brooklyn. It's too early to complete a diagnosis. It should not have taken her this long. I'll call the nurse to find her to see if she is okay."

"Doctor, there is no need. She's okay now."

"Getting a soda from the machine doesn't take five minutes. How do you know your Sister is okay?"

"Doctor, my Sister rarely wants a soda and only with David. She was at least honest. Her favorite is Chocolate Cherry soda."

Taken by surprise, the Doctor dashed out of the room.

Jacquie mused, "For a medical man, he is slow on the uptake."

After calling Annabelle and Jaz, Jacquie went into the waiting room to get Suzanne in to see David.

"Miss Brooke, sorry, only a wife or immediate family is allowed. Doctor's orders."

"Nurse Ratchet,"

"Nurse Rachel."

"Oh, sorry, Nurse Rachel. I respect you and truly apologize. However, Feck Off!"

Suzanne walked around the nurse and came face-to-face with a soldier guarding the entrance to David's room for additional security.

"Miss, that was courageous and a most unexpected and creative way to get around the head nurse. No one has ever tried this before. That was a classic movie.

Haven't heard this expletive in a long time. It reminds me of home."

Her tone was a soft Irish Brogue. Suzanne glanced at the name tag on her uniform.

"Sargent Murphy."

"Miss, Private-First Class Murphy."

"Private, may I ask your first name?"

"Yes, Miss, Eileen Murphy."

"You are teaghlach, family."

"Miss, all he says is 'I'm sorry, Suzanne. Where is my Irish Angel?'

Do you know who Suzanne is? I believe he will respond to her."

"I'm Suzanne Brooke."

"I'll keep everyone out for as long as I can."

"Private Murphy, "May God hold you in the palm of his hand. Please let my Sister enter too. Her name is Jacqueline."

Suzanne walked into David's room, fearing it would be cold, stark, and dark. Surprisingly, a beautiful flower arrangement on his bedside table and three Van Gogh paintings hung on a blue wall. Ostensibly, to create a serene atmosphere.

David was seated in an oversized leather chair facing the window, which could only open six inches. Which was not comforting.

"Suzanne, oh Suzanne, I'm sorry, I'm so deeply sorry. Where is my Irish Angel?"

"My love, I'm here now."

"Oh F*CK, now I hear things."

David was too weak to stand, and the chair was too heavy to turn around, so I walked around the chair to stand in front of him.

"David, it's me."

Tears emerged behind his closed eyes. He wiped them and opened his eyes.

Seeing his beloved again, "Oh, my Suzie, I missed those bluest blue eyes. Suzie, kiss me and dance with me before my hallucination fades."

Tears now flowed down both of their faces.

"Love, you are not strong enough to dance."

Suzanne leaned over to kiss him on his lips and found herself in his lap, not wanting it to end.

"Love, why haven't you spoken to the Doctor? That is the reason why they transferred you to this building."

"The terrorists tortured me day and night. They had little use for an American Jew and would kill me. The beatings never lasted for long. But the torture was constant day and night. They asked me to make a video denouncing American Jewry.

But they had no video equipment. When I refused, the terrorists threatened to shoot me in the head. They put a gun to my head and pulled the trigger. Each time it was blank. I never knew when I was to die.

They used the video as a ruse. The real intent was to torture me for disrupting their plan to kill everyone at the airport gate. A terrorist dragged a hostage from another room and made her kneel before me for no reason. A woman around forty, and they shot her in the head."

"That broke my spirit, but not my desire and promise to return home to you. These bastards would kill a hostage every hour. Didn't know how many hostages they were holding.

I couldn't, Suzie…, they wouldn't kill me because this was a slower death. Kept seeing your face and my promise to you, so fought hard to live.

Knew I needed to stall for time so Special Forces could rescue the hostages and me.

Suzie, so deeply sorry. Lost count of the days and reconciled with my death. Please forgive me."

"I'm here now, and you are safe."

Jacqueline smiled as she walked into the room. Saw tears and weariness on David's face.

"You look knackered, but I've seen you worse. In any case, it is grand to see you."

Jacquie's way of saying so, I'm worried about you. Her fear for my safety faded as soon as she was with me.

For the first time in a long while, David laughed. "Oh, my Jacquie, missed you too and worried about you and Suzanne."

"Suzanne, may I have permission for a long hug and kiss?"

Jacquie walked over to me and started to cry.

"David, you must stop finding ways to get into a hospital."

"Jacquie, are you all right? My Annabelle, how is she? Did you tell her I'm coming home? Thank you for looking after Suzie. Knowing you and Suzie had each other, you wouldn't be alone. Kept me from going insane."

"Yes, David, we both are good, and she is excited you are coming home soon."

Suzie held his hand, and Jacquie kissed David on the lips, in a tender, loving kiss, and started to cry again.

"David was so scared. Suzanne never lost her faith, and she helped me."

"And kissed her Sister.

Truthfully, we helped each other not to give up, and she hardly left my side. Jacquie kept me calm. She ensured my meds were refilled when they ran out and kept me from going into a more profound deepening of the blues."

"Jacquie got my David back, and you got your best buddy back."

"Suzanne, My Angel, get me out of here, and take me home."

The Chief Doctor knocked on the door as he entered.

"Is it okay for me to come in?"

"David, waiting outside your door, did not want to rush your reunion. The good news is your release papers have been started, so you can leave today.

But, young lady, you disrespected the Doctor in charge of this unit and told a nurse to go Feck herself. However, you made a friend for life. Private Murphy was willing to get a court-martial because she refused the Doctor and Nurse entry."

"Doctor, how did you convince her to let you in?"

"Suzie, " I told her, I was one of the good guys and gave her a wink. Ensured she would not get into trouble."

"David, you are physically fit, considering what you endured. All tests are negative. The weight you lost, well, a few good meals, can remedy that.

Regardless, wanted you under observation for another week. However, after observing your act, I went home and watched the movie Chance Return."

"Doctor followed the movie, and everyone but you believed me."

"Thirty-five years as an Army psychiatry practitioner and a fan of the movie, plus your skill at keeping others at bay from interviewing or debriefing you. Recommended your debriefing occur next week in the States."

"Suzie, how did you find out?"

"Doctor, he asked for a kiss to ensure this wasn't a hallucination. David and I watched the movie together."

"When can I leave?"

"Anytime today, your discharge papers will be ready in an hour. Married an Irish lass, and David, you are in good hands if the two Sisters represent the love and care you'll get.

David, with your permission, Dr. Kelley will arrange for your therapy and check up on you for a few weeks. You have a good relationship and trust the doctor. However, you will need treatment for at least a month. The therapist can decide from there.

With your girlfriend working with Dr. Kelly's wife to help elect her as the next President of the United States, David, you'll have the support required for a fast recovery."

"Thank you, doctor, for helping get a speedy release for David."

"Miss Suzanne and Miss Jacqueline, David, you are the luckiest man to have your girlfriend and Miss Jacquie look after you.

I'll check the status of your release papers. Jacqueline, come with me, and I'll expedite them."

Jacqueline kissed Suzie and David. "Please lock the door."

"Angel, don't have anything to pack. Come to keep me company."

"David, you almost went to the angels."

Remained silent. Suzanne had justifiable feelings that needed to be expressed. Just put her through emotional agony.

Jacquie heard her Sister through the door, maddened with worry for David.

"Sis, David is safe."

"Now, Jacquie, what about next time?

The Doctor said your girlfriend would take care of you. I DON'T WANT TO BE YOUR GIRLFRIEND.

I want to be your wife. I want us to get married."

"Suzie, would you ask Dr. Kelley and the Senator to find out the arrangements for our flight home and inquire when they could see David!"

"Promised myself not to be distressed when I found you alive and hugged you. David, please, you don't have to say anything.

I love you and need you, and I'm sorry. A New York man would have sounded better with a Bronx accent to show how bloody scared I was. An Irish Brogue does not sound as emotional."

"Angel couldn't walk away from this mission."

"Love, the Senator explained. I love you more for who you are. But, David, are we going to be all right? Didn't want you upset."

"Suzanne, having you on my mind prevented them from breaking me. Your emotional outburst means you trust I'll be okay."

"You are impossible to engage in an argument. I love you, David." She kissed me and turned to her Sister.

"I'll look for the Senator and Dr. Robert. David talks a good game but doesn't want to be left alone. He is not as strong as he pretends."

"Suzanne, let me read the touching letter you left behind. All your love letters reveal your heart, making you vulnerable, yet you write them anyhow. She will not leave you. I did not disappear. In fact, our relationship grew more intimate, got even closer."

"Jacquie."

"Listen and don't speak. Trust yourself and your relationship. Your love for each other has grown more profound, spiritual, and loving, and one day will bless you with a family.

Say what's in your heart. Not out of your kindness. Instead, from the center of your soul. Genuine affection and love lie in the heart.

David, please do not suppress your feelings out of fear. She loves you, and your love for each other will create not a 'romantic storybook' relationship but a tangible, touchable, and your enduring love will nurture your future children."

"Jacquie, I'm always angry, and the slightest thing sets me off, and my jealousy overwhelms me. The terrorists crushed my strength, leaving me with anger and despair. I can't, Jacquie, I can't feel her love. I can't hear the loving words she says to me.

My jealousy and misguided anger may lead me to lash out at Suzanne. The cycle of jealousy causes emotional pain and wears me down. It is fuel for depression. I can't remember feeling normal.

One of them shot an innocent woman hostage in front of me because she wouldn't make a video for them denouncing American Jewry, but they had no video camera. Would keep killing hostages, but was in an untenable situation. No choice but to endure their hatred.

If Special Forces hadn't rescued the hostages and me at that moment, I wouldn't be confident that I would live.

Jacquie, can't stop my nightmares. Suzie making love in the arms of another man. Each time, Suzanne woke up screaming, Suzanne, no, please come back to me. She said you drove me away. Terrified, I lost my Angel."

Jacquie took him into her arms and kissed him. Though she knew she could not kiss away any of his nightmares.

"Why is it every time you two are left alone, you find yourselves in each other's arms in an embrace, kissing?" Of course, said in an exaggerated Irish Brogue, which David loves.

"Suzanne, what did the Senator say?"

"Sis, there will be a government car from the US Embassy with a US Army terrorist team in front and behind us to take us to our plane. Which will be searched and guarded to take every precaution."

"Angel, I'm afraid for you to ride with me."

"Love, coming with you."

Her look said, Like hell, will I lose you without being by your side.

"The car will be here in a little over two hours. An agent will drive us in the opposite direction to the plane and then double back, taking another route to prevent an ambush.

As soon as we board the plane, it will take off."

"This reassures me. Special Forces and the US Army are here for you and Jacquie's protection. Nevertheless, not going into a bubble of protection. Would rather take a taxi."

"David, this is serious."

"Yes, Suzie, I know; however, it would make me too nervous."

"Love called Noreen and told her our estimated arrival time. She and Jessica will meet us at the San Francisco Airport to drive us home.

The Senator and Dr. Robert will depart shortly to meet with the Heads of State. She has plans for layovers in Germany, France, and England, first to provide condolences to the French President, meet the Prime Ministers of Germany and England, and personally deliver a message from POTUS. She will see you, me, and Jacquie before they depart."

David's weeping released feelings of failure and shame.

"So sorry, botched this mission and let the Senator down. Most of all, you, Suzie."

"Sweetheart, you had no control over events. You didn't fail.

David, the Senator, said I could work from home to be with you and help restore your health."

David emotionally choked up, and words blurted out in short bursts.

"Suzanne, sincerely sorry. You are the love of my life, but I have nothing left of myself. The terrorists took it all from me and left me maddened. Can't feel what it means to be normal anymore. Please proceed. Work in your office. Can not bear you seeing me this way."

"Are you finished? No one except Annabelle is to visit and come and go as she wishes. The family will respect your privacy. Jacquie and I will help you downstairs to my office each morning and set up a comfortable place for you while I work.

You will have the draft of your romance novel, along with any necessary notes and work, and any notes and work you need for you to reschedule or conduct radio and TV interviews. Sweetheart, returning to your regular daily routine will be necessary for your recovery."

"Suzanne, please don't treat me as damaged. Damn it! I will work where I want."

"David, this is not the way you talk to Suzie. Did you see Suzanne blink? These anger outbursts will subside. You will feel safer, and the family will honor your wishes.

Suzanne and I are not treating you as damaged or fragile, and do you see us walking on eggshells around you? It may take two Irish women who love you and will not tell you what to do unless you do something not in your best interest."

"Suzie, please tell this mean Irish lady still too weak to argue."

"Lover, keep holding on to your sense of humor. As it is your lifeline back to your life."

"Angel, so sorry to be unreasonable, but I still want to go by taxi and not be placed in a protective bubble."

The Senator was patiently listening before she stepped into the room with her husband.

"What is this request? To ride in a taxi? I understand. Robert explained how you would react to being surrounded by men and women with guns."

"Senator, so you will allow me to travel by taxi."

"You are the most stubborn man, and my Suzie is the queen of stubbornness. There is a little girl who can convince you. Do this not for yourself, or me, or your Angel.

Let this be a gift for Annabelle. With my concern about you, I forgot to give you her message. She made me guarantee her a half dozen times I would not fail."

"Suzie, please read what Jacquie wrote down from my Sweetpea."

Dear Daddy,

I told Mommy Jaz you are coming home soon. She told me how much she loves and misses you. I hope soon you can read me my favorite bedtime stories, tuck me in, and check for cookie monsters, chocolate chip cookies, and milk before bed. I kept our secret of two cookies.

Mommy Jaz sneaks the second cookie to me. I miss you, Daddy.

Hurry home. I Love You. Hugs and kisses, Annabelle.

"That was not fair."

"I'm sorry, sweetie. I promised Annabelle."

"Not that. Why didn't you give our daughter a second cookie?"

"Senator, he is all right now and will travel with security."

"No, can't do this. Suzie, what if an outburst of anger occurs and I'm out of control? Angel, I could not protect you, Jacquie, or Annabelle."

"You cannot always safeguard those you love from harm. But, honey, Annabelle is the sunniest therapy for you. Your love for your daughter and Anabelle's love for you will quell your anger."

"Jacquie, your little girl reminds me of my girls when they were small. She is an exceptional child, David. We all understand.

Suzie, Jacquie, assume you were not watching the news because I always informed you of verified facts, except for what I just learned from a recent debriefing.

First, want to say how proud POTUS and I are of David's actions that morning.

David, you made a substantive life-saving difference! We now learned more and pieced together events as we believe they happened. Until we get to debrief you and confirm what we know.

David saved the lives of ten girls and their parents, a Rabbi and his wife, and two Catholic Sisters from a humanitarian nonprofit. David was chatting with the girls when a suspicious man left a piece of carry-on luggage by the large window closest to the plane. Dodgy quickly walked away.

A young woman who joined your conversation turned nineteen that day. She enjoyed hearing about the girls' conference.

She is Israeli, serves in the Israeli Air Force, recognizes the same potential danger, and responds automatically to your voice's sense of urgency. And helped children and parents reach safety quietly.

David used a calm and authoritative voice to get the girls moving quickly. He told them to run into the Women's bathroom, get as far from the door as possible, and get down and cover.

Then picked up the youngest, about the same age as Annabelle, and shouted to all the passengers, 'This is real, not a drill, take cover.'

Your instinct saved countless lives. Before the first bomb exploded, you got the girls to safety, their parents, a young Israeli woman, Rabbi, his wife, and the two Sisters.

Lying on the floor, a few feet into the Jet Bridge, a woman and a man identified as FBI were injured and stunned by the explosion. Emergency Responders and German police were on standby because I had requested that the German Prime Minister do so, so they were on the scene within seconds.

One of the Special Forces team placed closest to you took your arm as you were bleeding from the head from the explosion. She said, You told her there were children in the ladies' room. She left you to ensure that emergency responders would go to them.

You ran to see if you could help the agents, risking your own life.

The female agent was dazed, and the other agent couldn't walk. So he put his arm around the female agent's waist and asked a nurse, one of the passengers, whose life he had saved, to help the agent.

Suzie then, David returned to the Jet Bridge to rescue the male FBI agent.

'Dr. David, a bomb is planted near the door at the end of the Jet Bridge behind children's strollers.'

A German police officer tried to get you to safety."

'Officer, this is an FBI Agent who cannot move.'

"The policeman lifted our FBI agent and carried him out of harm's way. Heard you say I'll be right behind you.

And you turned as you responded to the pilot's call for help.

The male FBI agent shouted to David, 'Getaway as quickly as possible. The bomb could detonate anytime.'

Amid the chaos, the pilot frantically waited for help. Due to the first explosion, the Jet Bridge jammed shut against the plane's door and could not pull away."

'Please release the Jet Bridge? My co-pilot and flight attendants are preparing for emergency exit deployment.'

"David anxiously tried to figure out which lever to use. The pilot calmly said,"

'It is the red lever for emergency release. An explosion of two canisters, 200 PSI pressurized air will free and push the Jet Bridge, so hold on tight.'

"Once freed, the plane immediately backed up and turned to safely deploy the emergency slides. Ambulances were parked next to the plane, and a bomb-trained dog found a bomb with a timer set to go off in less than ten minutes.

The bomb placed near the opening of the Jet Bridge did discharge with enough force to rattle and break windows. Thanks to David, the parents, and their babies and children, they all safely disembarked from the plane.

After running all the security videotapes, one showed David's disappearance. Two men with masks abducted you. How they escaped with you is yet unknown."

Tears were streaming down Suzie and Jacquie's faces as they did not know what to say.

"Senator, it was just what was needed at the moment. My only thought was to save as many innocent lives as possible. Did what any other person would do. For God's sake, Senator, please do not make anything more of this."

Suzie came over to me,

"Love, you made a difference, saving many lives."

With a trembling voice, "Senator, thank you for the security and for saving my life with a Special Forces rescue."

Nonetheless, infuriated, crying, frustrated, in a raised voice,

"But it wasn't enough, damn it. Why couldn't I save more lives?

Not a hero.

Senator, please, FBI agents put their lives at risk. Along with the emergency responders doing their job, risking their lives, even after the second bomb. Not a fecking hero, don't turn me into one.

Suzie, Jacquie, I tried but lost another chance to save more lives when a second explosion knocked me off my feet. So many innocent people died. I see them in my nightmares, so much death.

A woman hostage was shot in the head in front of me. And I can't get her face out of my head. But I don't want to forget or think of her as a faceless victim. Someone who had so much to live for. Being so young. As soon as my eyes close, her face appears.

A terrorist put a gun to her head, and she said, 'Don't feel guilty. I don't blame you. They would kill all of us anyhow.'

Maddened by the image of this young woman killed before him, "Who the F*CK should I blame? Doctor, you're an expert. Whom should I f*cking blame?"

"Julia, meet me outside in the car and let me talk to David alone. Will be there shortly. Suzie, you and Jacquie wait just outside the door."

"Suzie, don't leave me alone. I'm sorry, Doctor, not angry at you. You saved my life not so long ago."

She rested my head on her breast and softly stroked my hair. "Dr. Robert wants to speak with you. It's all right. Remember, this is the one Doctor you like and respect."

"Suzie, you have tears. I'm sorry, but I'm struggling to control my anger. I don't know who I am."

"Honey, Jacquie, and I will be right outside the door. Dr. Robert wants to talk to you alone."

"Dr. Robert, I am sorry and should not have used that language. But I anguish over her death."

"Suzie, it's okay. You and Jacquie wait just outside the room. I'll call you back in just a few minutes."

"Dr. Robert, I'm frightened when I lose control. There is no magic cure to vanquish nightmares. The only way I know is by fighting back using New York street talk to express my feelings, but not giving in to my anger. Doing whatever it takes for me to survive.

Where did the Senator go?"

"She is waiting for me in the car. David, the Senator, was anxious and concerned. Was there something else she could do? She hardly slept and kept a 24/7 watch to ensure everything went smoothly and the rescue was fast and safe.

She did not want Suzie sensing her anxiety during the search and rescue operation so as not to unduly upset her."

"I, too, want to avoid unnecessary worry about the time for your complete recovery.

"Doctor, I can keep a secret for Suzie's sake."

"David, the trauma in your case was severe. Regrettably, you received the wrong diagnosis. A severe shock stemming from what you suffered, a correct diagnosis is traumatic grief syndrome.

Your lifelong battle with depression has amplified the seriousness. Your anger is controllable. The nightmares will stop. It will take time, and I will monitor and adjust your therapy as required. You can rest knowing you have competent and reliable emotional support.

Recovery won't be easy. Perhaps more than one relapse is probable, but have confidence in your reservoir of inner strength when you need it. One more thing, no one blames your actions. You saved many lives, and parents with children are asking the White House where to send their sincere gratitude. It would be worrisome if you didn't feel why you couldn't save more lives.

I know exactly how you feel, as in my work, I have saved lives and watched helplessly when some patients die."

"Doctor, how do you cope?"

"Sometimes, not well, so I placed my focus on those saved. David, your anger is a symptom, not who you are. Everything I'm saying now will take time for you to work out.

I'll check in on you or have my nurse call you daily. You don't even have to take the call. Let Suzie feel she participates in your recovery."

"Doctor Robert, I love her so much. My anger will drive me away, and my jealousy feeds the anger. But she would never leave me, and fight alongside or without her until I give her the love she desires."

"Good sounds normal, and more of you."

"Doctor, you have to go. I have already told the Senator, Sorry about the bloodstains. Hope most of it stayed on my tuxedo."

"Thank you, David. Apology accepted. You are remarkable.

No matter how faint, your New York wit is alive and well.

So take solace, Suzie and Jacquie love you. Call you tomorrow to check.

Ladies, you may come in now."

"Doctor Robert, is my David all right?"

"Suzie, he is a most extraordinary man. Apologized for the blood he may have left on our living room floor months ago. Look for his wit and sense of humor. It lies embedded in his responses.

His spirit signifies his love will not diminish, nor will David give in to dark blues. Have you noticed that his words and tone sound like those of a stereotypical native Bronx boy once he gets angry? Right now, give him space and let him get fractious.

David will be all right, but it may take a while. Have a safe trip back."

"Doctor Robert, thank you."

An orderly unexpectedly came into the room with a wheelchair.

"Excuse me, but we didn't order a wheelchair."

"Miss, hospital policy. Every patient leaves in a wheelchair."

"Let me enlighten you on what you can do with your hospital policy."

"David, please, I will push you."

Jacquie came into the room and heard me, with my best Irish accent, say,

"Take your fecking chair…."

"Your Irish brogue has improved."

"Sir, leave it for you to finish packing. And come back when you are ready to leave."

"Sorry, orderly, for my rudeness. Could you please remove the wheelchair and refrain from quoting a hospital policy to me?

Admiration for your positive attitude. I'll remove the chair instead."

Standing, I intended to take away the wheelchair, but my legs buckled underneath me.

"Love, I have you."

"I'm all right. Suzie, please don't let me fall, but let me struggle if I need to walk alone.

Blindsided to ride with security. Dr. Robert said he has confidence in my sense of humor to help me heal. Then do it for Annabelle."

"David, honey, what is bothering you? You wouldn't leave Jacquie and me in the car without you.

"Going in the taxi with you."

"Jacquie, he listens to you because he trusts you. Opens up knowing you always share with me. David wants to hide his weakness from me."

"My Love, what is bothering you? When Suzanne walked into the room, you immediately stopped your act. What can't you say to Suzanne or me? Sweetie, your anger is real. I feel it. But you are not alone unless it is your choice.

David, please, don't choose to be alone. Suzie and I will give you space for healing. Not for you to be alone."

"Jacquie, my Jacquie, how is Annabelle?"

"David, she is ecstatic about your homecoming."

"Would you and Suzie keep me company when she is with me? Annabelle will feel better; everything is back to normal."

"You silly New Yorker, just say you don't want to be alone."

"Thought I just did."

The phone rang, and David realized his taxi ride would not happen.

Suzanne answered, "Hello, madam. This is Dr. David Benjamin Bradley's room. Suzanne speaking. Okay, yes, at the Emergency room exit of the hospital."

"Well, good news, the cars are here with undercover police and the US Army Terrorist Response Team. They told us to stay in the room until two FBI agents arrive to escort us."

"Suzie and Jacquie sit next to me. Hear me out in full before you say anything. Angry all the time. Some days, it can be kept in check. Assumed you both would pick up on my feelings. Since they would not allow me a phone call, I thought the repetition of one question would convey all you needed to know. I was all right.

Repeating your name and calling out for you provided me with temporary peace. It helped to keep horrific thoughts and images out of my head. Yeah, expletives are a bad habit from a New York upbringing. However, the upside prevented anyone from debriefing me.

After a short debriefing session, I overheard the head nurse tell the Psychiatrist, 'Doctor, David is crazy like a fox.'

She turned to me and in a low voice, 'My husband, raised in The Bronx, taught me how to survive all situations.' And she gave me a smile of understanding.

The wheelchair reminds me of my torture.

Suzie, can't walk out myself. Would you please aid me?"

"Yes, David, I'll be at your side, if needed, hold on to you so you can walk."

"Suzie, please let me finish. The extra over-the-top security was my request to the Senator. I wanted to strengthen the protection for you and Jacquie. With this much security in place to prevent reprisals, there must be chatter being picked up by the CIA or FBI. I did not want to be in the same car, so I want to be as far away from both of you as possible. Keeping you both safe."

"Sweetheart, are you strong enough so I can sit in your lap?"

"Angel scared me that my nightmare would come true. Still so angry all the time. Fearing a loss of control over what I say or do. Unforgivable not by either you or Jacquie, just by me."

"There is nothing I can say to relieve all your anxiety. Your emotions are being held hostage by your anger. This too shall pass, which you say to Annabelle when she cries over a hurt or disappointment: 'This too will pass.' Nothing lasts forever."

"Sweetie, Oh, how much I adore and love you. You mistakenly believe your jealousy drives me into another man's arms. Could never leave you, my beloved. David, in your heart, you know I would help you find your way back to me. You said periodic blue episodes can be controlled.

David, words, actions, or anger will not push me away. It will not affect the rest of our lives. In time, trust my David will return to me."

"Suzie, no longer the same man, and dubious if it is even possible to find my way out of a cycle of anger, jealousy, and blues.

Remember, no matter what, my trust and love for you are sacrosanct. Angel, in my heart of hearts, you would never leave me. You would not allow this to happen. Jealousy and anger are not rational emotions, and collapsing into the blues is devoid of emotions. The combination, if you can work it out, well, welcome to my life.

Jacquie and Suzie, thank you for taking care of Annabelle. It gave me peace of mind.

Won't ride in the damn wheelchair!"

"Suzanne will check on his release papers, ensuring the doctor has signed them. While you're gone, take that New Yorker and don't say a word, and kiss. Remember to lock the door. Shall call Jaz and speak to Annabelle again. She wants to know exactly what time her dad will arrive home.

Suzie found a comfortable position and started kissing. Suddenly stopped and whispered, "New York man, Jacquie, and I support your decision not to ride in the wheelchair. Breaking the rules, as you always do, because they are absurd, is intoxicating. David, would I go to the hospital jail?"

"Suzie, you used to be a normal woman with Irish wit, a sense of humor, and well-behaved. Inherited the best of your character traits and thinking, and you indulged yourself in my not-so-subtle New Yorkness.”

“Sweetheart, it's exciting. We both understand each other in ways most couples don’t explore.”

After ninety minutes of kissing Suzie in my lap, Jacquie knocked lightly.

“Come in, Sis. It is unlocked.”

“Love, FBI agents are waiting for us outside the door when both of you are ready. Sis, are you okay?”

“So is David.”

“Suzie, can we go to our Sanctuary?”

“Of course, when you are stronger?”

Suzie took hold of one of my arms.

“David, let’s take you home.”

“Please, first, let me try to stand alone, and would you move the wheelchair to the front door?”

Suzie was pleased that David was determined to walk, driven by sheer force of will.

“Love, Jacquie, and I will stand by the door.”

I stood up slowly first to clear my head. So far, so good. Took short steps and then walked a little easier. As I reached Suzie, she opened the door and took hold of the wheelchair.

“Agents, please move a few steps to the left.”

Suzie and Jacquie pushed the wheelchair, and it rolled down the hall past the orderly.

Luckily, it didn't crash into anyone; it just hit a laundry bin.

"Dr. Bradley, hospital policy."

"Just David, Nurse, has been arrested by two FBI agents assigned to bring me back."

The female FBI agent confessed in a whisper,

"Miss Suzie, have one like your David at home, and he fought and defied every doctor and got well faster."

The two FBI agents walked behind me.

"Agents, if you want to walk faster, feel free to bypass me. I'll meet you at the elevator."

Suzie was proud of my resolve to stand and walk on my own. Jacquie and Suzie supported my decision not to sit in the damn chair.

Suzie and Jacquie mused and accepted me wanting the discharge nurse to watch me walk to the elevator.

The male FBI agent understood, "Sir, take it slow. You will get stronger. Realize you want to do everything to prove your mind is stronger than any limitation. Although it sounds counterintuitive, going slow initially will make healing go faster."

"Thank you. Your advice is appreciated."

"Suzie, since we haven't hugged in a while, this would be a good time."

As we walked out of the elevator, just twenty-five feet to freedom, the Chief Doctor and Director of the hospital stood before us.

"Doctor, sorry to break hospital rules. Well, actually, not sorry, but I sincerely apologize. Didn't intend to get you in trouble. Encouraged by the aggressiveness, you get stronger regardless of the hospital policy.

I'll pretend you just slipped by. David Benjamin Bradley has an intense understanding of survivor's guilt. It is essential to give it a name. So you can fight what you acknowledge.

Mr. David, I've not given a military salute to anyone in the last ten years. Sir, thank you for your service."

A proud, smart military salute was kept until Suzie supported me so I could salute back.

With tears slowly flowing down my face, "Never received and never again experience the depth of respect you have shown me. Doctor, God bless you."

Regaining confidence, we walked out with Suzie's hand in hand wherever we went. Jacquie was waiting to be checked in by a Secret Service agent to speed up our departure.

"Sir, this is Suzie, Jacquie, two FBI agents, Roxana from the newspaper Washington Record, and me. We are ready to leave."

Agent Phyllis whispered, "Miss Suzie, no one passes Secret Service, no matter who they are, unless he was the President. So, how did David get them to let him pass and then help him into the car?"

"Agent, the Secret Service knows David risked his life to save two of your colleagues."

As soon as we were on board, a Marine was on duty to meet our needs.

"Sir, when you and the ladies are settled, I'll call the cockpit and inform the Captain. She is finishing her take-off checklist procedures. We will shortly be taxiing down the runway.

Miss Jacquie, Miss Suzie, as soon as it is safe after take-off and we level off, I'll serve lunch."

"Thank you."

The Marine picked up the phone and said, "Captain, we're good for takeoff."

"Marine Ramirez, would you bring me a Chocolate Cherry soda and drinks for the ladies? Please ask what drink Ms. Roxana and the FBI agents would prefer. What's for lunch?"

"Dr. David, selections for lunch were already made in advance by Miss Suzie, and as soon as we level off, we will come back to serve your drinks and bring lunch. Sir, we found an Italian restaurant serving fresh pineapple on pizza. Your DS pizzas are in the oven, heating up."

"Sweetheart, Jacquie and I wanted to surprise you, so we kept it a secret. Was it okay that we ordered our DS pizza for everyone?"

"A perfect choice."

"New York man, so proud of you."

"Can you tell me why?"

"This is the first time you have not corrected someone who says, Dr. David."

"Oh, I didn't notice."

"David, it's all right. Yes, you did. Why this Marine?"

"His use of Doctor is a show of respect and serves to protect at the risk of his safety. FBI and Special Forces risked their life to ensure my life was safe. It hit home.

Growing up, I was influenced by my British grandfather, who told me stories of his service as a pilot for the RAF during World War II. Granddad was, in fact, a highly decorated pilot. He affected me, saying, 'Don't make me a hero thousands of times.' Granddad was, in fact, a highly decorated pilot. Don't talk about this much because my granddad never did, except for my grandmother.

Admire and respect men and women who serve to protect the nation. They do not seek praise; they do their duty.

Rang for the Marine.

"Yes, sir."

"Can we make a call to the States?"

"As soon as we level off, we will bring you a phone. Just pick up the phone, and a military operator will place your call. We should be leveling off in a few minutes."

"David, who do you want to call?"

"No one, Jacquie. You want to call the love of your heart. Tell my Sweetpea, I love her and miss her and will see her soon."

"David, how I love you so. Jacquie had been anxious all morning, wondering how she would call Annabelle once we were in the air.

The DS pizza may taste different, not made by Vincent at our favorite pizzeria."

"Suzie, it will be the best DS pizza because you share it with me."

About two hours into the flight, David was sleepy, a combination of a sedative and walking further than he should have. Placed his head on my lap and soon was fast asleep.

The pilot came over, introduced herself, and asked Suzie to wake David.

"No problems, Miss Suzie. I have a message for him."

"Sweetheart, the pilot wants a word with you."

"Where is she?"

"Sir, standing in the aisle."

"Captain, everything all right?"

"Yes, Sir, I have the White House on line one. Pick up the phone, and the operator will connect you to the President."

"Is there a speakerphone I can use?"

"Yes, sir, this button here."

"Thank you, Captain."

"Yes, Dr. David Benjamin Bradley, on speakerphone. Is this permissible?"

"Yes, sir, please hold for the President."

"Jacquie, are you awake? The President will be on the phone in a minute."

"David, Suzie, my hair, I'm a mess."

"Never possible. You are always beautiful, don't worry, Luv, the President, will be on speakerphone."

"Now putting you through to the President."

"David, this is President Garcia. I'm pleased to have this opportunity to talk to you. First, I would like to extend on behalf of the United States a warm welcome home. Susie and Jacquie, the First Lady, relay her regards and look forward to having you over to the White House for an informal lunch."

"Thank you, Mr. President."

"Never heard Senator Harrison use such colorful language. She must care for you, and your loyalty to her is required for her to get angry. Been trying to get her to be more outgoing."

"Mr. President, if this is your sense of humor, I love it."

"David, thank you for the children's lives you saved and countless others."

"Mr. President, I appreciate you saying this. Thank you. Grateful you made it possible to ensure the hostages, and I were rescued."

"When you feel you are up for it, I will invite you, Suzanne, Jacquie, Annabelle, Jessica, and all Sisters and family to the White House. But, first, I want to acknowledge you for your bravery."

Suzie took my hand and looked nervous about my answer.

"With all due respect, Mr. President, these are not empty words. I voted for you twice, and it's a singular honor for me to speak with you. Not a hero, many brave special forces and two FBI agents risked their lives. Give them an award."

"The difference is they are trained and have chosen their career to serve the country. You did not, and their service will be recognized. However, this is The Presidential Medal of Freedom."

"Mr. President heard you once quote Ralph Waldo Emerson in one of your speeches: "A hero is no braver than an ordinary man, but he is brave five minutes longer." Please, Mr. President, no award ceremony."

"David, empathize with you about survivor's guilt. I spoke with men and women who saved lives, but could not save everyone; yet, you survived, while many others did not. You understand this intellectually. This is not a philosophical problem.

Served in Vietnam. No declaration of gratitude or medal can explain why I survived, while so many Vietnamese didn't. Why couldn't I save more civilians? I didn't want a Purple Heart; it's in the same box in a closet, and I never looked at it again.

Survivors and their families want to thank you. The country needs heroes, and importantly, children need to look up to someone selfless who cares about others first, even at the risk of their own life."

"Mr. President, thank you. Read your autobiography, and know you appreciate why I don't want a medal. You can decide not to have this ceremony."

"David, you saved an indispensable member of the Senator's team. You jumped in front of Suzie, took two bullets, almost died, and saved many lives at the Frankfurt airport at your own grave risk. The public already considers you a hero. The media has featured you and is expecting an award ceremony. Don't quote me, but it is not the Press I care about.

As soon as the Press ban was lifted, letters of appreciation poured into the White House Mail Room daily. Calling you an American Hero, someone whom they can believe in. There is hope for our society.

Hundreds of letters written by children from the United States, Israel, Germany, France, and the United Kingdom praised your bravery.

"Mr. President, appreciation from children means more to me. Love to share the goodness from children's hearts with my daughter." May I have the letters?

"Personally, I will ensure the necessary arrangements are made.

David won't say anything else. As President, I would not use emotional manipulation. Talk it over with Suzie, and will honor your decision."

"Thank you, Mr. President; I am grateful."

"David, let me say what has been kept from the media, with only a few people aware of the confidentiality.

One of the girls whose life you saved is my granddaughter. I wanted the opportunity to thank you personally."

"Thank you for telling me. I'm pleased that this was a happy outcome for you and your family. This gives me some solace."

"Whatever you decide, you have my 100% support. Your decision, no reason necessary."

"Need some time to process this. You can expect a response from me within 24 hours. Thank you, Mr. President."

"Suzie, Jacqueline, God bless you. Goodbye."

"Goodbye, Mr. President."

Annabelle stayed up late, way past her bedtime, until I came home. My daughter ran from her bedroom straight into our bedroom, jumped up on the bed,

"Daddy!" and right into my arms. "I love you, Daddy. Welcome home!"

Her enticing welcome-home kiss is always a special treat. Today, even more so.

Seeing tears in my daughter's eyes, started to cry, and we hugged for what seemed like forever.

"Annabelle, I love you more."

"Sweetpea, let Aunt Suzie tuck you in, and you and I will spend all day together until you go to bed. Your mom,

Mommy Jaz, and Aunt Suzie will join us for family time too."

"Suzie feels so good to be back in our bed. Come here, Angel. I heard you haven't been in our bed. I love you: I would have acted the same. Oh, Angel, I made life difficult and upset you. Let me kiss you and hold you in my arms. Are you sure you got the right bloke who asked for a kiss and a dance?"

"David, do you want to talk about it now or later?"

"Stay in my arms. Want you to call the President. Say will attend out of respect on the following conditions."

"Lover, the President doesn't operate on conditions."

"Of course, what about this subsequent request? Attending will be my honor if the award is done privately and meets your approval."

"David, you are almost the most intelligent man."

"Angel, why almost?"

"Had to deduct points for jumping in front of a loaded gun aimed at killing me. Additionally, running through an area where a bomb had been detonated, when everyone was going the opposite direction. I can't express how proud and admiring I am of your bravery."

"Yes, they are tears. Hand me a damn tissue."

"Love, what else do you want me to say?"

"Inviting and showing appreciation for the two FBI agents. Plus, the ceremony focuses on celebrating survivors' lives and remembrance of those whose lives were taken from them. Don't want people asking to take a picture with me."

"Honey, what if another Annabelle or fatherless child is out there?"

"You didn't add children with special needs. Suzie don't want to do this. I get why. People want a selfie with me.

Attention should be solely focused on survivors and the many men, women, and children who lost their lives. No one reported on the many brave men and women returning into harm's way to carry out the wounded. There were not enough emergency responders in the first few minutes."

"Love, do understand how you feel and agree with you. And love you because you are so empathetic. How about this? If you don't like it, won't say anything.

What if you were to stand in as your proxy, answer questions, and take photos with survivors and their families if asked? I would also be happy to stand in as your proxy, answering questions and taking pictures with survivors and their families if needed. Also, would love to have Jacqueline and Annabelle at the White House beside me.

I would like to invite Senator Harrison and Dr. Robert to attend. This will give her positive press, as she prefers not to, as she doesn't want to go public, about the hundreds of acts making a difference in people's lives. She tells me, Suzie, it's just who I am. Sound like anyone you know?"

"My mom always told me just to do, let others say, your deeds speak for you.

Suzie, thank you for letting me know. Wow, didn't see that coming. That is why you never lost faith in her becoming President. As you got to work more with her, you could see more of her compassion and kindness."

"She is even more remarkable, but yes, you are right.

Ask the President to present the Medal to Annabelle as your proxy and place it around her neck.

And make a short announcement to the Press. You want Annabelle to represent me as an inspiration for children. The Press will appreciate having questions answered."

"Who taught you to work the room this well?"

"Silly, it's my job as assistant communication director for the Senator."

"Of course, the Press is already aware of your credibility and reputation for honesty. One essential thing, please do not remain silent if the Press asks direct questions concerning me, and answer truthfully. Just be yourself."

"I asked the President to give me 24 hrs. Could you call now? It would be late morning in Washington."

"Do you feel like taking a walk today before spending time with Annabelle?

Arrived shortly before we came home. The physical therapist sent a walker for you. How about we donate it to the local senior community center?"

"This is my bad influence."

Uncommonly sarcastic, "It feels good talking and not slowing down to consider other people's intentions or feelings."

She flashed a sly smile, and I started laughing and couldn't stop.

"This is the first real laugh in a long time. You are gorgeous. Do you have any plans before we take our walk?"

"My calendar is clear, and my assistant communications intern will handle my agenda. David, she is brilliant. And have faith she will become a senator one day."

"What did she say when you told her?"

"She shyly said, Please don't say that. I could never become a senator. Oh, and guess what? Walking by her desk, she didn't notice me. Has written Senator Patricia Plath in perfect script on her desk's legal pad."

"You are her mentor. I'm proud of you."

"David, my love, spoke to the President. I let you sleep. It is just 11:00 a.m., and after our lunch with Annabelle, we can all walk to the stream at Live Oaks."

"What did the President say?"

"He said it was a perfect compromise. Seems like Senator Harrison's thinking.

The President laughed and with pride added, Understand why the Senator has a deep abiding affection for you and speaks highly of your keen wit and intellect."

"Thank you, my love. I'm so proud of you.

Before our lunch, hold me in your arms."

"David, are you sure?"

"Just be gentle with me."

"I'll start slow and kiss you, and if you feel like driving, you can take the wheel. That made it sound silly, actually going for romantic."

Twelve
"If You Believe Nothing Else, Accept US True

"She imagined she could taste the storm in him, the battering winds of desperation and frustration that met her own, blow for blow." Alexandra Bracken

Driving back from San Diego after bookstore signings and several TV and radio interviews for a new novel, Jacquie called to tell me she would pick up Suzie from work to attend Megan's birthday celebration.

"Jacquie, inform Suzie and Megan. I apologize, but I won't arrive until 7:00 pm. Do I need to pick up Suzanne at work?"

"Actually, on my way to get her. After the party, she wants to go home with you."

"Jacquie, my dark blues are back. Couldn't I arrive at the end of the party and get Suzanne?"

"No, love, you cannot. Two beautiful women will look after you."

"I know, but…."

"Love, there are no buts. Megan would be hurt if you were not there. Megan has been touting your books to all of her friends. She hopes it will mean a few more books sold."

"Megan should be enjoying her party instead.

Jacquie, feelings of insecurity cloud my sense of Suzie's love. Don't want Suzanne to find out about my losing emotional control."

"Did you stop sleeping together?"

"What do you mean?"

"She already cared for you and spoke to me, ensuring not to leave you alone when she talked with friends. Suzanne is protecting you by not feeling like you have to socialize."

In a slightly raised voice, "Don't want to be treated as fragile."

"Love, she does not treat you as fragile. David, please, you are still healing."

"Damn it, Jacquie, you don't have to remind me.

Sorry, can no longer control my anger. With frequent nightmares of Suzanne making love to a new boyfriend, I can't constrain my emotions."

"Dreams are not reality. Let's speak as soon as you arrive."

"If I arrive, if not, take Suzanne home with you."

"Honey, of course. What do you mean by "if I arrive?""

"Jacquie, please forgive me. Apologize for raising my voice."

"Always, do not see yourself submerged in the blues or your anger. You know this; you are much more to me, and never tire of sharing my love and belief in you."

"Got to go. Love you, bye."

Promptly hung up before Jacquie realized how deep I fell into a blue whirlwind. Losing my ability to restrain reactions. No longer will take the new antidepressant with my previous meds, and will call my doctor. That was not smart of me, and the consequences were the side effects of combining a new antidepressant with regular meds. Lost control of keeping at bay my darkest thoughts, nightmares, anger, and suicidal thoughts if I lost Suzanne.

"Did you reach David?"

"Yes, Sis, let's find a private place to talk."

"David, oh my David."

"He is getting flashbacks from the side effects of his medications. Suzie, never heard him in such an agitated state, even with his brief lapses into depression."

"Prayed Megan's party would help."

"We will surround him in love and get Megan and Jaz too. He loves them both."

"Jacquie, I'm worried."

"Sis, so am I."

People stood in small groups at Megan's party, talking, eating, laughing, and dancing.

Suzanne trusted David would be himself, surrounded by people who love him. She let go of her concerns. Then her world transformed into her worst fear.

When she turned fourteen, Jack tried to sexually molest her. Ryan's friend Jack evidently didn't care much about a teenager's age and treated her with despicable sexual advances.

"Sue, it's me, Jack."

He was the same asshole. Jack knows I don't like to be called Sue.

"Come on, dance with me, Susan."

"Thank you for your kind offer, but no, thank you. Waiting for my boyfriend."

"Oh, he won't mind. Come on, just one short dance."

Jacquie saw the unfolding peril, ran, and stood between her Sister and a fecking excuse of a human.

"Oh, big Sister, do you want to dance?"

"You are drunk and leave my Sister alone."

"Or what?"

Jack caught Jacquie off guard and shoved her callously aside. And yanked Suzanne up. She struggled as hard as she could, but Jack wrapped his arms around her, limiting her freedom. He started to drag her around in circles. If she refused to dance with him, Jack threatened to harm Jacquie, so she was afraid to scream for help.

David had arrived and did not see Suzie, so he first went to Megan.

"Happy Birthday, Doctor Megan."

"David, silly, I have a few more years as an intern."

"Did Suzanne give you our birthday gift? I was out of town and don't remember if I was supposed to."

With an expectation to find Suzie with friends, instead, my worst nightmare played out before me. Suzanne was in the arms of a man, keeping her in a kiss and holding and groping her.

This was my world, collapsing before my eyes, unleashing an uncontrollable, painful, emotional reaction.

Felt helpless, believing I had failed Suzie. Lost the ability for rational thinking and fell prey to my darkest emotions, blinded by an agony of anger. Jealousy also clouded my thinking, so nothing mattered.

Lamentably, I didn't stay long enough to see how hard Suzanne resisted and struggled. As best as she could, she finally had broken free with a knee to his privates. Jacquie ran over to get James, her sister's girlfriend Gabriella's husband. Suzie had not yet seen David arrive.

"Oh, good, so you want to play rough. With Jack's hand in the air about to slap Suzie, you are asking for a..."

Jack never finished the sentence. James, who played college football, had his former teammates there. James grabbed him by the collar and yanked him away from Suzanne. His mates dragged Jack unceremoniously out of the Banquet Hall, tossed him into a dumpster, and slammed the lid shut.

Megan ran to Suzanne. "David just arrived and was talking with me. Are you all right? Suzie, I'm sorry this happened to you. Jack is an old acquaintance of Ryan and must have told him about my party."

"Megan, sweetheart, don't worry for even a second. There is nothing more to say. I love you. Oh, Megan, sorry for the upset on your birthday."

Megan, nevertheless, remained upset. Suzanne had just fought off an abusive attack from Ryan's friend.

"At least let me come over and cook dinner for you both."

Worried, James asked, "Suzie, are you sure you are okay?"

"Yes, James, thank you for coming to my rescue."

Suzanne was anxious about what David may have seen.

"Jacquie, pray David did not see that."

Gabriella, her closest childhood friend, "Love, do you want James to stay with you until David arrives?"

"Love birds, go ahead and have a good time. James, escort your beautiful bride back to the party. And James, I appreciate you coming to my rescue and will join you both shortly. First, I want to speak with Jacquie."

A moment later, Gabriella asked, "Suzanne, doesn't David drive a convertible?"

"Yes, why?"

"James saw David with the roof down driving fast out of the parking lot."

David left the party painfully trapped in a nightmarish vision. Replaying his worst nightmare in his mind intensified his despair."

"Cheers, Gabriella. Get some food for you and your husband."

"Jacquie, he was standing next to Megan, and with loud music, oh, Jacquie, in his state of mind. It was his worst fear unfolding in front of him. I'm leaving to find him. Can I borrow your car?"

"Meet me by my car, and will explain to Megan."

Driving out of the Honor Banquet Hall parking lot wasn't possible.

"That scum bastard Jack flattened my tire. I'll call for a tow truck.

Go inside and ask one of our friends to drive you home, and meet you there as soon as possible."

"Gabriella, you are a lifesaver."

"Call David and tell him to wait for you to explain."

"No answer. Davide must have turned off his phone."

"Try sending a text."

I'm getting increasingly anxious and worried by the minute.

"Gabriella, he is not answering. So why doesn't he answer?"

"You will be home in less than an hour."

She shouted, "his car is not here. Stop the car."

Suzanne jumped out and ran straight into their bedroom. His laptop, briefcase, suitcase, and garment bag were missing. Empty wooden hangers were what she feared.

His new shirts and jeans, including his favorite suits and shoes, were gone.

She turned and ran to check their bathroom. David's toiletry bag and robe were missing.

She flopped onto the bathroom floor and burst into tears.

Gabriella said softly, "Suzie, your Sister just drove up. Hear her now coming up the stairs."

Crying for emotions not voiced. "Jacquie, he took some clothes and left. Why would he leave?"

Jacquie saw the empty hangers and the missing briefcase and laptop.

Gabriella gently said goodbye, "Not a word, Suzie. I'll keep this confidential.

Jacquie, you have my number. It will be all right, and I will call you in the morning to check on Suzie. Please don't hesitate to contact me if there is anything I can do to help."

"Thank you, love. I'll tell Suzanne."

Suzanne cried for a few more minutes before she could stop.

"Where is Gabriella?"

"She left a few minutes ago and said she would keep this confidential and check on you tomorrow.

Sis, sit with me. David and I spoke when he was on his way to the party. He sounded irritated and told me his nightmares were more frequent. When he entered the hall, his worst fear played out. Well, you can imagine his reaction."

"Why doesn't he answer his phone? David is not himself. His normal antidepressant does not have side effects of altering behavior."

"Sis, but the new antidepressant prescribed in Germany has serious side effects. A psychotic reaction to imagining the worst. David's jealousy and anger have intensified, and he has lost command of his emotions. For David, it must be terrifying, feelings no longer under his control. Susie, call Doctor Robert."

"No, please, don't want Senator Harrison to find out before the election. She has more than enough on her plate. He wants to keep this confidential to protect his reputation. We will find a doctor who doesn't know me."

"Sis, your name and face are all over the news. You have been with the Senator for over ten years."

"Did you look for a note?"

"Yes, there was none."

"Look under your and his pillow."

Her anxiety intensified, "I already have no notes."

"Oh, Jacquie," barely able to contain her fear, "what should I do?"

"Try his dresser drawer, the one with socks and underwear. David used to hide presents for me, assuming a man's underwear drawer is the best hiding place."

"Really?"

"No, frightened for him too, and want to lighten the stress, but my Irish wit is failing me."

Suzanne smiled. Jacquie's joking meant somehow it would be okay.

"Jacquie can't get it without permission. We respect each other's privacy. And he still hides gifts there."

"If he didn't want you to find and read, he would not have placed it under his socks. He put it in a place I would tell you to look."

Suzie found an envelope with her name in David's handwriting.

A quivering voice,

"Sis, afraid it's a goodbye letter. I can't, Jacquie. Please read this for me."

"Before I do, hold on to my hands. Never have a sugar-coated reality or give you false hope. Breathe in and out. That's good. Now sit with me on the sofa."

"Jacquie, will it be all right?"

"Suzie, don't know, wish I did, but trust you are in his heart. Leaving you no matter what it says to you now, trust his letter will provide you with answers.

You gave David love and tenderness. Your hearts are intertwined, there is no way to tell where his ends and yours begins."

"And I gave him sex better than you."

Jacquie and Suzanne stared at each other and burst out laughing.

"I don't know why I said that."

"Sis, I know why. You want to keep your faith and hope alive. I love your sense of humor."

"Jacquie, afraid of what he wrote in his letter."

"Take my hand, Suzie. Try not to squeeze too hard."

They both smiled and took a deep breath.

Jacquie opened the envelope, which contained two pages, and started to read.

'Dear Suzanne, my Angel,

You soothed me back to sleep, but my demons started to torment me in dreams with more frequency. Our hearts beat in sync, but if you are reading this, I'm afraid I lost control over my emotions and went off to heal. Nightmares have gotten much worse.

My beautiful Angel, each time we watched *Lord of the Rings*, we kissed when Arwen said, 'If you trust nothing else, trust us.' Love, I also want you to hear 'to that I hold,' as our love for each other is everlasting.

How would it be possible to read your letter through my tears if you left me? Suzie, I'd weep for our love.

Sweetheart, my love for you enables me to find a way back to our lives. Unfortunately, it will take time to emerge from my despair. There are no quick cures.

I'm relieved that you and Jacquie will be able to hearten Anabelle, as she won't understand why I left. She needs reassurance and reminders of how much I love and already miss her. So don't have to worry.

Suzie, now you're asking yourself. Then why did you leave, David? I can only answer. It was necessary to find my way back to you. Because I have no control over my emotions, jealousy surrounds me in a shroud of blue darkness. Trust you understand.

Thank God your natural tendency is to radiate love and joy in life. Sweetheart, I want to be by your side as much as you want to be by my side.

Seeing me sinking deeper into the blues each day would upset you more. I would rather get lost in your blue eyes to soften my despair. Trust what I am saying is best for you. Not running away and will heal once and for all. Pray to God, this will not end us.

Ironically, the din of New York will calmly nurse me back to mental health. How could I live with myself if my actions hurt you? You would forgive me, but I could not forgive myself.

I need time. Please don't come after me. Let me restore my life on my own. I trust that I will find a way back to our lives.

Promise to send a text message asking you to come to me when I have conquered what now torments me day and night. I feel I have lost

myself. Tears drop from my eyes onto this
letter....

My heart cannot connect to feelings except
anger, jealousy, and emotional pain. Searching
for a way back to you. I have no answers for you,
but I will never leave you.

Please take Jacquie's hand, as it will bring
comfort to both of you. It's reassuring to know
you aren't alone. But it was Hobson's choice. If I
stay, I will drive you away with my jealousy. If I
leave, you will find another love. This isn't true
intellectually, but my heart is hidden, and I can
no longer see.

Have recently had suicidal thoughts.
Leaving me means you're going into another
man's arms. Just having this thought terrifies
me. Probably a severe side effect of the
medication. It doesn't matter. I would never hurt
you by taking my life, nor Jacquie's, or my
sweetpea.

You have an essential job you love. Taking
care of me is too much of a burden. As it risks
robbing you of every moment of your life. Even
though it may be hard to concentrate, it would
help me know that it has not entirely disrupted
your life.

Angel, the very thing you taught me to do—
stop and reflect before acting and speaking, and
not act and speak from emotions, I have done.
Although I am in New York, I can still heal. But
I've tears because I'm not convinced I've done
the right thing.

Suzanne, I allowed myself to lose this fight
because I f*cked up and mixed antidepressants,
believing I'd get better faster. This was not
intelligent and dangerous, but it reduced the
severity of my depression. Then, side effects
rebounded with a vengeance. And was sent to
Dante's hell, all hope was left behind.

Oh, Suzanne, please forgive me. I had no
choice. Continuing with your work will be
challenging, but it is essential. You have a
senator running to get elected as President.

I will feel relieved if you move on with your
life, knowing you are safe and have your Sisters
and my love. Trust you are right here in my
heart.

I will never stop loving you. How do I
exorcize you from my life? Not possible. My life is
tightly intertwined with yours; a bridge of love
binds us.

This is me stripped down to my fear. Trying to face my fear of losing you, which is why I am weeping, and no one hears but you.

Angel, don't judge me harshly when reading this. I love you too much to lose you by not healing. My worst nightmare is failing you, not the faux suffering created by jealousy. We're never going to let go of our love. Keep your trust in us.

Jacquie, I apologize if I said anything or if my tone upset you. I upset you, dear friend, but you would never admit that.

Ended the call abruptly before getting entirely out of control.

Jacquie, don't want forgiveness because you didn't hear any affront, as it was in my head. Did that sound right?

Sweetheart, ask Jacquie, or if you are reading this together, love, tell the love of your heart, my Sweetpea, the truth. She doesn't need details until she is old enough, just a watered-down version. Daddy went to New York to rest.

I will send her many postcards, letters, books, New York chachkas, toys, and things.

Suzie, trust me, I had no choice. What else could I have done? I hated myself for putting you through this. Not that I fear you could not be strong, but I fear my weakness. Anger and jealousy are insidious opposite sides of the blues. Cannot and will not have my Angel, whom I adore and cherish, cope with my flailing to find a light in a circular tunnel.

Have now run out of words and placed this letter in my sock and underwear drawer. Jacquie figured out that anything I wanted her to find would be there.

If you are reading this, she already has. Please, Angel, know this is a devastating emotional decision for us. I go off to heal and take you with me in my heart.

Counterintuitive, intense emotional pain will motivate me to find peace of mind. Then I can give you all the love and life you deserve.

Your Loving David.'

Suzanne cried, "Oh dear lord, Sis, I can't soothe his heart. Why didn't he text me that he was safe?"

"Suzie, there is a second page. It is a love letter to you."

'My Dearest Angel,

The reasons for my abrupt departure are unclear. My decision was emotional and not rational. I fixate on imagining you in the arms of another man. Suzanne, don't want you to explain. Nothing said could take away jealousy and the image I'm obsessed with. Why me?

Of all men who would love you, they could not love you as much as I. Reasoning in my heart is blocked as black-blue depression dominates my emotions. My head felt wrapped in the darkness of dejection, and it blinded me. Realize it is my weakness, and I am ashamed if I am not by your side, protecting you. My God, if someone forced himself on you and turned away my Angel, how could I ever make it up to you? My heart believes and trusts you with my life.

Please don't be annoyed with me.

Not leaving you, would not know how. Instead, ran away from myself. I have friends, a job, a place to live in New York City, and therapy. Still, this madness torments me; I run to hide it from you, Annabelle, Jacqueline, Jazmine, Megan, Victoria, Noreen, Jessica, your mom, and Nana, but not so much from and Annabelle, Jacqueline, Jazmine, Megan, Victoria, Noreen, Jessica, your mom, and Nana, and not so much your dad.

When healed, I'll come back to you, not if, not maybe, but when I come back to you, we shall be happy.

Sweetheart, this is a storm of my own making. I win my struggle when I stop images haunting me day and night. It is the only way to burn out my jealousy, as painful as it is to be apart. Please, let me win my fight and find a way out of a blue sinkhole.

For any suicidal thoughts, promise to seek immediate help. The idea of never seeing you again is intolerable. However, my greatest fear is that you will be angry with me. Someone will take you into their arms, and I will lose you forever. If I stayed, my jealousy would drive you away, and I would lose you.

Please do not go looking for me; I need you to promise that you will think of yourself first.

I cannot guarantee anything, except that I'll never stop loving and searching for a way back to you. Kiss Jacquie for me and hug her every chance you get. Both of you will care for each other and keep strong.

Please tell her not to be upset with me. Tell her how much I love her. She brought us together and helped me become more thoughtful about life. Tell her I am so sorry that I failed her and you. I promise you, I will find my way back to you.

When I wake, you will be my first and last thought before closing my eyes at night. The stains on my letter are my tears of weeping for you.

I love you beyond what any person could love another.

Don't cry – let me for both of us.

Your David, who is forever in love with you.'

Suzanne's tears slowly rolled down both sides of her face. She said nothing and handed Jacquie my letter to read.

Jacquie took many tissues to get through reading, and between the two of them, they emptied half a box.

"Suzie, David sent you a reassurance of hope because he still has a sense of humor. Written in his memoir, should the last light of humor go out, I would be afraid of taking my life."

"How can you be convinced? Didn't find any hope in David's words except to reassure me to remain strong and trust our love. But he almost lost his fight for his life. Jacquie, couldn't live if I had lost him. Why tell me why? You know him as well as I do? What did you read that I didn't see?"

"Sis, not sure why. I also read about the despair in his struggle to stay alive, but he could not yet know how. David signaled he would find a way back to you."

"I want to have faith that there is a message. What did you read that I didn't pick up? You sound so confident and worried at the same time. Upset even with our deep love, David doesn't let me be by his side. I feel helpless and numb."

"Suzie, reread this and remember what you said as you arrived at Woodland Cottage."

"Can't remember! Why can't I remember?"

"Hold my hand, don't say anything; if you have to read it more than once, it's okay."

'...I run to hide it from you and Annabelle, Jacqueline, Jazmine, Megan, Victoria, Noreen, Jessica, your mom, and Nana, and not so much your dad.'

"Oh my God, Jacquie, I didn't see this the first time, David in a dark blue episode, but his New York sarcastic wit is a sign to me."

"The same as placing this note under his underwear. David wanted you to find it."

"Suzie, *not so much your dad?* Now, remember what you said."

"We parked in front of the garages, and turned to him. My father will love you once he gets over his anger sleeping with his first-born daughter, and soon his last-born."

"Sis, he is creative and intelligent with a keen, sarcastic wit and sense of humor. You have now read so much of his writing, knowing he writes layer upon layer and adds a thread of himself to everything he writes. Only you and I understand his complex multilayer constructions of humor to convey messages."

"Jacquie, oh, thank God for you. I love you. Of the two pages, he said everything he trusted I would see as hope. Five simple, one-syllable words: 'Not so much your dad.'"

For dinner, both managed to eat a small salad.

"Do you want me to be with you tonight?"

"Jacquie, I can't sleep in our bed until we are back together."

"Where then?"

"The family room's doors can be closed, and we can sleep on the sofa in front of the large fireplace."

"Remember when you and I were wee children?

During a winter snowstorm, you want to hear the fireplace crackling. We slept under an oversized down comforter with our heads side by side. Our pillows are on the armrest with our legs wrapped around each other.

Do you want to watch a movie?"

"*The Fellowship of the Ring.*"

"Suzanne, promise to keep looking for David. He returned to New York and will find work at the UN. He has childhood friends who would look after him. David will send you a message to go to him, but his life won't be easy for now. He will find a place and, when depressed, isolate himself. Hope David visits friends to talk to about his feelings."

Weeks slowly passed into a month, which became two months, and into the middle of a new month. Suzanne slept on the sofa each night, holding his pillow, crying herself to sleep.

Jacquie was proofreading a speech Suzanne had written for the President-Elect when a text message appeared on Suzie's smartphone. Jacquie monitored for signs of David.

Jacquie excitedly said, "Suzanne, this is for you." Every time Jacquie read a text on her mobile, Suzanne hardly breathed.

165 2nd Ave, Apartment 4158. The doorman has your name.

"Jacquie, what should I do? Don't know what to do if he is still distressed and wants to end our relationship. Come with me to New York."

"Of course, but first, close your eyes and take a deep breath. Now, what does your heart tell you?"

Suzanne opened her eyes and ran up the stairs to pack.

"What should I wear? I will wear my hair down the way he loves. Should I pack casual or formal if he takes me to a Broadway play? Which shoes, and how much should I take? Will he want me to stay in New York?"

Three light knocks on her bedroom door. "Come in, Megan. It's open."

Suzie has never seen Megan as animated. I just got this letter. The return address is 165 2nd Ave, Apartment 4158, from David, in his handwriting."

"Jacquie, too nervous about opening it."

Jacquie looked inside and handed her Sister the envelope.

Inside, two tickets to a Tony Award-winning Broadway play. Imperial Theatre, Saturday evening show, center orchestra seats.

"Well, you know you must pack a dress for a play. Love, there is a letter here, too. Suzanne, do you want me to read this? Megan, get comfortable as David gets wordy."

Dear Suzie,

My feelings, intentions, and thoughts are the songs you sang to me.

I Love You. Please play our CD, which was made for our intimate dinners. I hope our songs can help alleviate the sorrow I caused. Our song. "The First Time Ever I Saw Your Face, "I Want To Know What Love Is, and Baby Don't Go. It's Cold Outside."

Lost all connections to reality when you were with another man dancing. Afraid had driven you away. Please forgive me for not checking to see if you were safe, or for allowing you to talk to me and calm my unfounded fears. Don't need or want an explanation.

Living in New York without you has become bleaker and intolerable because of an unfounded fear of losing you.

My heart was shredded, and I searched but couldn't find you anywhere. Blinded by jealousy and anger, not of your making. Yes, there are tears in my eyes., I didn't want to lose sight of our love.

Needed time to completely heal, so we could be together again.

My love never diminished. In fact, it deepened. Left because I needed to purge the last of my demons, which kept me jealous and prevented healing. I was worried that you would not come when I sent you a text message.

Preparing a soft landing for your arrival. I love you and want us to take a more profound step to deepen our commitment to our romantic relationship. Look to your heart for the path back to me.

Angel, you made our dream come true.

Cried and cursed the Gods for this affliction. Fought day and night through therapy and antidepressants until I reached a place where I found my way back to our life together.

Faith speaks to me of your desire to come to New York, yet you are afraid you won't.

Overwhelmingly in love, I will follow you and shower you with red rose petals. Place a sign at the end of our hallway.

My Irish Angel, you caught my breath and captured my soul when our eyes first met. I'm anxious to tell you that I dropped the two $50 bills and asked the Senator to donate them to the charity of her choice.

My love for you is unbreakable. You have taught me what this means.

Your beloved, David.'

"Today is Tuesday, and the play is in four days.

David wanted to leave to go to New York. David needed time to be apart from me to heal. Remember Jacquie? I said it was my dream to see a Broadway play. I know now it will be all right."

"That's right, JFK, the first available flight in First Class, oh excellent Red Eye leaving SFO to JFK arriving tomorrow, for my Sister. Do you have a flight leaving from Sacramento, Red Eye? Great, what is the departure time? Departing tonight at 11:05 pm non-stop, arriving at 7:10 am, Wednesday?

Can I book a seat now, window, First Class? I will charge it to my Platinum credit card. Does she need to bring my credit card? Just her California Real ID-compliant driver's license and the reservation confirmation number you will email to her. Her ticket will be waiting at the counter. Perfect, she will take that flight. Thank you."

"Okay, Suzie, we have 14 hours before you need to be at the departure gate. Let's get you packed."

Thirteen
New York, New York

"If I can make it there, I can make it anywhere."

"I can never read all the books I want; I can never be all the people I want and live all the lives I want. I can never train myself in all the skills I want. And why do I want? I want to live and feel all the shades, tones, and variations of mental and physical experiences possible in my life. And I am horribly limited." Sylvia Plath

"Angel, growing up in New York, was an education on creating opportunities for a meaningful life.

However, opportunities and achieving such dreams were not readily available on either side of *The Cross Bronx Expressway*. International travel at an early age made me more conscious of more cultures, more inclusive than my hometown.'

Immediately, Suzie felt an overwhelming surge of people's energy as Suzie stepped off the NYC Express bus from JFK airport to Grand Central Station at Lexington Avenue and 42nd Street.

Suzanne finally understood what David meant about the city's vitality. A flow of hundreds of people walking down well-known New York City avenues or crossing streets, never bumping into each other. No one looked at the eyes of a passing stranger, content with the person they were with or where they were going.

David lives close to the United Nations, where people from around the world pass each other. Governmental Leaders, Ministers of Parliament, and Ambassadors, yet not one native city dweller seemed to care.

New Yorkers grumble, but at the end of the day, reluctantly accept the inconvenience of a Diplomat using their privilege and taking advantage when driving or parking. Except for a few days each September, streets get blocked off when the U.S. President and world leaders arrive to speak at the United Nations.

City dwellers love to (kvetch) complain to each other. The intensity of their words mirrors the chaos affecting their lives.

New Yorkers often encounter well-known individuals frequently. It is an unspoken rule to honor their privacy. Not to mention celebrities who live in Manhattan. They're just part of the city's cultural identity.

Walking those same streets in Manhattan has become crystal clear to Suzie why people love New York City. David acknowledges New Yorkers are friendly because he is one of the 8 million. New Yorkers are misperceived as rude or boastful. Everything you may want in New York was not arrogance but pride.

'Angel, if you don't speak up and walk fast and push through, you can't walk down streets or get on subway cars or buses during rush hours.'

This metropolis nurtured David as a boy and gave him a New York state of mind. I'm looking forward to seeing, hearing, and experiencing everything the city has to offer.

People in this city have shown kindness by helping strangers and neighbors. But, on the other hand, people who are softer-spoken could become rude in a friendlier, less populated town. For example, 'bless your heart, is the Southern way to politely dismiss you."

'Love, New Yorkers want to be perceived as friendly. Frankly, New Yorkers' nature is gregarious. Strangers inelegantly ask where I was born to confirm their guesses about my accent. So I use humor as a golden thread to keep hearts open. At least temporarily.

In New York City, it is prudent not to look others in the eyes because you must protect yourself emotionally from a sudden unwelcome interest in knowing why. It is sensible not to indicate you are looking with contempt. 'What are you looking at?' It is the best outcome. It could be much worse. New people to the city are not always warned to avoid directly looking into a person's eyes when they visit the city.'

David speaks to strangers wherever he is and thus meets interesting and kindhearted people worldwide.

During a rare blackout or a severe weather event, this city comes alive as strangers direct traffic and ensure people are safe and have food to eat, which is given away for free. It's hard to comprehend if you don't live in this crazy, wonderful city. Of course, people care. It's just that New Yorkers only talk to other New Yorkers and are not accustomed to talking to people brought up in a more polite culture.

Walked into a small neighborhood bodega, David's favorite grocery for its welcoming conviviality, to buy a Chocolate Cherry soda. I'm not surprised people actually talked to each other. David is friends with local shop owners, waitresses, and chefs at his favorite restaurants. An animated middle-aged woman who owns the Bodega is a friend of David.

'How is your mom? Haven't seen her in a while. Is everyone good? Don't worry. The gourmet specialty food ordered for your daughter's wedding will arrive on time.' And, of course, passionately debating in typical New York style about the *Yankees, Mets, Knicks, Giants,* and *Jets.*

In a city full of life, people share the same concerns as those of any other town. Or, for that matter, anywhere in the world.

David's school of life's lessons were gained growing up in this city throughout childhood and adolescence.

New York City, which purportedly never slept even with New York's multiple tempting cultural distractions, could wait. Nothing beckoned me except being with my

David. Strolling in the sun's warmth down Second Avenue, filled with hope for my future with David, was a good sign.

'Suzie, you can get anything from anywhere when you come to New York. So don't pack a large suitcase. Instead, go shopping in Herald Square or treat yourself and shop on Fifth Avenue.'

David prepared me for a future trip to his hometown.

In the short time it took to walk to the building on Second Avenue, she saw hundreds of people, each walking purposefully to different locations. So many things to experience. Each person had their own story to tell. However, Suzie simply intended to understand why New Yorkers take pride in their city.

Lost in contemplation about New York's sense of aliveness, suddenly found myself standing under a canopy at Williams Plaza, 165 Second Avenue, a twenty-story apartment building.

Placed her handbag, garment bag, and suitcase down and took a deep breath as the doorman opened magnificent brass and glass doors.

Living in a New York doorman building, it reassured me that David was living in a safe and secure place.

"Good Morning. Is Dr. David Benjamin Bradley home? He is expecting me."

"You must be Miss Suzanne. Welcome to New York City. I am Mr. Charles.

Yes, Miss, he left word to ensure you are comfortable and safe until he arrives home. Miss Suzanne, David, is currently at work and will be home early this evening. I must have seen over two dozen of your photos. He shows me every chance he gets."

David took the time to bring our photo album. As he wrote, he took me with him.

"Dr. David showed you our photos?"

"Yes, Miss Suzanne, he said he had these photos as an emotional bond to his angel.

Oh, and he has told me I am David. He never uses Doctor."

"I'm sorry I upset you. David told me that if you cry, they are called tears. Do you understand what that means?"

"It means he loves me."

"Never met anyone like David, and I see why you missed him. That is saying a lot in this city."

"He would come to talk when I was on the night shift, when he couldn't sleep. We talked for hours. I am going on and on, and you must be tired. David left something for you that I'm supposed to give you. I will retrieve it, as it will only take a minute. Here are your keys and my direct telephone number to reach me if you need anything."

"He left this bag and told me to make sure it's the first thing to give you, and he is a Meshugana; I Love New York T-Shirt."

"David said for me to tell you to look at the back of the T-shirt, but he bought the wrong size."

Suzanne took the T-shirt out of the bag.

"You see what I mean? It's an XL size."

Suzanne turned over the T-shirt.

Large Lavender and Blue Letters, New York Loves Suzanne.

"Mr. Charles, he got the right size. It's perfect."

"Fresh as last night, kept them in the staff refrigerator. They're a dozen red roses. He asked me what kind to buy, and when I said Red Roses, 'Yes, of course, her favorite flower.' And handed me a fifty-dollar tip.

Your man always surprises me. For sure, Miss Suzanne, David is one of a kind. I am sorry for being forward. He told me about you and would cry, saying, 'Charles, would she come if I called her? He was miserable the day he arrived, but had become a new man for the last few weeks.

Miss Suzanne, when a mother and her baby needed assistance, David was there before me, no matter the time of night. Her baby was sick, so David stayed awake in the living room watching over the baby because her husband was away. She was afraid to be alone with the baby if she needed a doctor or to go to a hospital. No person in this apartment building doesn't appreciate your David's random acts of kindness."

"Mr. Charles, thank you for telling me."

"Miss Suzanne, you have access to two elevators. One opens in front of the apartment door. This second key allows you to bypass the entrance and proceed directly into the Penthouse. A perk of having your elevator open in front of or in your penthouse is that it provides an additional layer of security.

He said something the new President would appreciate. But Miss Suzanne was evasive and would not explain. Mr. Charles, read somewhere that the President likes security."

"Mr. Charles, David was protecting my privacy. He meant my job at the White House."

"Miss Suzanne thought that was what he meant. However, I respected Mr. David for wanting to be just a person. Does this make sense to you?"

"More than you would realize."

"Mr. David put fresh fruits and vegetables in the fridge, and everything else you and David may need to prepare meals.

He told me that more than three-fourths of the closet is empty, and a separate dresser for you. David will arrive home by 7 p.m. He requested that I make a reservation at Evergreen, his favorite Chinese restaurant, for tomorrow night. I was to change the restaurant if you had a different preference."

"No, that's perfect. Thank you very much, Mr. Charles," and reached into her handbag and placed a fifty-dollar bill into his hand.

"Go raibh maith agat."

Mr. Charles knew I would understand that it was Irish for thank you.

"After all, it's my job to know how to say thank you in different languages. The United Nations is only ten blocks and one avenue over."

"When he first moved in, he asked, 'Can you get me a second set of keys?'

'Dr. David?'

'No, just David.'

'Are you having another person move in with you now, or can it wait a day or two? I like my new tenants' family to feel welcomed and comfortable.'

"Miss Suzanne, I am sixty, a wife for 35 years, and two grown girls with their children. Throughout my lifetime, I've witnessed a wide range of emotions; David expressed hope and tears, willing them not to fall."

As I handed him the extra set of keys, 'Mr. David, if you like, can keep them in a locked key box, so you never have to worry if you are not home.'

Miss Suzanne, he handed me back the keys."

'Good idea. Saving them for my angelic lady for when she arrives.'

Thought this was for his lover, the way he mentioned his lady. We became friends from that day on."

"David said that?" Her eyes started to well up again.

'Five new tissue boxes, Mr. Charles. Can you order them and have them delivered no later than Tuesday?'

'Isn't five boxes a lot of tissues?'

'Mr. Charles, there will be two of us.'

"You both sure are all that, and once more, welcome to New York, Miss Suzanne. Happy you two are finally together. My wife kept asking if you had arrived. Even my two daughters wondered. Don't hesitate to call me if you need anything."

Suzanne set her luggage down inside the apartment next to the front door.

Mr. Charles boasted that this was the most oversized apartment in the building. The building owner 75 years ago had blueprints drawn up to create a spacious penthouse for his large family.

She started exploring David's apartment and became speechless, overcome with emotion. His mom would say 'Verklempt,' though the phrase loses its full impact in translation from Yiddish. David shared about the overwhelming feeling the first time I took him to my home.

Standing in the foyer of his apartment, now understood how he felt. An envelope contained a note from my beloved.

Dearest Suzie, I'm happy you are finally here. Anything you want to change or add to your dream New York apartment, you have carte blanche.

The 7,500 sq ft apartment and penthouse have oak hardwood floors, thick shag carpets, and marble countertops. A famous chef designed the kitchen. Jaz will love cooking here. Wanted to have plenty of room for your family, with a formal dining room, den, two offices, a nursery, two family rooms, four full bathrooms, and eight bedrooms, each with large windows.

Plus, our primary bedroom has a panoramic view of the East River. A definite for you and me is a fireplace in the living room, family room, and bedroom. And Suzie, this apartment is rent-controlled because it is in an older building.

A graceful, curved stairway with a mahogany banister led up to the second floor and another to the third level. From the second floor, you could look down into the living room. An elegant straight banister ended at a window facing the East River. Picture David in his tuxedo, and me in my formal gown, walking downstairs, my right hand touching the banister.

Easy access to a private elevator in the lobby led straight to the third level. In effect, it has a self-contained apartment.

Under the stairs, a spandrel opened to a fully stocked pantry galley, including a wine rack with several of my sisters and my favorite wines.

On the second floor was a large hallway, a fifteen-foot-wide space running the length of the apartment. A touch of elegance was added with a round antique end table, Tiffany lamp, and loveseat.

The primary bedroom's tall windows have a ledge wide enough to lie on pillows. Ceiling-to-floor drapes, once shown to David, would be perfect. A room-sized walk-in closet, a twelve-foot-high ceiling, and two steps up to a magnificent king-sized romantic canopy bed.

A bedroom door opened to a full-size bathroom with a separate glass-enclosed shower with double glass doors.

The bathroom was designed with romance in mind, including a European bidet and two sink countertops. Loved the oyster colored large jacuzzi bathtub with a handheld showerhead featuring multiple settings. A window at eye level, so when you are in the tub at night, there is a stunning view of the city lights.

The bathroom leads to a family room, designed for cozy movie nights, with an LED television and soundbar speakers in each corner. A comfy sofa chair, the same as in our bedroom at Woodland Cottage, an oversized leather sofa with plenty of room to lie side by side. Four people could comfortably watch a movie or use it as an alternative sleeping place.

Astonished, with tears of joy, I walked back into the bedroom. At first, I didn't notice that against the wall was a tall mahogany bookcase. Books were our favorites. One book had my name and David's name on the book spine, and the title was "Baby Nursery, the Room Down the Hall." Did David author another book? Excited to take it off the shelf to read later.

I could only pull the book out six inches, and with a click, the bookcase swung open. A beam of sunlight lit up the room. Tears welled up. Not able to utter a word, just sobs of joy.

This room was partially furnished with a baby's crib, a changing table, and a comfortable rocking chair. A view of the East River, a room waiting for its new occupant.

In a wooden frame, in calligraphy, "The Room Down the Hall - Baby Nursery." Suzanne reached for more tissues.

Remember the Secret of Childhood

You wander the world in your imagination as it gradually reveals its secrets. So you won't be caught unaware. Faith is your guide.

You create a magical land and travel wherever your imagination takes you.

The famous storybook, Kings and Queens, greets you to tell you their stories. Even little boy Blue's friends, Jack and Jill, and the little old lady and her children, who live in a shoe, smile as you play together in laughter. Cinderella looks for her lost glass shoe, and the Fairy Godmother showers you with her fairy powder.

Your road map to life is locked away in your world of imagination, and my beloved baby, you have the key.

If you have questions, teachers and parents can help you find answers. Perhaps in your imagination, ask Peter Pan the way "to the third star on the left," and he says you are already there. And Tinker Bell embraces you with her unbounded love.

In your mind's eye of wonder, you view the world from a unique vantage point. You sail the ocean blue all day and explore Saturn's rings and moons before bedtime.

Sandcastles built in the air are where your hopes are realized; you find your way when you have the secret. Your dreams can come true. Ask the Blue Wizard.

Desires from your dreams give you courage. All of your life starts over a rainbow, where bluebirds fly.

The door to this magical land will open; the key is your imagination.

Love

Mom and Dad

Suzie hoped David meant to start our family. Her thoughts turned to the first day she showed him the room down the hall at Woodland Cottage.

'Love, this room can show her the secret. A room of imagination where a baby can be nurtured and loved.'

Walked out of the room at the end of the hall, hand in hand. Kissed me gently on the lips, and tears filled my eyes. Surprised and so happy, a baby's nursery touched him so profoundly.

Noticing another tall mahogany bookcase filled with children's books, David read as a child, children's books he wrote, a book of nursery rhymes, and some teddy bears.

Emotions with no words were David's soft landing. She opened doors you could only enter from the landing, David's office, Annabelle's bedroom, two rooms that could become additional bedrooms, and a magnificent library with a king-size sleeper sofa. Sat down on the top step and cried tears of delight.

'Jacquie, is it going to be okay?'

'Suzanne, expect the unexpected, don't start imagining a worst-case scenario. You and David are beginning a new chapter of your romance, continuing your love.'

Sitting on the stairs, an unexpected impulse led her to look at the wooden bookcase a second time. At the top of the right side of the shelf, she noticed the title of a book, *Suzanne Siobhan Brooke*. Anticipating the unexpected, she pulled the book lever down. With a click, the bookcase swung open.

Tears prevented her from uttering a word. Oh, dear David. My office includes a desk, the same office chair, file cabinets, connections for three phones, and ample space for whatever I need. Shared my wishes as we rode to Jacquie's and Jaz's for dinner.

'Love, always wanted my home office next to our baby's nursery to keep our baby close to me when I work.

My office requires top-secret security for confidential calls and soundproofing for the President's video conferences. Or when receiving calls from the White House.

Could it be possible for my dream of having our New York apartment to come true?'

David asked what I would want.

'Is that all? Anything else?'

'I'm being silly. It is just a dream.'

David believes dreams are just doors that open a heart's desire.

'Remember, *Tinker Bell* is alive because children believe. Your only job is to keep dreaming and believing, the rest is for you to do.'

'Even the most impossible dream?'

'Particularly, the impossible dream.'

David wrote he had found the perfect office for me.

'Love, your office has been made soundproof with double-paned windows and soundproof curtains.

Angel, this room was once a recording studio. The reason for over-the-top soundproofing is that our neighbors are famous. Prior tenants were the children of a famous rock and roll singer, and, together with their mother, would jam and make recordings.

Soundproofing was already in place, and they went overboard, going to the extent of triple-soundproofing. Everything is copasetic, a secure place for your work.'

Sitting on his hospital bed when he was recovering from two gunshot wounds, we talked about my dream becoming our reality.

An audible "Dear Lord," precisely my dream apartment in New York.

She went to retrieve her luggage and carried it up the stairs into the bedroom. Hadn't yet noticed the envelope on the pillow before. She slid the sealed envelope open with her fingernail.

'Angel, not sure of the order, you will discover things. Please, love, let me show you the rest of the apartment together. Save the downstairs and third level for us.

It's just a feeling; the beautiful staircase is irresistible, and I bet you started upstairs on the second floor.

Intuition reassures me we are ok, and you are happy you came to New York. Couldn't wait for you to arrive. Love, two and a half months to catch up. At long last, I plan a joyful visit for you when you come to New York. A Broadway play and a ride to my childhood neighborhood to start your long-awaited introduction to the *Big Apple*.

A heartfelt yearning to hear your lyrical brogue. My wish once again is to laugh with you and kiss you while we make love day and night. Once again, hear your melodious singing while we jog, cook meals, or walk hand in hand. Mind you, we love our mind-blowing sex, but it was your love I ache for. You are loved and cherished.

Since I arrived in New York, I have designed a home for us every free moment, fighting through heartache and tears. For your first time in New York, it is intended for you to walk into one of your dreams, especially an impossible one. The empty spaces, walls, kitchen, and bedrooms are left for you to decorate your New York home with your artistic, creative style. Your wish has come true. We will be together now, living in New York.

Suzie, what would New York be without its famous foods?

A fully packed refrigerator, our favorite freshly made bread from the local bakery, different kinds of juice, a six-pack of chocolate cherry sodas, and Chinese food from Chinatown. Yes, fresh fish from the New Fulton Fish Market, homemade pasta from Little Italy, and your favorite fresh vegetables and fruits, from a farmer's market on Long Island. Last night, purchased a large DS pizza from my favorite pizzeria in The Bronx.

Looking forward to eating meals together again.

Of course, your favorite wines, with one chilled in the refrigerator.

Blue Eye Lady, I love you. Your David, forever in your heart.'

"David, dear David, you put your love into everything, even the food."

A blue and white porcelain vase stood in the middle of the dining room table, the same Chinese design that had been shown to David from a Home Decorating catalog. Seemed not to be paying attention to the vase but staring at my boobs. 'Sweetheart, your eyes missed the vase. Smiled like a little boy caught looking up a girl's skirt.'

'What?'

'The Chinese vase would look good in our bedroom.'

'Are you giving me a hint you are horny?'

'No, truly it would, and yeah, I am horny.'

'Well?'

Kissed me, touched my leg, and slowly moved his hand closer to the top of my panties. We cuddled, lying in front of him while his hands gently massaged my breasts.

'Angel, turn and look at me, so I can start kissing you from the top of your face to your lips and bring you to orgasm.'

David's eyes started to wander. 'Love, where did you go?'

'To Manhattan.'

With the same vase, he imagined our future New York apartment for the two of us.

Suzanne prepared her roses and lifted the white and blue Chinese porcelain vase to take to the sink when an envelope with a business-sized card fell onto the dining table. *'Look behind you.'*

The marble counter only had what you expected: the same mixer he saw in Jaz's kitchen, a six-slot toaster large enough for bagels, a coffee maker, a microwave, a wooden walnut breadbox with a glass window,, the same mixer he saw in Jaz's kitchen, a six-slot toaster, large enough for bagels, a coffee maker, a microwave, a wooden walnut breadbox with a glass window, and a blender.

David shared nostalgia with his father on hot summer nights in the Bronx. His dad would call him into the kitchen. He let David help by holding the lid and turning the blender on to make his favorite chocolate ice cream milkshake.

Dearest David, how did I miss my favorite New York Rye bread, bagels, challah, and a chocolate babka? Ordered from New York, and it was mustard, never mayonnaise.

Opened the glass door of a large wooden bread box and immediately saw a beautifully wrapped package in my favorite colors of blue and lavender.

After placing my roses on the bedroom dresser, I sat in the living room. Anxious to open a small velvet box.

Shit left my tissues somewhere.

Inside was a heart-shaped 18k gold locket with a picture of us. David kept his promise to keep me in his heart.

A glass wall in the living room heightened my love of the apartment. Suzanne became aware of the living room window's pleated linen drapery filtering the setting sun's rays.

As she turned, she saw a real wood-burning fireplace with a marble mantel for the first time.

Prayed each night for David to propose for two and a half months, but we have been apart. Yet this apartment was made to order for our relationship. David would want to return to California and have this as our second home, no matter where we lived, as long as we were together. Could we live here for part of the year? Should I ask him?

I hadn't eaten except on the plane, so I went into the kitchen to make lunch. There were still seven hours before David would come home.

After eating a tomato and egg bagel sandwich, I took a refreshing hot shower. Curious to see what is on David's bookshelf in the downstairs living room. There are dozens of our favorite books and many on our must-read list.

Running her fingers over the titles, recognized her favorites and stopped at Harmony and Music Within, David's memoir.

Suzanne had not read the hardbound copy, which had a beautiful cover jacket, David's author photo on the back cover, along with a Five Star review and praise from well-known authors. Sitting down to read, David knew I would need many tissues. Five boxes now didn't seem like a lot.

The first book of the first printing of his memoir. Delicately, as not to bend the pages, David's pet peeve opened to the dedication page.

Dedicated to Suzanne,

My Angel, lover, muse, confidant, and best friend.

I now know what love is because of you.

Placed a box of tissues next to me and started to read.

Weary from a lack of sleep for the last 24 hours, my eyes decided they had had enough and closed. The book lay open across my chest. Before sleep took over, I pondered what to say first to David.

Fell asleep in mid-thought and dreamt of David.

"Angel," a delicate kiss on my lips. David held me in his arms with tenderness and fondness, and when his lips were free, "Suzie, I Love You," and he placed his lips on mine again.

"This feels too real to be a dream."

"Open the bluest blue eyes. It's not a dream. I'm here."

"David! Oh, my dear sweet love, missed you so much."

He stayed on top and kissed me; our mouths blended into one.

We remained in a passionate embrace. Did not want David to stop.

"Angel pondered what to say once we were in each other's arms. Finally, figured, kiss and let my love speak through kisses."

"David, yearning for your embrace, keep kissing and never let go."

"Suzanne overlooked saying something important."

"New York man?"

"Suzanne, don't want you to believe there was a relapse into the rude habits of New Yorkers."

"David?"

"With you asleep on the couch, I couldn't resist kissing *Cinderella* awake. But, Suzanne, have been apprehensive; I would never see you again if I couldn't purge my jealousy and depression. But I have, and you are here in my arms.

It's lovely to see you. How have you been?"

Started to cry, "Oh, David, your New York humor needs practice. David, will we be okay? Anxious and worried, you found a woman who nursed you back to health and would leave you."

"Suzanne, remember, trust me, trust us, and your vision of us since we first met. Sorry, our romance took a detour. Yet my love never wavered, and I missed you every second of every day, waking up and falling asleep thinking of you."

"Sweetheart, I've ached for you to hold me in your arms and make love to me. Promise me, you will never leave me again when trapped in the blues."

"Promise always stay with you. Love, we are back together. Can't guess what the future may have in store for us. No matter what, it will always be with you as you pursue your career."

"David, please don't do that again."

"Don't do what?"

"Hiding fears of losing me. It's safe to let your walls down. You have fought and won another bout of significant depression, made worse because of the horrific side effects of the meds.

You never have to be afraid of what lies ahead. Will always face it together. David, my faith in you kept my world from collapsing into despair."

"Oh, my love, how I have missed how you start in one direction toward upset, but switch back to your heart. Comforted you were not alone. You had Jacquie and your Sisters."

"David, my Sisters, send their love and impatiently wait to speak to you. Vickie, chosen as spokesperson, wants to tell you how much the girls missed you. They were worried and promised you would call them. They miss hearing your voice."

"Suzie, I missed them too, and Jaz and Megan. And will call each of them tomorrow morning."

"My love, Jacquie told me you already called Annabelle and have been calling her, she guessed multiple times a week. You ensured she had her smartphone, so you could stay in touch whenever you were on a trip. David, your Sweetpea would sometimes let something slip, only to reveal that it could only be coming from you. When Jacquie asked if she spoke to David, she said, "Mommy, daddy said, if you asked to say whoops."

"Well, can you imagine that? A Brooke girl that can keep a secret."

"Love, each time Annabelle spoke with you came to me and said, 'Aunt Suzie, don't worry.'"

"She would never say more than that, and Jacquie and I thought it was her creative imagination. It was natural for her to say loving things, and she got better at not saying too much after you called her.

Whenever a package of dolls, children's picture books, toys, or New York postcards arrived, my dear New York man kept her reassured that you were safe."

"Angel called Annabelle before leaving work today and told her you and I are coming home in a few weeks. And for her to inform her moms, aunts, Megan, Jessica, grandmother, and Nana. Reassured her that she would visit me soon. Subsequently, we would talk and hug, play, and kiss all day."

"Finally, we can start our family. Oh, David, this is the first time you didn't pull away when talking about having children."

"Walk with me, want to show you something."

"Never got the phrase out of my mind and heart. *The room down the hall.*"

"The first time I took you home."

"That is your home, not ours."

"Thought you were happy. You love Megan as your Sister. Jacquie is closer to you than you first met. Vickie loves and adores you and adopted you as her brother the day you arrived. Noreen and Jaz love and cherish you. They also embraced you as their brother."

"I am happy and love them more than I can express. Don't take their love for granted."

"You want to start a family. We talked about it, and you pull away each time we get closer to making plans."

"Not from my love to you."

"But a promise of love sealed by marriage scares you. David, I'm sorry, it's your fault. It is this blasted city. Starting to speak like you from emotions with no consequences for what you may feel. Because you tough New Yorkers, imagine no one gets wounded with words."

"When did you learn to speak like that?"

"Don't know. I love you so much, fighting with all my heart for us."

"No, don't mean that."

"Then what?"

"You switched from your Irish brogue to sound like you came from The Bronx. You said because you're tough New Yorkers, imagine no one gets wounded with words, with a New York accent."

We both stared at each other and started laughing.

"You said that to get me to laugh, didn't you?"

"Yes, I understand the depth of your feelings. I, too, share them with you."

"You have not listened, not to me, then you listen to me, but you don't trust yourself to listen because you know you want all I want."

"When you go into *Suzie Speak*, it makes sense. This is what I call love."

"You are impossible to engage in an argument."

Wrapped my arms around my love.

"David, what are you thinking?"

"Nothing, just listening to you. I missed you."

"You never were good at hiding your real feelings from me."

"Suzie, sorry if I have."

"You don't hide your feelings. Sometimes, say the opposite of what I'm feeling. I love you, and you always show me patience. We are two of a kind. Oh, David, what is going to become of us? You miss Annabelle, reading her bedtime stories, chasing away her monsters in the closet, taking her places with us, am I right?"

"Suzanne, not fair."

"Love, remember I would never stop fighting for you. Look at us. Any other couple would have stormed out of the room and slammed doors. We are opening doors, two and a half months' worth. Hated not being with you. You created a home where we both could live happily. Take your time. All I care about is we are together, and a few hours ago, I would have been afraid to be so."

"Blunt."

"Stop that, David.

When you think about Annabelle, you wish she were truly our daughter. The fact that she is Jacqueline's has captured your heart, for she has also captured mine.

David, I want a daughter. Let's have a baby. I don't care if we are not married yet. David, you are my heart, and I could not continue without you. I want to give us the family you dream about every day—the baby we want, to provide her with the room down the hall. You also speak to me in written words, and the songs you sing for me.

You have been in New York too long by yourself. Please, David, I'm serious. I love you. Tell me you love me. Have not heard those words from you in a long time. My fear is losing you, and you do not own the marketplace for blues."

David tenderly placed his finger over my lips, took me by the hand, and led us into our new bedroom. We kissed as he unbuttoned my silk blouse, revealing my push-up bra, and I wore the lace panties he loves. Mainly wanted to be sexy for him.

Softly and seductively, "David Benjamin."

Took my beloved by the hand to lead him back to the living room. Love, wait here. Want to look my sexy best."

Suzie wore my favorite silk shirt, four buttons open, barely covering her lace panties, and alluring red lipstick. Our song *"The First Time Ever I Saw Your Face"* played softly to recreate a similar ambiance for our first kiss and dance. With curtains drawn closed, lights dimmed, and candles creating flickering shadows that danced on the walls.

"My blue eye lady, perhaps incorrect French but my precise thoughts, La premie're fois que j'ai vu ton visage, the first time ever I saw your face, je t'aime beaucoup. I love you so much.

Longed to run my fingers through your luxuriant, wavy, reddish auburn brown hair, kissing you until your lipstick was more on my mouth than on your lips. Suzie, you are erotic and tantalizing. "Parfum de Montagne Rouge," my favorite."

David and I cuddled and placed ourselves so we could lie with my back to him. This was his favorite position; he could wrap his arms around me.

My love set the stage for a long-anticipated mood. Love songs played softly, intoxicating the air, as our favorite romantic incense hung sensually in the room.

Lying in his arms for the first time in months, he was content and wanted this moment never to end. Time stopped for us, and my body softened to be as close as possible.

Enchanté, my favorite cologne, made him smell sexy. Nothing was of importance except that we were in each other's arms. Turning to face him, placed my head on his shoulder. In my softest voice, "David, please let me explain."

"Love chastened, letting you down and not coming to your defense. There are no excuses, and not being in control of my emotions isn't an excuse. Please, love, forgive me, but nightmares trapped me in a void of helplessness. How could I not have waited to see that you were safe?

My sacred promise, nothing in the future will prevent me from protecting you. Made aware of what happened that night, Gabriella, James, and Jacquie were also there to protect you.

Suzanne, this night is for us.

There's no need to give me details; I love you. Was a bloody moron, a twit. You can say whatever to me tomorrow."

"How do you have knowledge about Gabriella and James?"

"Love, how is my Sweetpea? Is Annabelle doing well in school? What is she learning?"

"David, our sweet Annabelle, listens attentively to learn new words from you. She already teaches her favorite doll, Margaret, how to say Fuhgeddaboudit in an Irish Brogue."

"That is so cute. My sweetpea always loved talking like an Irish New Yorker. She giggles, "Daddy, can I talk like you?" Jacquie and Jaz had already resigned to my influence. Tried correcting her. Sweetpea, instead, say forget about it."

"Oh dear, you can never say no to that child. I agree she will hear no way too often in her life. However, when speaking to her teacher, David, she uses words you taught her. Sometimes in an Irish, French, or Bronx accent. Recently, she has been practicing a British accent with you."

'Did your daddy teach you these words?'

"Can you guess how she answered?"

"No, but bet my sweet multilingual daughter responded creatively."

'Miss Marie learned them from Mommy Jaz. She teaches me French.'

"David, her teacher, spoke with Jaz and told her Annabelle's father is a bad influence."

"Ouch, that was a mistake. How did Jaz answer Miss Marie?"

"She got angry at the implication that she should not learn from you. She replied in French. Jacquie told me she was thankful her teacher did not understand.

Jaz once told me she translates your Bronx and Yiddish words into French. Jaz has become fascinated by deciphering your Bronx talk into French."

How I missed your Bronx accent. Personally, would have responded to Miss Marie in Yiddish with the words you taught me. The teacher picks on one slang expression from Brooklyn, so now you are a corrupting influence on your daughter.

New York man, Annabelle, has learned to recognize thousands of new words and developed the beginning of non-linear critical thinking from you. She is writing and reading several grades above kindergarten.

Oh, lost the gist of my thought. Started to explain what had happened. You switched our conversation to Annabelle's choice of words."

"Please, David, be a little more judicious in your words."

"So, guess sending Annabelle the *Definitive New York Book of Slang* was not good?"

"You're serious? What am I going to do with you? Proud of Annabelle, too, for defending her dad.

David, you are getting good at deflection."

"Sorry, love, didn't realize all this about my Sweetpea. Glad you told me. Promise to have a talk with her about respecting her teachers."

After a few moments of silence, "Suzie, I lost control of my emotions while talking with Jacquie. Did not want to attend Megan's birthday party. Just to come to get you after the party. Your Sister tried to get me to feel safe and loved. Afraid I may lash out from my pain and anger directed at Jacquie. During our conversation, I couldn't feel her affection. It scared me to speak this way to Jacquie, so I promptly hung up."

"When I arrived in New York, I called Jacquie to say I was safe. David, haven't heard Jacquie this happy in a long time. She was worried but never said how much. Jacquie was with me 24/7 the first week. She slept on the sofa with me like we did when I was a little girl. Your pillow comforted me. I could not be in our bedroom without you."

"Now, feeling your love, safe in your embrace inside your apartment."

"Angel, our apartment."

"Oh, David, you are not kidding. Is our apartment for us? How could you possibly know I would fall in love with this apartment?"

"Well, dozens of times, at night before we go to bed, I shared your idealized must-haves for a future New York apartment.

Plus, hundreds of photos cut out of magazines of what you wished for. Suzie, you never admit to my listening to every word and feeling you have. Even though it doesn't appear that way at the time."

"Love, why didn't you say you would make my dream real for us?"

"Life happened and undermined me. Since arriving in New York, my darkest depression has motivated me to make this come true for us. Working to transform this apartment into our home was a lifeline back to you. Angel wanted you to feel at home as you crossed the apartment's threshold.

Suzanne, understand your dread of losing our chance for a life together when I got shot. Not having you with me scared the shit out of me. Sorry, but don't have a better descriptor.

"David, and the room at the end of the hall?"

"That was your making when you first shared the room down the hall from your bedroom. It was hard to put into words walking into that room. The nursery created an epiphany that didn't scare me."

"David, you made me happy. You looked content and comfortable in the room."

"Because Suzie knew in my heart that having a baby would be the beginning of a new chapter of our romance. I'm unsure if this makes sense, but our first dance, our first kiss, the shock of getting shot, and falling in love with you, and my life forever changed. Angel, my fear, this was just a dream, and my emotions ran in all directions, and life kept occurring. Whether I wanted it to or not."

"New York man, let life emerge. It will become our roadmap. When needed, we ask each other for directions.

My sweet, loving David, you always surprise me when I am sure you are not paying attention; your mind is thinking of ways to make us happy."

"The room down the hall is the essence of our love. Want our baby's nursery ready when we come to New York with her."

"David, what did I do to deserve your love and a life with you?"

Suzanne kissed me; it seemed different from the other kisses that night. Don't have the words to describe the feeling. It was similar to Noreen kissing me in her living room while Jacquie cooked dinner. Suzie's whole body was in this kiss, sending a message of love through her lips.

"Angel, how emotionally difficult for you to wait until vanquishing fear of rejection and depression. Together, we are better and happier.

Suzie, I wanted to confirm you received your apartment keys when you entered the lobby. Those are yours to keep. Did not want Mr. Charles to open our front door for you as if you were a guest.

Suzie, welcome to your New York home, and no, Suzie, no woman was a guest."

"David, Mr. Charles explained on the first day you arrived, you asked him to make an extra set of keys for me to truly feel at home."

"Of course, anxious for you and me to be together. Assume he told you I was a crazy man?"

"Yes, surprised he used the Yiddish word, Meshugana."

"Our lease has always included you and only requires your signature. The rental lease agreement is in our bedroom, so we will take care of this first thing tomorrow morning. I love you so much and wanted my actions to show that my love is not ephemeral. Suzie, our relationship has flourished. I missed you and love you for your trust in us."

"David, please tell me so as not to make me wait until tomorrow. How could you find out that what happened at Megan's party was an assault and not what you imagined?"

"Angel could never have foreseen how beatings and torture affected me. Never spoke about it. Didn't say anything, because it would have upset you too much. Dreadful jealousy returned with vengeance.

I knew when we met you had relationships and were not the only man in your life. My jealousy was held in check.

Secure in your love for me. Our relationship will flourish regardless. Details of how badly the terrorists tortured me with glee and hate and came close to breaking my remaining hope. They wanted to have nothing left of me."

Tears flowed. "Love this was inside me for quite a while, needed to start telling you."

"It will be okay. I'm here for you.

David, there was no other man in my life, you know this. We can discuss this further another time. It is upsetting you."

"You are with me, so I'm all right. Did the show's tickets arrive in time to take them with you? Sent them to you so you could arrive as soon as possible. Missed your twists and turns, jumping over and back again in a conversation. Still, all of it is interconnected."

"I love you so much. You had no one to voice your fears and joys, but you knew you had Jacquie and me. Can I come after you and remain stubborn, not taking no for an answer, so you don't slip away from me again?"

"Yes, love, hoping you would."

"Knowing Charles, told you I sat up all night in my neighbor's apartment. She was apprehensive because her baby daughter had a slight temperature. Her husband, Kevin, an active-duty Marine, was on a special duty assignment at the US Embassy across from the United Nations."

'My husband has Marine friends whose wives support each other. They had their concerns and children. Didn't want to place an additional burden on them.'

"Suzie, that touched my heart. She was a young new mother, tearful as she told me she didn't know where to take her baby if her temperature worsened. She had no friends besides a few military wives in New York. Her husband, on special duty, could not be reached. However, her mother and mother-in-law would arrive the next day.

Therefore, asked Sherry, 'Do you want to hear good or better news first?' She hesitantly said, 'The bad news first.'

'Sherry, good news or better news? Her shoulders demonstratively relaxed as she placed her baby in the pram.

I'll babysit so you can sleep peacefully. Stay on your sofa, move the baby's crib to the living room, and stay close to your baby for your peace of mind. Also asked Mr. Charles for the number of the best pediatricians in the area. The Doctor has the night off, spending it with her family.

Sherry, this is the best news. She lives in our building. Mr. Charles called the doctor and gave her your name and phone number, asking if she could be on standby.

The Doctor called me and explained how to reduce her temperature. She kindly provided me with her answering service number and personal smartphone number. The Doctor wasn't worried and said it sounded like the baby was teething. It was not unusual for her temperature to rise slightly, but it was not a fever. Since it is an average temperature for a teething baby, you can rest easy.'

"Megan called friends in New York, searching for me. She had just returned from visiting her intern friends. She had recently been placed in a well-known Mental Health Department at New York City Hospital. Before leaving for home, Megan spoke to her friend Sherry to spread the word among her military wives' friends."

"She is brilliant, as is all your family. Angel, you must have been praying. Megan's close friend Sherry and her husband, Kevin, are the same ones who live in my building."

"Sherry and Kevin had me over many times to dinner. He and I had become close friends."

When he got permission to call his wife, she told Kevin that her friend was trying to find her Sister's lover, who had come to New York. She reminded her husband of David's kindness, said, 'Honey, how Megan described Dr. David Benjamin Bradley sounds much like our friend David. Who made sure our baby was safe and sat up all night with her so I could rest?'

"Guess a light came on."

'Kevin, we do not know Dr. David Benjamin Bradley, but let me make a hunch. When David gets home in a few hours, knock on his door and ask. Everyone in the building knows him. Maybe perchance he knows this Doctor.'

"In New York City, among millions of people, sometimes you hear people connecting or bumping into each other accidentally in the most unlikely places."

"She told me the story and hopefully asked, 'Do you know a Dr. David Benjamin Bradley?'

'Yes, I do.'

"She was overjoyed by my awareness of the doctor."

'David, do you have his number? Where is he now?'

'You are talking to him. I am Dr. David Benjamin Bradley.'

'OH MY GOD,'

"Showed my driver's license because I'm still getting a lot of, oh my God."

'Can I give you Megan's number? She is worried and wants to reach you.'

'Sherry, sorry you have been taken by surprise. But I hope it was a pleasant one. Thank you for coming to me. I have her number and will call right away.'

"Suzanne was frightened that something had happened. You were in trouble or sick. When I called Megan, she first cried, happy to have found me, angry at me for not calling you, then crying again, and said, David, please call Suzanne."

"That was about ten days before sending a message to your phone.

'Megan, promise to text her in a week or so, and hope she will come.'

"This was a mistake, and I need to let my mouth sync up to my brain."

"Megan asked why I hadn't called you."

"Sweetheart, she was worried; thankful she talked to you. Why didn't Megan tell me?"

"That part was not so easy."

'Megan, please promise for now, don't say anything. She raised her voice and said in Irish, *David, tá tú as do mheabhair dá mbeinn chun ligean do Suzanne a bheith bertha ar feadh soicind eile,* David, you are out of your mind if I was going to let Suzanne worry for another second.'

"We argued, and sometimes she responded in *Irish*, not to hurt my feelings, at her intensity, telling me how crazy I was. And so it went back and forth, and finally, she said,"

'David, you are so irrepressible. I forgot why we searched for you. Just got lucky before Jacqueline.'

"Oh shit, Jacquie, the pain of you and Jacquie not knowing. Started to become tearful."

"Megan told me everything about how that bastard grabbed you to dance, how hard you struggled, his threatening you with physically harming Jacquie if you shouted for help."

'David, it was dreadful for Suzie.'

"Megan told me all the details of how our brave Jacquie stood before her baby sister to protect her. Jack pushed her away, intending to harm her.

That is when Jacquie went for help.

She asked your friend's husband, James, to rescue you.

He grabbed Jack as he was about to hit you. Megan thinks a knee to his privates got you free.'

"That's my Suzie."

"David, what am I going to do with you? My arms were pinned, and I am sorry because I wanted the satisfaction of slapping his face. You, of all people, appreciate how much it upsets me to have to protect myself with all my strength."

"Angel, proud of you. Well, back to how I found out. James played college football and had some of his buddies throw him unceremoniously into a dumpster."

"Suzanne, the side effects of the drugs darkened my thinking. Perhaps I can tell you more about how horrible it got for me one day, but not now. Don't want to worry you. There are no words to express my regret for not being there and coming to your aid. So deeply sorry I didn't wait. Megan figured if I stayed a few more seconds."

She soothed me, 'Please don't blame yourself. No one does. You told me true love doesn't break. Bear in mind, this was not your fault.'

"My childhood friend Roberta, our friend, had terrific dinners with her and her two adorable girls. As a result of asking for a favor, you can probably guess Roberta agreed not to call you, but was displeased and disappointed with me. I made her a promise that I'd contact her as soon as I knew you'd arrived."

Invited her family over for dinner as soon as possible. When finally told you were coming, she cried joyfully, and said her daughters were enthusiastic about meeting their Aunt Suzie."

"Oh, dear David, our friend Roberta and family hearten me. You were not alone."

"In my work at the United Nations, I met a permanent representative working with her country's ambassador, who lived with her family. She told me to call her landlord as she had recently informed me that this apartment had become vacant. She said you and Suzanne would be happy living there."

"You shared our relationship. Oh, David, this was hard for you. Worried about your nightmares. Frightened as days and weeks pass, you may unintentionally harm yourself, being so distraught."

"Angel, hug me, and you are holding me in your arms. Okay?"

"Okay, New York Man, understand."

Briefly contemplated suicide. In my nightmares, I drove down a highway and turned the steering wheel toward an embankment. Each time, Suzanne woke up screaming."

"David, your nightmares, when did they stop?"

"About a month ago, bad dreams were infrequently occurring. Talked to my therapist, and she told me that when I woke and screamed, Suzie, because you were my 'break glass in case of danger', ensuring I remained safe. She reassured me it might take a few more weeks to get the bad meds entirely out of my system. My therapist also said my nightmares are a drug withdrawal symptom, and life will improve."

"David, how did you get Megan to agree not to say anything?"

"That was reasonably straightforward. Megan and I have always been honest and have unconditionally trusted each other. Your family's strong determination is a quality I respect.

I'd love to hear her out, but first, she allows me to speak. Would love her more if she wanted to tell you afterward. It was up to her. Explained how we needed more time to have everything ready, including the locket, and finish setting up our apartment. She agreed."

Megan said, 'Suzanne will be delighted,' and asked what she could do.

'Could I mail you a letter to give to Suzie?

Megan, it's two tickets to a Broadway play, Suzanne's long-held dream.'

"David, she knocked on our bedroom door, though she never knocks. She said this was from David. It is in his handwriting and has a New York address. With tears and excitement, it never occurred to me to look more closely.

Later, before placing the tickets in my purse, I noticed that the addresses were printed and not handwritten. Thought this odd but got distracted and didn't give it a second thought."

Uncontrolled tears flowed down my face. "Love, so sorry I didn't stop him. Suzanne, how can you ever forgive me? I let you down. There is no excuse.

But my worst nightmare unfolded in front of me. Overwhelmed with intense emotional pain due to the severity of the horrific side effects. Please, love, forgive me."

With her tender kiss, "It's okay, sweetheart. We are together now. There is nothing to forgive. How horrible you must have felt."

"Lost control of my emotions and put you and everyone through hell. Nothing would have penetrated until I got my life back and on my regular antidepressants. Megan found me: if not for a teething baby, a connection might not have occurred."

Suzanne and I embraced and danced slowly about the room. Before the music ended, she led me back upstairs into our bedroom. Suzie and I suffered the ache of missing being together. We couldn't satisfy our sexual desires. Exhausted, we didn't want to stop to eat or sleep.

"David, want you deep inside me and to feel your penis throbbing. Lay on top of me and let me put you inside me. Make love to me all night."

We had watched erotic movies, and our lovemaking the first night we reunited was our erotic movie. Nothing in our past lovemaking was as sensual. Suzie introduced new sexual positions from a Kama Sutra book she had bought for us. She and I moaned in delight and were insatiable.

Overwhelming sexual passion can't be described in words alone. It was like making love for the first time. I was a virgin, and she was an experienced lover. After she climaxed, she slowly turned her attention to my pleasure and release.

Caressing with my hands on her boobs, reached a most exquisite orgasm. When ejaculating, David held Suzie closer. After a while, he carried her into the bathroom for a candle-lit sensual bubble bath."

Suzie slid her soapy body all over me, her breasts rubbing against my chest and genitals. We climaxed again and got back into bed.

Kissed her neck, and our lips gently met. "I love you."

Slipped my hand under my pillow, retrieved an envelope, and read Suzie a love sonnet.

Suzanne, Cry, and I dry your tears with kisses.

Laugh, and I laugh with you and love you more for your joy.

Suzanne, you are every love song.

Your brogue is an Irish melody when Blue embraces me in tenderness.

I love the child in you who loves the child in me.

Each day without you deepened my love and burned away the madness of jealousy.

Follow you across time and space.

With our pure love, our world becomes our love nest.

We celebrate our sacred love and share intimacy with sensuality.

Each sexual encounter is unique in its energy, bringing untold joy into our hearts.

Suzanne, like sweet dreams, you shine a beacon to lead us out of the darkness if life challenges our love.

"David, can't speak through tears of heartfelt emotions of your love."

"Sweet angel, may I ask a delicate question?"

"Love, ask anything of me."

"Are you as peckish…? Because we didn't eat dinner, and some wonderful Chinese food is in the fridge."

"David, just hungry for more lovemaking. I love you."

Fourteen
You are a New Yorker

"Do I love you? My God, if your love were a grain of sand, mine would be a universe of beaches." William Goldman

Suzie quickly adapted to the New York lifestyle and enjoyed living in the chaos of a harmonious but noisy Manhattan.

A long-awaited dream of finally attending her first Broadway play came true.

Suzie experienced her first New York pizza, an egg cream (no egg or cream, a New York classic drink), and ate an iconic New York City roast beef on rye. Black and White cookie, plus her first subway ride on the shuttle from Grand Central Station to Times Square.

Drove to the middle-class neighborhood where I grew up. She wanted to share the entirety of my experiences as a native New Yorker.

Suzie quickly mastered an essential skill, navigating sidewalks packed with people. My Angel walked like a New Yorker, with purpose and a clearer idea of where she was going.

"These darn slow-walking tourists, they are infuriating."

"Suzie, cheers, you are a New Yorker."

"David, love the energy on the sidewalks in Times Square!"

"This is the world's crossroads, mostly tourists out of half a million people daily.

"Suzie, before we eat dinner, let's take a short walk to where you can get tickets for Broadway shows at a discount. This is a typical experience for visitors to the city, standing in line to buy cheap Broadway show tickets. New Yorkers know you can now do this online instead of waiting in the heat, rain, snow, or cold."

"Of course, New Yorkers kept this a secret."

"Love, you are a New Yorker, and knowing these things makes life easier."

"Why are we waiting in line?"

Purchased three tickets to another Broadway play and made reservations for three at a New York Little Italy spaghetti dinner

Suzie loved living in our New York apartment these last two weeks. Megan, Jacquie, Jaz, Noreen, Jessica, and my sweet Annabelle have already visited.

Vickie was a godsend living downstairs. She wanted Suzie to go with her, as she was still intimidated about moving around the city alone and visiting law schools to determine which ones she should apply to.

Of course, the Sisters loved being together.

"David, a ticket to a Broadway play? With you and Suzie, I love you both. Need to buy a new dress and shoes, and will Suzie be able to go shopping with me?"

"Vickie arranged for a sedan from the Limo company, Susie and I occasionally used, and asked for our favorite driver. Miss Linda can take you and Suzie anywhere you want to shop. She will wait for you and, if you like, even take you sightseeing from the George Washington Bridge to a view of the Statue of Liberty."

"Dear brother, how could I thank you?"

"Vickie, you already have since my arrival at Woodland Cottage. You have your house key, and if you want, leave it when you go out with Mr. Charles or Miss Chole, the doorwoman with whom you have already made friends."

"Vickie, my love, David and I are pleased you are here. You are not our guest or family visiting; this is now your home."

Ensuring a fluid move into the White House for the President-Elect. The election was over, and President-Elect Harrison formed a transition team. Suzie was asked to join.

Suzie was rewarded for her unwavering faith and tireless work over the past ten years.

"Madam President-Elect, never been as happy for you. David and I celebrated with dinner and dancing."

"As soon as I'm officially sworn in as President of the United States, Suzie, I want you to bring David to the White House to celebrate over ten years of service and belief in me since you were a child. Dinner is in my private residence on the second floor. Also, arrange for Jacqueline, Jaz, Noreen, Victoria, and Megan to join us.

And Suzie, we have good news: your stellar work performance record, combined with your experience as the most qualified candidate, has been unanimously agreed upon by the Vice President-Elect, Press Secretary, Director of Communications, and Chief of Staff, who have unanimously decided to promote you to President's Communications Director. You report directly to the Press Secretary. Your salary is commensurate with over ten years of government service.

Did not participate in the selection process to ensure there was no appearance of bias. I have authorized the promotion and your new salary to take effect on January 1st solely on your expertise, experience, intelligence, and dedication as a dedicated public servant. Proud of how much you have grown professionally."

"Thank you, Madam President-Elect."

"I want you and David to undergo another round of background checks. Once cleared, permits a Top-Secret security-level clearance. Becomes easier to assign occasional assignments where David becomes part of a significant exigency team with tighter security protocols.

Suzie, you and David should go on a well-deserved vacation. Concerned that you haven't had one since you met David. Use your vacation days, as you have more than necessary to receive full pay. Take time off until January 2nd. Leave has been granted, and you will receive a copy for your records.

In the meantime, Suzie, you will be contacted by the transition team as needed. Enjoy your vacation."

"Was that our new President?"

"Honey, she granted me leave, which is government jargon for paid time off, from Thanksgiving to Jan 2nd, and David, guess what? She promoted me to become Communications Director to officially start in the new year."

"Well done, love, let's celebrate your promotion and dine in a fancy restaurant."

"Love, Vickie met a college friend, and they picked up where they left off as best girlfriends. But they won't get together until this weekend. Ask her to join us for dinner. She hardly takes breaks studying for her Law School Admission Test. Vickie will appreciate a few hours off from her studies."

Over dinner, we made plans to fly back to California to spend the Thanksgiving and Christmas holidays. Unbeknownst to me, Suzie had made other plans.

With the excitement of her promotion and time off until the new year, she couldn't sleep.

"How about a relaxing massage?"

"Can we talk first? Have something to ask you."

Delaying my massage could only mean she had something exciting she wanted to share with me.

"Before you say anything, the answer is yes."

"Silly, you don't know what I will say."

"Angel, your eyes are smiling, which tells me you have something you are enthusiastic about, and I'm not sure what my response is."

"Honey, can we take a winter holiday in the Sierra Nevada mountains, just you and me? Rent a cabin and get snowed in for Thanksgiving, Christmas, and New Year's Eve. The cabin I showed you is available.

We need to arrive before twilight. David, the outside staircase leads up to the cottage, and in the garage, everything we need is stored. Spare generators, fuel, a cord of wood, a freezer, a small, powered snowplow, with a fully stocked pantry.

Encircled by a silence of snow, sheltered by pine trees as wind sentinels. The cottage has an awe-inspiring view of the Sierra Nevada Mountains. It is a picture-perfect hideaway, snowflakes falling outside our window, cozy and warm in front of a stone fireplace's crackling fire. A large bathroom and a sunken tub, and you would not believe this. Also has a small wood-burning fireplace.

This is a perfect romantic getaway for you and me. Love, is it all right? Do you have any conflicts with your work?"

"No conflict, as such, all my assignments are writing speeches, and my consulting jobs can be done virtually."

"Wonderful, can't wait. The cottage will be prepared with what we need. I have already placed a down payment to hold the cabin.

Love, there is both a shortwave radio and a CB Radio. If we should get snowed in, the Sheriff will send a four-wheel vehicle with a plow when ready to go home."

"Remember to pack your favorite incense, bath aromatherapy bubble bath we love, and books."

"David, do you imagine we do much reading?"

"My Angel, I'll read you romantic poetry by the fireplace."

"Anticipating that you are as excited," we ordered our favorite food, hot cocoa, fruits, cheeses, chocolates, and fresh vegetables, from the local rural grocery store. Love, I'll cook you wonderful romantic dinners. Of course, wine, a bottle of champagne, and your favorite South African beer for New Year's Eve.

When I called the store, you would not believe it. The store's owner asked to give his regards and love to Julia and Robert.

'David and I don't have friends with those names. Did you mean the President-Elect and First Husband?'

'Miss Suzanne should not have been so informal. Attended elementary school with the President-Elect from Kindergarten through High School. She went to a different college. With occasional calls to say hello, and she sends my wife and me a birthday and Christmas card each year.'

'Miss Suzanne, order anything you need, it is my gift.'

'Mr. Lopez, your generosity is fondly remembered by the President-elect, and David and I are grateful. However, as a Federal government employee, I respectfully cannot accept gifts, in-kind, cash, or free delivery.'

'My apologies, and I will charge you the full price. However, Miss Suzanne, the delivery is free for orders over $250.00.'

'Thank you for understanding. Can I cut the number of bottles of wine to one?'

"David, he laughed," and said, 'Of course, your total will be $275.44. It will be ready when you arrive, unpacked, and placed in the pantry, refrigerator, or freezer, as needed. Ask my customers for an extra $25.00 as a tip for the college girl who will deliver everything. Miss

Suzanne, is there anything else? If not, can I have your credit card number?'

"You made a friend. Did you order what we need to make our DS pizza?"

"Even pineapple, is it okay if it is out of a can?

I'll pack some extra surprises for romantic dinners, breakfast, and lunch.

We got lucky; a cabin became available during the holiday season. The couple who rented it decided to go to Vail in the Rocky Mountains instead. So, placed a deposit to hold it until we could speak."

Suzie was uncharacteristically serene since the holiday season is her favorite time with family. But she won't be with them for the first time.

"Sweetheart, we can drive back for the holidays if you want. It is less than a four-hour drive round trip."

"Silly, couldn't be happier, together to celebrate the holidays alone for our first time."

"Suzie, won't Annabelle be heartbroken not sharing our birthdays, Thanksgiving, Christmas, and New Year's Eve with us?"

"Our Sweetpea won't be disappointed. Annabelle can have Jacquie send a text or email, and we have video get-togethers on those days. Jacqueline told her that she couldn't talk whenever she wanted. But anytime she misses us, Annabelle can call to chat."

Annabelle replied, 'I understand, Mommy. They won't have time to make their baby if I bother them.'

Fifteen
Two Sisters

"Courage is the most important of all the virtues because, without courage, you can't practice any other virtue consistently." Maya Angelou

"David, President-Elect Harrison wants us to fly to New York and host a dinner dance party. She asked us to thank the couples as her spokespersons who contributed to her presidential campaign.

We leave on Thursday, with the donor dinner dance on Saturday."

"You have already committed us to attend?"

"Are you upset I did not consult you? Remember what we talked about the other night? Jacquie and Megan are eager to spend time with us in New York."

"Angel, is this what you meant before falling asleep?"

"David, it's all right then. You can attend?"

"My publisher wants to meet in the Manhattan office on Friday. I'll ask my editor to reschedule our meeting for the morning. This frees up the rest of the day."

"The dinner dance party is at the world-class five-star Hotel Le Luxe, with spectacular views of Central Park. The President-elect arranged for us to stay overnight in a nearby hotel for security reasons. Is this okay?"

"Lover, every dress you like is too sexy for a donor party."

"Only pointing out my favorites for future reference. What about this one you overlooked?"

"Perfect color, a green-blue Jade, a formal Chiffon Evening Dress, oh my goodness, this is perfect. You are getting good at choosing dresses."

"My preference is the off-the-shoulder black evening gown with the slit showing off your sexy leg."

"Silly, this dress is like the peacock dress you love, silky and sheer, and remember how light I said it is to wear."

"Seriously, where do you learn this stuff?"

"Reading women's magazines and Jacquie and Noreen let me try on their dresses."

Suzanne began speaking with married couples who helped elect the President-Elect. A personal thank you on behalf of the President for their volunteerism or a donation to her Presidential campaign.

There were over 200 people, including the press and couples, whose contributions totaled $35,000. Additionally, individual donors contributed $15,000, and personal donations totaled, $25,000.

Megan and Jacquie were busy chatting and thanking donors and volunteers. Suzie asked me to socialize and note if a donor or volunteer wanted to have the President-elect informed about an issue.

Megan and Jacquie unexpectedly appeared, standing on either side of me. Jacquie kissed and hugged me, turning me ever so gently to face the opposite direction. While trying not to arouse my curiosity.

"Jacqueline Carolyn, this doesn't feel kosher. What is it you two don't want me to see?"

"Excuse me, ladies. There is no way this will happen to Suzie." Rushed to protect my Suzanne.

"David, please, Suzie is a personal representative of the President-elect."

In a less convincing voice, "Megan, I'll behave."

"David, let Jacqueline handle this."

Jacquie was less than three feet from Suzie, and I was right behind her. This giant pig of a man stood over six feet and towered over everyone in the room.

With sincere apologies to pigs, a good friend who works for a humane animal society told me pigs are full of fun, sociable, sensitive, and intelligent.

"No, thank you. Your wife, standing right over there, looks like she wants to talk to you."

"Love, I dance with whom I please, and you please me."

"Oh, shit, he's drunk and outweighs David by over 100 pounds."

Megan stepped before me and gave me a long, sensual kiss, holding me like we were lovers. Megan always wanted to have a sexual kiss. Her tongue touched mine as she hoped it would delay me enough for Secret Service agents to deal with this.

"Did you say Oh shit? Megan, I love you. Come with me, and scouts' honor will not instigate trouble."

Megan reluctantly put her arm through mine, as her kiss did not slow me down.

Jacqueline was standing fearlessly by Suzanne's side.

"Mr. Fox, heard my Sister say no a few times."

"Now, this is what I like, a fiery temper and both you Sisters in bed with me. Come on, little lady, just one dance."

"Who talks like that anymore?"

Every muscle has an endorphin rush. Suzanne was visibly upset, her eyes locked on mine, pleading with me not to do anything. Please let the Secret Service handle this.

"So what do you ladies say? I'll order some champagne and food, and both of you can make yourselves comfortable in my room."

Megan took my hand and held on tight.

"Sorry, Megan, Susie, and Jacquie will not be molested by this pig of a man."

Patted him persuasively on his shoulder.

"Excuse me, the two ladies said no thank you three times now."

"Who the hell are you?"

In a matter-of-fact tone, "Just someone in a second will knock you on your ass."

"You? A puny little runt. Take your best shot. Then I will beat your face until it becomes unrecognizable."

If he thinks I'm puny, this won't end well, sending me to the emergency room.

This mountain of a man was six feet and three inches, 280 pounds, and three sheets to the wind. He had the advantage of alcohol to soften any effects of my punch.

Jacquie tried to de-escalate and avoid having Suzie or me get hurt.

"Mr. Fox, the Secret Service protects this woman as she is the personal representative of the President-Elect."

"F*CK the Secret Service. Little lady, you will dance with me, and we can talk about the rest while we dance."

"Megan, before I get knocked unconscious, thank you for the kiss."

He was staggering, more intoxicated than I thought. There was no way this was going to happen to Suzanne a second time. Determined to protect my love. Standing confidently in front of Suzanne, I told her to stay behind me.

"Get the feck away from this woman, you pig of a man."

He laughed. Shit, what can I do to provoke this guy and keep Suzanne safe?

"Is this your Jewish boyfriend? What a f**king wussy."

With all my strength, this Goliath asshole forgot the Biblical story and got the full force of my fist in his face, and he laughed. This would not end well, as he grabbed me by the throat and lifted me inches above the floor.

Suzanne saw my breath slip away as my legs kicked frantically for air. She tapped him hard enough on his shoulder to ensure he would face her, with an alluring tone, "Mr. Fox, I have something for you."

He released his grip on my throat, and as he turned, Suzanne gave her famous five-fingered slap on the face. Took him by surprise long enough for a Secret Service agent to pull Suzie out of danger. It took four agents to handcuff him and escort him out the door.

Megan and Jacqueline quickly went to Suzie. Someone got the music playing. Oddly, there was not one flash of a camera.

One of the print reporters, a friend of Suzie, walked over to me.

"Dr. David, as soon as we saw it was Suzanne and what was happening, all the Press, including Cable News and print journalists, by tacit consent, agreed to keep this private for Suzie and the President-Elect.

On behalf of my colleagues, we are pleased, Suzanne, and you are safe."

"Thank you, I'll tell Suzie she will be appreciative, as am I."

Megan was astonished, "That would have been page one above the fold worldwide."

"Miss Megan, Suzie provides frequent access, briefings, and exclusives for our news reporting to be placed above the fold. She is truthful and open, making herself available, and has done personal, supportive things for reporters or their children."

Suzanne was upset and worried about David. Jacquie stood by her sister until David came over to her.

"Sis, Megan, and I will continue thanking the donors."

The Secret Service talked briefly with David, then escorted him to Suzanne.

"Honey, what did the agents say to you?

David, your silence means it is something that would upset me."

In a soft tone, Suzie speaks frankly of what is in her heart as an equal partner in our relationship.

Never afraid to show her emotions, "You almost got yourself killed. Mr. Fox was both drunk and homicidal. The Secret Service was a few feet away. What did you suppose you were doing?"

"A simple thank you would have sufficed."

"David Benjamin!"

"Made a solemn promise to you in New York. But, Suzie, damn if I do and damn if I don't, got street creds, and why are you upset with me?"

"Street creds. It sounds like you're proud of the respect you have from the old neighborhood. But love, your Bronx approach didn't work this time. You should be proud, but you rushed in and almost got yourself beaten up or killed.

David, terrified, seeing you with your feet dangling in the air and choking to death in front of my eyes. David, please, you don't have to make up for anything.

New York man, my hand is throbbing. David, I need fresh air."

"I'll take you someplace private."

Wrapping my arm around her, we walked across the banquet hall.

"A ladies' room. You take us to a ladies' room for fresh air?"

"Well, it is private, it has a window, and you are a Lady."

"David was afraid he could have choked you to death."

"Wanted to get him away from you."

"So your solution was to hit him. A man three inches taller than you and a hundred pounds heavier."

"Closer to a hundred and fifteen."

"David Benjamin, I'm serious. Stop making light of this. Everything is fantastic for us, and I don't want to lose you.

Please don't tell me how great my slap was. Would have cracked Fox's head open with a baseball bat to protect you!"

Suzanne started crying,

"Don't know why I said that."

"Because you are upset with me."

"Because I could have lost you in front of my eyes again. This won't be the last man to say sexist things and try to have me…, can't finish that sentence. Women have always lived in a male-dominated world. There are misogynistic men; women have to fight every day. What are we going to do?

Please, David, there are men and women with guns protecting me, and the President-Elect has talked to the Secret Service for you to be protected. A right not ordinarily granted for my position, the President will declare you and me family."

"Suzanne promised I'd never let jealousy or anyone prevent me from getting you to safety, no matter the risk. Cannot and will not stand by when you are in trouble. The angst of seeing you in danger, standing by and doing nothing, is intolerable. No way in hell that will happen. At least he didn't have a gun."

"David, don't you dare joke about placing yourself in harm's way."

"That was no joke. Would have a different approach if he had a gun."

"This is not who you are. Don't play *Clark Kent* to my *Lois Lane*."

"You mean *Superman*?"

"No, *Clark Kent*. He cannot reveal his superpowers. But did you notice you don't have a cape?"

"Suzie, what if Jacquie or Annabelle were in danger? There is no fecking way you would stand by and do nothing."

"You are changing the subject."

"I'm sorry to use that word. Don't make me impotent."

"Oh my God, is this a male ego testosterone trip you are on?

Oh, David, I'm sorry, you don't act out of ego, but out of love. But you are still a man with testosterone."

"Suzie, this is one thing I will not compromise. Why did you slap this pig of a man when you saw me choking?"

"David, you are changing the subject again; I was attempting to save your life."

"Thank you. I was close to passing out."

In a confrontational tone, upset and scared for David. "Damn it, David! Accept that I am not going to allow you to get hurt."

Suzanne dropped to the floor with tears flowing.

"David, is this the intensity of your feelings for me each time you say those words?

Come down here and hold me. Le Luxe maintenance people keep a clean floor."

"Honey, he is a multi-billionaire. Talked about a billionaire being so fat he could fit all of his money in his stomach. You told me to be nice because he is the CEO and founder of one of the largest energy companies and a major donor to President-Elect Harrison.

You punched him, and then he tried to kill you in front of me.

A Secret Service agent informed me he was anti-Semitic. With the Secret Service protection, why would you confront him?

Love slapped his face so hard that my hand hurts."

Held her hand, kissed it, and gently massaged it.

"Is that better?"

"It's a start."

Her tears flowed, and her nose was runny. She handed Suzie some tissues from the counter.

"Not going to stop crying. Embarrassed the President-elect, and she may lose this donor. But all I cared about was that you were hurt. David didn't want you to ruin your reputation. Like it or not, you are a public figure; your books are on the bestseller list, and you are interviewed regularly on the radio and TV. Don't consider myself, I never do with you."

"Angel, I love you, too."

"David, can we please live a life of no drama?"

"Where would the fun be in that?"

"Oh, I don't know. Perhaps we both stay out of trouble?"

Tears flowed again.

"Sweetheart, you don't have to be apprehensive."

The President will have my resignation on her desk first thing in the morning."

Gently kissed Suzie to assure her everything would be all right.

"But David, this is a lady's room. Why hasn't anyone come in?"

Just at that moment, a gentle knock on the door.

"A lady would not expect a man to be in here."

Before Suzanne had a chance to reach for the door, it opened.

"Miss Suzie, have been guarding the door since you and David entered. Take all the time you need."

"Thank you, I guess."

"Suzie, does this Secret Service agent look and sound familiar?"

"Oh my God, Agent Murphy! I've heard you are now working for the Secret Service. Congratulations.

How could you know I was here in New York? Or David would take me into a Lady's room?"

"Miss Suzie, the President-elect, assigned me to stay with you 24/7. Other agents would relieve me. You didn't see me as I had just returned to duty when the incident happened. The President-elect said, 'Those two have a penchant for getting into trouble.' You have to teach me your technique with that hand slap. Good, I wanted to see your smile.

Miss Suzie and Mr. David got word that the President was briefed about the incident tonight. She would like to talk with you and Mr. David at your earliest convenience, anytime tonight. The President added to tell Miss Suzanne there is nothing to be concerned about and to rip up that resignation letter."

"Thank you, Agent Murphy. Suzanne and I are thankful and pleased you are watching over us."

"Miss Suzie, lock the door, and I'll stand out in front."

"David," in a tantalizing whisper, "New York man, we never did it in a public bathroom."

"Why are women's zippers so hard to find? She reached the back of her dress and pulled the zipper halfway down.

"Don't worry, you have improved with all the recent practice. David, take it off over my head."

She wore her sensual lace thong, nylon stockings, garter belt, and a matching bra that was sexy and suggestive.

"Expecting romance with some man who falls for your beauty?"

A mischievous smile. "Yes, just not in a lady's room. Silly goose, since you're already here, you might as well do. There is hearsay about how women fall in love with you. All they want is to kiss your delicious lips and be close to you, then shag you until they cannot stand straight."

She pressed her body close to mine, removed my suit jacket, and wrapped my tie around her forehead to hold back her hair. My left shoe, then my right, threw my socks over a stall and accidentally landed in a toilet.

"Whoops."

The art of lovemaking is more than just sex. Suzie gently kisses, our favorite way to show affection, as no other touch could be as loving. She tenderly started French kissing.

"Oh, shit, have to pee. Where do I pee? There are no urinals."

Led me by hand to the last stall and took my penis in her hand. She tightened her grip as my stream started flowing to hold back my peeing. She held on tight until I was on the brink of exploding and sensed it. She let go of her grip, still in hand, and watched a strong stream. She shook it, wet some tissues, and she cleaned me. Suzie got on her knees, her mouth on my penis down to my pubic hair, and started sucking slowly.

"Never saw you with your piss so strong. Can we try?"

"It's called a golden shower."

"Can we take turns? It is my new fantasy, so kinky and erotic."

"Love, keep this as our secret."

She nodded, breathing heavier. Two fingers were going in and out of her vagina, and my other hand had a finger in her butt.

"Never have I been so turned on in a lady's room."

She fretted, "How many ladies did you have sex with in a lady's room?"

We kissed.

"Oh, just me.

David, want you to F*CK me hard."

Suzie had pent-up emotions. Knowing the incident upset her, plus we were making love in a lady's room. She thought it sounded sexy. Surprised by her choice of words, but enjoyed how stimulated and wet she was.

"My language won't improve when these words are arousing for us. Love put the toilet seat down and sat facing the front. F**k me in my anus."

She moaned, "It feels so good. Keep going, don't stop, faster."

Suzie turned to look into my eyes, held me tighter, rubbed my penis on her vulva and clitoris, and put me inside her.

"I'm cumming," her arms wrapped around me. She wiggled her hips to keep me hard as long as possible.

"Suzie, love our lovemaking."

"Sweetheart, I'll clean up."

Agent Murphy knocked on the door, opened it, and poked her head inside.

"It's okay, we are in the back stall getting dressed. What's wrong?"

"There are two Sisters who want to ask, do you want us all to ride back to the hotel, or shall we walk?'

"Sis, we are waiting to go with you. The party has been over for the past 30 minutes. All the guests have left. We have just finished speaking to the last donors.

Are you two okay?"

"Yes, Sis, we are wonderful. What do you mean by the last few donors?"

"You have been in there four hours."

"Oh my Goodness."

"It is shortly after 1:00 a.m., don't worry. We made sure everything went well. Megan and I are glad you are together and safe."

Suzanne and David finished dressing and opened the door, so Jacquie and Megan could enter."

"This may be the longest shagging in a hotel's luxury lady's room."

Jacquie confidently replied, "Megan, not in this city."

"Agent Murphy, what time do you get off your shift?"

"A few minutes ago, the agent on duty would have had to take you back to the hotel. Miss Suzie, I would rather you, David, and your Sisters not walk. The donor who tried to assault you is out on bail. He is distraught as his wife left him."

"How did you find out?"

Her Secret Service Agent face would never reveal anything.

"Oh no, your dinner."

"Miss Jacquie brought me a salad, main course, dessert, bread basket, and something to drink."

"Thank you, Jacquie, for ensuring Agent Murphy's dinner."

"David, by the look on your face and Suzie not standing steady on her legs, you are both happy."

"Where is Megan?"

"She went to get our coats. Agent Langley is waiting to take us back to the hotel."

Sixteen
Lovers Intimacy

"They slipped briskly into an intimacy from which they never recovered." F. Scott Fitzgerald

"David, do you want anything? You haven't eaten. Room service has a 10 p.m. to 5:00 a.m. menu."

"Angel, what would you like to eat? I'm too tired."

"Me too, love."

"Go ahead and get comfortable in bed. I'll be right there.

Breakfast at ten o'clock. Iis okay? Orange Juice, black coffee, and since we are in New York, lox, onions, and bagels with a few different schmears."

"David, do you want me to run a bath for us?"

"I'm sorry, I couldn't hear. Running a hot bath for us."

"I love you, silly."

"David, let me lie on your chest facing you."

At 2:00 a.m., both of us, she in a bra and panties and I in briefs, climbed into bed.

"Sweetie, can we have breakfast at noon?"

"Already have."

"Honey, did you put the Do Not Disturb sign and lock the door?

Could you message Jacquie and Megan to meet us in the lobby at 3:00 p.m.?

They would love a slow day, and Jacquie can talk to Annabelle and catch up with Jaz."

"Suzie, everything is as you wish.

You keep bringing me home from gun shootings, and terrorist bombs, now getting choked.

Love, get some rest. We will talk in the morning. Good night, Suzie. Sleep with the angels."

She loves to snuggle up to me so I can wrap my arm around her.

"Love, are you awake?"

"Can this wait until later today?

Okay, turn on the bed lamp. Tell me what is on your mind."

"Beautiful women flirt with you all the time. They want to be with you."

"Suzanne, you are my beautiful lady."

"Scared someone will tell you whatever you want and take you away from me."

"Angel, it is you whom I want. Megan's kiss was to divert me from jumping on that pig of a man, and she was afraid I would do what I did. Sorry, but couldn't just stand by."

"Her kiss was more than to prevent you from getting hurt; it was longer and more passionate, and she started French kissing. She is in love with you, and with Ryan gone, she has romantic ideas."

"It wasn't with ardor."

"Why then was your tongue in her mouth, David? I know how you French kiss."

"Angel, I'm sorry, but her kiss turned me on. Would never embarrass her in front of everyone."

"You love her, and Megan is a pretty woman."

"Sweetheart, love her as my sister and friend. You saw the look on my face when she let go. Jacquie had already stepped out of the way. About to get smashed to give time for a Secret Service agent to get you out of harm's way. So you would be safe, and couldn't deal with hurting Megan while ensuring you were protected."

"So you thought getting a wet kiss from a beautiful woman, then getting the life choked out of you, was a good rescue strategy?"

"Yeah, but thought he would throw a punch at me, then you could get away."

"Do you suppose this is why Ryan left her for another woman? She kissed you in front of him. Megan came to me crying, apologizing for being in love with you."

"Suzanne, know all of this, saw you watching, and wanted to talk about it over breakfast."

"David, a minute more, and she would have taken you to a quiet place and shag the shit out of you."

"Don't be angry. She asked me if it was okay."

"No, she didn't. There was no time."

"Don't want you upset. I'm truly sorry. Didn't mean to worry you."

"David, leaving me is my most dreadful fear."

"Suzanne Siobhan!"

"You are annoyed with me."

"Never. You always know if I hide my feelings."

"This is different."

"Have I ever lied to you or kept secrets? Suzanne, I love you, and you are crying. I am sorry I worried and upset you.

Have something important to share, and prefer you not tell your Sisters for now."

"Cross my heart."

"Now, you can only tell Vickie she can keep a secret."

"Why, just Vickie?"

"Intuition and her worried expression. She wants to speak to us when we return home."

"My hand on our love."

"A simple okay would have worked."

"First, tell me what you are not saying, as I'm missing bits of what you know."

"It was I who was afraid to tell you because you would let her get passionate. But, David, you have wanted to sleep with her, and she with you."

"Suzanne, you are still not telling me everything."

"Megan came to me crying last week. She said David never initiated anything and would never hurt you, nor would I. Then Megan said, but I'm in love with him. David is everything Ryan is not. Ryan wants to divorce me.

Love, don't get upset with me, promise."

"Angel, there is no more need for promises. I love you deeply and trust you with my life. Sweetie, we don't get angry at each other. That is not how we respond, and, oh!

So you aren't gossiping. It's a Sisterhood, so everything is shared to know how to best protect, defend, and support each other. Each of you will understand why or how."

"When did you figure that out?"

"Just now, I had an epiphany."

"New York man, you really are slow on the uptake."

"Waiting for you, watching Ryan bale hay for Whisper and Shadow. He asked if I would ever leave you.

This was only a few days after my arrival. Wondered why he would ask this peculiar question, as we just met."

"David, do I need to hear this?"

"Angel, not if you don't want to, but believe you should. You are upset."

"Love not at you."

"I know, Ryan."

"Out of the blue, he told me, 'Megan's kisses are passionate, and she wants sex.' This annoyed me. The tone in his voice was obvious. This wasn't going to end well. The bastard wanted me to have an affair with his wife.

Newlyweds have only been together for a little over a year, and he asks, 'Do I want to sleep with his wife?' Not accusing me, mind you, sounded as if he was permitting me. He angered me, but it was just a few days after I was discharged from the hospital, so I kept quiet. Ryan was already saying more than I wanted to hear."

'David, you and Megan can even feck, I don't care. Met someone and fell in love, and plan to divorce my wife.'

"It is this moment, walking toward me, remember what you said."

"Happy, you are getting to know each other."

"Exactly, but soon after, Ryan started missing family gatherings and dinners. He was always working late and hardly spent time with Megan. Returning at sunrise to feed

Whisper and Shadow. Can't imagine he wanted your mom or Nana to know."

"How did you realize he was not sleeping with Megan? Oh, David, you had trouble sleeping some nights. Your pain gets worse if you lie down in bed too long."

"Watching the sunrise, observed him as he drove up to the Barn."

"Why didn't you say anything?"

"Because, at that time, he wasn't accustomed to his habits. An ex-girlfriend didn't worry since she sometimes arrived home late from a conference. Sorry, Suzie, this was a few years before we met. You, my vixen, see me at the window and get out of bed just in your lace panties. Forgot about Ryan or cared."

"Hold me, David. Don't want you tempted. It's not fair. I'd never get upset with you. Wouldn't want you worried about my leaving you."

"My precious love, the kiss was my fault. Megan's beauty, charm, and wit are attractive. Nevertheless, I must reiterate I'm not at all tempted. Nor do I wish to be, and Angel would never sleep with her.

Maybe should have stopped her by not becoming intimate in the first place.

Suzie, every emotional, spiritual, and sexual feeling, and my love for you. Afraid this asshole was about to grab you and wanted to protect you. Megan hoped a Secret

Service agent would rescue you only if she was able to slow me down. The agents were only a few feet from you, and she got caught up in her love for you and her emotions for me. It was not conscious, and she reacted instinctively."

"Her instinct was to kiss you."

"Angel averted the heartache of unrequited love. Let's talk to her later. But Suzie couldn't let her feel unwanted. So, I embraced and kissed her back."

"Thank you for being honest. This was hard for you to say. But already knew all of this."

"Suzie, for God's sake, why did you let me go on? Never said anything."

"My lovely New York man, jumping in front of me because it would not be possible for you to live if I were killed. Standing up to my enraged father to protect Jaz, every tear you shed when Annabelle is upset hurts you, and you hold her and tell her it will be all right, plus the nightmares you share, and guess the rest. I love you even more. You place the well-being of my family first and would not allow me to be harmed even at the cost of your safety."

"Suzie, you didn't answer my question."

"You would be more upset if you thought I would not forgive you."

"Never cease to surprise. How deep is your love?"

"David, Megan wants to have sex with you and me.

'That would allow me to become emotionally closer to you and David.'

"Megan asked more than a few times. 'Would it be all right to sleep with you and David? It would be hot and sexy.'

Megan shared that Ryan has been sleeping with a woman for two years. Afraid, David, you would throw him out of the apartment if she said anything. Then, terrified, you would ask her to leave.

Honey, Ryan berated her because she asked him to come back to her. In a rage, he angrily shouted, he can be with you. David, he didn't care."

"Doesn't make sense. First, why would Megan think she is to blame? Let alone suggest leaving her home. Secondly, don't own Woodland Cottage; this is your sister's inheritance.

This has been Megan's home since she was a girl. Never mind, all of us share insecurity and quickly imagine the worst scenario."

"Ryan has been having an affair with a woman at his office. Told Megan he wanted a divorce to marry her."

'Suzie believed Ryan. We are meant for each other. Ryan used your David as an excuse.'

'Megan, when did this begin?'

'Six months after our honeymoon.'

"Sweetheart used your affection to justify cheating on his wife.

David didn't realize she was hurting all this time."

"How is Megan now?"

"Relieved she could not keep up a pretext, they were happy. Or continue to make excuses because Ryan was never home."

"Megan talks incessantly about a bloke she met at one of her conferences eight months ago. They spend time conversing about all sorts of things and, most days, eat lunch and dinner together.

There are signs of a woman in love. She insists he is only a friend. That man is her love interest."

"Be honest with me. Do you want to sleep with Megan?"

"No, my love, I love you."

"Love, honest, you would not say no. If you want to, I would also."

"Suzie, please, this is your insecurity talking because I experienced similar fears. Would say no without the slightest hesitation. Do not want another woman. You are everything I ever wished for in a relationship. It is your love I want. Angel, it would never cause you distress; I'm truly deeply in love with you.

Suzie, sex with Megan would not be lovemaking. Sex may hurt your friendship. Worse, you could become estranged from Megan. You could not endure this, and were worried that I would want other sexual affairs.

Though your love for her as a Sister is unconditional, you are mortal. Watching me having sexual intercourse with any woman, let alone Megan, well, sex is not a solution.

It is only a physical pleasure and not a remedy. It may fracture your lifelong friendship.

Suzie, it is you who has my heart. My relationship with Jacquie is one of love. Yes, we have occasional nights where we are emotionally close, not sexually intimate.

Suzie, you asked if you could be with Jacquie and me.

Jaz had mixed feelings, as she had never been with a man and wanted to, especially since it was Jacquie, you, and me.

Our intimacy grew to include her, but we held hands, kissed, cuddled, gave massages, and shared a hot tub. Never caused jealousy because of mutual love and affection. We mostly cuddle together while watching movies.

Your Sisters are already comfortable with each other. Sometimes we show our fondness and comfort each other after a long work week. Not sexual, a kiss is a more profound connection of love. It is spontaneous and not set up as Megan wants. Suzie, what should we say to her?"

"Megan has yet to become intimate with this new man in her life. This guy wants to have a relationship with Megan. This means taking a risk. She blames herself for the failure of her marriage. Not having been with another man, she fears it won't work out, and she'll be left alone.

"I understand her anxiety. I'm safe and reassuring; she loves me and sees us happy. Megan also wants a deeper connection and security of love. She already has an intimate closeness with you. She has rationalized never being alone by spending time sexually with us. She doesn't have to risk getting hurt and would never be rejected."

"David, had you spoken with her?"

"A few weeks ago, I reassured her she could always come to us and cuddle, kiss, have dinner, or watch a movie if she was lonely. Suzie, as much as you love her, she loves you even more. Last night, she and Jacquie ran to me, hugged and kissed me, and turned me around, so I couldn't help but see your discomfort and fear. Jacquie ran up to you and confronted the Pigman fearlessly, like a mother protecting her child.

Megan was not like Jacquie and watched me, ready to fight. Panicked and afraid, and yes, she loves me, and I love her as my Sister, and we always had sexual tension. Megan acted on our mutual affection and love, not to see you assaulted."

Love, she said, as I tapped the pigman on the shoulder, 'David, careful, for Suzanne's sake.'

David, I'm accosted by men with political power and money who want sex. Like every woman, I don't wish to deal with unpropitious advances. Love, these men believe they are alluring with dinner invitations.

David, hold me, so frightened. When a man rapes or tries to dominate a woman, it is not sex. It's an act of violence and hate directed at a woman. Been lucky so far, love, but petrified a man will physically keep me from escaping or scream for help and rape me. What if I got pregnant? I would have an abortion, couldn't bear being forced by a man's act of violence, and not being our baby would devastate me."

"Suzie, I will always love you."

"David, I am terrified. Someone muscular or more than one man would beat and choke me to death because I would vehemently resist and fight back.

When I saw him start to choke you, I had never felt so helpless, vulnerable, alone, and afraid.

David, hold me closer. Would you want me if a man raped me? I would be damaged goods. I lost you for 2 ½ months because a man used force to dance with me.

Jacquie told me that after her rape, she was wary of physical contact and wouldn't let Jaz touch her. It took her four years and therapy to be intimate with a man of her choosing, to let him kiss or touch her.

You were the first man who made love to her after revealing your love for her baby. She had hoped, but couldn't believe a man unconditionally accepted her baby girl. She opened up and became vulnerable, as you were the first person she ever talked to about the rape outside of her Sisters.

I love your first thought about arranging a fun place to take Annabelle when you meet her. You thought of her little girl and Jacquie's love for her child. My Sister quickly fell in love and had sex within hours after meeting.

What if it took me that long? How would you be able to stay with me, or would you have a baby with me? I couldn't live with that."

"Suzie, you are and will always be the woman I love with all my heart and soul. You would never, in my eyes, be damaged goods.

Please let go of this feeling. Angel, my love is absolute and unconditional. And I would move heaven and earth to ensure you get whatever support you need, God forbid. You would never have to cope alone with that horrific scenario. Sweet Angel, my help would be gentle, loving, and supportive of your feelings. Promise patience and deep compassion."

"Don't leave me."

"I'm here, just getting tissues."

"Please don't let go. I am all right."

"No, you are not."

"I have wanted to tell you how afraid I was for you. And couldn't protect you if you experienced an asshole who is wealthy, bullies women, and uses force to have sex. Your deep pain is beyond my reach, but not my love for you. I couldn't bear to lose you again because of another man's misogyny.

I was not afraid and dared to slap him because you were there to defend me, deeply in love with you. Reach over to me for the tissues. They are on my side of the bed."

"You are cute when you gently blow your nose.

I'll take this smile, however small."

"David, what is going to become of us? Jealous of beautiful women who love to hug and kiss you longer than they should if they can. Have to ward off men who want to persuade me to dance, date, or kiss, and don't want to think about what else.

Mr. Fox reeked of alcohol and being large and powerful. David, I panicked, but you were there, so I felt safeguarded. What if he grabs me again? A drunk, now an angry drunk, couldn't bear being sexually forced by another man. Terrified someone treats me with contempt for no reason other than my being attractive. Scared of being beaten or killed, since I will fight back.

Love, I never flirt, except for you and our pleasure. Men don't care what I wear, no make-up, or wear faded Jeans with one of your shirts. Still, attract despicable men for my breasts and tight butt who wish they could get me as a trophy."

"You added the breasts and a tight ass to flirt with me."

"David, please, don't try now to make me smile. This is not easy for me. You are my love, and we are destined to be with each other.

Never told you all your gibberish about my eyes and how I took your breath away because it allowed you to hide your true feelings, and you trust this is true because you saved my life.

You don't argue, make me feel wrong, or see me as a sex object. You value and cherish who I am, and you're the first person, not even my Sisters, to understand why I say I'm silly. Because I am the beautiful woman you dreamed of, and thought would never come.

David, you encourage me to embrace my potential and not be afraid that I may overshadow you with my success. You tenderly love me and are caring, and let me dress sexy to make myself attractive. I get myself pretty, sexy, and feminine for you. Yet, you understand I like to look feminine and sexy for myself."

"Suzie, this was not easy for you. Since your teenage years, you have had to protect yourself. Learn how to cope with sexual harassment just because you are gorgeous. That is just how you always looked, even as a girl.

Strong emotions built up over the years got trapped inside you, seeking expression. Your deep-seated fear is that you are regarded as a sex object and violated. I don't want you to deal with this alone.

Angel, didn't realize the extent of your fear of being raped. I hear terror and helplessness in your voice. Suzie, I am aware now and will protect you. Angel, my love is unconditional. My passion is genuine.

React vehemently against anyone who attempts to harm you. Falsely reassured that no harm could reach you as you have, Secret Service and the auspices of the President's authority for your protection.

However, this wasn't enough to quell your worst nightmare. First thoughts and inclinations would be of how you are feeling each day. I don't know my exact reaction, but rage for sure at anyone who harmed you.

Helpless, what to say, merge my patience with empathy. Ensure you feel secure, safe, and loved. Listen and let you take all the time you need.

When faced with intense stress and pain, fearful people respond emotionally and shut everyone out. You've lived through this with me recently, yet never lost your love or trust in us. Two and a half months is a long time not to hear from me. Still, your love is unbreakable, as is mine, and together, indestructible.

Remember, true love doesn't break; our love will prevail. No matter how long, trust that you will come to me and ask me to hold you when you are ready.

Jacquie said we have something unique that few people ever have, and we would appreciate it as we become more intimate. This is what she meant."

"David, you said what I needed to hear. In my heart, I knew those were your thoughts. You couldn't help but be jealous and get depressed. It would be hard for you to overcome when deep-seated depression gets triggered. Though grateful, our love is unbreakable.

Honey, why risk getting hurt when Agent Murphy was assigned to protect me? The agents were never more than a few feet away."

"You were in their line of attack. The Agents could not risk you getting injured. So the Secret Service watched as the situation unfolded. You became their diversion. A female agent grabbed you and took you to safety after you slapped him. That was Agent Murphy."

"David, how could you know? He was choking to kill you."

"I didn't, Agent Murphy told me. Suzanne, they were close to drawing guns, but too many innocent people were nearby."

"Oh, my love, thank you for telling me this. Even my Sister and Megan's passionate kiss and her physically holding you back couldn't prevent you from coming to my rescue. It was asinine and dangerous, and once again, you throw yourself into danger."

"To safeguard you."

"I know it's your unbreakable promise, New York man. What can I do to prevent you from getting hurt? I get jealous like you, but I am secure in our love."

"Wait, what did you say? Gibberish? I have never talked this way except with you. Your heart trusted that I was the man you waited for when we met. It was different for me. Afraid to reveal my true feelings, I emerged a little at a time.

Yeah, guess it was gibberish because, sweetheart, what do you say to a woman who walked out of a dream and let me kiss and dance with her? My emotional state was difficult to express. Though you have the bluest blue eyes, my way of saying I'm falling in love. Didn't believe in love at first sight, this was before we met."

"My Beloved, you just made love to me with your words. You are right, love is not romance or sex. They are just fringe benefits.

David, oh my David, I wish I'd known you when you were a boy. This was the most vulnerable you have allowed yourself to be. The boy still inside you, understand, I say, silly like you say, bluest blue eyes.

"David, we still have Megan's emotional dilemma to contend with, and a part of me wants her to join us in bed."

"The three of us will talk tomorrow. Jacquie is good at resolving things we mere mortals cannot.

Sexual pleasure is one thing, but getting emotionally involved is too high a price to pay. Then the hurt will be much more intense. Megan risks possibly ending your close relationship if she spends time with us. Love and family are a formidable bond, but you both would be miserable for a long time."

"David, what do you want to say to her?"

"Start with her feelings. Megan watched you almost get sexually molested and saw me inches off the ground, choking to death. Of course, she will be upset and troubled. Did she do the right thing by kissing me? Angel, she needs to be reassured that you still love her."

"I love you, New York man."

"Not as much as I love my blue-eyed lady."

"Oh my God, David, we didn't call the President."

"Tomorrow after breakfast. The Secret Service agent guarding our hotel door would inform us if the President wanted to speak to us."

Due to the lateness of the hour, an unexpected tapping on our hotel door.

"Miss Suzanne, Dr. David, good morning. Sorry to bother you, but the President just finished her work and is waiting to speak with you both. Pick up the phone and dial zero. You will directly connect to the White House operator, who'll transfer the call to the President-elect."

The current president generously offered additional resources as a courtesy, part of their planned smooth transition of administrations.

"Thank you, Agent."

"Good morning, Madam President-Elect. David and I have you on speakerphone. Is that alright?"

"Good morning, Suzie and David. Yes, that's good, because I'd like to speak to you both. First and most important, you are safe. Suzie, before you say your mea culpa, David, I'm proud of you, as it seems that no human intervention, not even two Sisters and a passionate kiss, stopped you from running to protect Suzie. We will discuss that in a few minutes."

"How are you aware, Madam President-Elect, of the kiss?"

"Suzie authorized the Secret Service to report to me all details. You two are public figures. As a ten-year-old, a teenager, and now a young woman, like my daughters, you have learned to protect yourself. However, we live in a more perilous world, and some basic, unobtrusive security measures are in place. Unobtrusive security is there to protect you and David.

Suzie, enjoy New York as you planned with your Sisters. You may work out of your home office when you return home. I need you to write speeches that you can do at home. We will have video conferences when you have something to show me."

"Thank you, Madam President."

"David, you told me your mother would repeat your name in threes, as she wanted to be assured you heard her. So, as President-Elect, I only need to say this once."

"Madam President, the Secret Service used me as a diversion. I will not stand by if Suzie is in imminent danger."

"David, respect you to the highest degree, so this is not a rebuke. You couldn't know because, at that moment, a Secret Service agent was about to snatch Suzie from harm when you confronted Mr. Fox. Agents now needed to protect you. Before acting, they waited to see what you would do as a distraction.

David, it seems there is a family history with your illustrious grandfather, who served in the Royal Air Force during World War Two, and risked his life to repeatedly save his crew. That almost got him killed several times.

David, Secret Service agents trained and wait for it, have guns to protect Suzanne. You are responsible for not placing them in harm's way through impulsive, reactive behavior. I do not want to see you running into danger. Of course, you will, so agents have been assigned to you for your protection.

Suzie, please stay calm. Your safety is more important to me, and I don't want to accept your resignation, as I would miss you and lose the benefit of your advice and friendship.

Mr. Fox was told all his campaign donations, every dollar, would be returned. He was read the riot act. Suppose he threatens, coerces, abuses, or touches you. In that case, if he threatens or sounds like a veiled threat, coerces, abuses, or touches you, he will be arrested for interfering with the duties of the President of the United States. It's a serious charge of sexual abuse and attempted assault on a federal employee.

David, I have arranged for a Secret Service agent trained with Special Forces to teach you to defend yourself and subdue any attacker. Having the confidence of knowing you can keep Suzie safe may convince you to act strategically. For example, you call for backup.

Robert and my daughters send their love. Two agents will be on the plane with you and see you get home safely. I must take a call from the Prime Minister of India with the Vice President-elect. The time difference sometimes means long nights.

David, you, and Suzie, irrational as it sounds, have angered a forceful and influential man used to getting his way with women by force. This is to be kept confidential, as his wife has left him and turned over many financial papers, documents, and business dealings, which are now under strict scrutiny. With Mr. Fox in court battles, I would guess you are safe for a long time. Good night, stay out of trouble, and get some sleep."

"The most beautiful people we have known are those who have known defeat, known suffering, known struggle, known loss, and have found their way out of the depths. These individuals possess an appreciation, sensitivity, and understanding of life that fills them with compassion, gentleness, and profound lovepersons have an appreciation, sensitivity, and understanding of life that fills them with compassion, gentleness, and deep loving concern. Beautiful people do not just happen." Elisabeth Kübler-Ross.

Seventeen
The Demands of the Loveless

"The demand of the loveless and the self-imprisoned that they should be allowed to blackmail the universe: that till they consent to be happy (on their terms), no one else shall taste joy: that theirs should be the final power; that Hell should be able to veto Heaven." C.S. Lewis

Crying and visibly shaken, Suzanne rode Whisper bareback out of the barn. She wanted time to be by herself. Suzie knew she needed to speak to David, uncertain of his reaction to those who would hurt her.

"Angel, Good Morning. Enjoyed your ride? Made us coffee. What would you like for breakfast?"

"Love, I'm not hungry; I need time to be alone. David, don't know what to do."

She ran up the staircase and locked our bedroom door, an uncharacteristic move that turned the door into a solid barrier.

A worrying sign, our bedroom became inaccessible. We never lock the door, as our privacy has always been respected. What could cause Suzie to be this upset? She needed time to herself, and with great reluctance, left her alone.

Almost everyone had already left for the weekend and wouldn't be home until the next day.

Nana and her mom invited Jacqueline, Jaz, Annabelle, Noreen, and Jessica to San Francisco to shop for school clothes in Union Square. A ride on a cable car up Nob Hill to go to the girls' favorite toy store, The Wendy Hut, was always a welcome treat; the girls looked forward to having lunch in Fisherman's Wharf.

'Daddy, I'm buying a surprise for Aunt Suzie.'

Megan and Vickie were upstairs packing. They were fussing over which Bed and Breakfast, but were delighted when they found a spa near the Napa River to spend the weekend. They plan to drive around Napa for wine tasting and to search for vintage wine bottles to make into candle holders. Vickie loved selecting a few bottles of wine for select occasions and storing them in the Sanctuary.

"Suzie, come with us. David is working on a speech and wants to come to pick you up Sunday afternoon."

Suzie didn't answer, only tears in her eyes. Concerned, Vickie knocked on her door after she found it locked.

The bedroom only locks in our intimacies when Annabelle is home.

"Suzie dear, what is wrong? I'm not going to leave until you let me in. Megan is finishing packing. Sweetheart, listen to me. As a little girl, you ran into my bedroom, upset about something. Remember, since I was the closest age, you shared heartaches when you had troubles."

Suzie unlocked her bedroom door, tears streaming down her face.

"Vickie, don't know what to say to David. Scared, and my hands are shaking. Don't know the word being mailed black."

"Blackmailed, sweetie, take your time."

Vickie held her hand to go to the sofa, where the two Sisters sat in silence.

"Vickie, I'm frightened. The blackmailers want $500,000 each and have sex on demand."

Her intensity of trepidation held back her tears, preventing any from escaping.

"Those bastards, Mr. Fox, Ryan, and Jack, want sex with me one-on-one or simultaneously.

They want me to give Jack and Ryan money. Mr. Fox doesn't need money. He wants a menage with Jacquie and me."

"Menage de Trois, I'm not going anywhere. Suzie, take your time."

"Suzie, can I come in?"

Vickie spoke softly, "Megan, close and lock the door behind you."

"Suzie, A phone call for David got him visibly fuming. Walked past me, not saying a word. That was him driving off."

"Vickie, he knows."

Megan was livid since Ryan was involved in the extortion.

"Vickie, what should I say to David?"

Forty-five minutes later, David drove back home carrying a package, went directly into the living room, and made a phone call.

"Vickie, please, just a few more minutes alone."

"Mr. Charles, thank you for waiting. Can you speak in private?"

Annabelle likes to answer the phone and push buttons, so the speakerphone volume is usually turned up.

"Mr. Charles, I require help to contact your friend from childhood and ask if you can speak with his son, your two police buddies, and Kevin. But, Mr. Charles, first, you must assure that under no circumstances will you take credit."

"No problem, Mr. David, which would be easy to arrang. I recently handled a similar situation. She was stalked by an ex-boyfriend who threatened to harm her. My friend's daughter is now safe from serious trouble."

"This is my plan, and everybody needs to remain flexible. Please inform Mr. Charles of the need to use discretion. Charles, remind everyone, unquestionably no violence."

"Mr. David, appreciate the importance and will see this done right. And call later tonight with confirmation."

"Seriously, consider Suzie and my work with the White House. The FBI will likely interview you.

Mr. Charles, please agree unequivocally that there are no heroic acts. I accept 100% responsibility.

The truth is that one of your tenants' lives was in imminent danger. Due to the sensitivity of avoiding involvement with the White House, everyone agrees that Mr. David takes 100% culpability when pressed. Primarily, you, Mr. Charles, please don't take any accountability. The FBI would not interview you unless they already have evidence."

"Yes, Mr. David, understood."

"It's imperative to keep Kevin downstairs. It is essential as the sole witness to the Bar conversation. As a Marine, he requires a credible explanation to avoid culpability.

Please contact your two police officers' friends whose duty station is in the neighborhood. Consider that they have to file a truthful police report.

The gang members won't have weapons or drugs, ensuring they are not charged. Comforted that they know how to care for themselves.

Kevin says it's personal and is happy to return it to the rightful owner. Doubtful Ryan, Jack, and Mr. Pigman claim ownership of the DVD. Or even file charges because their kidnapping sex trafficking scheme will land them in jail much quicker. Confident due to the severity of the crime of human sex trafficking, the FBI will apprehend and charge all three."

Vicki stood with her hand on her mouth, afraid to utter a word.

"Stay calm, Mr. David; my friend's son is a specialist in matters like this."

"Mr. Charles, wait for a second. I need to adjust the speaker volume. Who is this expert?"

"The son of a childhood friend went to school with and was part of one of the worst gangs in the South Bronx. He left the gang a few years ago, after getting arrested the third time. The judge offered an alternative; he got rehabilitated, and presently is called upon to speak to high school at-risk students, about the reality of the street."

"Mr. David, they are from The Bronx and know not to ask questions. Promise absolutely no violence, just a street conversation of the mind."

"When will I hear how this came down?"

"On the midnight shift from 10:00 p.m. to 5:00 a.m., my guess is sometime after 10:00 p.m. your time. The critical factor for Suzie's reputation is that she shouldn't know the details. So, if all goes well, and it will, Mr. David, this will remain confidential, and the extortion will end this evening."

"Understand asking a lot, but these three threatened sexual assault and kidnapping and have careened headfirst into an impenetrable Bronx barrier. Soon they will find out what a Bronx man is capable of to protect his lover.

Sorry, Mr. Charles, for the repetition. No violence must be clearly understood. Remind the gang members to walk right up to the line, but under no circumstances to cross the line to make this illegal. No one is to get hurt.

Kevin needs to be at least one city block from the building. These are honest police officers who follow the rules; they mustn't know what's in the package. This is an unknowable variable: how your police friends respond. My slight advantage is that we are street brothers."

"Mr. David, no one will hurt Miss Suzie. Wait for my call."

Turned to face Vickie, who surely would be critical of my plan.

"Hi Vickie, where is Suzie?"

"Mr. Charles, how is he? David, she is frantic with worry. She is in your bedroom with Megan. Tell her whatever you and Mr. Charles are cooking up. We are about to leave for the spa."

"Vickie, please, it will be all right."

"What are you and Mr. Charles up to, David? Are you okay?"

"As soon as Suzie is safe."

"Megan and I will be home no later than 9:00 pm."

"Please keep your plans for the weekend."

"Like that is going to happen."

Vickie kissed me gently to reassure me she would stand with Suzie and me regardless of any lingering concerns.

Suzie came downstairs and ran sobbing into David's arms.

"Vickie, she is now safe."

"Megan, is it okay if we don't stay overnight as we planned?"

"Exactly what I thought. Suzie, talk to David."

Suzie led us to sit on the sofa, hugging me tightly.

"David, did you eat breakfast?

I'll make our favorite mushroom omelet with toast, cherry jam, orange juice, and Café Mocha. Come keep me company."

One egg dropped from her hand onto the floor.

"Shit"

Suzie dropped a second egg onto the floor. After it broke in her hand, the third egg yolk slipped into the sink.

"How about cinnamon toast with strawberry jam, with French Press coffee for brunch? How does that sound?"

"Yes, it does sound good, sweetheart. I'd rather make us an omelet."

She turned on her favorite soft jazz radio station, as music generally calms Suzie.

"I'm sorry, silly me, it will only take a few minutes. You can help me by making toast and fresh orange juice. Would you like coffee also? I'll make us a fresh pot; please get the plates and forks, and we' will make us a fresh pot, please get the plates and forks, and we will eat in the kitchen. Is that okay?"

"Sounds good to me."

"Love, the pantry has a new ketchup bottle for your eggs."

We ate breakfast in silence. Suzie took small bites, which did not prevent her from blowing her nose.

"Honey, leave the dishes soaking in the sink and come into the living room. I'll open the windows, and we will take our walk later."

After a few minutes of weeping, silent tears flowed from her eyes, and she spoke in a soft voice as if to calm herself.

"David, got a threatening phone call early this morning. You were in the shower, so you took Whisper for a ride. Whisper took me to the far end of our property, our favorite grove of Live Oak trees, with a stream eventually meandering into the Sacramento River. Whisper knew to bring me here. You and I love it because it's peaceful. It's always fun to watch you try to catch a King Salmon, even though they live in the river and not the stream."

Her hands were shaking, and more tears flowed down her face.

"You don't have to say anything right now. Did you ride Whisper bareback?"

"Yes, why?"

"Tack up Shadow for me since she is calmer when you do. Whisper is comfortable with you riding her bareback, in the mood to put my feet into a cool running stream. Give me a minute. Want to retrieve something from our bedroom?"

We rode slowly through the luscious green meadow to the edge of the woodland before dismounting. Suzie never ties her horses up because Whisper and Shadow never wander far from her.

"Girls, get some fresh water. David forgot their apple."

"Just by chance, I passed the apple bucket, and it reminded me to take a few apples to feed Shadow. Took too many for her. Here, take two apples for Whisper."

"Just passed the apple bucket on the other side of the barn. How I love you so."

"Remember when you first took me here and read your favorite Coleridge poem, *'Sonnet: To the River Otter.'* You always laughed and were amused that there was a poem to read to the otters in the stream. Would you read the poem? I brought the handwritten copy you gave me."

Samuel Taylor Coleridge's "Sonnet: To the River Otter."

"Dear native Brook! wild Streamlet of the West! How many various-fated years have passed? What happy and mournful hours since last I skimmed the smooth thin stone along with thy breast, Numbering its light leaps! Yet so deep imprest Sink the sweet scenes of childhood, that mine eyes I never shut amid the sunny day."

"Damn, don't have tissues."

"You keep a small pack in Shadow's saddle."

"Love, please finish the poem for me."

Continuing, "But straight with all their tints thy waters rise, Thy crossing plank, thy marge with willows gray, And bedded sand, that veined with various dyes, Gleamed through thy bright transparency! On my way, Visions of childhood! Oft have ye beguiled Love manhood's cares yet waking fondest sighs: Ah! That once more I was a careless child!"

"David was afraid to tell you. I didn't want you to do something that places your life at risk. Frightened, I'm being extorted. Ryan, Jack, and Mr. Fox demanded $500,000 in cash and sex. Fox doesn't need the money, just wants Jacquie and me to have a Menage de Trois, do anything they want, and have sex anytime."

Tears ran unremittingly down Suzie's face.

"Suzanne, promise it will be alright, and whenever you want to talk, I'm not going anywhere."

"No, I need to let you know. David, hold me. I'm terrified.

My worst nightmare, the bastards want me for on-demand sex.

Wouldn't they have to kill me to keep me from testifying? Oh, my God, what are we going to do?"

"Suzie, take hold of my hands. No one is going to harm you. There is nothing to fear because I will protect you. Trust me, as you always have. I won't leave your side.

Additionally, Secret Service agents are protecting the perimeter of our home. You are safe and shall remain secure. Tell me what they said to you."

"The night we made love in the Lady's room in the Hotel Le Luxe's bathroom. A security camera recorded us as part of the standard procedure in case the FBI or Secret Service needed it as evidence. David, our lovemaking was captured on tape, and you could see all we did. We innocently made a sex tape."

"It will be all right. I'm sorry I didn't take the phone call."

"Disgusted by his demand, used Bronx street language and told Jack to F*CK off, and go to hell. Do what you want, and tell those two sons of a bitch, Ryan and Fox.

Did I say the right thing? Did it get him angrier?"

'You have one week; I have a DVD in an envelope addressed with postage to The London Sun to ensure it gets international coverage. The clock is ticking.'

"After the phone call, I ran out and rode Whisper."

"Suzie, don't repeat this because your Sisters and boss already think you have transformed into a Bronx Lady. But proud of your defiance and language. That was the correct reply for the New Yorker. Regardless of his response, you cannot show fear. Questioning why you are not the least bit afraid. Will ever so slightly place doubt in his twisted mind. It is just enough to keep him off balance."

"David, learning from you how to be street smart. Isn't that right?"

"Yes, you are, and the President does not blame you. Though she doesn't enjoy your vernacular, she is no stranger to the words."

"David, can you help me stop talking like a deranged New Yorker? Oh, sorry, didn't mean you."

She started to laugh but stopped almost as soon as she began.

"David, why are they doing this?"

"Fox and Jack were humiliated and defeated and want revenge, and Ryan wants to hurt Megan, and you and I would be my guess."

Suzie, fearful my reaction would be perilous and place me in harm's way, "David, I know the *city that never sleeps. Your* mind switches on automatically, thinking like a New Yorker without realizing it."

"The Bronx code of the street will handle this for us. Trust me. Be assured, this is over tonight, and you are safe. But, in the meantime, I'll share all I know."

"David, please, no violence."

"Angel, physical force is not required when applying appropriate street persuasion."

"How? Will it only make them more determined to ruin your reputation?"

"I'm not concerned. Your safety and peace of mind are of the utmost importance. Suzie, nothing will sully your reputation or career, dealing with the Press, or your work in the White House. As an important public servant working with the President and the love of my life, this will stop tonight, so you will never have to worry."

"You are going to kill them or get them killed. Oh God, no, I'm silly. You have another way. Tell me."

"Angel, I will share details as soon as I receive confirmation. I will tell you everything."

"David, what confirmation? I don't want to involve the President or the White House. Should I go to the FBI? I don't know what to do."

"Promise me you can't tell anyone, ever. This means your Sisters, this is vital. The fewer people who have knowledge of this escapade, the safer this becomes."

"David, keep holding me. No one will know. Except for Vickie, she was frightened on my behalf. Used to go to her as a child when scared. She always took care of what was troubling me. She is as stubborn as I am and wouldn't leave me until I told her why I was so distraught. Vickie is the only one of us who has kept every secret told to her. So frightened, I didn't know how to tell you. Megan also knows. Did I do the right thing?"

"Yes, love, Vickie and Megan will keep this secret.

You should never second-guess yourself. Suzie, you're more intelligent and strategic than I am. Plus, you have unassailable common sense. Suzie, you are not working for the President of the United States only because she loves you. The President relies on your critical analysis and advice."

"When you were upstairs, you probably heard me drive off. That was a coincidence, and don't worry.

Mr. Charles called me while you were upstairs with Vickie. He told me, Kevin…."

"Sherry's Kevin?"

"Yes, he was having dinner and a few beers in an Italian restaurant on Bleeker Street in the East Village with a few of his Marine friends. Three men, already intoxicated, bragged about how they could get a large sum of money and gain control over a sex Goddess."

Kevin was conversing with his buddies when he heard muttering about a woman named Suzanne. She is for our sexual pleasure. Her precious boyfriend will be humiliated.

"David, they mean to kill me."

"Suzie will never happen. They are *The Three Stooges*."

"The old black and white 1950s television shows you liked as a boy."

"Can't believe you don't think they're funny."

"Love, women don't like to watch such foolishness. They demean women. As someone who schemes or gets a pie in her face."

"Oh, my God, you are right. Sorry. They're three imbeciles. Is that better?"

"There are his delusions troublesome to bear; it was for me. Never been as infuriated. Suzie, I'd like you to listen to this.

Kevin didn't give the bragging any credence. Guys boast about sexual conquests when drunk because they have contempt for women.

As this man turned his head, Kevin turned away to talk with his buddies. Recognize Ryan from the photos shown to him and Sherry. How beautiful you are. Kevin asked who these women were. 'They are Suzie's Sisters, and you, Sherry, and your sweet baby will come for dinner when they are in New York. Suzie would love to introduce you to her Sisters. She is full of pride in their loving friendship.'

Angel, maybe it was his Marine training to identify intentions based on facial expressions."

"David, who is this person standing next to this woman?"

"She is Megan."

"No, you told me about her, this man?"

"Ryan, her husband."

"Look, this is only a gut feeling, but personally, I wouldn't trust this guy or let him near my wife or baby." Sherry diplomatically changed the subject."

"That is how he remembered Ryan."

"David, what did Kevin do?"

"This part of the story is why I'm confident you will be safe. Kevin told his buddies I'd be right back."

He needed to do something private. All three of his Marine friends had served together since Boot Camp, which was good enough for them.

Kevin spilled a little beer on his hands and wiped them on his face and shirt. Walked over to them, not to appear drunk, just tipsy.

With a slight drunken tone, 'Excuse me, gents. Heard about a sex Goddess available for sex. Sitting close to your table with my drinking buddies. Volunteered to see if we could also get on this action.'

"Jack spoke first." 'Yeah, the bitch broke up with me, and her beloved wussy of a boyfriend, David, took her away from me. Ryan married her first cousin and hates this sex Goddess boyfriend. Thrown out of a party unceremoniously because of him. The only way to teach him a lesson is to feck his girl.'

"Suzie, hold my hand.

Kevin decided to call his buddies over and beat the crap out of them; however, something seemed amiss, and he needed more details, so he continued to play along."

'Goddam, you must be pissed. How are you going to make this happen, and where?'

Ryan pointed to Fox, who was not paying attention and was already drunk, 'a rich bastard with a lot of money, who bought a video surveillance sex tape. This was made very clear. The bitch will do what we say and give her a week to comply.'

'Hey guys, what do you say? Here are Jack's number and address. He has the DVD; call a week from now, and he will tell you the time and date.'

'Thanks. Okay to share with my buddies?'

'Hell yeah.'

"Kevin walked back to his friends, and they asked what that was all about. Casually replied,

'Just a friend who needs some help. I'll take care of it when I get home. How about one last beer?

See you guys tomorrow. Your wives and mine planned for all of us to go out for dinner.'

"Suzie, Kevin was outraged and thought about unleashing his three Marine friends on them. His honor as a Marine gave him pause, as he knew someone who could confidentially handle this for you and me.

That evening, Kevin informed Mr. Charles of everything he had learned. 'Mr. Charles, would you speak to David and forewarn him? I'll do whatever is called for to protect Suzie.'

Kevin copied the telephone number and address and handed over the information. He had held on to the original in Ryan's handwriting. All Mr. Charles said was for him not to worry. No one would hurt Miss Suzie."

"New York justice, oh, David, this may not go as planned and make matters worse. Call and stop Mr. Charles and Kevin from getting in trouble."

"Angel, it is already in play. Trust Mr. Charles, growing up in the streets, has a friend whose son was a member of one of the gangs in the hood. He got shot a few years ago by a rival gang, and when he recovered, he discovered his girlfriend was pregnant. A judge gave him a chance, and he made the most of it. Honor among the gang let him leave, trusting he would never betray them."

"You can skip over this part. I understand."

"Kevin has a childhood friend who was a detective before joining the Marines. This friend has two police friends. Once they learned this was for Kevin and his wife's friend, they asked how they could help."

"How will this not make this worse? It sounds more and more frightening."

"Love, don't have any names of gang members. Mr. Charles thought it was best."

"New Yorkers taking care of their own."

"Something like that. In a few hours, this ex-gang member bangs on Jack's door. When he opens his door, a former gang member and two gang members enter his apartment."

"David, this is serious. They could get arrested."

"Angel trusts they are experts."

"Of beating Jack to death?"

"Suzie, Gang members understand how to protect one of their own when someone threatens their lady."

"So I'm one of those ladies? You will go to jail as an accessory to a crime. And I lose you and won't be able to protect you."

"Love, grew up in the streets, not so far away from their mean streets. And had gang member friends who protected me. We became friends because we didn't treat each other with contempt or fear, but rather with only friendship. And respect as a person, not their choices as part of a gang."

"New York man, was this where you gained knowledge of Bronx gang etiquette?"

"Yes, being saved from being beaten up or robbed in High School. Never saw them again once I attended university."

"David, your top security clearance, everyone you talked with, going back to high school, was interviewed. How did these gang guys avoid talking to the FBI and the Secret Service? Honor among thieves, oh my David, I'm scared for you."

"Good, that will stop you from being afraid."

"So, you've decided it's reasonable to trade my fear of being extorted into having sex and ruining our lives with a fear of you losing your reputation and work for the government and landing you in jail. The Press would hound you and uncover everything you ever did."

"Yes, it was what I thought. Suzie never broke any laws or belonged to a gang. Guilt by association was my only risk. My relationship was having guys protect me from being beaten to death or robbed. Friendly and grateful, they accepted me as a friend and trusted me. When the FBI interviewed, they would learn some are still in jail."

"David, be serious."

"Sorry, they would never say anything as they are street smart and probably said, 'You mean the skinny guy, who was always getting beat up, what about him?'

There is no police record, not even an appearance. Never broke local, state, or federal laws and have my clearance, so it's not a problem."

"You are impossible, and you are making this up to stop me from worrying."

"Yes, to stop you from worrying, sweetheart. None of this is made up. Would you like to listen to the last part? Because, in a few hours, I can tell you it's over."

"An Irish girl and a Bronx boy, we would have made a cute high school couple. Implicitly trust you'll protect me from them ever touching me, even if it lands you in jail. Oh

Shit, David, this is not reassuring. You would languish in prison."

"Angel, the worst will not happen; Jack would not dare file charges, exposing his blackmail plot much sooner."

"Plus, with a police record, the President could not protect you and would have to let you go. The Press will badger her until I, too, resign."

"Sweetie, this may be hard to hear, but not surprising. I love this, as it is New York street at its finest."

"David, please stop your New York tough guy talk, and believe in your New Yorkness., can resolve something as complex as this is for you and me."

"New York tough talk is to protect and out of respect for you."

"By gang members?"

"Yes, love, they have mothers, sisters, and girlfriends. Women are strictly off-limits. If an outsider harms any woman, they immediately take actions that won't land them in jail or a sentence.

So, when we return to New York, we can have the gang guys and their ladies over for dinner to thank them."

"You serious?"

"Yes, they are better people than those who commit financial investment crypto scams that deceive vulnerable citizens, taking their life savings. This gang protects older adults from mugging and also feeds poor kids. Suzie, they help save High School kids from impoverished areas of The Bronx, so they do not repeat the same mistakes they had made. He and the gang leader are in a documentary. They're the New York Bronx Angels. Meeting you would be a privilege and honor."

"David, why did you make me believe they were hoodlums and dangerous?"

"I didn't, Suzie, you assume."

"Oh, David, I did, and you told me they were doing this out of respect. Why didn't you tell me this first?"

"Suzie, love is multi-dimensional and includes all types of people. They have the same capacity to love."

"*West Side Story,* the movie we recently watched."

"Hoped you would not obsess because you will remain safe.

Perhaps Angel, could you please speak to the President to release federal grants for the Bronx's poverty islands?"

"Of course, if I'm still working for her after this. David, you never put anyone in harm's way. Except for these bastards. You wanted to extract more dire consequences."

"It was important to balance your safety and reputation, and people doing this for us. This was a perfect solution."

"You won't include yourself. Why not? You never think about your safety. Please, David, consider yourself."

"Angel, by ensuring you are safe."

"I'm your Mall then."

"Moll."

"Love, don't you dare make this into another day in The Bronx. Trust you, but I'm not familiar with this life you lived. Reading your memoir, you did include this part of your life. I love you, but I'm still nervous."

"Honey, there is nothing to go wrong."

"Don't tell me because they are practitioners of the street and know what they are doing."

"Just experts on the realities of life on the street.

Scripted out this last part, and if it develops, according to my instructions, believe everything will get resolved tonight. Remember, don't have names except for Kevin."

"Oh, David, why is Kevin involved? He can lose everything, his rank being court-martialled, and what about Sherry and their baby?"

"Because he can bear witness against them and is the best person to protect the DVD until he hands it over to Mr. Charles."

"Mr. Charles's friend's son is going to Jack's apartment. Once inside, he, along with two gang members, should worry Jack as he watches his life unraveling in front of him. Don't know the exact dialogue. Mr. Charles, based on my instructions, informed them what they should say and do."

"Mr. Charles, oh, David, this is getting perilous."

"Angel, you don't need to fret. Mr. Charles grew up in the streets, too. And won't let them break any laws. The gang leader of this escapade's instructions allow him discretion to ad-lib when required."

"The Ex-Gang member says Where is the sex DVD of my lady and the lady you are blackmailing?"

"Jack denies having a tape and says, 'Don't know your girlfriend.'

Next, the gang leader looks around the room for any expensive item that easily shatters. Then pick one up, 'Don't lie to me!'

Jack, a bully confronted by three gang members, will turn into a whimpering coward.

Jack nervously says, 'Telling you the truth. I have no sex tape of your lady.'

'Rumor on the streets is you also have a sex Goddess. You're offering any man or woman to have sex as much as they want.'

"Mr. Charles added 'or woman' because it sounded like real street talk."

"Holding a vase now by his fingertips,"

'How will you get this woman to approach your sorry ass? You have a sex tape on her, too?'

"He will deny that, and..."

'Oh, what a shame. Sorry, slipped out of my hand. Want to see this make-believe DVD and give me the tape of my lady?'

"I'll bet he holds out, hoping some neighbor calls the police. After multiple broken items, the ex-gang member says,"

'My associates are not as patient or forgiving and may reduce your apartment to unrecognizable trash. We'll start easy with the kitchen.'

"With broken glass, plates, and food thrown on the floor, and anything that can be shattered is smashed, Jack won't give up the tape so easily. It is his only chance for money and to have sex with you. Jack hasn't yet lost anything of real value that's irreplaceable."

"This is my favorite part."

"David, you promised no violence."

"There will be nothing barbarian, just street persuasion and broken household items. Sorry, love, this is gentle compared to what personally would inflict on Jack."

"New York man, you want to hurt and beat the DVD out of him. But you could never do that, nor would you allow these guys."

"Suzie, honestly, don't have the self-confidence to control my anger. That is why I didn't go to New York."

"David, you are scaring me."

"Angel, sorry, but they crossed a red line where no possible redemption exists. They were never going to have you live through your worst nightmare. The only solution was to make their threatening nightmares come true in front of them."

"Angel found a better solution to haunt them for the rest of their lives. But not by me. The courts will do that legally."

"David, this is not making me any happier, yet trust your instincts and judgment."

"Sorry, honey, let me share my favorite part. The gang leader gives Jack a final warning as two gang members enter his bedroom, searching for the DVD. However, that still doesn't break his defiance.

Mr. Charles told them that if this was the case, turn up street persuasion without physical violence, just psychological tactics."

'Ok, let's make it really easy. If we find it first, you will not recognize your face.'

"The coward in him will plead that there is only one DVD he hid and will retrieve it. Safe bet he swears there is no tape of his lady. Ironically, the truth.

Mr. Charles's police friends will know when to bang on the door."

'Police, open the door. Received a call from your neighbor complaining it sounded like someone was smashing up your apartment.'

"Jack will run to the police for protection, and before he says anything,"

'Okay, gentlemen, you know the routine.' One policeman pats them down.

'Sarge, no weapons except this manila-padded envelope.'

"The Sargent says,"

'Drugs, ok, hands behind your back.'

"Jack will believe he is safe and unknowingly places himself in jeopardy," says

'Sargent, this is my property.'

'This is now evidence. Two detectives will come to talk to you if this proves to be yours.'

"Suzie, one of the actual gang members, who was led out the door handcuffed, in a barely audible threatening voice, 'We know where you live.'

Handcuffs are removed once out of the apartment and into the hallway."

'Thanks, we owe you one.'

"Downstairs, Kevin is patiently waiting. The next moment, he gets his hands on the package to deliver to Mr. Charles. That is the phone call we have been waiting to hear: that the DVD is in hand.

Suzie, the FBI, will find Ryan, read him his Miranda rights, and arrest him for sex trafficking and attempted kidnapping. Exact charges will also be filed against Jack and Mr. Pigman. Sorry, I know it's not gracious, but I can say it is the kindest name.

Kevin is an essential witness to their involvement in attempted sex trafficking. Assuming Mr. Pigman denies all knowledge and claims he never met Jack or Ryan. A detective will visit him tomorrow. Bet Mr. Pigman runs for his life. His lawyers will deal with sex trafficking charges on top of his Internal Revenue problems, and his sorry ass goes to jail. Jack will be advised not to leave town."

Honey, you can't control what Jack and his conspirators say or how they respond to being arrested. But of course, you are The Bronx Child."

"You are the most talented communicator, and I love your prose. 'The Bronx Child' is perfect for when this episode is written into my romance novel."

"You mean in a written note to your lawyer when you get arrested. The FBI is more rigorous in its procedures than your police friends. David, can a girlfriend testify in favor of her boyfriend?"

"Susie, the President is frustrated with me as she already knows I'm influencing your choice of words. Now you are getting good at New York sarcasm."

"Trust you understand what you are doing, and no matter what happens, seriously, going to say I'm involved with you in this escapade and it is my scheme."

"Angel, Mr. Charles didn't want me to tell you details to prevent this exact reaction. I'm not letting you incriminate yourself. Promise me."

"David, can't let anything happen to you."

"Suzie, I'll be alright, please, for me, promise."

"New York man, can I testify you were insane with worry for me?"

"I'll take that as your promise."

"We won't hear anything until at least 10:00 pm."

"How about we have a picnic? Honey, too nervous to sit and wait. Can we also go to the Sanctuary? Have been wanting to paint the upstairs loft a deep sky blue."

Our favorite place for a picnic was under the live oak trees by the stream. Suzie was serene, as this was our favorite place on the property.

With the sun shining bright, we walked hand in hand silently to our Sanctuary. "David, how about painting a mural on the wall opposite our bed?"

Being creative is soothing and therapeutic for Suzie when she is anxious or upset.

There are always unintended consequences. Suzie and I comforted each other. Why hadn't the FBI come to interview? That seems odd. Put these unsettling premonitions of doom aside. Especially didn't want Suzie to become disquieted. There was another shoe to drop, but my priority was to focus on protecting Suzie and having the DVD obliterated.

The sky was turning silently into twilight when we decided to walk back to Woodland Cottage.

"What time is it?"

"We have at least four more hours to wait."

"New York man, tell me more about what you were like when you lived in The Bronx as a boy."

Suzie laid her head on my lap and reminisced randomly about my childhood. She liked to have my fingers run through her long, wavy hair, along with some gentle kissing.

Megan and Vickie were concerned and arrived home earlier than expected.

"Suzie, are you ok? Thankfully, you look calmer."

"Vickie, I'm The Bronx Man's Mall."

"Moll."

"Right, his moll."

"David, did you break our Sister?"

Suzie looked at Vickie and started giggling.

"Megan and I were anxious but glad you sound better."

"Sis, David broke me months ago," and winked at David.

David, could you tell us how Suzie changed from frantic a few hours ago to telling nasty, bad sexual innuendos clichés?"

"Vickie, did you ladies eat anything today?"

"We had breakfast here and had lunch."

"Vickie, stay with David. What he told me both upset me and calmed me a little. Is a salad okay? We can choose from several different kinds of dressings. How about a tomato, avocado, and mozzarella salad?

Megan, come to the kitchen and share what I know."

"Could you have devised a riskier scheme to get you into jail, sued, or both?"

"Vickie agreed with Mr. Charles, as he would do this regardless of whether I want him to. After hearing what

Kevin told him, they both were determined to do something. Mr. Charles had an idea."

"David, my dear brother, you know you well enough; this is your idea, and a foolproof plan, I assume. To use a real police officer, a Marine, and three gang members. This plan comes directly from your author's creative mind, with Mr. Charles providing the characters you need to make this happen."

"Two, one is an ex-gang member."

"As if that makes this a reasonable plan. One former and two gang members enter by force into an apartment, thus risking angering the President of the United States because you surmised a New York approach was strategic and risk-free. Please don't give me the Bronx tough talk, and this whole scheme depends on three gang members tearing up an apartment to procure a DVD to save Suzie. You are an unmanageable, most reckless man."

Vickie started to tear up and was rightfully upset. Suzie was her baby Sister.

"David, hug me. I need to feel your heart beating. It will calm me if you stay tranquil. Trust your ability to safeguard Suzie.

God help me. You know what you are doing. Otherwise, you would never have allowed this half-brained lunatic's plan to take place. David, I'm sorry. I love you so much, and Suzie is my life. Not upset with you. You are an uncontrollable and resilient New Yorker who saved Suzie's life. Thank goodness you survived."

Vickie kissed me gently as tears ran down her face. "After this, David, please promise you and Suzie will spend time with me and go to New York. Perhaps see another Broadway play?"

"Vickie would love to, and so will Suzie. Decide and book a flight. You will also stay with us when we go to our cabin in the mountains.

I love you, too, Vickie. You are cherished, and we are more than best friends. Sweetie, you and I have a lot in common, protecting Suzie and your sisters.

Sis, don't cry, it will all come out well. Have never told you of my unbounded love and affection for you, which began the first day we met, having just arrived at Woodland Cottage."

'Suzie, can't wait to meet your David.'

'Sis, David is upstairs. He will come downstairs in a few moments. He calls his mom to give her our telephone number and address.'

'Your beautiful, long, curly red hair, cute freckles, and smile are as welcoming as the start of Springtime. Delighted to meet you. Sorry for the schmaltz greeting. Suzie always tells me everything you are up to. Bet we already know a little about each other.'

'David, all the girls kiss and hug you when they meet
you. So do I, but first, I want to say I'm your sister in every
sense; friend, confidant, someone to laugh and cry together.

Bonded with you not because you jumped in front
of our Suzie to save her life. Jumping in front of Suzie was
an act of impressive bravery. It's because of your heart.

The girls, at first, didn't want a brother. We were
happy, just the four of us. After Noreen and Jacquie told
me about you, especially how pleased they were to have
you in their life, I wanted to adopt you as my brother.
David, can I have a hug and a kiss?'

"Want to share something private with you. Let's take
a walk before our dinner."

"David, you want to tell me about your special
romantic plan for Suzie?"

"Vickie, how could you possibly know?"

"Sweetie, next time, cover the store's name. That is
one of Jaz's boutiques, which sells romantic bridal and
evening gowns."

"Vickie, your love and friendship mean a lot to me.
You have been there for me when I needed to learn how to
adjust to your home. I knew you were standing in the hall,
but didn't turn the package around, so the store's name
would show. And you would notice. My dear sister, shows
how much trust and love I have for you."

"David, love you too."

Suzie walked in and heard Vickie say she loved David, and their kissing and hugging made Suzie happy. Vickie and David were good friends.

"Vickie, you gave David the strength to do these stupid things. You are close, intimate friends, brother, and sister. Your love and affection for him mean more to him than you may realize. Constantly expresses his feelings for you and Noreen to me.

David has shown me romantic love. As part of life, he says love is expansive, adding and never taking away. Our joyous family life has been woven into our romance. Vickie, move over a little so I can also hug David."

"Stupid, half-brained, and lunatic?"

"Hush, David, and you know what I meant. You're witty, intelligent, intuitive, and loving. I'm sorry I used those words, though they are accurate. Suzie and I did not grow up in a city where everything we feared was part of our normal life."

"A United States Marine, a doorman, three gang members, and two police officers are trusted to risk a lot to save me because of their friendship with David."

Sounding confident or pretending to, Suzie asked, "Since we have two hours to wait, who is hungry?

We can do nothing but hope, and even if this backfires, I'm sure David is already thinking about option two. That is why there is hope."

"Angel, while you set the table, Vickie and I shall go outside for a few minutes. She wants to ask my opinion about a guy she is dating and get a male point of view."

"It will take ten minutes before dinner is ready. Is that enough time to share your secret?"

"David, you have to get better at coming up with excuses. Not dating just one man, this was so transparent. Suzie knows I'm not yet ready to give up dating. How she lets you by and does not try to find out what you are up to is beyond my power of understanding."

"Vickie, it's easy. Suzie presumes all my planning and secrets are for her, and she loves to be surprised, so she doesn't give it a second thought."

"David, what do you want me to do?"

After a light supper, the clock slowly ticked away minutes with no phone call. Finally, at 10:22 p.m., the phone rang.

"May I have each of your permissions to put this on speaker? Whatever occurred, we always have each other."

A ringing phone sounds more ominous when you expect news that may change your life.

"Suzie, hold my hand. No matter what, it will be okay."

"Good evening, Mr. David. Miss Suzie with you?"

"Good evening, Mr. Charles. Yes, and you are on speakerphone. Vickie and Megan are also here."

"Evening, Miss Vickie and Miss Megan. Thank you for your support of your sister.

Suzie is hardly able to sit.

Mr. Charles said, "Good evening, Miss Suzie. This was not my idea, and sorry, but Mr. David requested I say this."

Letting out her fear in a low voice, "Oh, my God, David."

"Miss Suzie, *the Eagle has landed.*

"Mr. Charles, please, what eagle? What does an eagle landing have to do with the most important news of my life?"

"Mr. David told you she would not be old enough to recognize this famous quote."

"Miss Suzie, I'm sorry your David is. Don't have a word."

Vickie said, "Mr. Charles, the word you seek is unmanageable."

"Everyone hush, Mr. Charles. Your news, please, dear God."

"Don't cry, Miss Suzie. You are now 100% safe. The package is in my possession. And can now confirm it is the correct DVD. It has been effectively erased three times.

Watched for a few minutes up to the time you started kissing Mr. David.

Waiting for Mr. David's permission to destroy the DVD. Remember, a UN representative lives in the building, so my office has a highly classified documents shredder. The shredder will destroy it, and a safe way to burn what comes out, so nothing remains."

"Mr. Charles, thank you. I'm nervous about you getting into trouble. Did you see enough of the tape to see how my hair looked from above?"

"Understand now what you mean, Mr. David. She sometimes uses humor to hide her feelings."

"Mr. Charles, this is Vickie. My sister is serious."

"Yes, thank you, Miss Vickie. Mr. David also told me her sisters sometimes would extend the humor. But, Miss Suzie, only watched once and briefly.

You were walking in and turned to face Mr. David.

Miss Suzie, you were the Belle of the Ball. Dear folks, it is all over. I must take my leave and return to work, but first, I need to shred the DVD. Miss Suzie, you can now rest easy."

"Mr. Charles, we will talk in person when we come to New York, but let me say thank you now."

"Good night, all."

Suzie's tears flowed from her blue, bluest eyes, and she couldn't stop crying. She buried her head in my chest for comfort.

"Angel, don't cry, it's over."

"Not crying for that. Afraid my hair didn't look good."

"David, you did break our Suzie."

"Anyone hungry for some hot food? Megan and I can cook something delicious. Meanwhile, you two celebrate."

"New York man, dear lover, we must check for security cameras for the next public bathroom."

"Suzie, Megan, and I swore to never reveal this secret. So, no sister, mom, or Nana will be told. Besides, this is such an unrealistic story. David must have put us up to this."

"Dinner will take less than 45 minutes to prepare."

"Megan, Vickie, adore you both. Come here, let me give you a hug. David and I will tell Jacquie and Noreen over dinner when they come home. Jaz will help calm Jacquie as she will be upset and worried for David and me. Noreen doesn't show worry; she will just hug David and me and cry. It is important not to give details until it is known how the President will handle this."

"David, the Secret Service, would monitor and playback to watch every tape, specifically since there was an attack on my life. Oh, David, the President must know and be told about a stolen sex video DVD of us."

"Angel, she wouldn't watch."

"Secret Service would report to her that there was nothing to worry about. It was the sexual shenanigans of Suzie and David."

"Why, then, are there no follow-up interviews from the Secret Service? The security company must have reported it stolen."

"Angel can only guess it was Mr. Pigman who called to arrange to get the tape, probably for a large amount of cash."

"Love, how would he find out whom to call?"

"Don't know. But, Suzie, you realize what we must do right now."

"Call my boss."

"Megan and Vickie, I'm calling the President."

"Operator, this is Suzanne Siobhan Brooke. Can you please put me through to the President?"

"Hold, Miss Brooke."

"David, it was an excellent ten-year gig while it lasted. I'm not going to get upset."

"Miss Brooke, the President, is in her residence with family and said to take a message.

Miss Brooke, this is Joan. What is wrong? Is this an emergency?"

"Joan, no, not really, well yes, it's personal and rather important."

"Please hold, Miss Brooke. Sending a message to the President's intern, who has access to her residence. She will relay your message to the President."

A few minutes passed. "Hold, Miss Brooke, I'm now connecting you to the President."

"Suzie, if you cry, you can't talk. Please hand the phone to David."

"David. Good evening. My daughters and Dr. Robert send their love. We had just finished a late dinner when Suzie notified me that she wanted to speak to me. David, are you in Suzie's office on a secure phone?"

"Yes, Madam President, may I put us on speakerphone?"

"Suzie, are you better?"

"Yes, Madam President."

"My daughters send their warm regards. They are by my side now, as is Dr. Robert. With your permission, place this call on speakerphone as well."

"Yes, of course."

"My girls said, 'Mom, Suzie is in distress.' So I asked them, How do you know?"

'Mom, look at the time on a Saturday.'

"Apologies, forgot the time difference. Call you tomorrow with your permission."

"Suzie, you have access to me 24/7. Not once did you call without it being urgent or important this late. I wanted to explain that when you called, I was going to call you and David tomorrow. This news is better to deal with now, so you can get any stress out of the way and be aware that you are tearing up, expecting doom. Go ahead. I'm listening."

"Madam President, it started at the donor party, David and I."

"Suzie, the Secret Service kept me informed."

"David, can you confirm from a reliable source someone you trust implicitly destroyed the DVD?"

"Yes, Madam President, Mr. Charles, my doorman in New York."

"He must think highly of you and Suzie to risk so much. Suzie, afraid that when protecting David, you wounded a powerful, wealthy, unbalanced, fixated man in search of women he can dominate. I'll disclose new information, and when I can inform you how I know, I'll tell you."

"Thank you, Madam President. You'll have my resignation first thing in the morning."

"My dearest Suzie and David, you two get into more complex situations than kittens in a box full of yarn. Suzie, please sit and relax. After the donor dinner, extra Secret Service personnel were assigned to you and David. They obtained legal permission from the court to monitor Mr. Fox's communications to ascertain if he was plotting revenge.

Agent Murphy knew of the security camera in the hotel's ladies' room, ironically for your protection, and reported it to her supervisor, leaving what David was doing there to our imagination. Assigned agents to retrieve it, but it was too late, it was missing.

The Secret Service reported that Mr. Fox spoke to the President of the surveillance company and offered a substantial bribe. Hid the tape minutes before our agents arrived.

His behavior was suspicious, as he stuttered and perspired profusely. Nonetheless, he provided the agents with all the neccessary information. He was then charged with accepting a bribe to prevent Secret Service agents from retrieving a DVD made for their use.

They don't react well if someone interferes with their duty. The FBI was instructed to follow the tape to determine its destination. It led the agents directly to Mr. Fox, Ryan, and Jack. Ordered not to release names to the Press. The targets for the FBI were surveilled 24/7 and followed if they left town.

Suzie, this may be difficult as Ryan was married to your cousin. I'll leave it to you how much you want to tell her.

Interestingly and coincidentally, but somehow not surprisingly, in the same building in New York as your apartment, a Sargent from the Marines was bragging about harming Suzie.

An FBI agent paid a visit and asked for permission for an interview. The Marine honored her request, answered all questions with specificity, and handed over a piece of paper with Jack's address and telephone number in Ryan's handwriting.

Kevin is a recipient of a Purple Heart and should be awarded a second one for placing himself at risk to pay back David's kindness. Asked his commander only to reprimand, not escalate further action against him.

Also requested that the commander consider that David stayed up all night with Kevin's unwell baby, to ensure his wife could catch up on her sleep. David watched over the baby and successfully lowered her slightly elevated temperature. He didn't tell you, Suzie. It seemed that the baby was the most significant person in the world, as he stayed awake by her crib all night.

Mr. Charles, a doorman, a sergeant in the United States Marine Corps, two police officers, and three gang members. I'm not surprised you could put together a unique operation right up to the line of remaining legal.

The gang members got a reprieve from an interview due to their well-known community work for the elderly and children. They would not divulge anything as they are loyal to their word.

Suzie, while recovering from gunshot wounds, David asked for history books of the Second World War to read while you slept. That reminded me of the Mafia, who were asked to help in the U.S. campaign in Sicily during World War II. Intriguingly, David has been an avid student of this War. One book sent to him included that fact. As you know, his grandfather flew for the Royal Air Force of the United Kingdom.

I need to remember that you received a Ph.D. because you refuse to use Doctor David unless it's official.

Suzie, there was never a time any member of David's faux S.W.A.T. team was in danger. There were FBI agents there as backup. The FBI Director shared the contents of the DVD with me, as it seems they had obtained a copy that has now been destroyed. Unfortunately, can't reveal how they received a copy.

The Director advised me to allow this to unfold. To keep it from the White House. The Director added,

'Madam President, wish my husband were that romantic.'

"Perhaps it is my fault for assigning you on missions where you have had minimal Special Forces training needed to stay hyper-aware. The FBI Director stated that much of your strategy was derived from an FBI Special Forces training manual.

Both frustrated and proud of you. David, you've gained the support of my two daughters for the romantic bathroom adventure, and my husband reminded me of your adeptness and intelligence in protecting Susie and me. At the same time, do not put anyone in harm's way.

The gang members were a brilliant addition and made the whole thing work. Understood it was not good for the President to praise them. After all, they have street creds to protect, and God only knows how you convinced them, as they are not prone to allow police to handcuff them.

A Presidential order was signed to release additional funding for use in The Bronx and provide access to government grants to aid local nonprofits. Providing educational support for low-income adults and children. Additionally, ensure that the underemployed are referred for job training and placement.

Mr. Charles appears as stubborn as you and took 100% responsibility for cooking up this scheme. Mr. Charles initially refused to talk. The FBI informed him he would not face any charges. Even then, stayed loyal. The FBI knew you didn't want him to be involved, just to reach his contacts. Once shown evidence, he cooperated.

The FBI was ready to seize the DVD and arrest this Jack fellow, who was not my favorite person after harming

Suzie. Still, the FBI Director told me that it would lead to the White House.'

The Director also convinced me they had not devised a better scheme to catch Ryan, Jack, and Mr. Fox. Regarding Mr. Fox, there was no direct evidence, and he was released. However, until police could gather proof of his involvement, a judge ordered him to report to the court if he left the state.

The FBI Director wanted to recruit you, but relented because you were already working with the White House."

"Suzie."

"Yes, Madam President."

"You must issue a press release to explain an in-progress life-threatening sex trafficking scheme. To answer questions of the Press before they ask them. You know what should remain confidential. Since they will not have access to the DVD for collaboration, the story will soon die. You shall say it compromised you and David and endangered your life. You are too close to this. Have your supervisor review it before releasing it to ensure there is no bias.

Years ago, two Press members, now happily married, used Air Force One as a place to show their affection. David, get this thought out of your head.

You are both to watch every word and sentence you speak, not construed as anything other than your life in danger. That is the truth. The dishonorable Press will spread lies, but that started the day David jumped in front of you. You are not to disclose anything about this conversation or the security measures you have taken. It is legal and approved by the Intelligence Committee.

Due to David's penchant for finding trouble, he is now protected by the Secret Service. An agent will be assigned to David until we get evidence of Mr. Fox's participation and arrest.

Mr. Fox paid a bribe to obtain a surveillance tape reserved only for Secret Service use. The three are part of a sex trafficking plot, and Kevin has provided his account. Now it is up to a prosecutor.

Grant an exclusive interview to Roxanne Morris, your reporter friend. Her colleagues trust her to check sources.

David and Suzie, I would like to thank you and appreciate your reasons for not coming to me.

Suzie wanted the White House to remain uninformed, and no way to be knowledgeable.

You both must be hungry. Have dinner.

"Madam President, how do you know we did not have dinner?"

"I know, Suzie."

"Suzie."

"Yes, Madam President."

"Glad you are safe, and this is over. Good night and enjoy your dinner."

"Hey, you two, perfect timing. We are just serving dinner. Is everything good with the President? You only go to your office to make urgent calls or receive confidential calls."

"Vickie, even after these many years, she still surprised me with her depth of empathy."

Eighteen
Too Precious to Forget

"Some say you are too painful to remember. I say you are too precious to forget. I carried you every second of your life, and I will love you every second of mine." Unknown

Sacramento, California, is twenty miles away. Made a mental note of how close to home. Driving Northbound on I-5 was the fastest route from San Diego to Woodland Cottage in South Lake Tahoe. After attending an educational leadership workshop, I would often find that my route home became familiar and comfortable.

Looking forward to surprising Suzie with a present.

My smartphone rang as I thought about the best time to give it to her.

"Hello, Jacquie. I was going to call you. And tell you hid Suzanne's gift in Annabelle's room."

"David, two California State Police Motorcycles should catch up with you any minute., Don't pull over, and follow them."

"Suzanne, oh my God."

"David, I hear police sirens., The police will get you there faster."

"Suzanne! Where is she? What happened?"

"She is in the Emergency Operating Room at Mercy General. David, I know nothing. No one will tell us anything. Dr. Robert was in the hospital meeting with doctors, so thank God he is in the Emergency Room. Promised to tell me as soon as he knew something."

"David, he had tears in his eyes. Doctors don't get emotional. I'm frightened. The police will speed up, so please focus on your driving."

"Jacquie, are you and Jaz okay? Are you both safe? Where is Annabelle? Is she home?"

After receiving reassurance, my concern solely focused on Suzie.

"Jaz and I are in the Emergency Lounge."

"David took the phone from her. She is crying and can't talk. Waiting for you outside the Emergency Entrance. How far away are you?"

"Jaz, the police are going over ninety-five miles per hour, less than eight minutes. Why this urgency, my Suzie?"

"As carefully as you can, please drive safely. David, a policewoman, is guarding the door to the Emergency Room. There is a Secret Service agent here and a Detective waiting to speak to you. They only appear after a crime has taken place. The Press has somehow found out and just arrived. They are behind a police line away from the

Hospital Emergency Entrance. Oh, David, please get here as fast as you can."

"Jaz, stay strong. Suzie and I need you. We can cry once we learn, Suzie, and our baby will be all right."

Two police motorcycles stopped at the front door of the hospital's emergency entrance five minutes later. Dismounted from their motorcycles and stood by the door.

"Sir, you have to move your car. This is only for ambulances."

"Here, move it yourself." Tossing the car keys.

"Sir, it will be towed."

"Then tow the F*CKing car."

Jaz was standing at the open sliding doors. Kissed her and started running inside, turned, and said,

"Are you okay, Jaz?"

She forced a smile. Reacting to David's impatience, "Officer, I'm sorry. Let me have his car keys to properly park the car."

Jacquie heard me before she saw me and wiped tears from her eyes.

"Love, they don't have anything to report. Dr. Robert came out and said it was still too early to make a statement. And returned to the Emergency Surgery Room."

"Thank God Dr. Robert is here with her. This should be calming for her."

We looked at each other.

"Well, he is a friendly face."

With my arm around Jacquie, "For Suzanne's sake, hold on to your faith."

"For God's sake, don't you pray it should have been you and not Suzanne?"

Quietly spoken, "Jacquie was praying for our baby."

"David, forgive me. I'm so upset."

"Sweetheart, there is nothing to forgive."

Jaz walked over to David and slipped the car keys into his pocket along with a note indicating where she had parked the car. Sat next to Jacquie, and no one spoke.

"Dr. David, I am Detective Johansen."

"She already interviewed me because I was there that night."

"What night?"

"Sir, no questions. Miss Jacquie told me what was needed for now. We can talk later after you visit with Suzanne."

"How do you know Suzanne is all right?"

"Dr. David, read an early police report and interviewed the Emergency Responders, Police and Fire Response and Recovery, and an Emergency Room Nurse.

The White House was immediately informed by the Secret Service. President Harrison requested that we provide you with updated information. Dr. David and Miss Brooke were, and Miss Brooke, was forced off the highway. She was stable and alert at the scene and taken to Mercy General Emergency.

I don't have more recent news on her condition, but a nurse informed me that they are still conducting tests.

"What about our baby?"

"The doctor will speak with you shortly."

"What are you saying, Detective? What do you mean she got run off the road?"

"David, please, hold my hand."

"Jacquie, what happened to Suzanne?"

"Sir, she was driving home when forced to take defensive measures. Miss Suzie has been trained to defensively avoid car attacks.

She spun her car to evade crashing into any vehicle in front or behind her. That sent her car careening down an incline, and she hit a tree. The airbag deployed, which an Emergency Responder said saved her life. Miss Suzie received emergency care on the scene. She has been in the operating theater for the last hour."

"Was it intentional? Please tell me if it was intentional and who it was."

"Sir, it was Mr. Fox, the Texan."

"Where is the Pigman? You will certainly want to come with me."

"Sir, Mr. Fox didn't survive. Pronounced dead at the scene.

Suzanne gets training each year on defensive driving by the Secret Service. It started as soon as she obtained her learner's permit. President Harrison, as a Senator, ensured she received training and refresher training twice a year.

She turned the steering hard to the right, and her car hit Mr. Fox's car. All we know now is that momentum forced him into the left lane. He turned to go after Miss Suzanne when an 80,000-pound eighteen-wheel tractor-trailer careened into him and he died instantly."

"Jacquie, does Suzanne know?"

"Sir, the doctor does not want anyone to tell her until she is in her room and stable."

"She will take full culpability for killing him."

"No, she has no blame. She used her defensive driving instincts to escape, which saved her life. The truck would never have smashed into him if he hadn't turned after her."

"David, understand how angry you were with her. He is dead. It's over."

"That is all for now, except this piece of information: Hope provides solace in the coming days. One of the senior officers, a sergeant, was positioned at the right angle to see it all. Good enough to become certified as an instructor. Textbook perfect. She was trained, prepared, and surrounded by security. This enabled emergency responders to quickly administer triage."

"Detective, appreciate your honesty in providing me with details. Thank you."

"Of course, Dr. David, even without White House permission, in her free time, Miss Suzanne shows up at the end of the year before the winter school holiday vacation at a local public elementary school our precinct sponsors with toys and children's books.

She reads stories to children with learning disabilities, encouraging them to believe they can succeed and excel in their academic pursuits. One of those children is my niece."

"Jacquie, your sister asks me if I can give her a ride. My Angel helps colleagues and school children and exclaims in her sweet Irish way, 'Oh David, it's just what I do. Sound familiar?' Your sister and I have a mutual harmony of caring that enriches our relationship."

Another hour passed, and no one would update us.

"I'm sorry, the doctor will speak with you shortly."

Trying to keep a civil tone, "Nurse, you just came out of the emergency surgery room."

"The Emergency Room Doctor and Dr. Kelly are just coming now."

"Dr. Bradley, Jacqueline, and Jaz, let's talk where it is private."

"Doctor, don't need privacy. No disrespect, really don't give a shit about privacy.

Please, what I want are answers about Suzanne and our baby."

Dr. Robert interrupted David, "he follows hospital policy, which you rarely do. So please sit and listen to the Head Emergency Doctor."

Jaz gently tugged his jacket. "Please sit down."

Jacquie acknowledged that only a few close to him could get him to sit. Jaz was one of the few.

"Here is a place for you between Jacquie and me."

All three of us have developed a visual language with our eyes and facial expressions.

Jacquie urged, "David, just for a minute, please stay calm so we can find out how Suzanne and your baby are. The Doctor is not your enemy."

"Doctor, forgive me."

Benignly, "Please tell me about Suzanne and our baby."

"I understand. Don't know how otherwise you could respond.

Lamentably, she lost the baby. My sincere condolences, sorry for your loss.

This occurred during her car accident. It's uncommon, but a severe shock may cause enough trauma to lead to a miscarriage. Wanted to check to ensure no more internal bleeding and conducted tests for signs of trauma to her head. Successful operation. I was able to stop minor internal bleeding. She lost little blood. All tests returned negative, and Suzanne suffered no internal or head injuries."

Dr. Robert reassures David before he dashes off to Suzie. "There is no medical reason she cannot give birth to a healthy full-term baby. Prescribed a mild sedative for her to sleep. Need to leave but will keep the President updated."

Hearing Suzie could conceive again, David dashed out of the Emergency Waiting Room. Her room would be guarded by security, which was not a concern. Before a nurse went after him. First, he needed to locate Suzie's room before a nurse went after him. A sign, *ICU Recovery Rooms.*

"Doctor, please understand my sister and David have gone through a lot together."

"I have watched the news."

The Emergency Room Nurse said, "Doctor, the White House just called, and President Harrison wants to be informed every hour."

The nurse added,

"Miss Jacqueline and Miss Jaz, the President, said she is taking care of everything to pave the way for you to be with your sister. The President sends her heartfelt condolences to Suzie, David, and the family.

Dr. Robert called the President and updated her on the condition and the loss of her baby. The President would privately give her condolences to Suzanne and David. Dr. Robert has already left the hospital as he has a busy schedule. Though I will check up on her every day."

David eyed an open light-colored greyish canvas laundry bin with fresh white Doctor coats and grabbed one. Luckily, it was the correct size. Next, picked up a clipboard to look like a doctor on staff. A stethoscope was lying on a counter, and David placed it around his neck.

In a doctor-like tone, "Nurse, direct me to the room Miss Suzanne Brooke is in."

"You are?"

"Doctor Bradley."

"Is she your patient?"

"Thank you, Nurse, which is room number 2…?"

"Room 212 is down this hallway, the last room on the left. A private room requested by the White House."

"Yes, of course, thank you. Nurse Sanger, her distraught boyfriend, will try to convince you to see his beloved."

"Sorry, Doctor, strict orders, no one is allowed entry if the Secret Service does not first clear you."

"Agent, Doctor David Bradley, check this list."

"Dr. Bradley, she was given a sedative and will be asleep. Who gave you this list?"

"White House, thank you, Agent, for protecting my patient. Note her sisters have permission from the President to visit my patient."

David entered immediately as he didn't want her to realize she had allowed an unauthorized person to enter. Though his suspicion, when she smiled slightly, she recognized him and let him enter. The Secret Service doesn't get fooled so easily.

Suzanne was crying and knew she wouldn't take a sedative until my arrival.

"David, our baby, I'm devastated. Our baby girl. I had a miscarriage; we lost our baby. I'm devastated."

"Angel, I'm here." As I took her in my arms, she started to weep at the loss of our baby.

"Love, no one wanted me to know, but my body doesn't feel her anymore."

Hugging her, she held on to me tightly.

"Half dead now, for if I lost you, I couldn't imagine life without you. Thank God you are alive."

"David, need your strength and love. Please don't leave me alone."

Whispering, "Angel, not going anywhere, spending the night with you. Promise won't leave you until you get released, and we go home together. When you feel up to it, we can discuss what you prefer so Jacquie can start arranging a Jewish and Catholic funeral."

"David, could we have just a Jewish funeral? I want our baby buried in a Jewish Cemetery. Your mom would have liked that."

"Thank you, love, for considering my mom's wishes. Yes, she would have wanted a Jewish burial. Suzie, anything you want will be taken care of. You are to rest, and I will stay with you."

"Jacqueline is out in the waiting room with Jaz.

Jacquie already called your sisters, Megan, Nana, and your mom. Your sisters were on a conference call to divvy up chores so you can rest and not worry. Vickie, Noreen, your mom, and Nana are on their way now to Woodland Cottage to be there for Annabelle and Jessica. Megan has been watching the girls."

"David, please call them too. Tell them I am sorry."

Suzanne started crying again.

"Oh, my sisters, Mom, and Nana. David, how did you find out?"

"Jacquie has been texting me to keep me informed. The family doesn't want you to be worried. Megan will care for Whisper and Shadow with your sisters' support. Jacquie said the family was broken-hearted and sent hugs and kisses."

"David, the President, who told her?"

"Angel, Dr. Robert was in the Emergency Room with you, and he called her. Suzie, Jacquie said he had tears in his eyes."

"Whatever you do or tell me, please say again later. Can't think or feel anything, our baby, David. Let me lean on you, my sweet New York man. What about you? Please, the truth, tell me, are you all right?"

Did not answer because I would not be able to control my sobbing.

"David, does Jaz know? Want to see Jazmine? Please tell her I need her. Sleepy since swallowing the sedative a few minutes after you entered the room. Can't think, it hurts to think. Where is my Jacquie?"

"She is in the waiting room. Let me get her for you."

"David, please don't leave me alone! I need you by my side."

"Texted Jacquie, and she and Jaz are on their way. Be here in less than a minute."

Jacquie walked into the room and held back tears as far as her eyes would allow. Determined to remain serene for her sister's sake. Jacquie hugged and kissed her baby sister. Tears escaped from her eyes anyway, and the two sisters were closely bonded. Each felt the other's misfortunes intensely.

Suzanne collapsed into her arms.

"Hold me, oh God, Jacquie. I lost David's baby. Where is David?"

"He went to get Jaz, who is calling Annabelle."

"Jacquie, how is David? Please tell me. He won't tell me the truth and doesn't want me to worry about him. Sis, please tell me how David is."

"David is here for you and won't leave your side."

"The truth."

"Suzie, heartbroken for you and the loss of your baby. He could not imagine if he had lost you too. His only solace is that you will come home tomorrow. David wants to nurse you back to health."

"Sis, he cried, got angry at the Doctor, and used his favorite get-out-of-my-face Bronx words. That helps him to cope. But David will not let you see that side of him until he is sure you are better and stronger."

"Our family, we won't be able to have a family. Since I can't give him a baby, he should forget about me and find someone with whom he can have babies."

"Sis, he already found a woman. It's you."

"No, have to let him go."

"Sweetheart, at least wait for your Doctor to update you about your tests. Don't say anything yet. Doctor Robert informed David and me that there are no medical reasons why you can't have another healthy baby and bring her to term. You will get pregnant again."

"Jacquie, don't know what I'm saying."

"Wait for confirmations of all test results. You will feel better. I'll stay till David returns before calling Annabelle; she is worried about you."

"Jaz, she named our baby after my mom Rebecca, and her middle name Jacqueline Jazmine, and her mom's maiden name, Brooke. She is devastated that she has let you down.

"Disappoint me? That is not possible. She honored me by giving her first child my name, too."

"Suzanne, not going anywhere, and you don't want me to. The truth is, I don't like babies with another woman. You have stayed strong for me. Sweetheart, let me have my turn to take care of you. You can get pregnant, and we will have a baby.

You know my feelings before I do. I'm brokenhearted, the heartache of losing our baby, Rebecca."

"Oh my love, David, we will get through this together.

Excited but wondered, "Is it true we can still have babies?"

"Yes, love, healthy babies."

"Could never let you go. It's the sedative and shock-talking. Stay with me. It's getting harder to keep my eyes open. Don't leave me. David, sweetheart, I know you are heartbroken. We are going to face the loss of our baby together."

"Love, don't fight the sedative. Go to sleep. Right here by your side all night. I love you."

"David, do you know how I got pushed off the road? Oh, David, I killed our baby. Wasn't careful with our baby."

"The Doctor would disapprove and said not to tell you, as the truth would upset you more. My Suzie, you need to know what happened to have peace of mind."

"Honey, who did you upset?"

"Just a security officer who didn't like my leaving the car in the Ambulance lane and walked inside, and a nurse tricked into learning which room you are in. Oh, and I borrowed a Doctor's white coat just back from the laundry, and perhaps a doctor's stethoscope.

Then made up a list with my name to get past the Secret Service Agent who guards the door for your protection. However, she recognized me and let me in."

"Oh, David, what am I going to do with you? Promise me you will behave now."

"Sweetheart learned to get past doctors and nurses from you. I need a chocolate cherry soda. It calms me."

A small smile. "Love, thank you for remembering.

Don't know how long I can keep my eyes open."

"Take my hand, you are safe, and I'm here. There is no one to be afraid of."

"The detective has confirmed that pig of a man tried to run you off the road."

"Oh my God, David, he was coming to kill me. But, Mr. Fox, was he drunk?"

"Don't know, probably. You crashed the back left side of your car into him. Security said you turned the steering wheel hard to the right, spun, and saved lives. You aimed for the incline and crashed into a tree. An instinctive reaction from your training defending against car attacks protected you. The airbag, along with wearing your seatbelt, saved your life. A severe shock from the crash caused your miscarriage. That is how we lost our baby.

That pig of a man tried to run you off the road. You are faultless, and you did not kill our baby."

"David, where is Mr. Fox? Oh no, did I kill him? Did his car crash because of my defensive driving course? Oh God, David lost our baby because I killed a man. You must hate me; you could not save our baby."

"Sweetheart, it's all right. You are faultless. That pig of a man wanted to kill you. You had police, Secret Service, and FBI following behind you. Recent intelligence indicates that Pigman flew out of Dallas-Fort Worth International Airport and landed at San Francisco Airport. As a precaution, your security increased."

"David, why didn't they tell you?"

"Well, perhaps something said to the Secret Service in New York the night of the thank you donor gathering, if that fat pig came within 1000 feet of you, would blow his fecking head off."

"Honey, you wouldn't do that."

"Suzie, not so certain. Honestly, I don't know what I would do."

"Dear, you don't own a gun."

"Could buy a gun easily with my White House clearance."

"David, you would not have done that. So stop talking like this to blur the fact I killed him."

Looking into her eyes, she was terrified. Tears flowed randomly down her cheeks.

Nothing she was told could convince her it was not her fault. She turned away and cried.

"Hold me, oh, why, David, our baby? His contorted face filled with anger, and he was getting closer to me.

Afraid, only remember the car spinning and thought of you and our baby."

"Suzie, I love you more each day. Don't have words to express what is in my heart. Let me see your beautiful blue eyes. Now, look into my eyes. I, too, only have sadness and tears.

The doctor said you are too fragile and vulnerable. Let you convalesce. As I walked away, the Doctor said, 'Miss Suzanne is emotionally upset. Try not to upset her more.'

Emotionally upset, you *THINK*! We are both upset and need each other. My Suzie needs to hear what happened from me, not your imbecilic saying. Try not to upset her more. Doctor, how could I sadden her more? You fecking moron."

"Your Bronx tough talk. David, please tell me you didn't add that expletive."

"Yes, I did, actually. The exact words, Doctor, what is the f*cking matter with you?"

"Glad you have the intensity of the New York street, but honey, your reputation. We are not in New York. People don't understand that you are expressing your emotional feelings. You understand emotional fears need words to exit the body. Did that sound right?"

"Yes, love, you also have courage. After Paul shot me, and could have quickly re-shot. Regardless of the inherent danger to your life, you went to be by my side."

"Thank you for reminding me, I'm brave too."

"Was there any Press in the waiting room?"

"No, security kept them outside."

"Thank God.

David, I love you for reassuring me and explaining what happened. Even if it was not your best choice of words."

"Suzie, expressing outrage, then turned away and heard clapping from nurses, doctors, as well as people in the waiting room. Jacquie pointed out that every survival method ascertained in New York is needed more than ever. 'My sister needs your strength.'"

"You could have omitted one word, as a few reporters might have been there. Oh, David, they applauded."

"Sweetheart, are you ready for me to share facts?"

With some trepidation, "Yes, please tell me now, did I kill him?"

"No love, you are unequivocally not to blame. In fact, you saved your life and others following you because of an instinctive response from years of defensive driving training. You turned the steering wheel hard to the right, causing your car to spin.

The left rear of the trunk slammed into his vehicle, and momentum pushed his car into the far-left lane. Your car spun around, and somehow you managed to avoid hitting the security cars behind you. You then rolled down an incline and crashed into a tree.

Please don't be upset. Definitely won't express regret. Pigman, in a murderous rage, had him turning into the right lane to go after you again. An 80,000-pound eighteen-wheeler ran into him, demolished his car, and he died instantly."

"Ouch, that must have hurt! Bet that made a considerable amount of bacon."

"Really must be more careful of my influence, not to inspire you to go astray from your normal and respectful self. And not encourage you to speak like a New Yorker when upset or angry."

She was barely able to smile. "David. Am I safe? Is it over?"

"Yes, love, you are 100% out of harm's way."

"Sweet Suzie, I'm back."

"Jacquie, our baby. Stay close to me, Jacquie. Oh, dear God, Jacquie. I am miserable."

"David and I are here. Jaz is coming in a few seconds. We girls will surround you in love and take care of everything.

Suzie, what makes a lot of bacon?"

"Mr. Fox. David was worried, as I thought I killed him, so he told me what happened."

"David, I love you so much. My sister needed to hear this, and I don't trust anyone but you to ascertain what is best. The doctors will believe you lost your mind by not following their orders not to let Suzie hear gory details now."

"Love, come closer. Tired and can't keep my eyes open much longer. The sedative is finally taking full effect. It will take me some time to recover. Promise me you won't hide your feelings or shut me out. You feel the same amount of grief and hurt as I. David, our baby, I don't want you to go through this alone."

"Angel, I promise. Now stop fighting and let the sedative take effect, and sleep. I will be here when you wake up.

Susie, my mom used to say this to me when I was in one of my darkest depressions.

"May you see God's light on the path ahead? When the road you walk is dark. May you always hear, even in your sorrow, the gentle singing of the lark. When times are hard, may hardness never turn your heart to stone. May you always remember you do not walk alone.

Suzi, sweet dreams. I love you, and I'm staying with you tonight."

"David, you are going to get into bed with her and hold her all night. This room is in the intensive care ward, and you can't lock the door. As if you always do.

The night shift nurse will check on her every hour, and in the early morning, the doctor starts her early rounds. David, please be mindful that Suzie would not want you to get asked to leave her during the night. Suzie needs you to stay by her side, promise me.

President Harrison arranged for Jaz and me to stay in a guest room down the hall.

David, your Angel, wanted you to find someone to have your babies."

"No, she didn't, Jacquie. She wanted me to reassure her that we can still have a family."

"Love, so verklempt, overcome with emotion, is the right Yiddish word? I don't remember how intuitive you are to read Suzie's heart."

"Do you want us to bring you coffee?"

"Yes, thank you, Jaz, just coffee. No food for now. not hungry."

"David, try to get some rest, and I will bring you and Suzie breakfast in the morning.

Jaz and I will take turns checking up on her. Is that ok?"

"Of course, but only once. I want you both to get rest.

Don't know how long I can keep sadness at bay."

"Love, you lost your baby. We understand this is intensely painful. Please note we are not just coming in once. We are concerned for you and Suzie."

"Jacquie, David didn't answer you. So, how do you know he will sleep in bed with her?"

"Because he did not answer."

Nineteen
A Child's Heart Speaks

"A wife who loses a husband is called a widow. A husband who loses a wife is called a widower. A child who loses his parents is called an orphan. There is no word for a parent who loses a child. That's how awful the loss is." – Unknown.

The winter air was frigid, snow fell, blanketing the meadow and trees, and the tops of the Sierra Nevada Mountains were capped in a snowy white.

Whisper and Shadow got a visit and their apples each day from Suzie. Being with her beloved horses was consoling. She let them out in the meadow each sunny day, where her beloved Mare and her Filly foal loved to roll and play in the snow.

After writing speeches and performing other duties for the President, Suzie enjoyed sitting by the fireplace on snowy days. She felt warm and cozy and read her favorite Robert Frost poem.

"Stopping by Woods on a Snowy Evening."

"Whose woods these are, I think I know. His house is in the village, though. He will not see me stopping here. To watch his woods fill up with snow.

My little horse must think it queer. To stop without a farmhouse nearby. Between the woods and frozen lake, the darkest evening of the year. He gives his harness bells a shake. To ask if there is a mistake.

The only other sound is the sweep of easy wind and downy flake. The woods are lovely, dark, and deep, But I have promises to keep, And miles to go before I sleep, And miles to go before I sleep."

My Suzie healed slowly from the deep-seated grief of the loss of our Rebecca. Suzie was heartbroken because she had robbed her mom and Nana, a new family member. Most importantly, Suzie needed time to grieve with her sisters. At least able to get her to agree to be outside with Whisper and Shadow.

Some days are better than others, and today was one of the days that overwhelmed her emotions. Her sisters, mom, and Nana were concerned and found flimsy excuses to visit.

"Not able to face the family today." Everyone honored her wish except one.

"Honey, please check to see if our bedroom door is locked. My family is grieving too and worried about me. Still, but I don't have the emotional strength for a family visit today."

Suzie was depressed and immersed in grief, as starting a family with David was taken away. Her sisters lost a niece, her mom, Nana, a granddaughter, and Annabelle, a sister, causing her to descend deeper into a dark blue sea of sorrow.

As she started falling asleep, she read her a favorite Walt Whitman poem.

Angel, "This is thy hour, O Soul, thy free flight into the wordless, Away from books, away from art, the day erased, the lesson done, Thee fully forth emerging, silent, gazing, pondering the themes thou lovest best. Night, sleep, and the stars."

Escaping, mourning the loss of our baby, the only hope for a temporary release from the despair of grief, was sleep.

Startled and awakened, she screamed,

"REBECCA, my baby, I love you, oh God no."

"Suzie, it's just a bad dream. Do you want me to get one of your sleeping pills?"

"No, sweetie, you can fall asleep in my arms. Oh, David, how did you bear your suffocating pain? The heartache you escaped many times from your depression. How do I cope with being disquieted in my dreams? Can't find relief even for a few moments. How did you ever find a ray of hope in depression's darkness when disheartened?"

"Relieved you are imbued with love and joy of life. Promise it becomes easier one day. Our love for our baby inspires us to escape despair. After being rescued from terrorists, what did you do?"

"Stayed with you and let you cry. Your tears help express inner pain. To be of some comfort, sang to you. My love became a beacon leading you out of anguish. Just loved you.

David, is it possible one day to live without grief, talk about our baby, rejoice in her, and keep her alive in our hearts?"

"Yes, without a doubt, that day will come. In the meantime, heartache dominates emotions. Pain and unhappiness come from our loss of Rebecca. There is a natural healing process. Trust you are healing. Love is therapeutic. Stay quiet and mindful, and remember your grief doesn't define you. Staying cognizant, your heart will show you a way back to yourself.

One day, your grief lightens, your suffering less oppressive, and you have more minutes of peace. The bad dreams vanish into the nothingness from which they came. That day assuredly arrives, and on that day, you wake up realizing you are thinking of our Rebecca, not with mourning but in a new morning bathed in the warmth of loving remembrance."

"David can't see that day, devoid of hope."

"There is always hope. You nursed and loved me back to my life."

"No, didn't know how. It was you who found your way back out of depression. It was meditation that connected you to your higher self. My love, please do not say Angels are slow on the uptake."

Suzie smiled and even let out a giggle.

"David, don't believe you consciously accept how many hearts you touched with tenderness and love. You are a Love Whisperer. This is your superpower.

New York man, you once explained to your audience, 'Looking for a light to dissolve the darkness of depression is not found at the end of a tunnel but in the darkness where light is brighter.'

You spoke your truth, not a cure to end anyone's depression. You said the way I remember; silence is listening to your heart. Hope surfaces from faith, manifesting out of silence. Trust in silence, where recovery first appears."

"Be patient. You'll wake up from the nightmare of grief.

"Assured you'll experience more and more moments of peace. And in those extended periods, you become stronger through love and less grief. One day, awaken with serenity in your heart.

There is light in the blue darkness of depression, like shining stars in a dark universe. Trust your light never went out. Your essence emerges, and you gain freedom from grief.

Each day, growing closer to your loving self. In the meantime, your family, friends, and I are here for you. We shall feel joy when we speak of our Rebecca."

"David, please repeat the quote that inspired you not to give in to your depression."

"So stick to your struggle when you're the cruelest struck. It's when life seems worst that you must not quit."

"That was always your strength; you were able to pull yourself out of the deepest blue darkness of depression because you never quit."

A few knocks at our bedroom door as if someone didn't want to intrude on Suzie.

"Angel, someone asks if it is all right for her to see you?"

"Can't see anyone today. Tell Nana maybe tomorrow."

"It's not Nana; she looks like she won't take no for an answer."

"David, I can't. Whichever sister they will understand."

"She insists on seeing her Aunt Suzie. She is waiting."

"Annabelle, my dearest Annabelle, Sweetheart."

"Aunt Suzie, can I sit on the bed next to you?"

"Oh, my precious girl, my heart is always open for you. Daddy will lift you to sit next to me."

"I'm sorry, Aunt Suzie, your baby is now safe in God's hands. Mommy said it was all right to come to see you."

"Sweetheart, don't worry about me, I'm all right now, for you are visiting with me."

"Auntie, God called your baby to heaven because she wanted angels to teach her some stuff and return her to you soon. While we wait, I'll be your baby until your baby comes home."

"Darling, you are already my baby. Come closer so I can hug and kiss you."

Annabelle whispered to her Aunt, "Please take care of Daddy. He still pretends tears are called things, and doesn't take good care of himself."

"Sweetpea, would you help make it easier for Daddy? He hides tears from me, too."

A big hug. "I love you, Aunt Suzie. Daddy, can you please help me off the bed? Want to help Mommy Jaz cook my lunch?"

"What are you cooking, sweetpea?"

"Peanut butter and jelly had to teach her. Mommy said that when she was a girl in France, children didn't know about it.

Aunt Suzie, Mommy Jaz never uses enough jelly and cuts off the ends of the bread. I have to watch her, so she leaves them on."

"David, could you tell the family if they could set two settings for us to have lunch? Then come back and walk with me downstairs.

Annabelle, tell Mommy Jaz to leave those things on the end of the bread of our peanut butter sandwiches., Your daddy and I want lots of grape jelly."

As Annabelle closed the bedroom door, a child's love spoke lovingly to her Aunt Suzie and Daddy. Annabelle inherited a gift of prescience. No adult would conceive of something as simple as a peanut butter and jelly sandwich as a restorative. Healing for Suzie and me was a little faster than we believed possible, and it was as simple as a PBJ.

Twenty
Family is the heart of love

"Being a family means you are a part of something very wonderful. It means you will love and be loved for the rest of your life." Lisa Weed

This was a disconcerting letter, challenging to read.

'David, you cheated on your Suzie with my wife, but don't care; you only married her for sex and live rent-free. You can have her. She loves you.

Going to marry a real woman. Megan was good in bed, but he never loved her. Living with Megan, keeping up a charade to stall for time to be with the woman I love. Already moved out.

Nana and Mom know but don't care. They wanted to see me leave.

You are fecking another man's wife. You are rubbish and should have informed Suzie, but it would have created unnecessary drama.

Megan recently agreed, and divorce papers were filed after threatening to expose you and Suzie and ruin your reputations. Finally free of both her and your hypocrisy. The final divorce papers are expected to arrive within the next two months.

With your preaching and holier-than-thou attitude, you believe you are clever, a peacemaker. You had no idea until I told you to go sleep with her.

Ryan.'

"Love, Vickie is here and wants to speak to you. Says it's urgent.

She asked to help get the girls together for an emergency family meeting. Does this have to do with that letter Annabelle gave you?"

"Suzie, don't know. Vickie hasn't said anything yet. She first wanted us together."

"Need my sisters' counsel before we begin. Is it ok to start our family meeting?

Suzie, read this first, then let Jacquie."

"Love, it goes faster if we read in pairs."

"Sorry, of course, but before you do, let me explain how I came to this letter. Annabelle was handed an unopened white envelope that contained an odious letter. Ryan told her it was a letter to her dad.

Annabelle could read enough words that she became upset and asked many questions. She got distracted and put the letter in her *Cinderella* dollhouse. Because it would be safe until she could give it to me. Thank God Annabelle respects privacy, so it never occurred to her to look inside the envelope.

That was two months ago; this is a home with never-dull moments. She forgot about it until two days ago. Annabelle was upset and said, 'Sorry, the mail got delayed.'

Didn't know who had given it to her. There was no name on the envelope except mine. Annabelle sometimes writes letters, so I saved this one until this morning. When Vickie wanted to speak to us, Suzie was about to read this.

Anticipating that this letter would anger everyone, I nervously handed it over to Suzie and Jacquie. Sensing my concern, Jacquie moved closer to Suzie. Both started reading and looked at me, not knowing what to say, waiting for everyone to finish. Noreen and Vickie were next, and Vickie kept saying, Why that son of a bitch. How did he escape a prison sentence? That S.O.B. tried to harm Suzie and now attacked Megan.

Suzie was livid. All it takes is for someone to hurt her family or friends, and she rises to the occasion. She sounds like a scolding mom, don't get me wrong, because the fear of a scolding is ten times more intense than a real scolding.

"David, are you okay?

The damn word escapes me to express my rage. I'm beyond angry, that's how pissed off I am. You went out of your way to do him favors. And after my family treated him kindly, how dare he? Most of all, he hurt Megan."

"Suzie, it's with regret to share his bitterness with you and your sisters, but it's necessary to find a way to protect

Megan. My concern is whether I should show this to Megan. Or ignore and burn it, but Megan may learn the letter's content another way. One day, Ryan may say this to her in pique or out of spite, and may already have. Megan wouldn't want us to be upset.

Megan's feelings and reputation are hurt by impugning her dignity. She should not have to deal with this alone. Perhaps one day he will tell her his new love."

"David, my news is also upsetting, but it may provide a solution to shield Megan from any emotional hurt. Together, hope we can figure out what to do.

First, want to sit next to David; you are angry. Suppose this is good because we now have the truth. Then, knowing what is needed, we can support Megan."

Jacquie was anxious, "Vickie, go ahead and let us hear what you have to say."

"Let me start by saying you need to hear details. Don't know how to safeguard Megan.

Suzie's girlfriend, Gabriella's sister, shared confidences. We use the same beauty parlor."

"In a beauty parlor, why a beauty parlor?"

Noreen lovingly responded, "David, it's where women get their hair done."

"Noreen, yeah, but never mind, you didn't answer because it was a silly comment."

"Noreen, David, sweethearts, are you two finished?"

"Sorry, Vickie, everyone is nervous. It's David's fault."

"The two of you act like kids sitting in the back seat of a long car trip. The beauty parlor has nothing to do with this news."

"David, Gabriella's sister Cheryl has shared confidentially about a man she worked with who had continually harassed her and tried to have an affair. She said he wouldn't take no for an answer, and he refused to listen to me when I told him I'm in love with my husband, and we are happily married.'

'Oh, I can make you happier in bed.'

"Suzie, sweetheart, this occurred about the time he tried to extort you. We all know men with Ryan's repugnant behavior who want to dominate and make a woman submissive.

At each new beauty appointment, there was something that would upset her. Since many men act similarly, it didn't occur to me to ask questions.

A few weeks ago, her husband convinced her to go to court and get a restraining order. He became increasingly agitated, insistent, and started yelling at her. She wanted assurance from her husband not to do anything to get himself hurt."

"Vickie, oh my God, Gabriella told me about her sister but didn't mention details."

"Suzie, her husband, would rescue her and avoid upsetting you.

"Suzie, sweetheart, this is how I got to ask her what this guy's name is. In case I run into him."

"Vickie, what is it? You're shaking."

"Oh, Noreen. It was Ryan. So, what is this freak's last name? Afraid my suspicions were correct. She said, Ryan Michael O'Brien.

David asked her if she would allow me to give you her telephone number. I thought you would want to speak with my friend.

Here is her number and her husband's in case she is busy and doesn't pick up."

"Vickie, thank you, love. Please trust me. You do not have to do anything. Just follow my lead."

"David, what led? How will we know what to do?"

"Angel, all of you will know. This is why your trust is necessary. There is no other family in which I have assurance. Please know this will be resolved tonight."

"David, your look of 'I know what to do,' just now concocted in your New York mind, worries me."

"Jacqueline, I know what I'm doing."

"My sweet brother, your track record of running into danger where angels fear to tread is not comforting." Noreen worried., She knew David was cautious, but what about the unknowns?

"True enough, dear Noreen, please keep this letter secret for a few more hours until after dinner. Jacqueline will give Annabelle and Jessica their pizza dinner and let them eat it in front of the TV. Jaz will stay with the girls until bedtime and then come downstairs. Say I asked for this favor. Annabelle and Jessica love spending time with her. She will understand and not ask questions."

"David, dear, what love hold do you have on my Jaz?"

"Jacquie, you know how awesome she is, loving and trusting all of us, knowing she's told everything when she comes downstairs."

"New York man, knowing what?"

Standing at the screen door, called back to them, "Well, preparing dinner doesn't start by itself."

"Suzie, may I use your downstairs office? Please come with me. You need to know what I plan to do."

"David, do you know what you are doing?"

"Not 100%, but this is not a guess. Certainly wouldn't try something that could backfire and hurt Megan."

The girls were finally asleep after their bath, and Jaz read two bedtime stories. It was a little after 10:00 p.m.

when the doorbell rang. The sisters recently installed a new doorbell with a magical Fantasia sound, which Annabelle loves to ring.

"This must be the invited couple. I'll let them in.

Suzie, come with me, I want to introduce you to an old friend of yours."

A tall, attractive, slender woman who looked a little like her sister Gabriella and her good-looking husband, perhaps an inch taller, entered the foyer.

"David, my love, I hope you know what you are doing."

Under my breath, "Me too, Suzie."

"Thank you, Cheryl and Joe, for coming on short notice. First, let me introduce Vickie's sister and your sister's best childhood friend, the love of my life, Suzie."

"Oh, Suzie, I'm looking forward to our first reunion since we were teenagers.

My sister always brags about how proud she is of you. "

"By the way, David, cool doorbell. Cheryl shared the contents of the letter, and we both wanted to help Megan. Finally agreed not to beat the crap out of him. Words wouldn't hurt as much if ever I found Ryan...."

"Brooklyn?"

"How did you guess? My accent."

"Actually, your instinct is not to refrain from speaking your mind, doing what is necessary, and not worrying about feelings."

"Who is at the door?"

"Vickie, your friends Cheryl and Joe."

"Where are they now?"

"Suzie wanted to give them a brief tour of the house."

"Could you have come up with a more convincing cover? David, really need to teach the art of not being transparent. My wonderful brother. The problem, love, is you are too honest, and any deception gets caught in your throat."

"David, what are they keeping from me? She wouldn't show off the house after 10 p.m."

"Megan, would like you to read this letter."

After a few tears and tissues, Megan looked up.

"I'm so sorry, David., I knew he despised me. Just didn't appreciate how deep his hate ran."

"Ryan never had an affair and was rejected the first moment he tried. You did nothing wrong to drive him out of your arms. Ryan is emotionally disturbed, selfish to a fault, and egotistical, a delusional man. Who thinks every woman revolves around him? And believes he can command any woman. Only tried to extort Suzie because he had already moved out. Moreover, two deviants were with him, as well as an unexplained hatred of me."

"David, don't know why he feared attacking Jacquie, Jaz, Noreen, or Vickie. Why not? It doesn't make sense."

"Megan, have you noticed the look Nana gives when he enters the room? He wouldn't dare try anything; perhaps wanted to keep living rent-free."

Megan anxiously asked, "How do you know Ryan never had a love affair?"

"Megan would like to introduce a long-time friend of Vickie. If you would, please listen to her. I want you to understand this was never your fault or anything about you. Is it okay for me to introduce you to her?"

"The woman Suzie is talking to?"

Suzie walked in with Cheryl and Joe. Vickie introduced them to Megan.

Cheryl was beautiful, elegant, and confident, with a welcoming smile.

"Megan, I'm Cheryl, and this is my husband, Joe. Let me tell you a little about Joe and me. Is that okay?"

Megan looked at me and saw how calm I was, which put her at ease.

"Cheryl, please, I would like to hear."

"Two years ago, Joe and I separated because he was offered a promotion in his company's East Coast office. He would not accept the advancement, and it was a once-in-a-lifetime offer. My parents, family, and friends are here, and he would only take the job offer if I were to leave him.

Megan cried every night and made the most terrible mistake. Joe left, was angry and hurt, and slammed the door.

Started running after him, but he got in a taxi and left me in the street. He took his work Smartphone number and new address with him, and his company said they could not even give me his phone number. Joe did not leave permission for me or anyone to have access."

"Megan, as I turned around and saw Cheryl crying, I could not stop feeling empty. I immediately called my new boss and explained I wanted to resign. She said, 'What if you stay here for a few days while arranging for you to go back home and work at the same promotion in our Sacramento office?'

Anxious to call Cheryl right away with the good news. Each time I called, she didn't answer, so I left voice messages. She finally called and left a message asking to be left alone so she could heal. Booked the next flight back on a Friday as I had the weekend off.

Texted her my flight number and the time of my arrival. She was not there when I got off the plane, hoping she would be at baggage claim. My heart sank. Behind me and in her sweetest voice, 'What took you so long?'

We kissed until airport security asked her if we wanted a private room."

"Megan, dear, wanted my husband to tell you through his eyes, as this was almost two years ago. At about the same time, you got married. My husband and I have been married for a year and were apart for only a few days.

Ryan became obsessive. Joe and I had no idea who you were or how to reach you until Vickie and I talked because he was getting crazier and more unrelenting. Joe wanted to smash his face.

Megan, there was never love, sex, touching, a date, or even coffee or lunch. It was all in his mind. One day, he screamed at me, and that was when I got a restraining order. He told Joe I was terrible in bed and was moving in with a new girlfriend.

Ryan must have spoken about me because this woman called and asked me to help her get him out of her life. Ryan would not leave after forcing his way into her apartment. Our boss fired him, and she finally had her family and boyfriend physically remove him from the premises.

An FBI agent asked me sensitive, probing questions about Ryan. The agent said that if new information or he reappeared, call the FBI. Told all I knew, and they seemed interested. That was over a week ago. I heard that he lives with a woman in Tucson, Arizona. Imagine he caused somebody serious harm."

"Megan, permit me to answer. Cheryl and Joe, you are correct. Ryan committed a serious crime, and the FBI is closing in on him. I'm sure he is aware of what the FBI wants him for. Wish I'd known and saved you and Joe this grief."

"David, you know I'm from Brooklyn, so no need to say anything else."

"Joe, we just made new friends. Thank you, David, for inviting us to speak with Megan."

"Cheryl, this must have been hard for you to live with. Thank you for telling me."

"David felt that once you got rid of this misguided notion of having failed in your marriage, you would stop blaming yourself and get closer to your Rick."

"Cheryl, Joe, please stay over. There is a lot of pizza and Suzie's famous salad. None of us has eaten dinner."

"We've already been invited to have DS pizza, whatever that is."

"Suzie, may I have permission to kiss your David?"

"Megan, yes, my love deserves a kiss. Take as long as you like."

Megan put her arms around me, kissed me softly, buried her head in my shoulder, and wept.

Waited quietly for her to stop crying.

"Sweetie, I understand love, affection, and an intimate friendship do not mean sex. Ryan left you a despicable letter. Please rip it up."

"Suzie already took it from me."

"David, I still love you and want to be close."

"Megan, Suzie, Jacquie, and I will talk with you tomorrow. Promise it will be okay.

"Come with me. Annabelle pretends to sleep, but my Sweetpea listens when we have company and want to tuck her back into bed and kiss her goodnight."

Twenty-One
No, Not Now

"One must still have chaos in oneself to be able to give birth to a dancing star." Friedrich Nietzsche

Suzanne fretted over which gown to buy for President Harrison's inauguration, which was delayed due to the president's involvement in dealing with an international crisis. Finally, she let the plans for her inauguration ball proceed.

"Love, when are you going to pick up your new tuxedo? May I come with you? I'd like to show you the gown I'm planning to wear. The shop wanted to have one last fitting to ensure it was ideal. This is the store Jaz recommends.

Oh, David, what if it isn't exactly right? Can I exchange it for another?"

"Yes, of course. No problem. I, too, thought the formal style of my tuxedo wasn't best suited for this once-in-a-lifetime occasion. Want to keep shopping, since I have ten days. Don't have to worry about my appointment at a beauty parlor, having my nails done, buying the perfect shoes, or practicing ballroom dancing...."

"Are you done now? Will you tell me the truth?"

"Honey, every eye will be on you, and this is what you dreamed about for over ten years."

"New York Man, you are the most charming boyfriend as an escort and dancer."

At the Le Charme Dress Shop, Suzie was nervous that I would like it.

"You know I love your Black dress."

"Honey, the color is not right, and thanks for being here with me."

"Promise to give you my first honest impression."

Of all the shops sitting and waiting for Suzie, sitting in a women's bridal and gown shop is a new experience. This means staying attentive when Suzie steps out of the dressing room.

"Sir, Miss Suzie is ready. She looks lovely, the dress is a piece of art. An off-the-shoulder gown with a slit down one side. She looks beautiful."

Suzanne peeked out of the dressing room. "Ready."

"David, tell me, honestly, do you like it?"

"Gorgeous, you look so gorgeous."

"Honey, behave yourself. I know that look.

Can I take it with me now?

David, please pay the balance on our credit card.

Call Jaz to see if she can join us for lunch at our favorite Chinese restaurant."

Suzie was the most joyful in months. Her smile lit up the Ballroom, and alluring blue eyes shone in delight. We danced to every song.

Suzie was generous with her time for Press friends when they asked for an interview. Stayed in the background as this was her well-deserved moment.

Words such as 'proud' lost their meaning. Don't have words to describe the joy of watching Suzie's charming smile. Fashion magazine photographers took dozens of photographs. She was radiant, having never questioned if she would be present for this moment. For a moment, she had never faltered in her belief since she was ten years old.

This was Suzie's *Cinderella* Ball. We glided across the dance floor without a midnight curfew. She leaned closer to me and whispered,

"David, thank you for your love and for never leaving my side. Loving me while everyone worried about me, you were in as much pain and mourning. I could not have made it through my grief without you.

I wanted you to be interviewed by the Press, but you told them this night was all about me, and you had no comment.

Oh, love, did talk about you and permit the fashion photographers to take candid shots. Each one said no matter how much they tried, you were deliberately posing for them. Silly, but warned it would not be probable. You were so cute. They got a few beautiful shots and wanted to photograph the two of us. Already told them you would be happy too. Was it okay?"

"Of course, it would be my honor to have a photo taken with you, my precious love."

"Madam President, thank you for inviting my sisters, David, and me to dinner at the White House.

Thank you also for inviting my nieces, Annabelle and Jessica, to visit the Oval Office. They were thrilled."

"Suzie, who will babysit them?"

"My mother is taking the girls to our New York apartment. They get to ride on the Apple Line Cruise around Manhattan. Nana and Mom are in charge of bringing the girls home to Woodland Cottage. David and I should arrive by Sunday afternoon."

"Could you come to the office earlier? There are speeches to look over, and please take questions from the Press.

The Secret Service will transport your sisters and David by 7:00 p.m. Dr. Robert will also arrive at the same time. Please let David know when he and your sisters get picked up. Dinner is served at 8:00 p.m.

Suzie, your office has been moved closer to the Oval Office. Everything is in place for you exactly as you wanted."

"Thank you, Madam President."

"Suzie, work is left on your desk. I'll be in meetings most of the morning.

You never doubted your belief in my becoming President. It's overdue to celebrate your dedication and long years of service. The dinner is a recognition and appreciation of over ten years of public service."

An elegant table was set in the President's dining room, where Jacquie, Noreen, Victoria, Jaz, Megan, David, and I were seated. We all applauded when President Harrison and First Husband came into the room. This was our first dinner with the President since the election.

Jaz worked with the famous White House French Chef as her Sous Chef. The best part was that the President requested her after she obtained the Chef's approval. Jaz was giddy with delight. She had never imagined such an opportunity.

Unexpectedly, with a tone of sheer urgency.

"Oh my God, David! Excuse me, Madam President."

Suzie stood up with her hand over her mouth and quickly managed to reach the toilet in time.

"Madam President, Dr. Robert, if you also excuse me, I want to check on her."

"Your sister and David are always in motion. How do you keep up with them? It is hard for me, and I have the resources of the Federal Government."

"Madam President, she admired and respected you since she was ten. On behalf of my sisters, we appreciate all you have done for her."

"Jacquie, Dr. Robert, and I feel the same way."

"Oh, what are they quarreling about now? I am sorry, Madam President."

"Vickie, it's all right. I understand why."

"David, no, no, I don't want to lose you."

"Angel, the President, requested me to take this assignment. The Vice President and the Chair of the Foreign Relations Committee also wish for me to accompany them on this trip. It won't be more than five days."

"Don't Angel me, like the last mission was supposed to last only five days, and you almost got blown up and taken hostage."

"What are the odds of that happening again?"

"Don't joke with me. What is this assignment?"

"Can only say I'll be consulting and advising."

"To whom?"

"Suzie, I can't tell you even with your Top-Secret Clearance."

"On whose orders?"

"President Harrison."

"Is this dangerous?"

"No."

"Good, then coming with you."

"Suzanne, as much as I want to, you know I can't take you."

"Because it is dangerous. David, I can't live without you."

"Suzie, perhaps I can delay the mission a few days."

Suzie was never as obstinate and determined.

"David, please, no, I don't want you to go."

"Why the flood of tears? Suzie, I've never seen you this panic-stricken and resolute. Oh, my God, my Love, are you all right? Are you keeping any health problems from me?"

"David, you don't have to worry. I'm in perfect health."

"Then why are you so unyielding for me not to go on this mission?"

"Because we don't want our baby to grow up without her father!"

Jacqueline was glad when the noise level quieted down. "This is the second time she vomited today."

"Third time."

"Jaz, what secret do you have?"

"Can't say, Vickie, promised Suzie."

President Harrison interrupted.

"Ladies, two plus two?"

"Madam President?"

"Early morning vomiting, running to pee every ten minutes. I have had two daughters, Noreen and Jacquie, who should know now."

"Madam President, when did you find out?"

"Vickie, you don't vomit twice in a White House toilet and once in my residence to have trouble figuring it out."

"Then why do they quarrel?"

"Dr. Robert?"

"Vickie, doctor and patient confidentiality."

"I don't understand. Suzie wanted this since she met David, and after her miscarriage, she and David should be in the Lincoln bedroom now. Oh, sorry, Madam President."

"This is my fault. Imagine Suzanne just told David. She was waiting for confirmation, and David told her about his news before she had a chance."

"Ladies, I asked David to go on an assignment for the United States. He is an expert, has the experience, and once he has the Bronx talk out of the way, he is a master negotiator. Except it seems with our Suzie."

529

"Our Baby!"

"David wanted to tell you tonight in our hotel room. Dr. Robert relayed a phone call earlier from my doctor. She said we were going to have a baby. She is healthy and in perfect health."

"Our baby, Love, our baby, we are having a baby."

"Didn't want to say anything until I received a confirmation from my doctor. Told no one. Jaz walked into my office as I hung up the phone and slumped in my chair."

'When is your baby due? Does David know yet?'

"Didn't answer. Couldn't gather my thoughts on how to tell you. As we were having dinner tonight in the President's residence."

"President Harrison must already know, too."

"How could she?"

"Angel, she had two daughters, and you just threw up in her residence's White House toilet.

She, the doctor said, she, our baby, our baby is a girl!"

"They can do a test to determine the sex. Nana told me it's the Brooke genes that make it possible to have all girls. I waited for confirmation from my doctor. Knowing how much we both want a daughter."

"I'll speak to President Harrison. Can't accept this assignment or any other mission."

"David, not because I asked you. This is your life's work."

"But you did ask."

"David Benjamin! Want you to do this because you want to. Don't want you unhappy. This work is your passion."

"Suzie, have never been happier not to go on an assignment because you would be nervous. You and our baby are all that matters, and I love you so much. Won't put you through this worry."

Once Suzanne and I entered the dining room, all eyes were on us. The sisters' eyes were overflowing with tears.

The President stood., "Come, you two, to the living quarters. Excuse us for ten minutes. Robert, Ladies, please begin eating salad. Jaz, thank you for your recipe."

"Suzie, are we called into the principal's office?"

"David, not as bad. It is my living room."

"Sorry, Madam President."

"Dr. Robert, is the President upset at them for raising their voice?"

"Ladies, the President loves Suzie as a daughter and has adopted David into our family. He is the little boy who gets into mischief, which she has wanted. The four of you are our extended family. Which do you prefer, Blue Cheese, French, Italian, Vinaigrette, or some other type of dressing?"

"Madam President, sorry for raising my voice. It was my fault. Suzie tried to get me quieter. You know how stubborn you are, and you are not buying this."

"Suzanne, hold you in the highest regard ever since a forward ten-year-old girl came into my campaign office to tell me I was going to be the president one day. David, you almost died in my home, saving Suzanne's life.

You each saw a future together the moment you met. David, you risked your life for a love promised only in both of your dreams. Over the last year and a half, you two have faced challenges that most couples would have given up. It is I who needs to apologize, Suzanne. David did his best, arguing not to go; he did not want to be away from you."

"Madam President."

"It's all right, Suzie. I'll save you and David the discomfort of having to dismiss a presidential request. David has served the country well, more than he thought possible. You and I believe in him, grown beyond his high expectations. And not yet reached close to his potential."

Tears flowed from the bluest blue eyes.

"Suzie, there are extra boxes of tissues with you working more often in the White House. So, now you two sit down."

"Why, love, didn't you say, and it took a presidential order for you to agree? Why didn't you say? A man with a million beautiful words?"

"Because I gave in and said yes."

"Suzanne, can't tell you the details, but this is an urgent mission. David would have three FBI agents trained in protecting VIPs remain with him in his room and outside the door while he sleeps. Arranged this to occur in the US Embassy.

Marines at their present duty station will be reinforced with additional Marines flown in for this mission. The Military Police monitor his security. David will immediately be taken to a secure, safe, undisclosed location and airlifted out of the country to avoid potential danger.

Suzie, honestly, I can't say anything happens. This mission is of great consequence, and the Vice President, Secretary of State, and their security teams provide an additional layer of protection. Our intelligence indicates it will be secure."

"Madam President, thank you for informing me of the details. However, such a high level of security underscores the importance of this mission, which is also a testament to the inherent risks associated with it. Please, I understand you can't promise things you cannot control."

"Madam President, may I have some time alone with Suzanne?"

"I'll have both of your salads waiting."

"Suzanne, please be patient and let me finish before you say anything. My mind is made up. Will inform the President cannot travel out of the country. Instead, the team will retain access to me 24/7 for negotiations or consulting, as necessary.

"David, it's not my intention to give up your life's work."

"I'm not. You and our baby are the center of my life's work. I was uncomfortable accepting it, even when I was told of its importance. You realize the President is a hard person to say no to.

I gave you my word in New York to always share my feelings and make decisions together, not without you. I was about to say this, but became concerned you were not well. Then, hearing about us having a baby."

"David, this wasn't my plan on how to tell you about our baby."

We entered the dining room, kissing and holding hands.

"Before you two say anything, Suzie, due to international and domestic events unfolding all at once, there was an urgency to have expertise in educational policy for refugees. The Vice President and I agreed to add additional responsibilities to you as Special Advisor to the President of the United States. It is a higher pay level, and you can work from home and come to the White House as long as you are allowed to fly."

"Madam President, how do you know?"

"Suzie, you peed a lot and threw up three times in a White House toilet, and had two girls.

"Madam President, thank you. With your permission, I would like to promote my intern, Ms. Patricia Plath, to a full-time assistant, placing her in a higher salary level. She already has top security clearance. As my assistant, she broadens her experience and advances her career. Madam President, believe she has the potential to become a Senator. Or whatever in her career she decides to do."

"Approved. I'll initiate the hiring onboarding process tomorrow. Patricia would have been my first choice for the assistant position.

David, you can continue your consulting, teaching, writing, selling books, and caring for Susie and your baby.

We can discuss 50-75% of the time devoted to your career. David, work with the Secret Service to add more secure phone lines and set up whatever you need to take assignments from your New York and Woodland Cottage home.

When conducting government business, you are put on a per diem pay scale with an expense account. David, your priority is to care for Suzanne and your new baby."

Suzie, perhaps one day you'll share, as you have with David, your vision for your future. Like David, never speak about your exceptional skills, knowledge, expertise, or accomplishments. With each promotion, you become humbler. You have been this way since I have known you."

"Madam President, thank you. May I hug the President of the United States?"

"The Secret Service may not be happy, but you can hug your friend Julia."

"Girls, David doesn't understand what a baby shower is. Please explain his role."

"Too tired to undress."

"Oh, David, we both didn't eat dinner. Honey, would you order room service for us?"

"Why would it take 45 minutes at midnight?"

"Sweetheart, some people return to their hotel rooms after drinking and feel hungry.

Can we talk? David, how would you feel about using our first daughter's name, Rebecca, as our baby's middle name in remembrance? Believe she will like it when she is older. She wasn't able to know her firstborn sister. She'll appreciate more and more as she grows up."

"Brooke Rebecca Bradley, I love her name."

"How could you know? David, you never cease to surprise me."

"You have been scribbling BRB on every piece of paper. A perfect name for her."

"Is it okay for my sisters, Jaz, and Megan, and the President and Dr. Robert as her Godparents?"

"Of course, Suzie."

By the way, Angel, when do you introduce the President for her first official Educational Policy speech?"

"In two weeks, on Valentine's Day. The President told me it would be a perfect time. So excited, having waited over a decade. First time introducing her as President. But honey, she is going to surprise me. I don't know, but I have a sense in her voice that she has something she kept from me."

"Whatever it may be, enjoy the moment and don't let on that you sense something. You don't want to spoil the President's surprise."

"David, I'm happy you get to share my memorable moment."

"Of course, love, where and what time?"

"I'll give you the time and location as soon as it is confirmed."

"Love, our food will arrive in a few minutes."

"Glad you ordered scrambled eggs, bacon, roasted potatoes, cherry jam, and toast, with black coffee. David, it sounds scrumptious. Hold and kiss me long and tender. I love you, New York Man.

Twenty-Two
Lovely Lady Love

"Without a doubt, an inevitability of life is unpredictability. Why should the future be foreseeable? Where is the enjoyment in that? Even still, glorious romances are waiting to be received and embraced." David Kenneth Waldman

Since this was her first public appearance to introduce the President of the United States, every dress came out of her closet. Suzie had the 'oh my God panic' as none seemed suitable.

"The black dress with the slit is my favorite."

"David, it is your favorite choice for any occasion, and you know my wardrobe by now. Perhaps I'll wear my grey business pantsuit."

"This is her first major announcement in front of the Press for the roll-out of her education policy?"

"Yes, excited and allowed 30 seconds to introduce her."

"Oh, so the Press won't take photos of you."

"Honey, they always take photos. Why?"

"You were recently promoted to Educational Chief Advisor to the President of the United States. This is your first time in your new role in the public eye. Wearing a dress would highlight your personality and charismatic elegance. For sure, you'll attract the attention of everyone.

The Press, of course, wants to interview you about your never-faltering faith and foresight. This will be widely watched and televised. All photos will be in newspapers, also in her Presidential library one day."

Now, in an absolute panic, she had unintentionally created for her.

"Oh, God, what dress, red, beige, my blue dress? David, please see if Jacquie can help me pick out the perfect dress."

"Love, what are you up to? Secret meetings with Jaz, you stop talking when I walk into the room. She won't tell me anything."

"Suzanne is frantic, not knowing which dress to wear. She wants you to help her. Steer her towards the Galena dress. It has a slim-fitting bodice and a relaxed skirt. Tell her how beautiful and sophisticated it looks when she tries it on.

Sleeves are loose-fitting with smocking at the sleeve opening. She'll show her legs. Honestly, that is for me, plus it's a perfect color for her eyes."

Tell her how beautiful and sophisticated it looks when she tries it on."

"David, honey, sounds like a dress you saw on a website. Don't imagine you know what smocking at the sleeve opening means. More to the point, Suzie doesn't own a dress like this."

"She does now and is on my side of our closet. So, please take the dress and hang it on her side when she is not looking."

"David, sweetie, every woman knows every dress she has bought. So naturally, wonder how it got into her closet. But, of course, you have a plan without me having to lie to my sister."

"It's simple. Suzie showed me this dress, as she does when she wants my opinion. She loves this dress, and she won't figure this out until later."

"Later when?"

"Could say, sis, what about this dress? She'll get excited and say, this is the dress I showed to David. You don't have to say anything else once she tries it on."

"Why didn't you give this to her directly?"

"Jacquie, you realize how rare it is to keep something from your sister. She would ask questions about why this dress. After all, it is only an announcement she waited ten years for. She will want to know what's up. Please do this for me."

"Are you surprising her?"

"What do you mean?"

"David, you are transparent. It's easy to assume you'll take her to a fancy restaurant."

"Why?"

"You are impossible. Jaz and secret meetings, now this dress."

Jacquie took my hand, and we walked into her bedroom. Jaz finished dressing and was about to leave."

"Both of you are up to something. Suzie's announcement: She waited a decade. If what you are planning backfires? It would ruin her significant moment."

"Trust me, it won't backfire."

"Oh, mon Dieu, don't have a clue what you two are talking about." Jaz tried to sound innocent but was unsuccessful in doing so. A sidestep was not possible in her romantic-sounding French accent.

"David, love, how are you so confident? Mom and Nana will watch it on the public government cable network. There is local, national, cable news, and international Press and TV coverage, featuring the Vice President, Senators from California, the Secretary of Education, all congressional representatives from California, including the Press Secretary and Suzie's assistant, plus Secret Service and other VIP educational leaders in attendance.

Oh my God, oh my God, this is it, isn't it?"

"Isn't what."

"How are you going to pull this off? She is going to be nervous as it is."

"Pull what off?"

"David Benjamin, you are going to propose marriage to Suzie publicly."

"Jacquie, even with your sisterhood pledge, you would never tell her. Nevertheless, you may leave clues, and Suzie's intuition would alert her."

"Who else is on this? You need support. Oh, no, David, the President is in on this? That is why Suzie told me it's her intuition that the President has something she will surprise her with on this long-awaited day."

"Jacquie needed her to help for a quick approval from the Secret Service."

"Which sister? Don't tell me, Victoria. She is fearless and can keep a secret."

"Can't tell you more now. Vickie will fill you in."

"Megan, Noreen, and?"

"That is all, Jaz, and you and Vickie already have Secret Service clearance. Just needed clearance approved for Megan, Noreen, and the girls."

"You are not telling me everything."

"I'm sorry, no, only Jaz and Vickie know. Nothing can go wrong."

"How do I keep a secret from Suzie, as she is super intuitive?"

"Oh, that is an unforeseen problem. Should have realized the dress would be a giveaway."

Jaz confidently chimed in, "David, I have the perfect solution. I'll tell Suzie that Jacquie asked me because we have shopped together many times. Will go to her now. She loves that I teach her about French-style dresses to look elegant or sexy."

"Jacquie, please, I need you to keep this secret from Suzie. Got shot, almost blown up, and taken hostage, overcoming deep-seated jealousy and depression, creating our home in New York to advance our romance and relationship. Plus, events of the donor thank-you dinner, protecting her from extortion, and the painful loss of our baby Rebecca, finally, everything is perfect. Do not want Suzie to wait any longer."

"Oh, my lovely David, you made me so happy for the two of you. Why now, at a Presidential Press conference, her first time introducing the President, why not a romantic place, Paris, or Bora Bora Island in French Polynesia in the South Pacific?"

"That is all I can say. I love you."

"David, please propose to my sister since you met. Yet couldn't propose due to your fear of rejection. You want an atonement because you kept your depth of love between just you and Suzie. You couldn't say what your heart believed, so you want my baby sister to finally hear the depth of your love by declaring it in front of the world. She will be deliriously happy, and I love you, David., Where will our daughter be sitting?"

"Annabelle and Jessica, with Megan in the front row, Secret Service reserved seats. Jacquie, forgive me for keeping this from you.

You and Suzie have an intimate, mind-blending connection. But trust me, didn't leave you out. Oh shit, never mind, just excited."

"David, never doubted you would have some miraculous thing you cooked up to include me. This one time, I don't have a clue.

Knowing you, whatever you have in mind, will make me and Suzie super pleased."

"Jacquie, I love you more than can be expressed in words, and I cherish our relationship. From the moment we met, you opened my heart, allowing Suzie and me to be together. Let me keep this a secret and a surprise for Suzie."

"David, guess what? You will love it. Jaz said I have the perfect dress for tomorrow. It is a perfect fit. And compliments my blue eyes. Remember, showing you the green dress?"

"Is it the one that would show off your sexy leg?"

"Asked Jaz if she helped you, David. She only said it was a surprise. Jaz is an acclaimed international fashion expert, but she didn't buy the dress. She wouldn't say, but New York Man happened to mention I liked this dress, and it was you who bought this for me, and she is covering for you. Isn't she a wonderful sister? Thank you, love. So happy now, I won't consider what you are up to."

"Yes, Madam President, Belfast and leave Dulles International Airport in Washington, DC, to travel with a large contingency from the State Department. Yes, I'll look for the Briefing Book. Thank you.

Currently, no questions, Madam President."

Suzie found me in her office, overheard my conversation, turned on her heel, and went straight upstairs to our bedroom.

"Don't know if angrier at you for your broken promise, which by the way, didn't last more than two weeks, or frightened for your safety. Spoiler alert, it's your safety. Don't tell me it's Ireland. It is Northern Ireland, and the conflict has been ongoing for over a hundred years. All it takes is one person wanting to derail the talks with a bomb."

"Only for three days."

"Why do you always consider the number of days as if that will make me feel better? When are you leaving? No, don't tell me because you promised you would not go for my sake and our baby."

"Suzie, you know my calling is for the safety and education of vulnerable children. Felt compelled to go, and you know this, even with my promise."

"What about our baby?"

"It is for her I'm doing it for."

"How? She is not even born yet."

"Don't want our baby to grow up in a violent world. If I make only a tiny difference, I know it's Ireland, and religion and nationalism have divided one country. Too many lives were lost. The Peace Treaty Accord has been held for two decades, so it won't be dangerous."

"David, she will be born and raised in America. What do you mean?"

"How do I explain to our daughter her Irish culture inherited from Nana, her great-grandmother, that her father missed this opportunity to bring stability to Nana's native home country? Didn't even try? I couldn't say to her that it was because you weren't born yet.

How can we encourage her to pursue her dreams and make a positive impact, making a difference in the world? If only it's risk-free. Suzie could never tell our baby to be afraid of the world or not to follow her heart."

"That becomes moot if I have to explain to our daughter why she doesn't have a father. You can't even make peace with my father. No one can. Will the Irish people be easier to come to mutual terms?"

"Not easier. Presently, there is no conflict or war. The mission is to secure peace by finding additional paths to reunite the country one day. Couldn't live with me or look into our daughter's eyes and tell her I didn't even try. Want her to know her mother and father fought as best they could to make the world better for her, if only a little bit."

"No, you promised, but you can't prevent yourself from going. From the first day we met, I was aware of your determination to help vulnerable children. Although you want to save all children, unfortunately, it's impossible.

I appreciate your dedication to benefiting marginalized and vulnerable children who remain invisible to society. You know I'll never stand in your way. However, it doesn't mean I approve, not before our baby is born."

"Irresolvable choice to give up a lifetime of work and this opportunity to improve the lives of children in Northern Ireland. One in four children lives in poverty. Children's rights are my mission. Give me time to reflect on my career and my devoted love for you and our unborn baby. Need to be alone."

"David, fell in love with you for who you are. We share a passion for making a difference in the lives of marginalized children. The girls without access to education. I love you when you take risks to help vulnerable children in distress. It is what we will do together one day. I don't want to prevent you from future missions.

I know, being selfish. Just help me get through this year. After our baby is born, I'm coming with you. Even if that means resigning from my work in public service for the White House."

"Suzie, this has been a calling since you were ten. You have even surpassed the President's high expectations for you. Angel, you have a passion and a natural disposition for public service. After a decade of building a reputation and expertise and being promoted by the President of the United States, I don't want you to end your career you love.

Suzie, my precious love, you will significantly influence public policy for human rights for children working from the White House. This is your dream, and you worked hard to earn your reputation. Promise me you will stay working for the President as long as she is in office.

Suzie, this is something I have to reconcile. Everything we dreamed possible for us can shatter if you or I no longer follow our dreams. Your life's work, starting a family, and my career."

"David, where are you going?"

"Tahoe Bar and Grill, for a drink."

Honey, you don't drink. Please, talk to me."

"Angel, soon, just not now."

"Sis, where did David go? Walked past me and seemed troubled. What's wrong?"

"Jacquie, his life's work and my career are in the way of our romance and starting our family."

"Suzie, give him some time. David will find a solution."

"You and Jaz go and have dinner. Are you taking Annabelle with you?"

"She is getting dressed. Love, it will work out somehow."

"No, Jacquie, it doesn't always work out. We will not let the other sacrifice their calling."

"Do you know where David went? Jaz and I will drive you there instead of you taking your car. Be with David and accept his support and love for you. There is no problem, only if you make one. David will not let you give up your vocation. Trust you find a way to make this work."

"Hello, excuse me, looking for someone, but saw you, and honestly, I have not had many handsome men in my life. So, if you don't mind, I'd prefer to be with you. Are you waiting for anyone?"

"Oh, hello. Just waiting for a beautiful woman to kiss me. Sorry, I'm out of practice with what to say to a pretty woman."

Suzie's kiss lingered on his lips for half a minute.

"Do you come here often to meet women to kiss, or were you lucky when I walked over to your table?"

"No, this is my first time. I've heard this is a popular spot for picking up women. What about you?"

"I thought I could try my luck. My guy walked out and left me alone at home, and I felt like a drink."

"What do you drink? I'll buy you one."

"What are you drinking? It looks good. I'll have the same."

"Chocolate Cherry soda on the rocks, sound good?"

"Oh, that is my boyfriend's favorite. To clarify, buying me a drink does not imply any commitment.

By the way, what is your name?"

"I'm called Doctor.

Call me Suzanne, and we can see where this goes. If this works out, you can call me Suzie."

"May I ask you a question?"

"Sure, anything. You look stressed. Talking to a stranger helps. You can open up to me with no judgment."

"Tell me the truth, would you walk away from a profession you worked hard in and became successful to make your guy happy?"

"You are starting with the hardest questions first. Yeah, it would not be hard if I loved my man enough."

"The truth is I'm just a guy in a bar you just met, so no one will know."

"No, couldn't, and don't believe I just admitted that."

"Strangers are friends you haven't yet met. Secrets, stay safe. Me too, don't believe I could as well."

"What would you do? You are a beautiful woman. Do you love your work? Perhaps we can find each other's answers. Do you have time to hear me out, or need to be somewhere?"

"Since my guy left me alone, I have all night."

"If my idea works for you and your guy, can I have another kiss?"

"Slow down, fella, I love my man."

"Of course you do. This was not a pickup line. It's that you look like my love, and she kisses me a lot."

"You are in love with her?"

"She is part of my heart and sustained by our everlasting love, spiritually and sexually, my best friend and lover. So, yeah, deeply in love with her, and I'm here because I love her so much."

"Doctor, go ahead and tell me your idea."

"This may sound silly, but it's rather simple. Discuss with each other about why not giving up your life's work is positive. For any problems, you find solutions. There is no right or wrong. Just do what makes each other happy. Finding remedies is the solution to solving problems. Couples forget it doesn't have to be a binary decision, yes or no. Please tell me your thoughts. Does this sound like I'm on to something?"

"Yes, I do. What if work takes you away from the other? Or unexpected snags that always show up? Or other obligations, such as your family, may diminish your romance?"

"What if you continue date nights, like when you were getting to know each other?"

"Go on, and what if you work thousands of miles apart?"

"That used to be a problem, but not today for couples with texting, video calls, and flying to each other. Work is never 24 hours, and when apart, do things to enhance your life and dreams, to enrich your relationship."

"Like practicing playing piano, singing, and painting.

What do you do if you and your lady want a baby?"

"Suzanne, can you prioritize what is essential? This is a rhetorical question. Of course, having a baby is the priority.

Suzanne is your man, loving. You seem like you are. You find solutions together."

"Your woman must love you a great deal."

"Not half as much as I adore and cherish our love and time together.

Do you have any security clearance?"

"Yes, why? I'm of legal age to drink this soda."

"Just like the woman I love, playful. Really, do you have a security clearance?"

"Yes, top security clearance. Why?"

"There is a phone call I need to make on my secure mobile, and I would like you to listen."

"Operator, this is Dr. David Benjamin Bradley. Can you please put me through to the Vice President?

Oh, yes, I'll tell Suzanne. I'm good, thank you for asking. In fact, Suzie is doing well, with no more morning sickness. She is sitting next to me, and I'll pass on your best wishes. Yes, I'll hold the line. On Air Force Two, on his way to California, thank you.

This is your friend Joan, and one of the friendliest White House operators. She asked how my love was doing.

Mr. Vice President, thank you for taking my call. I'd like to propose a solution for my participation in the upcoming mission to Belfast. With your approval, would you bring this up to the President?"

"Doctor, you know the President. Wow."

"Yes, Mr. Vice President, Suzanne is sitting next to me. I will send your regards and remind her that she knows the President as well. Sir, no, Suzie only had one chocolate cherry soda. Yes, Mr. Vice President, she is in a playful mood.

Mr. Vice President, thank you for understanding. Yes, Sunday would be perfect. There will be someone home. Please inform the President that I will do my best to assist. Suzanne sends her regards and will see you and POTUS on Saturday. Yes, sir, thank you. Goodbye, Mr. Vice President."

"Miss Suzanne, this is forward as we just met. Do you want to eat here or go home with some takeout?"

"Oh, New York man, you are so sentimental. May we kiss before answering?"

"Does Chinese food sound good? Annabelle loves egg rolls and vegetable chow mein, as do Jacquie and Jaz. Let's also bring home their favorite vegetable dishes."

"How did the VP respond?"

"He said it is a practical solution and will ask POTUS, but believes she will agree."

"If it is OK with you, can we eat in the family room? The family is out doing something. We have the house to ourselves."

"David, whose turn is it to choose a movie?"

"The choice comes from the movies we both want to watch."

On the way home, Suzie softly sang, "Somewhere Over the Rainbow."

"Love, would you have let a woman you didn't know kiss you in a bar?"

"Oh, my dear sweet Suzie, the woman was you. Suzie, thank you for being honest. If we're out of town, we speak in the morning, and we're out of town, we speak in the morning and, if possible, after work and each night at bedtime. Date nights are sacred, celebrated by cuddles, kisses, and holding hands. Our child always comes first, no exceptions."

"What made you play along with me, talking like we were strangers? This made it easier not to become caught up in emotions."

"One of the benefits of a New York street education. You talk to strangers daily, and the density of people on the streets makes it inevitable. Eventually, you make a friend. They become your street friends, people in the grocery shop, restaurants, the man or woman you buy The New York newspaper from each day."

"Finally, a benefit of how New Yorkers communicate. Oh my dear God, David, you told me this, and I couldn't understand. New Yorkers discuss emotions that come to mind.

There is no mistrust of strangers because, in a city of over eight million, strangers to a New Yorker are just people they have not yet met. Talking to strangers creates safe havens to express peaceful emotions. New Yorkers adapted their lexicon in the same way that every culture is nurtured by its environment.

Why don't New Yorkers let people in on this secret?"

"Because to every New Yorker, it is not a secret. Rude, angry, or disrespectful behavior is not what tourists find acceptable. Surprisingly, people from other states believe New Yorkers aren't friendly.

New Yorkers are not arrogant. Just a character trait from living in the Big Apple. New Yorkers believe that anything you need is in Manhattan. If not, it is not worth having.

New Yorkers often live in self-imposed ghettos, such as the Upper West Side, the West Village, Hell's Kitchen, and the East Side, where our apartment is located. People rarely travel to another borough. In a way, the city that never sleeps is insular. We are a unique population because we have amalgamated cultures for over four hundred years. Trying to get along is not always possible in an imperfect world."

"New York man, you remember my first introduction to President Harrison is tomorrow?"

"My tomorrow is wide open for you. What time do you want me?"

"Come around 11:00 am. This allows ample time to spend with you."

"Where should I meet you?"

"Stage right in the wing so you can watch me. It means a lot to me that you'll share this moment. I've booked a room for us to have a romantic dinner, celebrating my long-awaited fate coming true.

"Perfect. I was just going to suggest we do something singular to rejoice. I'll be there. Any more worries that prevent me from talking to you?"

"Love, please tell me honestly, I'm unsure if the Galena dress suits me. Maybe the blue one you..."

"Not going. This was what the Vice President agreed to."

"The blue dress has bare shoulders, and it will make you frisky in public."

"Not going where?"

"You didn't hear the full conversation with the Vice President."

"David, this is harder for you than I thought. This is your life's work."

"The Vice President had a simple solution, but we did not discuss. A team of FBI agents will install a large screen monitor to attend meetings. This will be your new LED flat-screen monitor for video conferences. It's the same used in the Situation Room, so it is secure using state-of-the-art quantum cryptography."

"Are you sure this is what you want? Don't want to turn into a controlling girlfriend."

"You are never controlling, just a little stubborn, and I love you. You told me you would always fight for me. But you don't have to. I want to be with you. Suzie, you and our baby are my life.

"Are you hungry, Angel? Just got my appetite back."

"Me too. I love you."

"Suzie, let's make love."

"In our bedroom?"

"Here is perfect. Don't undress. Just let me hold you."

We hugged for hours with loving, long, tender kisses. Romantic, sensual lovemaking at its purest.

Twenty-Three
"The First Time Ever I Saw Your Face"

"I would rather spend one lifetime with you than face all the ages of this world alone." J.R.R. Tolkien

It was almost 11:30 a.m., and Suzie was concerned. I was always early.

"Jacquie, I'll introduce the President in 10 mins. Where is David? It is not like him to be late for me."

"David knows how important this moment is for you and will be here."

"Can you call or text him to see if he is all right? Here, use my phone."

As Jacquie took hold of her smartphone, "Sis, this text just came, Angel. I'm in the building. Be there on time."

"You see, David is not going to disappoint you."

Jacquie quickly texted, "Where are you?"

"Jacquie, look across the stage. Please say nothing to Suzie."

"Oh, David, you are on the wrong side."

"Jacquie, can't talk. It's 11:30, and there is Press here with a full President's agenda today."

Suzie started walking toward the podium. I worried about getting there first. Of course, had the advantage of surprise.

The Press, dignitaries Noreen, Jacquie, and Megan were speechless. Only Jaz and Vickie knew my plan, as they were needed to keep Suzie calm. Well, to be by her side in any case.

"Mr. Vice President, Secretary of Education, California Senators, Representatives from Congress, members of the Press, ladies and gentlemen, my beautiful daughter Annabelle and adorable niece Jessica sitting in the front row with their Aunt Megan.

It's my singular honor to introduce Suzanne Siobhan Brooke, who in a few minutes will introduce the President of the United States. I humbly ask for your indulgence to share a brief story about the day I met Suzanne. Indeed, the Press and most, if not all of you, also know a disturbed man shot me twice at President Harrison's home. But there was a more significant moment when I saw Suzanne."

Jaz excitedly said, "Vickie, go stand with Suzie. She is shaking."

"I saw the most beautiful woman, who rendered me speechless, and that is saying a lot. I was going to kiss her and ask her to dance. Her beauty radiated from the bluest of blue eyes, and her giggle wrapped in a laugh captivated me. Suzanne turned to face me and said, Doctor David, it's nice to finally meet you.

Her blue eyes seemed to say, "I know you." I have always known you. My heart was forever captured inside hers, beating in sync.

Suzanne, I have wanted to express what has been in my heart for a long time, ever since the first day we met. Your heart has waited too long to hear.

"Oh my God, Vickie, my David is opening up his heart in front of the world."

Vickie held her hand as she got teary and handed her a tissue.

"But was blinded and couldn't see through fears of rejection. Was this just a dream? You had no such fear.

When our eyes met, I felt braver saying, "hell, this is presumptuous, but I would like to kiss you and then dance with you."

In a year and a half, we experienced a lifetime of both the happiest and the saddest times. Your eyes always shone, with a heart filled with love.

We danced, and your body melted closer to mine, releasing loving emotions, laying dormant in my heart."

Vickie leaned closer to her sister, tearful from David's outpouring of love. Whispering to Suzie, "Walk over to David. Your sisters are here; you have been dreaming and praying for this moment all your life."

Suzie came nearer to David.

"The black gown you wore the first night we met was gorgeous. You, my Irish Angel, made the dress memorable. Regrettably, there was an unexpected interruption the night we met. Will you finish our first dance with these honorable people as a witness to my love?"

On cue, our song played, "The First Time Ever I Saw Your Face."

"And when I held you in my arms, all my emotions wanted to escape to you."

Dancing in front of the world was not scary once Suzie was in my arms, and no one else mattered. She trembled with palpable anticipation as we danced with her head on my shoulder.

"Suzanne Siobhan Brooke, my Angel, I have often dreamt of this moment."

I started looking for the engagement ring and panicked because it wasn't in any of the pockets.

Not to embarrass me in a soft, barely audible whisper in my ear, "My New York man, what you are looking for is in your top left inner coat jacket's pocket. We were dancing close."

And took out a little ring box.

With blurry eyes filled with tears of love, "Oh my God, David, your mother's engagement ring! David, oh my God. Yes, David."

"Suzie, I didn't ask you yet."

"Oh, sorry."

"Suzanne, the only words fit this moment. I love you. Will you marry me?"

"Yes! Oh, David, yes, you've made me the happiest woman, even though you are slow on the uptake. I love you so much."

Neither of us heard applause as we kissed. Wrapped my arm around Suzie and started to leave the stage.

Tears flowing down her face, Vickie ran out to us, holding a box of tissues.

"Suzie, love, did you forget someone?"

"Oh my God, the President."

Walked her back to the podium.

"Mr. Vice President, Secretary of Education, Senators, Congressional Representatives, members of the Press, and my dear, sweet nieces Annabelle and Jessica.

I waited for this moment, never doubting, and was finally able to introduce the President, my friend, to the public for the first time. Since I was ten years old, I had anticipated this particular moment, never doubting, and now, at last, I was able to introduce the President, my friend, my first time.

Only one thing could have put my head in the clouds. I've just received a marriage proposal from a man I deeply love.

Thank you, dear sister, Vickie, for freeing me of my disorientation.

Prepared a speech, but words alone on paper cannot express my sincere admiration and respect. Proud because the United States and the world will be better.

How to introduce the most powerful woman in the world? I don't have the gift of words my fiancé has, but I have an advantage: being Irish.

Appreciative of a woman who has confidence in a ten-year-old girl and was true to her word. Friend, mentor, and boss, a woman who has done hundreds of acts of kindness and refused publicity. A moment to tell my children and grandchildren of my sincere honor to be able to introduce the President of the United States, President Julia Liliana Harrison."

Suzie walked over and stood next to me to wait. She had the pleasure of introducing the President, a long-awaited dream come true, plus a proposal of marriage. Slipped a few tissues into her hand.

"Suzie, a memorable introduction anyone has given me, especially because you have said it.

David and Suzie, we have time to celebrate later. Congratulations, you two. My daughters and Robert send their love and hugs. Two Secret Service agents will take you to your room through the kitchen elevator to avoid the Press."

"Miss Suzie and Mr. David, please come with me. The other Agent is waiting in front of the kitchen service elevator."

"Oh, Agent Murphy! So happy it is you."

"The President asked for me.

Miss Suzie, you are not allowed to hug a Secret Service Agent. Fellow Agents would tackle you if you did.

No, just kidding. Every agent knows you, your work at the White House, during the presidential campaign, or watching over you when you two are into mischief."

Agent Murphy was the first agent to tell a modest joke. This was the first time an Agent smiled on duty in Secret Service memory. This meant so much to Suzie.

Suzie and I kissed until the elevator door opened, and we walked arm-in-arm down the hall.

"Agent Murphy, our room is on the 10th floor."

"Miss Suzie, your Sisters upgraded your room to an Executive Luxury Penthouse Suite. Congratulations, your luggage is in your room, and the Suite is yours until tomorrow. There is an Agent on duty 24/7 if you need anything."

"David, please text my Sisters. They are having lunch in the hotel restaurant, and ask them, please don't leave until we talk with them. I want to see Annabelle and Jessica."

"Know that look. Do you want to talk? Come and sit on the sofa with me."

"Are you happy?"

"That is code for something you want to ask me."

"Love, can we elope?"

"Been wondering when you would mention this. Tell me truthfully, would love to if this is what you want, but we should keep this secret."

"Oh, Annabelle, she's already told her she'll be my flower girl. Jacquie and Jaz, Noreen and Jessica, Vickie, Megan, oh, love, this is already spiraling out of control.

New York man, I do not want a traditional wedding. Wait months and months, shop for a dress for the maids of honor, arrange for a band, flowers, a photographer, and invitations, or consider a gift registry at a department store. Deciding whom to invite and include on our guest list for those who want a special meal is overwhelming! And takes my time away from being with you."

"Eloping sounds perfect. Suzie, are you sure you won't be disappointed? You dreamed of a traditional wedding."

"David, you are my dream. So, what do we do?"

Wrapped my arms around her as she began to tear up, turning her eyes into pools of deep blue.

"Angel, if you had to choose one person to marry us, no matter how improbable it may seem, whom would you want?"

"Jacquie, how is that possible?"

"Jacquie told me on the first day we met about how you love playing pretend, getting married. She conveyed your dream, which you had had since you were a little girl, and wanted Jacquie to marry you. Recently reminded Jacquie you never gave up your dream."

'Sis, my perfect wedding ceremony is for you to marry David and me.'

"This was a child's fantasy."

"If your dream becomes true, do you still want Jacquie to officiate our marriage ceremony?"

"David, it is only a dream. I want my Sister who raised me, and it would be a miracle if she could officiate our wedding."

"Dreams do come true."

"Love, this cannot happen. It is not possible."

"Jacquie told me how poignant you held on to your dream but were sad it could never come true. After some research, she can marry us."

"David, could you make this happen?"

"The State of California made it easy. Jacquie would get instructions, fill out a form, pay a fee, and be sworn in as a Deputy Marriage Commissioner. Just for our ceremony, and it could not have religious overtones."

"David, how did you know I wanted to elope? My Sisters, can they be at our eloping wedding? Does Jacquie know yet? No, you would want to speak to me first. But you couldn't know what I wanted."

"Kind of, late at night, you ask what a romantic way would be to get married."

"Love, you know my mind and heart, and always finish my sentences. You tell me frequently that, as long as you are happy. Your mom always said if you're happy, that's all that matters. Wish your mom could have been at our wedding."

"In a way, she is, as you carry her namesake, our unborn daughter Brooke's middle name."

"Can we call my Sisters before they leave the restaurant?"

"They are waiting for us to call. Asked Vickie to keep them waiting."

"How did you know? Was this part of the conversation you had before our dinner with her? David, you are the most wonderful, thoughtful, loving romantic man."

Held her closer and kissed her to slow her down and enjoy each moment. My Angel's mind was racing from one thought to another, happily listening to her excitement and questions.

"Oh, my goodness! Mom and Nana."

"What about your mom and Nana?"

"Stop teasing."

"Call them now, and I'll ask Jacquie to come up first and tell your Sisters to follow when they have finished eating."

"No religious ceremony permitted, and you don't mind not having a Rabbi marry us?"

"Not a bit. Having Jacquie is picture-perfect."

Jacquie anxiously knocked, and Suzie was excited to let her in.

"Sis, remember my dream as a girl for you to marry me."

"Suzie. Is this for real?"

"David learned it's legal for you to marry us in California."

"Sweetheart, we were both children pretending. But, David, is this really a thing? This is perfect. Suzie, this makes me the happiest Sister. We thought it would be impossible, but our David found a way."

"Jacquie, there is something else. David and I don't want a traditional wedding. So, we are going to elope. Couldn't imagine getting married by anyone but you."

"Mom and Nana?"

"Before you came up, spoke with them and swore them to secrecy."

"Were they disappointed?"

"Yes, at first, they were amiable when I told them elopement is romantic and sensual, a wedding is a ceremony and party, and they were relieved. However, they did not want to deal with changing my mind about every detail."

"You made up that last thing."

"David, you made Suzie and me the happiest Sisters."

There was some rather loud whispering behind the door.

The Sisters were impatient to enter our suite to hug and kiss their baby Sister.

Vickie, Noreen, Jaz, and Megan looked at Suzie, expressing excitement in unison, and cried out, "You are eloping!"

"Sweet Sisters, how could you possibly know?"

"We couldn't, listening at the door. Annabelle and Jessica's clever idea."

"Love, give me a few minutes. Want to look sexy for you."

"Honey, it's been such a long day. Let me prepare a hot bubble bath for the bride-to-be and give you a sensual massage."

"David, my groom-to-be, today I find my heart smiling for it heard the words I have longed to hear. Each love song we listen to is lovely, but we prefer the music of our love.

The day of our marriage and our baby's birth is just the beginning. You are right. Love cannot be expressed in words alone."

"We love with a love that was more than love." Edgar Allen Poe

"My heart is and always will be yours." Jane Austen

Twenty-Four
"So They Plighted their Troth."

"Let Love be Like a Moving Sea Between the Shores of Your Souls." Kahlil Gibran

"If you find a man who trusts you, who isn't afraid, who sees you for who you are, and if it feels like he knows you for who it is that you simply are and thinks all of that is beautiful, know that you have found a rare thing." C. Joy Bell C.

"A happy good morning to friends and family gathered today in France, Germany, England, and worldwide. To our Irish family in Ireland and the United States, Dia daoibh ar maidin! The idiomatic translation is 'Good Morning,' translated idiomatically in Irish Gaelic.

For the Bride and Groom's friends here with us today or via SOAR Livestream worldwide who do not know me, let me introduce myself: Jacqueline Carolyn Brooke, Suzanne's oldest Sister.

This is a blessed day for the bride and the groom-to-be.

David and Suzie's love embraces all of you as you share in their symbolic garden of love.

There were no words to express my emotions when my Sister and David asked me to officiate their marriage ceremony. Suzie has dreamt of her wedding since she was a child. Suzie pretended to get married, and I would perform the ceremony. My baby Sister said it was practice for when she got married for real.

Couldn't imagine our dream manifesting itself, yet today I'm performing the marriage ceremony for my Sister and David. I shared this dream with David the day we met, and he found a way to make our impossible dream come true.

On behalf of the couple, they wanted to share this moment with many they love. It is live-streamed and videotaped for loving remembrance.

Their decision to elope and not have a traditional wedding excluded their extended family and friends, as they found it was more romantic and sensual.

I'm deeply honored to welcome the President of the United States, First Husband, and their two daughters and family watching this online. Suzie and David have already personally shared sentiments with the First Family.

We are doubly honored to welcome the Vice President and the Second Lady, who are watching online.

My daughter Annabelle, my niece Jessica, my Sisters, and my Jaz, along with Suzanne and David, all gathered here today, or virtually. Even prose gifted by Suzanne and David could not find words to express their deep-seated feelings. Today, for all gathered here or virtually. Only three words could best describe what is in their hearts. We love you."

You can imagine that my Sister fretted over whom to acknowledge first. Her boss, the President of the United States, and her First Husband have been her second family since she was ten. So, love and protocol, thank goodness, were easy decisions for her.

Resolving who to welcome after the Vice President and Second Lady was impossible for the bride-to-be. She and the groom asked me to have you imagine you are in Times Square on New Year's Eve as the Ball drops, exploding into more than sixteen million colors by over 32,000 LEDs spelling out each of your names, all at once as the bride and groom's electronic gift of love.

Here to celebrate with the bride and groom and their union in matrimony are dear friends Mr. Charles and his family, Gabriella and James, Sherry and Kevin, Cheryl and Joe, and the bride's close colleague and friend, Patricia and her husband. Her friends from the White House Press Corps, well, a secret elopement was impossible for Suzie.

David and Suzie had already called to express their love and appreciation for the many friends watching virtually.

The couple wanted to express sincere respect, affection, and love for Agent Eileen Murphy, Roxanna Morris, White House operator Joan, and the Chief Head Doctor at the U.S. Army Hospital in Germany. Suzie and David are grateful to each of you for being with them in person or virtually on their happy day.

Suzie's beloved Whisper and Shadow have joined us today and will take the couple back to Woodland Cottage. Golf carts will bring family and friends to join them there. You are invited to join us for lunch and traditional Jewish and Irish dancing immediately after the ceremony, and share in the couple's joy on this special day.

David and Suzie will experience their first sunrise as a married couple before leaving for their honeymoon. The destination is kept secret for privacy and security, except for Annabelle, her mom, and Nana, where confidences are kept safe.

Oh, yes, I was reminded by my Sister. There are boxes of tissues available."

"We take ourselves out of the usual routines of daily living to witness a unique moment in the lives of Suzanne Siobhan Brooke and David Benjamin Bradley. Today, they join their lives in a union of marriage. As we weep in joy for their love.

Suzanne and David feel fortunate to share this moment with their family and friends. We are gathered in their abode of love, a grove of Live Oak trees and a stream with twists and turns that winds eventually into the Sacramento River. This wonderful place is where they laugh, cry, and share intimacies in the cool shade of the trees.

Since the day of her birth, Mom, Nana, and my Sisters have known just how out of the ordinary and extraordinary our last-born Suzanne is. We watched her grow up during her school years and shared unconditional love through the sadness, the joy of her life, and the delight of having her love mate step out of a dream of faith and ask her to dance. Each of you adopted David into the family and your hearts.

Because, dear Sisters, family, and friends, you are the ones who have supported and loved them, and know them so well; dear Sisters, family, and friends you are the ones who have supported and loved them and know them so well, it only fits that you are the ones to share this once-in-a-lifetime moment with them.

Suzanne and David are pleased to have their beloved mom and Nana in the front row, close to them, for the ceremony.

Suzanne appreciates and sends love to our mother and Nana for every opportunity to be the best mother and Nana anyone could ask for.

Suzanne also sends her love to Sisters Victoria and Noreen for being her Maids of Honor, Jaz, Megan, Jessica, and Gabriela as her bridesmaids, Annabelle, her flower girl, and the Honorable Dr. Robert Kelly, Her First Husband, attending virtually as David's best man.

A wedding day is when couples miss family members who are no longer with them. Of blessed memory, David's mom and dad, whose memories they hold dear and love the most.

Suzanne and David prepared for the wedding by reflecting on what they love about each other. This was the easiest part of planning their wedding ceremony.

Suzanne and David, the years will pass with deepening love and commitment to your future children, always supporting each other and sharing dreams.

Your love story is memorialized in a romance novel, David's *Weep for Love*, where endings become the beginning of a new chapter.

Suzanne and David, we come now to the words you have longed to hear. Words from their hearts take them across the threshold of their first kiss and dance to becoming engaged to be married."

"David, I love you. You are loving, romantic, and kindhearted, making me laugh when I want to cry. You taught me tears and laughter share the same coin. And you let me weep as wordless emotions need release.

David, you are always there for me as a comfort. Cherish and love you more each day. My sweet New York man, my arms and heart will always remain open when you need a hug, and my lips will be there for your tender kisses. Give you freedom, support, and love to achieve your dreams.

You are a warm breeze to dry my tears. My moonlight was on our romantic walks. I love you; you always want to share intimacies by hugging or kissing. I love how you laugh with me, enjoy my silliness, and share in my sense of humor. Always find ways to love me, even when faced with life's surprises.

You remember details, and even when I think you are not paying attention, you're planning for our mutual dreams. Your love for my family and close circle of friends means a great deal, and your love is reciprocated and appreciated.

The room down the hall, where our baby sleeps in our New York home, speaks without a need for words about how much I love you.

David, you always love me and become closer, especially when I'm silly or upset. You never argue or judge. Instead, you listen to understand my feelings.

Shining the limelight on my career, passions, and dreams. Never concerned that it might place you in the shadow. Standing by your side, our shadows blend into one.

My New York man, I love how we enjoy our romantic escapades. There's so much more to say about why I love you. I'll whisper lovingly what is in my heart when we are alone."

"Suzanne, to say I love you is insufficient to capture the depth of emotions I have for you.

I promise our romance won't end, but will grow to include our children. I promise not to hold secrets unless it's a surprise gift of love to you. I promise you independence, as you are a person in your own right. I promise you my love and faithfulness. Tenderness when you cry.

You are my guiding star when I am lost.

I love that you can be silly to underscore feelings lovingly, regardless of what they may be.

I love how you make me smile and laugh, and let me share our life through your eyes.

I love your intellect, Irish wit, smile, bluest blue eyes, and inner beauty.

I love every second of every day spent with you. Or when I travel, you are forever in my heart.

I love you for letting me be with all my New York peculiarities. I love your Irish Brogue, soft and loving when you express your passions, talents, and dreams. I love your sensual kisses.

My love for you is unbreakable! I love your patience in creating our family, a more profound expression of our love.

I love it when you are romantic or when we eat our DS pizza.

I love it when you spend time with your Sisters as you bring their joy back to me.

I love that we never argue about which movie to watch, although no one will believe it is possible. It is with you."

"I love how we rid ourselves of dragons guarding the gate of our ego, and what's beyond is ours to create. I love how our hearts beat as one."

"Suzanne will sing their song, '"The First Time Ever I Saw Your Face."

"Today, we witness the marriage of David and Suzie, a loving, equal commitment to each other in matrimony. Crafted in the most profound sense to the exclusion of all others, it is entered into with the desire to last for life.

Before you declare your vows to one another, I want to hear you confirm that it is indeed your intention to be married today.

David Benjamin Bradley, do you come here freely and without reservation to give yourself to Suzanne Siobhan Brooke in marriage? If so, answer I do."

"I do."

"Suzanne Siobhan Brooke, do you come here freely and without reservation to give yourself to David Benjamin Bradley in marriage? If so, answer, "I do."

"I do."

"Having heard your intention to marry each other, Suzanne and David, now I ask you to declare your marriage vows.

Please face each other and hold hands.

David, please repeat after me."

"I, David Benjamin Bradley, take you, Suzanne Siobhan Brooke, as my love partner. Without reservation, I will share my life with you and build our dreams together, support you through times of trouble, and share in your joy in times of happiness. I promise to give you respect, love, and fidelity. This commitment is made in love, kept in faith, and made new every day of our lives."

"Suzanne, please repeat after me."

"I, Suzanne Siobhan Brooke, take you, David Benjamin Bradley, as my love partner. Without reservation, I will share my life with you, build our dreams together, support you through times of trouble, and share in your joy in times of happiness. I promise to give you respect, love, and fidelity. This commitment is made in love, kept in faith, and made new every day of our lives."

"Your wedding ring is an outward and visible sign of the inward and invisible bond that already unites your two hearts in love.

David, place the ring on Suzanne's finger and repeat after me."

"I give you this ring.

Wear it with love and joy.

As this ring has no end,

My love is also forever."

"Suzanne, place the ring on David's finger and repeat after me."

"I give you this ring.

Wear it with love and joy.

As this ring has no end,

My love is also forever."

"May the wedding rings you exchanged today remind you constantly that you are surrounded by enduring love.

Suzanne and David,

Everyone has advice for newlyweds, and I have the privilege of sharing a few personal words with you.

Suzanne and David, I offer you this blessing on your special day.

May your life together be blessed with children, prosperity, and health. May you always share open and honest communication.

May you respect each other's talents and gifts and give each other full-throated support in their professional and personal pursuits.

May your love be a lifelong source of excitement, contentment, affection, respect, and devotion for one another.

May you cherish the home and family you will start together.

May all the years be filled with moments to celebrate and renew your love.

Now, by the power vested in me by the State of California as Deputy Marriage Commissioner, it is my honor and joy with eyes filled with tears and a heart overflowing with love to declare you husband and wife. You may now seal this affirmation of your love with a kiss.

Oh, David, no one expected you to wait. You may keep kissing the bride.

Breaking the Glass wrapped in a cloth bag is a centuries-old tradition. David and Suzanne, both of you have a glass in a cloth bag. You will break the glass to symbolize your absolute finality to your wedding covenant.

Mazel Tov!

Before I lose it, break down, and cry, I have the honor to present the newlyweds as a married couple for the first time, Suzanne Siobhan Brooke-Bradley and David Benjamin Bradley."

Epilogue
Beginning A New Chapter

"Ends are not bad things; they just mean that something else is about to begin. And many things don't really end, anyway; they just begin again in a new way. Ends are not bad, and many ends aren't really an ending; some things are never-ending." C. Joy Bell C.

Turning into the school's entrance, a black sedan limousine escorted by four police motorcycles and three police cars with sirens screaming and a high-pitched wailing noise heralded my arrival.

Everyone ran from the school auditorium to watch the excitement. Brooke enthusiastically went to her mom, who was carrying Victoria Jacqueline, our three-year-old daughter.

"Mommy, Daddy had police sirens."

All the children were jumping up and down, overjoyed to be part of something unusual. Annabelle was delighted at my arrival, and Jacquie, Jaz, and Suzanne were smiling. Since I was so late, they expected my appearance to be spectacular.

Suzie smiled. "Brooke, Victoria, Daddy certainly created interest, and this was without a doubt a different way for Daddy's arrival."

Parents and teachers were simply happy their children enjoyed themselves.

Mrs. Chaffee, the school principal, thought of some awful emergency and evacuated the auditorium. She was sanguine that everyone was safe. However, she was not easily forgiving.

Secret Service agents protecting Suzanne expected my arrival, so they didn't panic.

The black sedan's back door slowly opened.

In blue jeans, a grey shirt, a dark grey vest, and worn-out brown Oxford shoes, aviator sunglasses, David exited the Limo and found everyone staring at him.

The Press was there because Suzanne promised them a news briefing after our daughter's performance. They loved the spectacle created, as it was a chance to take up-front pictures of my unusual yet somehow expected arrival.

Oh, the President won't be pleased with me for the commotion I made. My advantage was that it was her goddaughter's first public performance.

A truly animating way for my daughters and wife to know I had arrived.

"Whoops, sorry, folks.

Promised my daughter would arrive on time. But my flight got delayed."

"President Harrison granted permission for me to fly back with the Vice President on Air Force Two. The sirens were due to the chief of Police's permission this one time. Always wanted to arrive with sirens blaring to my daughters' delight."

Even so, Principal Chaffee wasn't interested in my adult family fantasies.

"Two minutes to spare. Thank you, officers, for the escort."

"Sir, the police cars must leave, but the motorcycle police need to stay for Miss Brooke-Bradley."

Brooke shouted to Annabelle, "Sis, there's Daddy." And ran into my arms, lifted my precious baby girl, and gave her a warm hug and kiss hello.

"Precious, I love you and miss you so much. A surprise gift for you and your Sisters. Bought it in Washington, D.C., and will give it to you when we arrive home.

Put my beloved down as Annabelle ran into my arms and hugged and kissed me. She smiled her signature warm I love you smile, confident that her dad would be on time, just as for each of her performances. Anticipated her dad's arrival creatively.

"Sweetpea, I love and miss you so much."

"Daddy, I love you more. Here is another kiss and hug."

"Sweetheart, tell me, is your new Principal as mean as you told me?"

"Meaner," with a loving smile, my daughter adopted the playfulness of her Aunt Suzie. "Daddy, please comport yourself and toe the line. Please don't say anything to her," she said and giggled.

"Come along, Brooke, you have a performance to give. Daddy will take her backstage."

Parents and children had already returned to their seats.

Principal Chaffee, with a slightly annoyed tone, announced, 'Our performance will begin as soon as Dr. Bradley is seated.'

"I love you, New York Man, for wearing my favorite outfit."

"How I missed your bluest eyes and your kisses."

Suzie's kisses expressed her deep affection and love, and she didn't want them to stop.

"Daddee, Mommee, your baby is being squished!"

"Oh, sorry, sweetheart."

Love, let me hold Victoria. Sweet baby, I love you. Let me hug and kiss you."

"Daddee, Sis is going to sing with Mommee."

"Yes, how exciting. My adorable girl, you will be with your aunts, grandma, Nana, and me."

"My New York man, you cut it rather close to the start of the performance. So, how did you convince the President to authorize a motorcycle and police escort?"

"Texted the President and asked if she could arrange for me to arrive in time to see her Goddaughter's first public performance."

"The sirens?"

"Always wanted a police escort with sirens blaring to impress Annabelle, Brooke, and Victoria. Want my daughters to know that Dad arrived, and nothing would prevent me from being on time. And promised Brooke, afraid to be late.

After hearing my reason, the sergeant agreed to the sirens. Guess what?"

"Of course, he is Irish."

"A hardy-looking man with an Irish brogue. 'This is for your daughter.'"

"The aviator sunglasses were a nice touch. Looking so handsome, you made a lasting impression on parents, the PTA president, and teachers. Still, you, pissed off Mrs. Chaffee, the Principal. But, to be fair, the Vice Principal was smiling."

"President Harrison is on the phone, thanking Mrs. Chaffee for her leadership and care of her Goddaughter. Bet Brooke and Annabelle become her favorite children."

"Oh, David, you are incorrigible."

"Honey, the President asked me what she could do to smooth the way for my entrance. It seems she has a David gets out of trouble book. Really, the President did it for the girls."

"David, setting a romantic table for our date night.

When the girls bathe, please let them play for a while in the bathtub., Annabelle likes to shower, but she will help you while her Sisters bathe.

Would you also see that the girls are ready for bed?

David, remember just one bedtime story. That should give me ample time to prepare our dinner.

After dinner, Annabelle will be in the family room with Jacquie and Jaz. They promised her a movie night."

"Yes, of course, Suzie. Do I have time to…?"

"Down the hall to your right."

"Honey?"

"Yes, Love."

"Victoria?"

"Oh, sweetheart, let Mommy take you."

"Suzie, Annabelle took Brooke backstage to be with her class."

"David, joining her shortly for our performance.

Love, Brooke, and I are going to sing our favorite movie song. We are the finale this year for the children's end-of-the-year school performance."

"Sis, did you tell David about your new job offer and living in New York?"

"Tonight, Vickie, reconsider taking my girls to live in New York for a year instead of staying at Woodland Cottage."

Jacquie waited outside for her mom.

"Where are my beautiful grandchildren?"

"Your granddaughters, Brooke and Annabelle, are backstage, and Jessica is with Noreen and Megan, talking with Nana. Come sit next to David, as Victoria wants you to hug her."

"David, your arrival was a class act. I love you." Jacquie gave me a sweet kiss and sat next to Jaz and Megan.

Spoken softly, "Sis, when it comes to you, Brooke, Victoria, and Annabelle, he will use all his influence and any leverage he can gather to make you all happy. Trust David and you to find a solution."

"What solution? Suzie, are you hiding something from me?"

"Love, talk to Mom. Nana is having a chinwag with Megan, Noreen, and Jessica."

"Hello, Mom, you look beautiful as always. It looks like Victoria got comfortable, all snuggled in your lap."

"David heard about your unusual arrival. Are you sure you don't have hidden Irish genes?

"Yes, perhaps you are right. Elizabeth, how are you? Suzie and I would like you and Nana to come to stay for a long weekend."

"Love, honestly, want to tell you myself. Asked Vickie not to say anything."

"Say what?"

"David, have to go and prepare for my performance with Brooke. Tonight, after our dinner and dancing."

Vickie leaned over, "Trust David and yourself to know what you both want."

Suzie thought he couldn't have found out. My mother, Nana, and Sisters, except Vickie, don't know yet.

There wasn't a dry eye after Suzie and Brook's rendition of *Somewhere Over the Rainbow*.

After the girls were tucked in bed, "Let's dance and make love all night."

"New York man, first, I want to ask you something."

"Angel, may I first share my good news? Just heard the most wonderful news."

"You know."

"Know what."

"Suzie, due to my consulting experience at the United Nations for over six years, the U.S. Ambassador to the UN offered me a full-time position working in the United States Embassy.

We would be able to live in our New York apartment. Travel back on long weekends and holidays to visit your Sisters, mom, and Nana. What about having the whole family for both Thanksgiving and Christmas? That should make the girls happy."

"How did you find out who told you?"

"Love told the Ambassador needed time to talk to my wife and daughters. But, Suzie, you were anxious to tell me something."

"Oh, David, you always make me happy. You knew about my UN offer and arranged this position yourself, so you don't have to choose between family and working for the US Ambassador to the United Nations."

"United Nations, Suzie, sorry to upstage your news. Wow, a major step in your political career."

"David, hug me. How do you always make life easy, so I don't have to give up my career? You kept your promise before Brooke was born. We would find solutions, work, and travel together."

"Suzie, the President, called and wanted to speak with you after finishing your shower.

'Madam President Suzie said nothing yet.' Told her you would return her call in a few minutes. That is when she said to me,

'Glad you and Suzie made this happen.'

'Do you mean my position at the United Nations and living in New York?'

"That is when I handed over the phone to you."

"David, you are impossible. You shouldn't be bantering with the President. She can run rings around us. You can't fool her, and honey, you made it up, didn't you? You would never be sarcastic or play games with her."

"Angel, I love you so much, but didn't arrange this. Received a call a few days ago from the United States Ambassador to the United Nations. Over the years, she has been impressed with my consulting work for the President.

The Ambassador wanted to appoint a consultant on human rights for girls on behalf of the United States. The position includes meetings with Ambassadors from all over the world. She said my office would be on a different floor, but 'this was perfect because your Suzie is coming to work for me.'

'No, she has not yet said anything, and if you would permit me, Madam Ambassador, this sounds too coincidental and convenient. Was this the President's suggestion?'

'Yes, but already decided on you before she said anything, so everything came together. Arrangements for onboarding have started, and since you have an apartment close to the United Nations, I hope you both say yes.'

"Love, we deserve some good fortune. We have to ask Brooke. Have you spoken to her yet?"

"David, she loves her room in New York and has friends in the building and preschool. Victoria is still too young, so I told her as much as she could understand.

Would you be honest with me?"

"Of course, always."

"If you were not offered a position, would you?"

"Yes, unequivocally."

"You would move with me to keep us together for the year?"

"How could you for one second consider I would not? Promised to follow you anywhere to advance your career."

"The truth is, if you were not happy, you would have turned down this offer, but you wouldn't let me. So, we are happy. You are happy, aren't you?"

"Love, never been happier. We have our daughters and each other.

Suzie doesn't want to accept the U.S. Ambassador's offer. Advise and travel when required, but want to write more children's books, teach, consult, and advocate for vulnerable girls."

"I shall turn down my offer as well."

"Love, haven't finished what I want to tell you."

"Ok, I'm listening."

"This will allow me to be there for our girls when you work overtime. Then, when travel for work is necessary, coordinate with you and our daughters."

"David, love, did Vickie phone you while in Washington, DC?"

"Yes, and since you already are aware of her good news, Vickie was accepted into a prestigious Law practice in New York as a Junior Partner.

Vickie loves her bedroom in our New York apartment and all the privacy she wants.

Vickie can't wait to spend time with Brooke and Victoria. Best of all, she would be with us in New York."

"My Sweetpea is at an age when she should spend more time with her mom. Annabelle will spend long weekends, holidays, and summers with us in New York. So our girls grow up together."

"David, since Jaz and Jacquie expanded their business, owning twenty boutiques, with store managers, it is easier to be home with Annabelle at Woodland Cottage. I had hoped you shared my views. Jacquie and Jaz were excited to spend more time with Annabelle."

"What's wrong, Suzie? Your smile vanished."

"Honey, you don't want to stay in New York for a year. Don't want you unhappy. Going to turn down the offer. Instead, we can work out something with Vickie to have one of us visit her, so she won't be lonely. David, please tell me honestly."

"Angel, would rather not spend a winter, let alone a year, in New York. Our girls should grow up together at Woodland Cottage. That would make Annabelle and her Sisters happier."

"Tell me truthfully, what you want, and not worry about the President or me."

Initially excited, but worried. Didn't want our daughters to spend a year in New York. The girls and I would miss riding Whisper and Shadow. So would you. I love our home, and we visit New York a lot anyway.

"Love, let's have a conference call with the President and US Ambassador and propose how we have worked since our Brooke. We can work from Woodland Cottage and New York. So, we accept both offers and easily travel back and forth as we do now."

"David, this works out better for Vickie. It's brilliant; Vickie's Law firm has offices in Sacramento and New York. This allows her to work and live in Woodland Cottage and New York.

We girls, Megan, Jacquie, Jaz, Brooke, Victoria, Annabelle, and Jessica, are here.

The idea of not having her family close was insufferable. Vickie looks to us for moral support. She didn't want to disappoint you or me.

The Law Firm has already asked Vickie to work on legal cases in the New York and San Francisco offices. She becomes a more valuable asset to the firm. We all have the best of both worlds. How often does this happen in life?"

"David, once we are settled in our new positions, let's discuss our long-held dream. Just you and I working together to advocate and take action for the most vulnerable girls."

"Certainly, we don't have to wait and can start anytime.

Angel, how about traveling with the girls to Ireland during their next summer vacation? They will be older and will adore meeting Nana's massive family of aunts, uncles, nephews, nieces, and cousins. That would make our girls happy.

You once said I was a man with a million words, but there are no words to express the endless love held in my heart for you and our daughters.

Honey, even with our important talk, it wasn't all you wanted to discuss with me."

"Oh, David, how do you always know?"

"Angel, you wouldn't whisper to Vickie at the school performance if it were insignificant."

"David, can we try to have another baby?"

Suzie and I have a romance that had a providential, though turbulent, beginning with a first kiss and dance, which led us to become happy married lovers.

Our narrative doesn't end with the last few words on the book's final page. Suzie and I now weep with joy as tears and kisses have become one and the same.

Louis Armstrong – it's a Wonderful World.

The colors of the rainbow, So pretty in the sky
Are also of the faces of people going by
I see friends shaking hands
Saying, How do you do?
They're really saying
I love you...

Afterword

"I have learned that you can go anywhere you want to go and do anything you want to do and buy all the things that you want to buy and meet all the people that you want to meet and learn all the things that you desire to learn and if you do all these things but are not madly in love: you have still not begun to live." C. Joy Bell C.

We kept our love safe during challenging times, never doubting our passion for each other. Yet, we still struggle to put it into words. Even with all the love poems, sonnets, and songs, we still managed to keep our love secure in our hearts. It was our turn to create our own song with Harmony with Music.

Our lovemaking and romance continue to grow and become increasingly gratifying. Our girls bring us never-ending pleasure, and we spoil them. They are our love babies.

Suzie and I primarily live in California, where there are more singing gigs and art shows that cater to her passions..

She built a recording studio at the Sanctuary and named it Woodland Records. She has started to write lyrics and music, so she has original material. And has already recorded dozens of songs, enough for three CDs. Even made several elegant music videos.

Recently, Susie accepted a contract with a well-known streaming music distributor. Available across multiple media platforms. My love has begun her dream journey as a professional singer.

Of course, we have the same worries and problems as any family. Still, we are exuberant in our marriage and children. Our love rises above disagreement and fears, molding them into a love story patchwork.

Our intimacy nurtured us from a romantic partner to a girlfriend, fiancé, now my wife, and mother of our children. My relationship with Suzie is an intricate blend of lover, life partner, best friend, confidant, and romantic partner all rolled into one to share life with.

Above all, her talents, accomplishments, and career, what she loves and cherishes most, are being a mother of our children, whom she indulges. Suzie now understood what my mom meant when she told her she had a mother's love.

Therefore, she never objected to my spoiling our Annabelle because she and I adore and pamper our girls. We encourage our three girls to keep hope alive for a romantic future. You can't give too much love, ensuring they are healthy, safe, happy, and have multiple and diverse opportunities.

The secret to our romantic love story lies in the simple yet profound teachings from Relationship 101 at the University of Being. With the caveat, this is not just for one day or time, but for the entire relationship. These daily acts of love will bring you closer and keep you together. This is not just for one day or time; it's for the entire relationship. By giving love daily, you'll bring yourself closer and keep it close. Kiss every day, not just a peck, but for at least 15 to 20 seconds. Nothing else will bond you as closely,

Wishes come true, especially incredibly impossible ones.

*W*_{eep} *f*_{or} *L*_{ove}, David's first novel, is a Realistic

Contemporary Romance Novel. Somehow, David managed
to maintain a multilayered reservoir of passion and love as
research material for his novel. Weep for Love was an
endeavor to make sense of love gained and lost, joy and
depression, successes and failures, all spoken with humor
and humility in a Bronx accent.

It was hard for the author to let go of the characters of
his imagination. David wrote down their experiences,
feelings, and thoughts as they shared their life stories.
Trusting that he had liberated them to take on a life of their
own, he shared them. Trusting he liberated them to take on
a life of their own, to share with future readers.

Dr. David Benjamin Bradley is a romanticized fictional version of Dr. David Kenneth Waldman's life. Though written through a fictionalized lens, events and situations were based on personal encounters and actualities. However, no character or description portrays any natural person, living or deceased; it is a coincidence and not meant by the author as such.

David has lived an extraordinary life, not an exhaustive list; meeting and working with Members of the Uganda Parliament, His Royal Highness: a Ugandan King, and an Iranian Princess, U.S. Senators, and U.S. Ambassadors to Uganda, and Guatemala, California, as well as Hawaii State Educational leaders, speaking at numerous major academic conventions, and three times at the United Nations, and has presented dozens of educational development workshops for teachers.

Dr. David Kenneth Waldman's joy and cherished career are in instructing children. His one overriding passion and love is when David teaches. David takes pride in being a child whisperer.

During the 2019 COVID-19 pandemic, I taught onsite special needs children for five months at the Redwood School District, as there was a need to prevent these children from falling behind.

Yes, he prefers to be called David.

David has had a multifaceted career with over 47 years as a social entrepreneur, publisher, educator, host of two radio shows and a public access TV show, educational sales consultant, author of children's books, and now a romance novelist.

An international traveler to forty-seven countries, David, lived in Germany for five years, working as a civilian educational consultant for the U.S. Army.

Personal life experiences woven together inform who he is at heart: a boy from The Bronx. The author presently lives in San Francisco.

The author welcomes any feedback or comments. Stay connected and in communication with David. Although he cannot guarantee a response, he will make an effort to personally respond to each email.

Book Reviews

Reviewed by K.C. Finn
for Readers' Favorite
Four Stars ★★★★

Weep For Love is a work of fiction in the contemporary romance subgenre. It is best suited to the mature reading audience for its intense emotions and adult themes, and was penned by author David Kenneth Waldman.

The premise follows a central protagonist, David Benjamin Bradley, through a love affair that will leave lasting marks on his heart and soul. A series of tragic and trying events is interspersed with the passion, joy, and romanticism of faithful Love to deliver an all-encompassing love story that attempts to show Love from every realistic facet rather than just the central romantic elements.

Author David Kenneth Waldman delivers an in-depth novel that explores various perspectives on the nature of Love. In large part, it achieves a realistic. It provides a well-rounded view of how Love fits into daily life, but can also be a hugely disruptive influence.

The central protagonist, David's character development, is a significant focal point of the novel and a solid perspective from which to view the novel's major events.

Overall, Weep For Love is a detailed and dedicated portrayal of Love that fans of this subgenre will undoubtedly enjoy. But the close narrative skills and plot construction around the protagonist, David, make for compelling reading for those who want a male perspective. The novel's pacing is excellent as it delivers a storyline where there is never a dull moment, and it will play on the heartstrings of its audience well.

Reviewed by Idowu Adekunle

for Readers' Favorite

Four Stars ★★★★

Weep for Love by David Kenneth Waldman is a story of two people, David and Suzie, who are in Love with each other and looking to find the perfect passionate romance. The characters' raw emotions are written honestly, and it is worth noting that this novel is intended for a mature audience.

The characters are sophisticated, self-aware, and deeply romantic. The scandal of a leaked sex tape only adds more fun to the story. Jaz is my favorite character. I love her confidence and the way she defends the people she loves. Weep for Love is a well-written story about Love, friendship, romance, and sexuality. Overall, it is an exciting read, and I would recommend it to fans of romantic novels.

Books

by David Kenneth Waldman

Novels

Weep For Love Trilogy

Weep For Love (2024)

The Harmony and Music Within:
A Memoir of Perseverance (TBA)

Flyboy and the RAF Nurse (TBA)

Books Published by Rebecca House International

The Changer: A Young Adult Trilogy

 by Tatiana Strelkoff

The Changer (1997)

Jeremy and the Crow Nation (2016)

Kelly: Full Circle (2020)

Available on Amazon and all online booksellers internationally

Spring Catalogue 2024

Just for Now

Original Cartoons By David Kenneth Waldman

Illustrator Kimberly Spuhler

REBECCA HOUSE

San Francisco

Imagination is the Secret

David Kenneth Waldman, Founder & Publisher

Website: tolovechildren.org

Email: davidkennethwaldman@gmail.com

Author Website: davidkennethwaldman.com